SHROUDED IN THE DARK

ASPEN BLACK

FOREWORD

Hello, Wanderers. I can't begin to tell you how much of a whirlwind this book has been. I wrote part one back in April of 2020, but part two was silent for me until January 2021.
I know our world has been turned upside down. 2020 was a mess for a lot of people.
I know I struggled with my mother's diagnosis of cancer and her having to be in and out of the hospital and long term care for most of last year. For those unaware, I've been helping take care of my mom since 2015.
I've struggled with uncontrollable anxiety and depression the past few months. If it hadn't been for my writing, and my readers, I'm not sure how well I would be at this time.
Thank you for reading these words. Thank you for diving into this world that means everything to me.
Becca, the main character, suffers from some medical issues that I do, so she means a lot to me.
I hope you are ready to buckle up and enjoy this book.
Please make sure the fans are turned on in your room and the room is bright so you don't strain your eyes.

Thank you,
Aspen Black

*Thank you to my beta-readers! You ladies are amazing.
My alpha-readers! I have no idea how I'd do this without you.
Becca—Thank you for letting me use your name and for being on this journey with me.
Jenn— you know.*

Mom— I know you'll probably never get to see this, but I love you. Thank you for always supporting me, even when I drove you crazy. I miss you.

Copyright © 2021 Aspen Black
All rights reserved. This book or any portion thereof may
not be reproduced or used in any manner whatsoever
without the express written permission of the publisher
except for the use of brief quotations in a book review.
Any references to historical events, real people, or real
places are used fictitiously. Names, characters, and places
are products of the author's imagination.

Front cover image by CReya-tive Book Cover
Editing: Black Lotus Editing
Editing: Chantal Fleming
Facebook: Aspen Black
Facebook Group: Aspen Black and Adammeh's Wanderers Readers Group

❦ Created with Vellum

CHAPTER 1
Becca

"...Finish reading chapter fifteen of the textbook. I would like a minimum of a five page essay of your response to it." The lecture ended and the class groaned loudly. The professor chuckled. "The essay will be due at the end of next week. Be happy it's your final and not an actual test." The clock chimed to announce that it was four in the afternoon, signaling the end of the day. "That's all for today. See you next week and enjoy your weekend."

As the students began to file out through the doorway, I turned to Felicity. She was packing up her shoulder bag.

"Hey, since it's Friday, do you want to go to one of the frat parties tonight to celebrate? One last party before the end of the school year?"

I wouldn't normally suggest going to one of those parties, but Felicity's twenty-first birthday was last Friday and she'd not done anything to celebrate it. Her family had insisted she come home and spend the weekend with them. She'd been in a foul mood since she returned.

She looked up at me from where she was digging inside of her bag. "Really? But you hate the frat parties." Her eyes, which were such a deep brown they were almost black in some lights, filled with hope.

I shrugged as I stood, pulling my own shoulder bag on. "We're making it your redo birthday weekend! It's not about what I like." I grinned at her. "Just promise we go to karaoke next time."

Felicity dove on top of me, wrapping her arms around my neck. She squeezed so hard, I was pretty sure I turned blue. Even though she was petite, she was damn strong. If it had been anyone else trying to hug me, I'd have curled up in a ball.

"Thank you, Becca! Yes! Yes! Let's go!" She pulled back excitedly. "We have to get ready. Let's go." She grabbed my hand as she basically ran out the classroom door.

"Felicity!" I laughed as she dodged around other students. "We still have a few hours before any of the parties start."

"Yes, yes, but we have to find the perfect outfits!" She grinned over her shoulder at me. "We're both going to be gorgeous!"

I rolled my eyes, but couldn't stop the smile that spread across my face. Felicity and I met at the start of freshman year when we'd become dorm mates. I thought, at first, we'd never get along.

She was as perky, pink, and happy-go-lucky, most of the time, that you could get. I was the exact opposite. Total introvert, awkward, chubby, but I did like pink now after seeing it all the time when we were together.

Felicity didn't seem to care about our differences. She immediately latched onto me, demanding friendship. She hadn't even cared that I was an anxious mess.

At first, I thought she was weird. But as the days merged from weeks to months, she broke down my walls and we'd become best friends. She insisted we do everything together and I had finally given up protesting after the first month. She was still weird, but so was I. Now, I couldn't imagine not having her in my life.

"You know, all you have to do is smile and the guys all roll over on their backs for you, right?"

"Pish posh. I'm not that great," Felicity snorted as we finally made it to the dormitory that we'd currently lived in for the last year. "Besides, if you actually talked to a few, they'd be tripping over themselves to get to know you."

"Right." I gave my own snort, but I wouldn't have this conversation with her again, since we'd had this discussion multiple times already. "I'm going to miss this dorm." We went up the stairs instead of waiting for the slow elevator. Our room was on the second floor at the end of the hall.

"I won't!" Felicity chuckled. "We're going to be in the sophomore dorm. It has its own cafeteria and we'll have a private bathroom. No more communal bathroom for us! Just wait until after summer break! It can't go by fast enough."

Unlike Felicity, I couldn't wait for the summer break. I was getting away from everything in the city and spending it up in my family's cabin in the mountains, sans the family. I'd invited Felicity, but she was going off to some kind of family reunion she couldn't get out of.

So, it was going to be the first time I'd gotten to go on my own since the rest of my family was in California for the summer visiting my stepgrandparents.

I was looking forward to reading, working on my art portfolio, and enjoying the outside with no one around besides me. The cabin was located off main roads and several miles away from any kind of human contact.

The short trip up the stairs ended. As we stepped inside our room, I glanced around. Her side of the room was decorated up the wazoo with everything under the rainbow. Random posters hung up on the walls everywhere, a few of them looked to be about to drop. My side of the room had a few decorations, but most of the available surfaces were covered in books and my art supplies.

"Ok, let's figure out what we're going to wear." Felicity threw open her wardrobe closet. "How about we match? That cute purple dress-shirt you have with black leggings? I'll wear my hot pink dress with black leggings."

I shook my head smiling, but pulled out said clothes. "Alright."

Over the next two hours, we took showers, dressed, and for the last thirty minutes, Felicity had been putting makeup on both of us. If it was up to me, I'd go without it, but this night was about Felicity, not me.

"Annndd there!" Felicity finished putting some stain on my lips. "Perfect." She stood back with her hands on her hips. "I think it's my best yet. You can even hide your flashlight keychain in the dress' pockets."

I looked in the mirror and blinked. She'd contoured my face to make it look slimmer. It wasn't bad. I smiled at her.

"Thanks."

She grinned as she clapped her hands together. "Let's go!" She looked amazing in her pink dress and leggings that fit her hourglass figure perfectly. Her light blonde hair was curled around her face and ran down her back. She really was gorgeous.

I followed her out the door as we made our way out of the dorm. It was later in the afternoon. There were still a few hours before it would get dark.

We roamed the 'main street' where most of the sorority houses were located. Almost every building was lit up with lights that flashed. There was music pumping out of the doors. Students roamed the middle of the street, some already drunk and singing loudly.

"I was thinking we could stop by Axel's frat house," Felicity suggested as we walked. She was trying to be subtle.

I hid my smile. "That's fine. Let's go there."

Felicity had a huge crush on Axel. It didn't hurt that he was drop dead gorgeous and on the football team. I wasn't sure what position he was, I wasn't really interested in sports, so I never paid attention when Felicity talked about it. I'd never had a chance to talk to him, having only met once for about a minute. When they would go out, Felicity met him wherever they had planned to go.

After another ten minutes of walking, we stopped in front of a two-story Victorian house. There were students all over the front yard, and loud rap music blasted through the open windows and front door. There were plastic cups littering the yard and I wrinkled my nose in disgust. Was it that hard to throw away an empty cup?

"Come on, Becca! Stop spacing out!" Felicity grabbed my hand as she dragged me across the sidewalk, up the stairs, and into the house.

The house was even more jam-packed with people than it had looked like from the outside. You couldn't even hear yourself think without yelling in your head.

"Where do you think Axel is?" I leaned forward to yell into her ear. I pressed into her side to try to avoid being touched by other people. It also gave me a focus so I wouldn't have an anxiety attack.

"He's probably in the kitchen!" she yelled over her shoulder at me as she pushed her way through the crowd of dancing and mingling students. I was right on her tail.

There were a few curses from kids that Felicity basically shoved out of the way, but no one stopped her. Being hot had its perks. As soon as we went through two rooms, we were in the kitchen. I wouldn't have been able to step into this house without her pushing me past my comfort zone.

Axel leaned against the island, his right ankle over his left. His arms were crossed as he was talking with the guy to his left. I paused for a brief second to look at him. Felicity had good tastes. He was tall, hands taller than most of the boys at this party. He was almost as muscled as he was tall. His muscles were clearly defined in his black shirt that looked like it might be a size too small with how it clung to him, giving hints to the body underneath. He had a handsome face with strong features. His hair was light chestnut and was cut short. It was just long enough to look tussled. His eyes were a shade darker than his hair. His skin tone reminded me of caramel. He looked like the bad-boy jock.

It was significantly quieter in here; you could talk without having to yell. Axel looked over as we entered the room and his amber eyes lit up as a look of yearning flashed across his face.

"I didn't think you were coming." He didn't move from where he was as we walked to him. His white teeth flashed as he grinned, making them stand out against his darker skin tone. I had to admit, he was really hot and his voice was smooth as velvet.

"I wouldn't miss getting to see you before you left early for break." Felicity's tone had deepened as she fluttered her eyelashes up at him. She'd let go of my hand as she stepped up to him.

Axel chuckled as his arm went around Felicity's waist. "Well, we're just going to have to make the most of tonight, aren't we?"

The guy that Axel had been talking to cleared his throat, coughing into his hand. He was nearly as tall as Axel but leaner. He wasn't as wide as Axel, but still in great shape. His hair was only a little longer than his friend's. It was a light blonde with hints of natural red tint in the strands. I was too far away from him to see what color his eyes were in the low light, but his face was beautiful, with hints of Asian heritage. I'd love to draw him. He looked like he could be one of those old samurai with a katana, ready to strike. His skin was a light tan. Axel looked over at him and laughed.

"Sorry about that, Jasper." He motioned between the two. "Jasper, this is Felicity, the girl I've been telling you about. Felicity, this is Jasper. He's my best friend."

Felicity stuck her hand out to shake Jasper's. "Nice to meet you." She pressed against Axel's chest. "You talk about me, mmm?"

I had to admit. The girl was smooth. I looked around, maybe there was a quiet corner I could hide out until she was all partied out. I'd made sure my phone was charged all the way so I could read the new book I'd just downloaded onto it. It would be a good distraction to keep my anxiety at bay.

"It's awesome to meet you. You'll have to tell me how you got this dimwits attention. The only thing he's ever cared about is food and working out," Jasper had continued the conversation as I was looking for my escape. His voice reminded me of melting chocolate.

Felicity laughed before looking back. She narrowed her eyes at me because she knew exactly what I was doing. My shoulders slumped.

"Let me introduce you to my best friend!" She walked over, threw her arm over my shoulder and shuffled us forward. "This is Becca. She's in the arts program, one of the best artists I've ever seen, and probably the kindest I've ever met."

I looked at her. "Awww." That was really sweet of her. "I love you, too."

We laughed at each other, forgetting about the two guys for a second. Axel's chuckle joined ours and I ignored how his voice caused a lightness in my chest that tingled.

That hadn't been weird at all.

"Yeah, apparently, they're like that all the time, or so I've heard." He looked over at Jasper with a shrug as he grinned.

"Well, it's a pleasure to meet you, Becca." Jasper had stepped forward and he took my hand in his much larger one. "I'm just a simple man trying to make my way in the universe."

Our eyes met and my breath left me. His eyes reminded me of an emerald necklace my mother wore all the time. They were a deep green with flecks of brown. His lips were curved in a smile as we shook hands.

"Nice, Star Wars fan? Jango, right?" My mouth felt like it had cotton balls in it, but the look of shock on his face was priceless. I was a nerd. "It's nice to meet you too. Are you a football player like Axel?"

Our hands separated as he put both of his in his front pockets. "You are the first girl to get that reference!" He looked at Axel. "Where have you been hiding her?" He looked back at me. "To answer your question, hell no. This idiot takes enough whacks to the head for both of us. I'm in the engineering program."

Smart, nice, nerdy, and gorgeous. This guy was the total package, technically both of them were, I'd noticed as girls went in and out of the kitchen, most of them wouldn't take their eyes off of these two. It's a good thing Felicity was too busy staring at Axel to care.

"Hey," Felicity interrupted, "we're going to go dance. Jasper, don't let this one go hide in a corner and read." She shook her finger at me as Axel, with his arm around her waist again, pulled her toward the living room where it was loudest.

I flushed as she left before glancing up at Jasper with an awkward laugh. "Sorry about her. I'll let you get back to partying." I turned to go find that corner when Jasper grabbed my hand. I stiffened.

"Hey, you don't have to go." He tugged on my hand before letting it go. "I'm not much of a partier. Would you care to keep me company and talk? Promise, no pervy moves." He chuckled low.

I wasn't surprised about the promise for no pervy moves, but company would be a nice change at one of these things. "Sure. No pervy moves on either side." I winked at him. His smile almost split his face. I might not have a lot of experience with men, but I knew how to flirt when I felt like it. Didn't mean I wasn't awkward.

"A sense of humor. I thought those were rare, like tanzanite, amongst your kind." Jasper waved his hand, having me follow him through the back door in the kitchen.

"Like the tanzanite, it's the most revered amongst gemstones," I replied straight-laced.

His shoulders shook in silent laughter as I followed him.

We dodged our way around more students, couples gyrating on each other in the middle of the walk way, and a fight that had broken out. Jasper made sure I was on his other side as we passed the fight, so that if something happened, he'd be the one hit and not me. That was surprisingly chivalrous of him. He didn't even know that I was already so anxious about being separated from Felicity, I'd started to see black around my eyes, but that single act of kindness helped even my breathing.

He led us to the corner of the yard where there was a stone garden bench under a small, open-sided gazebo. There was a small flower garden around most of it.

"I didn't expect to see this in a boy's frat house," I spoke without thinking as I gazed around the gazebo. It had small lights hung around the inner area.

"Honestly, if it weren't for our landlady, it would probably be dead grass." He sat on the stone bench. "But, this will be the last place most of the guys will come, unless their bedroom is locked and they need a place to have sex."

I scrunched my nose at him. "Ew. Do you have any disinfecting wipes for that bench?"

The smile hadn't left his face since we left the kitchen. The amusement clear with his next words. "You're safe. No one's had sex out here for a few weeks and the sprinklers have cleaned it up. Come sit."

I sat on the other end, making sure my leg didn't touch his. I had big thighs and some people got annoyed or antsy if they're touched.

"You know you didn't have to hang out with me, right? I was going to go read in a corner."

"Nah, you seem to be the only one who wasn't interested in drinking or finding a hook-up. Not to mention, you got my reference. Most girls just look confused."

I leaned back slightly on the bench, my hands behind me, gripping the back. "Most girls weren't raised on Star Wars, Star Trek, and anything nerdy sci-fi you can think of. I hated Cartoon Network, except when they had Sailor Moon or Inuyasha playing."

"No shit?" Jasper copied my stance on the bench but his legs stretched out in front of him. The guy was tall.

From there, we talked about shows that we both liked. Turned out, a lot of my favorites were his too. Jasper told me about the classes he was taking. It went over my head, but he seemed passionate about it, so it was fun to listen to him. He listened as I told him about my art, which I told him about with a lot more enthusiasm than I usually did with strangers. We were talking about favorite types of restaurants when the sun finally disappeared. I hadn't even been paying attention to anything other than talking to Jasper.

My vision had been getting progressively worse through the evening as the sun's light disappeared but now, with it gone, I couldn't see. Nyctalopia was a bitch that I had suffered with since I was a baby. I can't see in the dark, which is why I always carried a few flashlights with me. I even had a mini-battery powered lantern in my purse for when I do go out in public. If the streets were brightly lit, I was usually ok as long as I had someone with me. If there were some lights, I could see them like they were really far away and looked fuzzy. Unlike most people who get diagnosed with nyctalopia, my doctors had never been able to fully make it go away. I was nearsighted, but even eye surgery didn't help my night vision.

I hadn't even noticed how dark it had become until my vision just went black. I'd been too engrossed with our conversation.

"Becca? You okay?" Jasper's tone was concerned since I suddenly just stopped talking.

"Uh, yeah, but do you mind if I turn on a flashlight?" I'd already had my hand in my pocket that held the flashlight.

"Oh." His tone was confused now. "Are you afraid of the dark?"

I barked out a self-deprecating laugh. "Something like that."

I could hear him shifting where he was. I'd just pulled out the flashlight when there was a click and the lights in the gazebo turned on. I needed to blink to focus. It wasn't the greatest light, but as I looked around, Jasper was in front of me, frowning.

"Is that alright?"

"Yeah, that helps." I nodded at him as I placed the flashlight next to me but left it off. As long as I could see a little bit, I could ignore the shadows further out into the yard.

"You're not really afraid of the dark." Jasper sat next to me again. "It isn't that dark yet."

I sighed. Here came the explanation part. Most people find out and think I'm even weirder since I also suffered from severe anxiety. Which suited me fine.

Not being able to see at night sucked. It meant I couldn't drive at night time, couldn't go to the movies. I'd never gone to a dance because they were usually dark inside wherever it was held.

I ran a hand through my hair. I should have put it in a braid. "I can't see at night. I have nyctalopia. I've had it since I was little. If it's dark, I'm blind. Even with these lights? You're pretty fuzzy to me. And no, you can't catch it."

Jasper scooted closer to me. My flashlight was the only thing separating his thigh from mine.

"Is that better?"

My nose scrunched again. "You're taking this really well."

He shrugged. "It's not a big deal to me. Anyways, you were telling me about that sushi place that actually has a revolving bar?"

Just like that, we were back to talking. It was nice to meet someone, besides Felicity, who learned about my partial blindness and just moved forward not caring. It didn't change who I was.

We'd moved onto where we'd grown up, when I heard my name being called. Felicity popped in the gazebo. Axel was right behind her.

"Becca! I'm sorry! I had no idea it had gotten so late!" She rushed forward, her face becoming clearer as she grabbed my hands in hers. Her lips looked swollen with her hair looking disheveled. Someone had had fun.

"It's ok, Fel. We were just talking."

She eyed Jasper before looking back at me. "You ready to head back?" She pulled out the bright pink flash light she'd bought shortly after she'd learned about my partial blindness. "Got mine ready!" She puffed her cheeks out proudly as I smiled.

"You're done?" I glanced between her and Axel. He had his hands in his pockets, but I couldn't really see his expression.

"Mhm. The party is still going, but now everyone is super drunk. I thought we could go get some dinner. Axel said he's buying."

"Well, if Axel is buying, I'm in," Jasper interjected and stood.

Felicity, keeping her hand in mine, turned on her flashlight as I did the same for mine, and started to lead the way.

I trusted Felicity as we walked through the backyard, around the house that music still seemed to be pulsing louder from, and around to the street. Where my flashlight hit, I could see a lot more students along the street, most of them drunk. Axel was next to Felicity, judging by the large shadowed figure next to her. Jasper had decided to walk next to me and he'd turned on his cell phone flashlight. It made my heart warm. I hoped he'd want to talk again. He seemed like a great guy to know.

Jasper

When Axel had pulled me from studying in my room to join the loud party downstairs, I was annoyed as hell. I had been studying for my final next week in my Differential Engineering class that was kicking my ass this semester. I'd told him I'd stay for an hour with him, the damn bear was taking full advantage of college life while he could.

I couldn't blame him, but it didn't mean that I had to like it. My fox certainly didn't like the noise. My hour had almost been up when Axel's crush walked in, making a beeline straight to him. She was pretty hot, smart too, according to him. I wasn't thrilled to meet her, but it was inevitable if Axel liked her. I had run my eyes over her body, trying to see what he saw in her. Then she'd stepped back to introduce the friend who'd been behind her that I hadn't noticed at first.

Her friend was taller than she was, coming up to my chin and probably Axel's shoulder. When Felicity had introduced her, I'd been polite and offered my standard greeting getting ready to say goodbye when she'd shot back, knowing my Star Wars reference.

I'd decided that talking to the friend might be worth the lost study time.

Her friend, Becca, had longer hair that was loose around her shoulders. It was a medium ginger color, straight, and reminded me of the sunset at home. My sister would have killed her for that hair. She had a round face that fit her body that she hid underneath clothes. Her hips were pear shaped. She was a little bigger than my last lay. Her eyes were a bright cobalt color that I had to blink for a second to make sure I was seeing correctly. My fox perked up in interest. Her body posture showed she was uncomfortable and it looked like she was getting ready to bolt.

Axel pushed his shoulder against mine when the two girls were talking. "Help me out here."

I'd sighed but nodded. Felicity had recommended just a few seconds later that I keep Becca company. We'd gone outside to the gazebo where it was less crowded since it was loud and Becca looked like she might appreciate a location that would be less congested with people. The next few hours had flown by and before I'd known it, it was night. I'd enjoyed myself a lot more than I thought I would. So did my fox.

When the girl had gone quiet and looked dazed, I'd thought she was having some kind of episode. Her eyes had gone glassy as she blinked rapidly. When she'd explained she was basically blind at night, I'd taken a deep breath. I'd thought she was hurt and here she was, blind as a bat.

Now, we'd walked to a small pizza joint. Felicity had led Becca through the street as we'd all used our flashlights for her, even though it wasn't that dark to Axel and me. We sat at a table near the back of the restaurant. Axel ended up next to Felicity and I sat next to Becca.

I was taking a drink of the water the waiter had left when Becca leaned into my side and whispered softly, "They kind of make you sick with the puppy eyes, don't they?"

I sputtered on a laugh as the water I'd been drinking got stuck. I coughed, clearing my throat, thumping my chest as I laughed through it. Axel lifted an eyebrow at me as I just shook my head at him.

"You did that on purpose." I leaned over, whispering to her, knowing Axel had heard what she'd said and my response.

When she tilted her head to look me in the eyes, she had a smirk on her round face that was oddly adorable. Her cobalt eyes sparked with her own amusement.

"I don't know what you're talking about." She looked back down at her menu, scrunching her nose in thought.

I'd noticed she'd done that a few times when we'd been talking when she was thinking about something. My fox wanted to boop her nose when she did that but I refused, pissing him off.

"Oh, how about we share a white pizza with pepperoni and pineapple?" Felicity looked up at Becca.

"That sounds yummy to me. Also, garlic bread." Becca's stomach rumbled just then, but it wasn't loud enough in the restaurant a human wouldn't have heard it but Axel and I did.

Axel laughed into his hand masking it as a cough as I just grinned. Talk about timing.

"Pepperoni sounds great. But pineapple? How dare you!" Axel had turned more in his seat to face Felicity and Becca.

Becca had set the menu down, looking like she was about to reply just as the waitress came to the table. She ran her eyes along Axel and me before licking her upper lip. She totally ignored the two girls.

"What can I get you?" Her voice was lowered in her version of sultry.

I'd leaned back in my chair, draping my arm over the back of Becca's, getting comfortable so I could enjoy what would happen based on how both girls had stiffened.

"You could grow some manners," Felicity clipped at the waitress. "You do notice that their GIRLFRIENDS are literally right here? And you know we can see you eyeing our men, right?" Her tiny lie slipped out, but I snickered as Axel's ears turned red.

"Now, Felicity. It's not her fault that the guys are so mouthwateringly yummy," Becca spoke up as she leaned back in her seat, her hair brushing along my arm. "We would like to order though." She gave our order to the waitress, whose face had progressively gotten angrier through the conversation.

"I'll get that in right away." She turned on quickly to rush off.

"I really hope she doesn't spit on our pizzas," Becca muttered softly.

I snorted this time, loud enough that she heard me. "Becca, I think that tonight is the start to a beautiful friendship."

She threw her head back and laughed, her hair covering my arm now. My fox started to purr and I had to hold my breath. He was far too interested in this girl. She wasn't even our normal type. She's going to be a friend, I reminded him silently. He ignored me and continued to purr. The lil' fucker.

The time passed quickly. Our food came out, spit free, we hoped, and we all ate hungrily. I even got Axel to try a bite of the pineapple pepperoni pizza. He had grudgingly admitted it wasn't horrible. The best thing about never being picky meant more food for me.

When it was time to pay, Felicity grabbed the check before either I or Axel could. Felicity pulled out several bills putting them into the fold. She winked at Axel.

"It was my idea. I get to pay." She stood stretching. Her dress rode up higher on her thighs and my eyes tracked it, but, instead of enjoying it like I thought I would, I didn't feel anything. "I saw a claw machine. Let's play one game before we leave?" Her grin was infectious with Axel and Becca.

"You go ahead," Becca laughed softly at her friend. "I'm going to use the restroom. I'll catch up."

Axel stood before wrapping an arm around Felicity's waist. "You coming?" He looked back at me.

I looked down at Becca with her nose scrunched. "Nah. I'll be there in a minute."

Axel shrugged as Felicity led him off to the front of the restaurant and I turned to Becca. "What are you thinking about so hard?"

Becca reached for the check. She counted the bills before sighing softly. She pulled out another five dollar bill with a few ones. She put it with the other bills and slid it to the middle of the table.

"Felicity sometimes has a temper. She looks and sounds fine, but that waitress really pissed her off." She stood, brushing something off her legs. "Even if the waitress was hitting on you guys, she's still working hard. She deserves a tip."

"That's damn mature." Surprise laced my tone.

She just shrugged. "My mom worked a second job waitressing for years. I get it." She looked up at me as I stood next to her. "Plus, you guys are eye candy. Can't blame her for having that reaction."

My grin was crooked as I laughed. "Damn. I'm starting to see you don't have a filter."

She pulled out her flashlight and returned my grin. "Not really."

I liked this girl.

CHAPTER 2

Becca

"Freedom!" As the clock hit four o'clock, the classroom erupted into chaos. It was officially summer break. The only one in the room who didn't look thrilled was Felicity.

"Hey, it can't be that bad." My hand squeezed hers as we stood. "You said you'll get a week at the end? You're coming up to the cabin and spending it with me still, right?"

Felicity had become increasingly withdrawn as the week had progressed. She never really talked about her family, except for small things. I knew she didn't get along with most of them and was being pressured into joining the family business. Whatever it was.

"Of course, I am." She offered a wistful smile. "I'm going to need it."

We dodged other students as we walked through the hallway toward the door.

"How's it going with Jasper?" A little bit of her spark was back as she threw me a teasing grin.

"Uh, ok? We're just friends. He's fun to talk to. He gets my nerd talk, even if someone I know doesn't." I emphasized the last sentence, which made her laugh. "Stop talking about me. How's it going with Axel? When are you going to make it official?"

There was a faint blush to her cheeks as we walked through the entrance to the building and out into the fresh air. "I'm not sure. This thing with my family is going to take all of my attention this summer, but, girl, I can tell you, the man can kiss." Her voice sounded like she was about to swoon.

"Did you talk to him about it?"

She nodded as we walked across the street toward our dormitory. "He said he'd wait for me." Her blush became more pronounced. "We'll still talk, even when I'm doing my family thing."

"Good. You deserve to be happy."

The dormitory common area was packed with bodies of students and some parents as everyone worked on getting ready to go home and leave their room for good. My heart sped up. Felicity grabbed my hand and wove through the crowds as quickly as she could get us through and up the stairs. The hallways on our floor were even worse with the amount of people.

I usually was ok with crowds as long as there was breathing room, but when bodies are packed together like tuna cans, my anxiety gets the best of me and I usually freak out. Felicity had experienced one attack and since that time, she'd been around to help me avoid them. They didn't happen often, but this situation started making me feel like I couldn't breathe. I know, the partial blind girl also has high anxiety. Who would have thought?

As soon as we got into our room, Felicity slammed the door shut. I laughed breathlessly in relief as I moved to stand in front of the window so I could see the open spaces. "Damn. That's a lot. That's even worse than the first day we were allowed to move in."

"No kidding. It's a good thing our families aren't coming to get us until later." She faced several empty boxes that we'd stacked in the middle of the floor this morning.

I went to grab a large trash bag for the things we'd throw away. "Yeah, about that."

Felicity turned to me, narrowing her eyes.

"I'm taking a Lyft back to Englewood, packing my stuff for the summer, and taking another Lyft in the morning up to the cabin." I had turned around to start packing my art supplies into one box that would be going with me up to the mountains.

"How does that work?" I could tell she was annoyed. She'd wanted to meet my family, but she didn't push. "What about groceries? It's in the mountains where there's nothing around for miles, right?"

My sketchbooks went on the bottom, followed by the smaller blank canvas I still had left. "We have a small truck we keep up at the cabin. I'll just have to connect the battery. We have one of those portable battery jumper things." I didn't look up from where I'd grabbed my watercolors, I was trying to decide if I'd put them in their own box. All of my finished artwork had been either shipped to my house, or stored in a small storage unit that my stepfather rented for me across town. "I'll come pick you up in Fraser if you don't want your family to know exactly where the cabin is."

I stumbled forward as Felicity threw herself on top of my back hugging me tightly. "YOU ARE THE ABSO-LUTE best!"

"You're just saying that because I have a cabin in the middle of nowhere, away from your family," I teased as she went back to her side of the room.

Cleaning out the room that had been home, for what seems like years, ready to be empty only took a little while after we were done packing. We'd done most of the cleaning the night before. It was nearing six in the evening when we both finished. I had four large boxes and a suitcase. Felicity had double that. Thank the person who had invented those vacuum seal bags or we'd both have a ton more boxes.

A knock sounded on our door just as I finished taping the last one up. Felicity wilted in front of my eyes. The bright energy dulled in her eyes but she forced a smile as she opened the door.

"Hey, Mom! Dad! You're right on time!" She stepped back letting in several people. "I see you brought help." She left the door open before walking to stand next to me. "Mom, Dad, this is my roommate that I told you about. Becca, this is my mom, Nina, and my dad, Ralph. The three other guys are my cousins, Bud, Charles, and Wyn."

Her mother was tall, taller than her father by at least an inch. She was willow thin, like Felicity, with lithe muscles. She wore a pressed pantsuit and her hair was perfectly braided with no hair out of place. Her father was broad in the shoulders, he wore a black business suit, and he had his hair shaved close to the sides of his head. Both of their eyes were deep set and the same exact color of Felicity's dark brown.

"Hi, Mr. and Mrs. Jager. It's great to meet you." I stepped forward to shake their hands.

Her mother's handshake was limp and her hand was cool. Her father's handshake was two rough shakes and I swear, he was trying to break my fingers, but I didn't rub my hand after I stepped back. Her cousins came forward to say hello.

"We've heard many things about you from Felicity. Thank you for helping her throughout the year." Mr. Jager nodded at me solemnly. "It's a shame we weren't able to meet you before on other breaks." He said this while looking over at Felicity. "But we're in a bit of a hurry. We're going to get going."

He and Mrs. Jager left without another word. Felicity's cousins stepped up. The last one, the biggest of the three, looked over at me. He walked over to us.

"Hey, Fel. It's good to see you."

He was tall, my head only came up to the middle of his wide chest. He gave off a scary leader vibe, but I couldn't help appreciate his forearm muscles when he looked at me.

"You only have four boxes? Why don't we carry those down when we're done with Felicity's boxes?" He had a strong face, square nose, and full lips. He was easy on the eyes. Speaking of eyes, his were the same dark brown as the rest of the family. That was starting to get a little weird since there was no variety in the eye colors at all.

"That's really nice of you. I'd appreciate any help!"

He nodded at me as he turned back to the other two. "Let's hurry up, boys, before Aunt Nina gets annoyed." They all grabbed two boxes each before going out the door.

Felicity looked at me. "That was the first time Wyn has ever said hi to one of my friends." She looked impressed before her face sobered. "Becca, my family," she looked at the door, tilting her head as if trying to hear something. "Don't talk to them except for me. My family, they aren't good people to be around." She looked at me for the first time with such intensity that I'd not seen from her before. "Even if Wyn is cute, he's not safe."

I was about to reply when she jerked her head, placing her finger over her lips. "I'll definitely miss you, too!"

I was confused for a second but understood when her cousins came back. They grabbed the rest of the boxes, save two of hers and mine. As soon as they were gone, I looked at Felicity.

"Do I need to be concerned for your safety, Felicity?" I kept my voice as soft as possible.

"No, it's just my family isn't like other families. It's just better to be safe than sorry." She placed her hand on my shoulder. "You're the first best friend I've ever had and I'd rather keep you away from that brand of crazy."

I touched her hand on my shoulder. "You're going to talk to

me more about this when you're at the cabin." My tone let her know I was serious.

She just nodded before grabbing her large bag that held more clothes. I grabbed my suitcase as her cousins came back in for the last of it.

"We'll take this down and put it where we're parked. Is that alright?" Wyn looked over at me. "You have someone coming to help you? Or a car we can take it too?"

"No, thanks, though. Where you're parked is fine. My Lyft should be here in about ten minutes. I'm sure I can get it in the car with their help."

Wyn lifted an eyebrow. "Where do you live?"

Felicity shot me a look that I ignored. "My parents live in Littleton. They're paying for the ride, so all I am spending is tip money." I only lied a little. Littleton was near Englewood.

Wyn just nodded. "Alright. We'll get these downstairs." He bent to pick up three of my four boxes. He glanced at Felicity. "Five minutes."

With that, they all left with the remaining boxes. I hugged Felicity tight for a few moments before pulling back.

"I don't have the best signal at the cabin, but I'll make sure to check in with you at night or whenever I go into town for anything."

Felicity nodded at me. "That'll work. I won't have my phone with me except for night anyway."

What was she going to be doing? What was her family doing? Were they drug dealers? I felt my face pale as I thought about it. I stopped Felicity as she began to walk out the door.

"Felicity, it's not drugs, is it?" My whisper sounded loud in my own ear.

She looked at me before bursting out in laughter. She laughed so hard that she doubled over clutching her stomach, and her bag hit the floor.

I tapped my foot at her, crossing my arms over my chest after letting my own suitcase down.

"It's a valid question," I snapped at her in annoyance. "With the way you're suddenly acting."

"No," she straightened as she breathed in, "it's not drugs." She picked up her bag. "Come on."

I followed her mumbling about buttheads and jerky friends, which just made her laugh harder as we walked outside of the dorm. Most of the other students had gone by now, with just a few stragglers. Some would leave tomorrow.

Her family was to the left of the building where the parking lot was located. They were pretty easy to spot in the middle of the almost empty lot. They were parked beside the street light. Her mom and dad were already in the front seats of the huge red SUV. Her cousins had just finished putting her boxes into the back. Charles and Bub got into the back. It looked like there was a third row that they climbed into. Wyn came over to us as we reached the car.

"We set your boxes next to the light." His tone was concerned. "I can convince Aunt Nina to wait until your ride gets here."

This guy was big, good looking, and scary, but a sweetheart. Felicity would have a lot of explaining to do when she came to the cabin at the end of summer as to why he wasn't to be trusted.

"Thank you, Wyn." I smiled at him as I pulled my phone out of my pocket. I pulled up the Lyft app. "My ride should be here in a minute. Shows that they're around the block."

Felicity pushed her bag into Wyn's arms. "Go on in the car. Let me say good bye to my friend."

Wyn rolled his eyes. He nodded his head at me with a soft smile before climbing into the back of the SUV. Felicity turned to me and hugged me tightly.

"Be safe in that cabin. Text me every night. If I don't hear from you in a two day period, I'll call the cops." I'd have laughed but I knew she was serious.

"Same goes for you." I hugged her back for a few more moments before stepping back. "Thank you for making this year awesome."

There was a loud honk behind us. Her dad looked at us and gestured at Felicity. She turned back to me and blew out a breath.

"Alright, I'll text you. Let me know when you're home and safe. And send me a screenshot of the Lyft driver's info and take a picture of his license plate." She waved to me as she got into the red SUV. Her face was drawn tight already. Whatever they were going to do this summer, she was not happy.

I waved until their car pulled out of the parking lot. A sedan pulled into the lot just as they pulled out. My phone beeped, letting me know that this was my Lyft driver.

The house was quiet when I walked through the garage. The Lyft driver had been a nice older man who entertained with me during the drive with stories about his grandkids. He'd been kind enough to help me pack and unpack my boxes and suitcase from the car. I'd sent a quick text to Felicity and Mom letting them know I'd made it.

The lights were all on. Mom always made sure we had automatic lights that turned on as soon as it started to get dark and could be controlled by an app on our phones. The security panel started to beep, letting me know I'd only have a few more seconds until it went off, which would be a huge hassle if it did. I hurriedly put in the code, my grandma's birthday, before it went off. I set it back on and went to the kitchen.

There was a note from Mom on the island.

. . .

There's lasagna in the fridge. Just reheat in the microwave. We also packed you a cooler with food and drinks for the cabin for the first two days. It's in the fridge in the garage. I'm sorry you didn't want to come to Cali with us, but we all love you. Call me when you get to the cabin.

--Love Mom, Gary, Milly, and Stephen

I smiled as I finished reading the note. The cooler was probably Gary's idea. He was pretty awesome for a stepdad. My stepbrother and sister were also pretty cute. They'd just turned eleven last month. So far, they hadn't started into the terrible pre-teens stage yet.

It was the first summer since Mom had married Gary that we weren't all spending it together, but I really needed to work on my art this summer for my portfolio since I'd received an internship to work with one of my heroes, Devon Mckenzie, for the second semester of the school year. I'd worked my ass off to be one of the two students who were selected for this semester and I wasn't going to blow it by not having a more diverse portfolio.

My stomach grumbled, interrupting my thoughts about what I'd be working on this summer. The lasagna was exactly where Mom said it was. It took only a few minutes to heat it up. I decided to eat at the island bar instead of going into the dining room. Setting the plate with my lasagna in front of me, I opened the bottle of Coke I'd gotten out of the fridge as well. It wasn't super healthy but after the long day, it was exactly what I needed.

Mom made lasagna from scratch with extra ricotta cheese because she knew that was my favorite part. I'd almost finished my plate when my phone vibrated. I'd thought it would be Felicity, but it turned out to be Jasper.

Hey! Happy summer! Sorry we didn't talk all that much this past week, finals really kicked our asses.

I chuckled. Him and every other student on campus.

It's cool. How'd they go? What are your plans this summer?

A few of my friends and I are heading to our summer house. Get away from the crowds. Go skinny dipping. The works. You?

I blushed as an image of Jasper skinny dipping flashed through my mind. *I'm spending time alone to work on my art and sing karaoke to my heart's content. I can't wait.*

His reply was almost immediate. *Sounds like we're both going to relax and have fun. I've gotta go, we're getting the stuff in the car for tomorrow. Ttyl!*

I smiled at the short conversation. Jasper was easy to talk to.

There was a beep from my phone again, my alarm went off reminding me that I needed to pack for tomorrow. I sighed. At least I only needed to pack clothes. I was going to take clothes from here and not the ones from school. The mountains were nice during the summer, but the night could still get a little nippy. Plus, it'd be nice to wear something else. Baggy clothes were my favorite to wear, but Felicity had started replacing my clothes at school with clothes that fit a bit more. Being a bigger girl with clothes that fit well made me self-conscious, but she was helping me step out of my comfort zone. But up at the cabin, I didn't have to be around people, so I could be comfortable.

When I opened the door to my room, I laughed. Mom had already packed my clothes that I'd need and they were in three large suitcases next to my bed with a sticky note on the biggest one with a heart on it. I shook my head as I grinned. I didn't need to pack much now. I'd take my art supplies from school and the suitcases Mom had packed. All I would need to do is grab the resin I'd had shipped here a few days ago and the polymer clay. I was going to work on sculpting this summer, too.

It was only a little after ten when I got into bed. I'd set the app for the lights to dim the ones outside of my room by fifty percent. I turned off the lights in my room with a clap, my phone's screen was the only light I could see. It was already plugged in so I didn't have to search for the charger. After placing the phone on the nightstand, using its flashlight app, I turned it off, and settled into bed to sleep.

CHAPTER 3

Becca

The ride to the cabin had taken almost two hours, but it had been relaxing. The female Lyft driver had been friendly and had been an avid artist as well. We had passed the time talking about our favorite artists, what our favorite era was, and mediums that we used. I'd given her the same amount in tip money as it had cost to get to the cabin.

It was only a little after eleven in the morning as I brought my suitcases inside. The outside was a classic cabin with wood logs while the inside was modern. It was a one story cabin, but it held four bedrooms and three bathrooms. It was more than enough room for all of us. The cabin had a soft spot in all our hearts because it was how Mom and Gary had met.

Gary had been looking to buy land here and Mom was selling the cabin because we'd been drowning in bills thanks to medical bills on both of our sides. She'd taken Gary on a tour, he'd asked her out, and the rest was history.

We'd worked two summers ago on renovating the cabin to bring it modern touches and appliances. Not to mention plumbing. The addition of a heat pump for when it was cold was one of my favorite parts.

Gary owned his own construction company that did well in Colorado, Arizona, and Washington. He was well off when he'd met Mom, and was smart when he saved his money. Mom had worked two jobs for years to support us both, and was too dedicated to ever let someone just take care of us, so she worked as Gary's assistant now. Mom never let me or the twins become spoiled enough that we didn't understand hard work for money that was earned.

I ran my hands along the artificial leather couch as I walked through the living room. The side of the cabin that faced the mountain was a wall of windows. Even though we were in warmer months, there was still snow on the tops of the Rockies. There was a sliding door in the middle of the wall of windows that led out to a large deck that held the hot tub, a table set near the barbeque with a built in umbrella that we changed out last year, a firepit, and the built-in outdoor furniture that surrounded the firepit. I'd need to bring out the cushions for the outdoor furniture, but could do that later.

The sliding door slid open as I unlocked it. The security system was already off, so I didn't have to worry about it until I left again. The air here was clean, free of the pollution of the city, and it made me smile as I tipped my face toward the sun. My hands touched the deck's rails. The grass was green, the trees were bright in color, the sky was a light blue with just specs of clouds. There was a small pond about a quarter of a mile in the backyard. I grinned as I watched some birds fly over it. It was fed by a small stream from higher up the mountain, so any time we went swimming, it was freezing.

Right now, the water reflected the sky and my hands ached to paint the scene, but I knew I'd have plenty of time later to do it. I needed to put away the food from the cooler that was packed, air out my bedroom's bedding, and get the battery hooked up to the old truck in the garage. I know Mom had packed the food so I wouldn't have to go into Fraser the first night, but I wanted to get a few things after I had dinner at a small café that'd been as much of a constant in my life as the cabin itself. With that thought as motivation, I kicked it into high gear.

It took about twenty minutes to air out the bedding in my room. The room was actually bigger than the one at the house in Englewood. The large bay window was, of course, my favorite part as well as the ceiling window. Gary had managed to hide it from me until after the renovations. The glass was reinforced like those glass bridges and bullet resistant. It was strong enough that the snow wouldn't make it cave in. Several full grown men had jumped up and down on it for about five minutes to show that it would hold up and satisfy Gary's protective nature.

I couldn't see the stars at night, but I loved laying there in the mornings or during the day to watch the sky.

The cooler took less time to unload and put the food away. All that was left before I headed into town was to get the battery in the truck.

I grabbed the keys, the portable car battery charger that I'd brought from home that had a full charge to it, my jacket, just in case, and the cooler. I rearmed the security system and went to the garage.

The truck had been my dad's. It was one of the few things we'd kept when he'd passed away. It was an old Chevy S-10 truck from 1986. It might be a small truck, but my dad had lovingly kept it in perfect shape. It'd been the first truck he'd bought when he'd gotten his license. Mom still had a mechanic out twice a year to make sure it was kept in perfect condition, even if we weren't here to drive it. The gas in the truck was only six months old, so I shouldn't have any trouble with it.

The building was only a two car garage, the other side of it held various items in storage. The battery I was looking for was located on a shelf near the truck. There were a lot more things scattered around the floor, a lot of trash. I'd have to tell Mom to talk to the mechanics about picking up before they left. I'd clean it back up when I got back.

I set the cooler in the back of the truck and threw my jacket into the cab. As I popped the hood, I remembered helping Dad change the oil. I'd only been 6 when he'd passed away in a car accident.

The battery was easy enough to get hooked up. It was the battery charger that gave me issues. It didn't want to connect properly. I finally got fed up, smacked the positive cable against the side of the truck, and tried again. I rolled my eyes as it connected just fine after that. After turning on the battery charger to full, I got into the cab and turned the ignition. The truck turned on in a loud roar before leveling out into a small purr. I whooped in victory and pulled out my phone.

I was surprised to see that I almost had full bars. Last year, I'd barely had one bar when I was outside. Looked like they'd improved cell service out here, which was awesome. I sent a quick text to Mom and Gary, letting them know the truck started right up. I waited a few minutes to give it time to charge before I took off the battery charger, placed it on the passenger side of the floor, just in case, and got into the truck.

The ride into Fraser was quiet. I didn't bother turning on the old radio. I had the window down and was just enjoying the breeze. Fraser was bigger than Tabernash, but not by much. They had four grocery stores, a few Starbucks, a spattering of banks, a theater that was also the bowling alley, more restaurants or bars you would think would be in a small town, and several ski and snowboarding shops. Otherwise, it was one of those towns you stopped to fill up on essentials and went through.

When I pulled up in front of Rocky Mountain Roastery Café, I locked the truck and walked into the cafe. The smells of freshly baked goods assaulted my senses with coffee and tea mixed in. I was in Heaven. A tall man with long blonde hair and a full beard to match was behind the counter.

"Hey! Welcome! What can I get for you today?"

I ordered a large steamed milk with cherry and a sweet croissant. I chose a table near the windows so I could watch outside. I'd brought my drawing pad and charcoal pencil for some sketching. Just as I bit into the croissant (which was Heaven in my mouth), I got a text from Jasper.

Hey. We finally got here. I hate riding in a car with a bunch of whiny guys. They're all jerks. Did you get to your place okay?

I smiled before I replied. *I did. Got the truck working and now I'm at a café. I love having a snack before I have to go get some groceries.*

Ugh. Food shopping. I don't mind cooking sometimes, but I hate grocery shopping.

I stifled a laugh as I took a sip of my drink. It was perfect.

I don't like long grocery trips, but I'm a good twenty miles from anything, so it's better to stock up.

He didn't reply as quickly as before so I picked up my charcoal and began to draw.

I didn't think about it, I just let my hand move. The world faded away as a dark piece started to reveal itself. The edges of the paper were all black, forming a circle. Inside the circle was the form of a woman sitting on her knees, feet pointed behind her, her arms at her sides as she stared up into the sky, and cried black tears.

When I finished, my right fingers were black from shading instead of using a tortillon. I hadn't even noticed I was doing it until the piece was done. I stared at the drawing for a few minutes, my brows furrowed. I didn't usually draw dark things. At least it could bring more diversity to my portfolio.

My drink was cold but I finished it with the food. I used the restroom to clean up before heading out. As I got into the truck,

I checked my phone for the time and noticed that Jasper had texted me back about thirty minutes ago.

Where is your vacation home that you had to get a truck working and you're that far out from anything?

I started up the truck before answering, letting it sit for a minute to make sure the battery was going to behave.

Our family cabin is in Tabernash. It's the middle of the mountains, about a half hour from Winter Park. I have a whole mountainside to myself for the summer.

I drove the half mile north to the Safeway we always went to when we were in town. I grabbed a cart before going through each aisle. They'd done a renovation since last year, so now it looked more modern, with cleaner lines. I grabbed my headphones in my pocket, put them on, and pulled up a playlist on my phone while I shopped. My head was bobbing to the music as my lips mouthed the words when I was in the chip aisle looking at the options when my phone buzzed again with a text. It was Jasper again.

You're shitting me? Our summer home is in Tabernash.

I blinked for a second. I was stunned.

Small world. Technically, it would be your vacation home if you visit it during the other seasons, too. Just saying.

Harhar. I forgot you have that sharp wit. You're right. It's our vacation home away from home. What are you doing right now? Still in town?

I bit my lower lip as I thought about how to reply. Did I want to tell him? We'd only hung out that once and talked a few times via text. It didn't make us friends, but it seemed like he was trying to be. I counted backwards from ten as I felt my anxiety start making me doubt myself again.

After I breathed out the last second, I replied, jumping in feet first. *I'm at the North Safeway getting groceries for the next few days. Would you like to come over for a BBQ later?*

He didn't reply after a minute, I put my phone back in my

pocket and continued shopping. I grabbed a few bags of chips, dips, and a case of soda. I picked up a pound of hamburger meat, two steaks, condiments, salad, and sandwich makings. The last stop was the bakery for some cookies. As I was picking out the different kinds, my phone buzzed again. I set the cookies down.

That sounds like a blast. My friends are with me, though. Is it alright to bring them? It'd be four of us. Axel's part of the group.

My anxiety had me breathing quickly and my hands started to shake. Ten, nine, eight... My eyes closed. It was Jasper and Axel. I'd met them, they both seemed nice. I sent a text to Mom first to tell her some guy friends wanted to come visit since they were in town too. I waited until she texted me back.

As long as you're comfortable, no objections from us. You're an adult, but I don't want you to have an anxiety attack with no one with you. Felicity has been working on you during school. Think you can do it?

I thought about it for a few moments. Before I'd started hanging with Felicity, I'd have never said yes or even entertained the idea of throwing a barbeque with some acquaintances, but now?

I was going to go for it. I had my breathing exercises and Jasper didn't seem the kind to be friends with assholes. I sent him a message with my address.

I'll see you there in two hours. I'll get the food started before you get there. Any drink preferences?

We'll bring some drinks. Don't worry about those. Thanks for the invite. See you soon!

I finished grabbing two dozen cookies and went back to the meat aisle. I would need a lot more meat if there were going to be four guys.

Jasper

"Hey, Seth," I yelled up the stairs. "Hurry up! We're going to be late!"

When we'd finally gotten to the house, we were all ready to smack Cody. He had a habit of singing annoying songs on long rides to get that reaction. My fox was having a fit. He wanted to get out to stretch his legs in the forest.

I'd forgotten that I'd texted Becca yesterday about getting here. When she'd told me she was in Tabernash, I'd shouted, making the other guys rush into the room.

"Remember Becca?" I'd asked Axel.

"Yeah, Felicity's friend. Why?"

"I've been texting her. She's spending the summer here too. Her family has a cabin near us."

Axel grunted. "No shit? Is Felicity with her?" His eyes lit up.

I rolled my eyes at him. "It's just Becca."

"Ah. Well, that's cool."

Seth just looked at me from where he leaned against the wall. "You like this girl?"

I shook my head. "Just as a friend. Met her at a party last weekend. She's the best friend of the girl Axel's been crushing on." My fox scoffed at me. He liked her.

Cody plopped himself down on the couch, almost hanging upside down. "Aw, Axel has a crush!"

I'd stepped out of the way when Axel had rushed at Cody. When Becca's barbeque question popped up, I'd looked over at Seth.

"What do you say about a barbeque at her place? Give us a breather from the car ride here. We can order groceries tomorrow?"

Seth was silent for a minute as he contemplated the request.

He was always so serious these days, I was hoping that the time here would loosen him up and get his mind off other things.

"Yeah, alright. Let's do it." He ran a hand through his hair. "I'm going to change." He turned, leaving me with the other two.

"Alright, guys, get ready!" I grinned as I sent the text to Becca. She'd given a two hour time frame, which worked out perfectly. We had some soda and beer in the car that we'd brought from the house.

Cody yelped from the floor where Axel had him in a headlock. I rolled my eyes as I went up to my room to change out my shirt.

Becca

I'd just finished putting away most of the groceries, when the doorbell rang. It was a little after three in the afternoon.

"It's open! Come on in!" I yelled over my shoulder from the kitchen as I poured one of the bags of chips into a large bowl. It gave me a second to take a deep breath to prepare myself to meet new people.

"Hey, Becca!" Jasper's chocolatey voice rang out. "Thanks for letting us come over!" His voice got closer as he came into the kitchen.

I turned around toward the center island with the bowl of chips when he came in carrying a large case of beer over one of his shoulders. He looked relaxed with a soft smile on his face. His blond hair was rustled, like he'd been running his hand through it all day. He wore black jeans with a loose dark red V-neck shirt.

"Hey." The grin that spread across my face was real. "Talk about a small world, huh?"

He set the case of beer down on the island as he threw his head back and barked out a short laugh. "You're telling me! We're literally down the road from you. Maybe a neighbor between us? How many acres is it here?"

I passed him the bowl of chips as I opened up the dip. "Twenty, give or take? It's been part of my mom's side of the family for a little over a hundred years. The original cabin was one of the first on this side of the mountain." The next dip was giving me issues. The top just wouldn't come off. "What about your house? Do you four own it? Belong to family?"

Jasper set the chips by the case of beer as he pulled the glass jar from my hands, easily popping the top off of it. "It's ours. Seth bought it a few years ago, but since we've all lived together most of our lives, he just put it in all of our names." He handed the dip back to me. "There you go."

I eyed his arms again. "Must be nice to be a boy sometimes," I grumbled as I turned to the fridge to pull out the hamburger patties I'd already formed and the steaks.

"I don't know about that," Jasper chuckled. "Hey, Cody. This is Becca."

My back froze up at the sound of another person walking into the kitchen but I just counted in my head before turning around with a strained smile.

"Hi."

My eyes roamed over the newcomer. He was only a few inches taller than me. The word that popped into my head for him was delicate. He had porcelain skin that was a beautiful contrast to his hair that was so black, it looked like it absorbed light. His eyes were grey, so light that they stood out against his face. He had blue jeans on and his hands were in the pockets of his overly large black hoodie. He had a stud piercing in his right eyebrow. He offered me a grin that showed off pearly white teeth.

"Hello there. Thanks for inviting us over." He came forward to shake my hand. His hand was warm and almost as big as Jasper's. His voice reminded me of when you ran your hand over water in the pool. I found myself staring into his eyes for a long moment. The grey seemed to reflect the light.

"Would you stop griping about the car? I already said I'd pay for the window." Axel's annoyed voice filled the area as he walked inside. He had circles under his eyes and his jaw had scruff. He looked pretty handsome with the scruff. I wondered if I could get a picture for Felicity. He was talking to another person behind him.

"I'll gripe about it because we're going to ride in a car with a broken window because you tried to punch Cody." The voice that responded to him rooted me to the spot.

My eyes widened slightly and my heart beat faster in a flutter as a taller man stepped inside, closing the front door behind him. He was only a little taller than Axel and only slightly leaner. He wore black slacks with a light crème long sleeved shirt. Even from where I stood, I could see his clear blue eyes. No, blue wasn't adequate. His eyes were azure, like the bottom of a clear lake. To add to that, his hair was curly in a dark copper color. He had a square jaw and was probably the hottest guy I'd seen before that wasn't on the movie screen. Not to mention his voice was every fantasy come true. It was low and commanding.

What was with these guys? Was it a requirement to be buff and hot? I forced myself to swallow and breathed slowly as he walked over to the island to join his friends. He met my eyes as he got closer.

"Hey, I'm Seth. Thanks for letting us come over. None of us wanted to go into town after that drive." He shook my hand twice but looked at Jasper for a second. "What can we do to help?"

"Well, I'm about to go out to the deck and turn on the barbeque. I have hamburgers and steak. What do you guys want?"

"Steak," they all said at the same time.

I burst out laughing. "Wow. Okay. That was so in sync, you sure you didn't practice that?"

Jasper snickered softly as he handed Cody the bowl of chips. He grabbed the plate that held the steaks and the hamburger plate as well. Seth had snickered as Cody just grinned. Axel just shrugged as he looked between all of us laughing.

"It looks like we can each have a steak and a hamburger or two." He winked at me. "Lead the way! These losers can get the drinks, ice, and everything else out to the table."

I showed the way to the deck, leaving the sliding door open. It was nice enough today that no air conditioning was needed. The fresh air would be nice inside, too. Jasper followed me to the large barbeque that was built into the side of the cabin in stone. He helped me get the propane tank and light lit. As he opened the lid to the grill, he sniffed.

"What is that lemon smell?"

"I cleaned the grill and wiped down the metal with lemons. It's a good way to clean and will give the meat a little extra taste. Are any of you guys allergic? I should have asked."

"No, but that's a neat idea." Jasper didn't sound like he was mad or anything, so my shoulders relaxed. "Now, we'll let it heat up and slap these babies on there. How do you like your steak?"

"Rare." I walked to the table set and started to crank open the umbrella after untying it. "If you eat steak, it's rare."

"How are you still single?" Jasper laughed, teasing me as he came to stand next to me.

I snorted. "Why are you?"

"Touchè." He grinned.

"Here's everything." Cody came outside, carrying the beer, and a paper towel roll.

Behind him came Axel, carrying the soda, plates, and utensils. Seth came out, narrowing his eyes against the sun for a second. He held the dips in one hand and the bowls of chips balanced on the other. Color me impressed. Before I could help, Axel had set up the plates and put a soda at each place and a beer. He stopped in front of me, holding one out.

I looked up at him, cracking my neck a little bit. This was the first time we'd been this close to each other. His brown eyes were warm as they met mine.

"Would you like a beer?" He held it out to me. There was perspiration on it; they must have kept the beers cool on the way up here.

Being this close to him, his velvety voice had me flushing slightly as I forced myself to look at the beer. I really needed to get over these guys being hot. Even if it was the first time I'd been around such hot guys without anyone else. Could you blame me?

"Thanks." I took the offered beer, used the table to pop the top and took a drink from it. It wasn't light beer, which was good because I liked darker beers.

The guys had all paused what they'd been doing and were looking at me. My heart rate kicked up as I looked around me.

"What?"

"You just popped the top off on the table like a pro." Cody's voice was laced in amusement. "Never seen a girl do that before. We usually have to open their drinks for them."

I snorted taking another drink. "You're hanging out with the wrong girls." I set it on the table and went back to the barbeque.

Jasper walked over to me, leaning over me to pull up the top before I could. An arm went around my waist all the way, which was surprising and pulled me back against a muscled front. I froze as I noticed that it wasn't Jasper who'd come over to help. It was Seth. I looked up at him as he was looking at the thermometer inside.

"Um, I could check it," I mumbled around the cotton that felt like it was growing inside of my mouth. His body was hard behind me as I tried to step to the side but his arm was snug.

"I know you can, but it'd be safer if one of us does it since we're taller."

My eye twitched slightly. "What does being taller have to do with checking the temperature of a barbeque?"

Seth set the top down as he stepped back, his arm leaving my waist. "We have longer arms than you do. Hence, less chance to get burned if the flames go up for some reason." The corner of his lip moved a little like he was fighting a smile.

My annoyance deflated. "Oh. Well. I guess that makes sense." I turned away from him with my face on fire and went back into the house quickly. "I'll put together the salad and be right out."

The guys were all talking but their voices were muffled by the time I was in the kitchen again. The salad only took a few minutes to put together. I pulled out the ranch, but didn't see the Italian dressing I'd bought. I went through several cabinets, wondering if I'd accidently placed it somewhere else. The only other place it could be is in the truck. It could have fallen out when I'd brought in all the bags in one trip because I was one of those people. All or nothing with grocery bags.

"Hey, I left the other dressing in the truck. I'm going to go grab it!" I yelled out before going out the front door to go to the garage.

I'd backed the truck into the garage instead of just pulling in this time. Before I looked for the dressing, I noticed the trash around the floor from earlier. I sighed as I started picking it up before throwing the food wrappers away in the trash. There'd even been a rotten leg of some kind of meat. I had no idea how I didn't smell it when I'd come in here earlier. I'd need to wash my hands when I got back inside. The Italian dressing was under the passenger side seat, I had to dig around to grab it.

After closing the garage door, I thought I heard a noise behind the building but when I looked around, I didn't see anything. I just shrugged and went back inside. I washed my hands quickly before bringing out the salad with the different dressings. The guys had finished setting up the table and had even brought out the French bread I'd left on the counter.

Cody smiled at me as I set the salad down. He winked as he started to dish the salad out on the plates. "If we don't force them to eat it, they'll not touch it." He paused for a brief moment as our hands briefly touched before moving on.

Axel just grunted when Cody plopped some salad on the plate in front of him. He was playing a game on his phone.

"Have you talked to Felicity?" I sat at the table across from him, grabbing my beer.

He looked up to meet my eyes. "Not yet. I know she was traveling somewhere with her family. Didn't want to bug her."

"I think it's awesome we have service out here. I actually get bars in the cabin," I chuckled before looking over to where Jasper and Seth were talking at the grill. "Can I do anything?" I spoke up loudly enough so they could hear me.

Jasper looked over at me and winked. "No way. You bought most of the food. Let us make the meat. It'll be ready in just a few minutes."

Cody sat next to me. "You go to the same school as Jasper and Axel, I take it?" He draped his arms across my chair and the other chair beside him.

As long as he didn't touch me suddenly, my anxiety didn't rear its ugly head.

I nodded. "Yeah, what about you? You don't?" I grabbed a chip before dipping it.

Cody looked out onto the backyard and the pond. "Kinda. I'm taking online courses and working. Haven't really decided what I want." He shrugged before tipping his head back. "Jasper says you're in the art program?"

"Yeah. I've got an internship for next semester too."

"You gonna show us some?" Cody looked back at me, tilting his head. That gesture reminded me of my mom's dog for some odd reason.

I cleared my throat as I finished my beer. "We'll see. What are you guys going to do while you're up here?"

"Hiking, more barbeques," Cody smirked at Axel, "and Axel will be doing a lot of fishing. It's one of his favorite things."

Axel didn't even look up from his phone but Cody yelped next to me as he pulled away from the table rubbing his left shin. I snorted suddenly but tried to cover it up with a cough.

"You just snorted!" Cody stopped rubbing his shin and laughed.

"And you just got your shin kicked for being an ass," Axel drawled and velvet rolled over me. "Leave her be."

I grabbed a soda, opened it, and took a sip to distract myself. "Thanks."

Axel nodded at me before looking back at his phone.

"Food's ready!" Jasper announced loudly as he and Seth brought the two plates with the hamburgers and steaks.

It smelled mouthwatering. There was more lemon smell mixed with some spices. Seth grabbed the top steak with the tongs and put it on my plate. His face was straight but his azure eyes had a warmth in them.

"Alright, guys, plate up." Seth sat across from me as he grabbed some of the food before the others did. The rest of them dived on the food like they were starving. Axel grabbed two hamburgers on top of the steak. He grabbed the ketchup as Jasper was reaching for it. Jasper scoffed at him but loaded up his plate without a word.

Dinner was mostly silent as we all dug in. The steak was

cooked just the way I liked it. There wasn't any blue in the meat, but it was as rare as it could be. I tried to be quiet as I ate but a small hum of appreciation here and there slipped out but I was too busy eating to care. It wasn't until I'd finished my steak that I looked up.

The guys were already done. All of the meat was gone and the salad was surprisingly almost gone. Seth was leaning back in his chair looking out to the yard. He seemed sad with his shoulders slumped forward slightly.

"Can you swim in the pond?" Cody asked, bringing my attention back to him.

"Yeah, it's fed by a small stream from higher up so it's not stagnant water."

"Awesome!" He stood and before I could blink, he took off his shirt.

My mouth opened a little in shock as my eyes took in his chest. He was slimmer than the other guys but wow. His skin gleamed against the sun, his muscles were defined even though he was skinny. He didn't have the abs that women drooled over but his chest was flat with the Adonis Belt that my eyes naturally followed down to his pant line. His hands were on his pants just then and pushed them down as he took them off, hopping on one foot for a few seconds. He was left in tight black briefs that as my eyes moved over them, I pulled them up quickly to look above his waist. Oh. My. God.

I grabbed my soda and forced myself to look at my now empty plate. There was a groan from Axel as he watched Cody run off the deck's stairs to the pond. He sighed as he glanced over to Seth before nodding at him. He stood and followed Cody at a walk.

"You okay there, Becca? That was a little more skin than any of us were expecting to see today." Jasper's smooth voice rolled over me, calming my blush.

I cleared my throat before giving up and laughing. "It was

certainly more eye candy than I thought I'd get in the mountains."

Jasper stood from where he sat and came to stand over by me. He picked up my empty plate and utensils. "Why don't I help with dishes? It's the least I can do since you bought the food."

I stood with him and grabbed what dishes I could before he grabbed them. "I'll help. I don't mind." I looked at Seth, who was watching us. His copper hair flashed in the sunlight. I had the sudden urge to play with the curls. "Thank you for cooking the meat, Seth. The steak was perfect."

A smile slowly spread across his face. "I could tell."

Jasper bumped his hip into the back of Seth's chair as he walked by and spoke over his shoulder. "Come on, Becca. Let the crazies play outside while you and I clean up."

I couldn't help the giggle that came out as I followed him. Seth growled at him but didn't move from his seat. Jasper already had the sink filling with water when I got to his side. The only downside to having a well for a water source was that Mom and Gary had decided that it would be a waste to have a dishwasher, so dishes had to be hand washed.

"Where are the dish towels?" Jasper put the dirty dishes in the other side of the sink while we waited for the left side to fill with soapy water.

I knelt next to him to open the cabinet. I grabbed several and handed him one. "I'll rinse?"

I don't know what it was about this guy, but it was like we'd known each other for years with how comfortable I felt around him. Now that I thought about it, my anxiety had spiked a few times with these new guys, but honestly, it was a lot better than I thought it would be.

"Deal." He turned off the faucet and started to move the dishes into the left side. "How was the café?"

I moved the faucet head to the right side of the sink and set it to a small flow as he handed me the first plate. "It was good. I got caught up with a new drawing. It turned out weird, though. I usually don't create dark pieces, but this one feels haunted."

"Is it a good dark?"

"I don't know. I could use a few more for a diverse portfolio. So it can't hurt."

I glanced up and noticed he somehow had gotten bubbles from the sink on his cheek.

"Jasper," I laughed as he looked at me, "hold still. Just a second." I reached up and wiped the bubbles off. He flashed a grin at me but just as I was bringing my hand down, he grabbed my wrist gently. Before I could ask him what was wrong, he brought my hand up to his nose and sniffed several times. "Uh, Jasper?

CHAPTER 4

Jasper

My fox bristled in anger at the faint smell of an unknown shifter. This side of the mountain was ours, so there shouldn't be any shifters up here. The closest shifter pack was in Montana and a mountain lion was forty miles outside of New Mexico. Still holding Becca's wrist in my hand, I looked at her seriously. There was the scent of possibly a wolf with rotten meat.

"What's this smell on your hand? It smells like rotten meat." I kept my voice light, so I didn't spook her.

"Huh? I thought I washed my hands enough. I guess I didn't." She scrunched her nose in thought. "There was some trash in the garage from the last time one of the mechanics came to do maintenance on the truck. I cleaned it up when I grabbed the dressing I left in the truck." She tugged her arm and I released her wrist.

"That's so gross." I tossed a grin at her as my mind whirled. Perhaps there was a lone wolf shifter who lived nearby that just didn't know this was our territory. That wasn't likely, but it was possible. The other possibility was we had a rogue shifter on our hands and that was dangerous for everyone who lived around the area. I needed to speak with Seth.

Washing the dishes was done quickly since Becca was rinsing and put them onto the dry rack. As I unplugged the sink, I dried my hands. "Ready to go back outside?"

Becca stifled a yawn but nodded. "Yup. There's still a good two hours or so of good light out. Do you guys mind if I try to draw a bit? Or is that rude?"

"Rude? It's your place. Why would it be rude?" I winked at her as we walked toward the open door. "Besides, I'd like to see you in action.""

She shrugged. "I'm sure you've noticed I'm a little awkward with new people." She'd picked up her art things, including a large pencil bag, that had been on the couch.

"I hadn't noticed at all." The lie was easy. She'd done really well with meeting the guys. Felicity had mentioned to Axel about how bad her anxiety sometimes got and we'd been prepared to step out if she'd said so, but she'd handled it pretty damn well.

She shook her head at me, but didn't say anything more as we stepped onto the deck. I had to admit, this place was nice. It had the feeling of a home filled with love.

Seth was still in his chair where we'd left him. Axel was standing near the pond where Cody had jumped in with just his black briefs. He'd almost given poor Becca a bloody nose when he'd stripped. My fox thought it was hilarious.

Becca set up on the outdoor couch. It was missing its cushions but with the curves in the wood, it would be comfortable for a little while without them. I sat next to Seth and kept my voice low as we began to talk.

"There's been a shifter in her garage."

Seth stiffened next to me as his eyes scanned the surrounding forest. "You're sure?"

My fox hissed in annoyance. Of course, we were. "Yes. She says she cleaned up some trash she thinks the mechanics who came out to work on the truck left. There was some rotten meat of some kind and it has the shifters scent all over it. I don't recognize it."

"Shit." Seth's cheek ticked as he thought. "I'll make some calls. See if I can find out anything that we may have missed."

"What are we going to do about her?" I motioned toward Becca. She was consumed with her drawing pad and hadn't paid any attention to us.

"For now, we'll keep an eye out. She didn't say anything?"

I shook my head. "But she just got here this morning like we did." I shrugged. "She didn't mention anything to me about anything out of the ordinary. But, Seth," I hedge slowly, "she's a girl alone on the mountain. She has an impressive security system in the house, but let's be real, against a shifter? She wouldn't stand a chance."

I eyed Seth as his face smoothed out until it was blank, even his eyes were blank. That was his thinking face. I leaned back in my chair, getting comfortable as I looked over to the pond where Cody was floating on his back. Axel had found a large rock to lay on. He was soaking in the sun as it slowly made its way across the sky. It would start to darken soon.

"One of us will patrol the area at night. We'll have to find an excuse to have someone around during the day, or have her visit us," Seth finally spoke softly. He was very close to growling. "This asshole isn't going to ruin our vacation."

I laughed. "Please. Seth, you would be bored out of your mind if we didn't have some kind of shifter business to handle."

Seth was obsessive over shifter politics and helping us survive without attracting the Venandi's attention. I couldn't blame him, really. He and his little brother were the last of their species. But the reason he was our leader besides being the most dominant? He was ruthless and hunted from the shadows when he had a target. Most of those who tried to go after him never had a chance because he had them six feet under before they knew it.

His lips twitched slightly before he looked back over to Becca. "Don't worry about your friend, Jasper. We'll make sure this shifter, whoever they are, doesn't harm her. I want them out of our territory. This is our safe space and no one violates that."

Becca

I just couldn't get the eyes right. My breath blew out in an annoyed huff. The fox was beautiful. I'd used shades of peach, soft reds, and white to blend the colors of the fur. It was on its side, batting at a ladybug that was flying by, its tail was in the air. The eyes needed to be playful, mysterious, and serious at the same time, but I was having difficulty with getting it right. Maybe it was the wrong color. That's when I thought of the perfect color.

I grabbed my jade green pencil and started to blend it with a few other colors. My nose scrunched as I concentrated. Time passed by as I focused on the fox's eyes. The blending took a little bit longer before I was finally satisfied with them. I leaned back as I finished and smiled down at the fox. The forest floor was faded so the focus of the picture was the fox and the ladybug.

"Hey, Becca!" Cody's voice yelled from across the back. "The water is so cold! Why don't you come swim?"

I looked over the decks rail to where Cody was standing, having just gotten out of the pond. Water droplets ran down his body, I couldn't see a lot of details but he was laughing as he waved.

"Come on, you guys too!" He yelled at Seth and Jasper, who were still sitting at the table.

I started to put up my supplies when Jasper walked over. I'd just shut my drawing pad when he reached me.

"We're not swimming, but did you want to swim with Cody?" Jasper leaned against the couch. "It'll get dark soon."

We both looked at the horizon. The sky's colors had started to merge orange with the blue. I sighed. The lights on the porch would be going off soon.

"Nah, by the time I get in the water, it'll be too close to dark. The porch lights don't extend that far." I smile up at him. "Maybe we can all go swimming sometime?" I surprised myself with how easy it was to ask him that. I didn't even think about it.

"I think we can do that." His voice was warm. "I appreciate you letting us come by. You could have fooled us, we couldn't tell you have severe anxiety." His tone turned apologetic.

I sighed. Felicity probably told Axel, who mentioned it to him. I couldn't even really get annoyed because I know she probably told him so that Axel didn't do anything to trigger it.

"It is what it is." I shrugged. "The partially blind girl who also has social anxiety. It'd make a good story, wouldn't it?" I laughed softly so he knew I wasn't upset.

Jasper placed his hand on my shoulder and I tensed automatically. He sensed it and removed his hand. Thankfully, he didn't say anything. I started to think about why I'd tensed. I liked Jasper. I was hoping we were going to be friends. He'd touched me before and I hadn't flinched or tensed. I wondered why I'd done it this time. I shook my head at myself. Possibly because we'd just been talking about my mental issue. There would be time to think about it later.

"Are you guys planning on heading out after Cody is done swimming?"

Jasper came around the couch and sat next to me. "Probably. We don't want to bug you so much on the first day, you won't hang out with us again." His tone was teasing again.

I smiled looking off to the pond where Axel had dunked his feet in. "It's been fun. Honestly, I just plan on working on my art and sleeping in. It's nice to know that you guys are close and want to hang out. Felicity won't be here until the last week of break."

I watched his eyes narrow before he grinned. "Well, now that I know you're here too, I think we'll have to work out times to hang out! Why don't you come have lunch with us tomorrow? That way we can show off our house to you."

"You sure that would be ok with the others?"

Jasper nodded. "Yup. It was Seth's idea." His voice went louder as he said this in a sing-song voice. He was messing with Seth for some reason.

"Sure. That would be fun." I stifled a yawn. I think the day was finally catching up to me.

"And that would be our cue to let you get some alone time." Jasper stood and I followed suit, carrying my supplies.

I looked over to the pond to see Cody and Axel lumbering over to the deck. As they got closer, I got a better look at wet Cody. My eyes took him all in before I turned abruptly as they climbed up the steps.

"Get dressed, you idiot." Next to me, Jasper threw Cody's clothes at him.

"Oh, man. That was refreshing. You guys need to go next time." Cody's voice was right behind me, followed with the sound of clothes rustling.

Seth stepped over to me. I looked up into his eyes, taking his offered hand. The lines around his eyes crinkled just a bit as he spoke softly.

"It was fun. I hope we'll see you tomorrow. Have a good night. Call Jasper if you need anything at any time of the day or night. We're probably a lot closer than the sheriff's department." He emphasized his words when he said to call. That was pretty sweet of him.

"Sure! I'll see you guys tomorrow. Looking forward to it."

Seth nodded as he walked through the back door to get to the front. Cody came up to me and before I knew how to react, he'd swept me up into a hard hug for several seconds before following Seth.

"Bye, Becca! See you!" He waved as he disappeared.

Axel was next. He stopped next to me and offered a smile. This guy was a heartbreaker with it.

"Thanks, Becca. I'll text Felicity when we get back." He winked at me as he followed the other two out. I felt my heart skip once at the wink. No wonder Felicity was head over heels for this guy.

Jasper grabbed my supplies from my hands. "After you, milady." He bowed extravagantly as I burst out laughing.

The three guys had already left out the front door. Jasper was right behind me as he closed the back door. I watched as he flipped the security lock on it. He eyed the wall of windows before he turned to me warily.

"I know the windows are great for the view but they don't seem very..." He paused like he was trying to think of a word. "...practical. They don't seem practical if someone were to try to break in. Aren't you worried about that when you guys aren't here?"

I grinned at him. "Usually it's not. But Gary, my stepdad, takes the security of the family seriously, so this glass is bullet resistant. It's ranked at B7, which means that it can resist armor piercing projectiles. Plus," I pointed to a thin slit in the ceiling, "when it's bedtime, all the windows in the house are covered by security roller shutters for additional security."

Jasper whistled low. "Damn. That's pretty impressive."

I nodded. "Yup. I even have the same type of glass in my room on the ceiling."

"Your ceiling?"

"Yeah, it'd be even better if I could see the stars," I hid the lost feeling I got every time I thought about seeing stars, "but during the day? I love watching the sky."

"Sounds like you have a cushy room." Jasper's light tone made me smile again.

"Yeah, I guess you're right. You can set my stuff on the island. I'll probably take a bath and hit the hay early."

"Honestly, I'm probably going to crash when we get home. I love Cody, but damn. He's a handful when trapped in small spaces with him for over an hour. Make sure to lock up and turn on your security after we leave."

I chuckled as I walked him to the front door. "I get it." I held the door open as I watched him step out and head to the SUV that was parked in front of the house.

It was a black Escalade. Fancy. One of the back windows looked like it was cracked. The other guys were inside with Seth sitting in the driver's seat. I waved as Jasper got into the front passenger seat and as they drove away.

It wasn't until I closed the door, set the system, and went to the restroom to wash my hands that I noticed when I looked in the mirror, I was still smiling. I had fun today. I'd not over thought much, and I think I'd made the first steps to making new friends. Felicity was going to go nuts when she heard.

Speaking of Felicity, I pulled my phone out and sent her a text.

Can we video chat tonight? I have service up here! Plus, you know, Wi-Fi.

I knew she wouldn't respond right away, she'd said that night was going to be the only time that she'd be able to talk. The clock on my phone showed that it was just after six in the evening. I wasn't hungry, the barbeque was filling enough that I wouldn't be hungry for the rest of the night. I walked back into the living room and looked at my art supplies on the island in the kitchen, thinking about what I wanted to do.

The fox's eyes were still in my head. I decided on what to work on as I left the living room to my bedroom. The box I labeled as 'canvas' was on the bottom of the stack. It took a few minutes but I got it moved to the living room in front of the windows. Canvases on their own usually aren't heavy, as long as you aren't talking about the really large ones, but when you have twenty or more together, it gets heavy.

I picked out one of the larger canvases I'd brought with me and started to set up my space. I always brought an old, thick sheet where I went to paint so that I could spread it out to prevent any paint mishaps from causing damage on the floors. I pushed out the large ottoman in the room to the corner and spread the sheet on the floor and draped on the couch where I was planning to sit as I painted. The easel was just a quick snap to set up, just muscle memory at this point. I set out acrylics I'd decided to use. I decided to leave my oil paints at home since those took longer to dry and I didn't want to have to worry about the bigger mess they could sometimes make.

With the supplies ready, I sat on the edge of the couch's seat, flipped open the drawing I'd worked on outside and started to work on the canvas. I didn't think about this one either. I let my mind empty as my brushes and, sometimes, my fingers took over with the colors of the paint. I didn't notice when the automatic lights flicked on an hour later. I'd just started on the shape of the fox when my phone started to go off. My hands were covered in red paint so I very carefully answered the phone on speaker.

"Hello?" I went back to mixing the red with a little of the yellow to lighten it just a bit to a more orange red.

"Hey, sweetie." Mom's voice echoed through the room. "Did

you hang out with those guys?" I heard the twins in the background arguing over a video game and I grinned.

"Yeah, actually. It was fun. They're all pretty chill. I didn't have any kind of attack." Even I could hear how proud I was in my tone.

"Really? That's great, hon!" There was a crash in the background and Mom pulled her phone away. "Dang it. Steve! It's Milly's turn!" Mom huffed before coming back to the phone. "What are you doing now?"

"I'm painting." I put the brush down and dipped my finger a bit in the paint and brushed it as I worked on the tail. "It's a fox. Not sure why, but it's cute. I didn't think I'd get to painting so quickly."

"That sounds like you're starting off on a great note, sweetie. I just wanted to check on you and make sure everything was ok for your first day. Everything fine with the house?"

That question reminded me about the trash in the garage.

"Yeah, the house is great. I got my bedroom all aired out earlier. But, Mom, I wanted to let you know whoever did the latest maintenance on the truck left a bunch of trash in the garage and rotten food. It was really gross."

"Huh." Mom paused. "That's weird. Sheldon usually doesn't do things like that. Maybe he sent one of his employees, but I'll talk to him about it for next time. You got the battery hooked up?"

"Yup. It runs perfectly." I grabbed my black paint and decided to use my smallest brush to start with the outside of the fox's eyes. "I'm just going to work on this painting and go to bed in a little bit."

"Ok, hon. Love you. Everyone says hi."

"Love you, too. I'll call you later."

I made sure the call ended before turning back to the canvas. Just as I started back up, the shutters started to lower slowly automatically. I turned to look out the windows. It was dark out besides the lights that lit up the deck. I wondered what kind of inspiration I could get if I worked in the night air but shrugged. No sense crying over spilt milk as grandma used to say. I was just about to start back painting when there was a flash of color on the deck.

I put my brush down on the easel as I narrowed my eyes. There was nothing out there now.

There was suddenly a flash of gray over the deck. My heart rate sped up and I stumbled over the old sheet and moved to the security panel near the front door. I pressed the button to make the shutters in the house lower quicker and lock down the house. My chest felt like it was constricting as I fought to keep my breath even to stop the anxiety attack I felt rising up.

What the hell was that? Maybe a bobcat? It had been pretty big for a bobcat. Mountain lions weren't grey. But, then again, my friggin' eye sight when it's dark is shit. Even with the lights outside, whatever it was may not have been grey.

I told myself that I was okay, regardless. Whatever it was might have just been chasing bugs that might have been attracted by the lights outside.

I rubbed my face with my hands, trying to focus instead of the freaking out that was happening. That's when I remembered my hands were covered in semi wet paint. I groaned as I pulled back to see that the paint had smeared all over my hands. That means it was all over my face now, too. I groaned, it was time for a shower and bed.

Since I was the only one here, I left the sheet and easel where it was. Packing up my paints took a few minutes and I cleaned my brushes at the sink. Not for the first time, I thanked Gary silently for the touch faucets so I didn't get the sink covered in paints as well. My phone case had a splotch of orange-red paint where I'd answered the phone but that was easy enough to clean off with the corner of the sheet.

The bathroom that I shared with the twin's room was a jack and jill set up. It was rather large with a separate shower and bathtub. The bathtub was a jacuzzi tub that I planned to take full advantage of while here but for tonight, a shower would do. It was a large walk in shower with a ceiling rain head. Even though we wanted to conserve water, showers could be ten minutes before Mom had an issue with it. The water was recycled and used for the plants outside.

The water took about a minute to heat up, I had time to scrub as much paint from my hands before I went to town on my face and hair. The hot water helped my muscles loosen up. I hadn't even known they were so tight up to that point. I didn't want to end the shower when the ten minute timer went off but I did. No rebelling tonight. I was starting to get tired as it was. I could be a rebel with the shower next week.

Drying my hair took a few minutes since I have to brush out the tangles before and after the hair dryer. My hair was one of the few things that I loved and didn't want to change. Don't get me wrong, I was perfectly happy with myself, but my hair was pretty and I never wanted to dye it. I'd gotten the color from Dad. It was reddish brown but natural highlights made it shine in the sun. I braided it over my shoulder so that I wouldn't end up yanking on it when I slept.

By the time I went back into my room, all of the lights in the house, besides mine, were dimmed. I crawled into my bed, pulling up the comforter after I grabbed my phone off the table. I'd missed a call from Jasper and there was a text from Felicity. I took a look at Felicity's text first.

Hey! Sorry, today went long. I'm pumped to hear you have actual service! I can't video chat tonight, but let's do tomorrow night? Luv ya with lots of kisses.

I grinned as I told her that would work and gave hugs and

kisses back. She was such a sweetie. I was so happy she'd basically adopted me as her best friend.

After responding to Felicity, I called Jasper back. He answered almost immediately.

"Hey! I just wanted to make sure you were alright for the night?" His tone was light but I could detect a little bit of concern.

"I'm fine. Thanks, worrywart. The house is all locked up. I was in the shower when you called, sorry."

Jasper cleared his throat. "Ah, sorry about that? Anyways, glad you're all set. You're still planning on coming over tomorrow? Maybe lunch time?"

I thought for a second. That would give me a few hours to work on the painting. "Yeah, that should be fine."

"Awesome! Today was fun. I know I said that already but, yeah." Now his tone sounded slightly worried. "Can I ask a weird question?"

"Shoot."

"I meant to ask but I didn't and now it's bugging me. Why is your stepfather so security conscious? I mean, don't get me wrong, the bullet proof glass is cool."

I bit my lip. Here came the part to see if he would think I was crazy and I'd get uninvited from their house or he'd be cool about it and I might have a new friend. This conversation usually didn't come around for a few months until people actually met my family, or Gary, specifically. Felicity hadn't even met any of them yet.

"Gary is a little bit of an end of the world guy. He believes there are things out there that go bump in the night. So, he takes security seriously for any house he works on. He's a good guy and makes my mom happy. I think it's silly, but right now, I'm thankful for it. Think of it kind of like the house from that movie

The Purge." The flash of grey from the porch ran through my mind.

"Wait." Jasper's tone was amused as I sighed internally. "He believes in, like, zombies and things like that? And yeah, being alone up here, I can see why extra security would be a comfort."

"No, more like things that aren't human? Not specifically zombies. I mean, if the end of the world came tomorrow, there could be zombies, right? Who knows?" I rubbed my temples. "So, now, you ask me if I believe it and if I believe in the tooth fairy, right?" There was a bit more bite to my tone, even though I tried to keep it funny.

Silence on the other end was my answer. My shoulders slumped as I slid under the comforter more. Guess that was my answer.

"I'll talk to you later, Jasper." I couldn't help the disappointment that welled up inside of my chest. I never thought Gary was crazy, it was just the way he thought. It didn't hurt anyone. I loved that he made my mom happy and that he was smart. Sometimes, though, it sucked how I had to explain the strange things to people.

"Wait. Wait." Jasper's voice had deepened and I ignored the shiver it gave me. "I didn't mean to make you uncomfortable. There's nothing wrong with being prepared. Besides, it's a free country, right? If your stepfather wants to make sure his family is protected up the wing wang, it's none of anyone's business, right? Please, don't make me keep saying right. Because, I will and it'll get annoying. Righttttt?"

A chortle was his answer and we both started to laugh. The tension that had built for a brief second went away as he joked. He wasn't going to be one of those pricks.

"Right."

He snorted this time.

I was grinning when I continued. "Thanks, Jasper. Some people are asshats about it."

"Nah. Don't thank me. I was kind of a jerk there for a minute. But it makes me feel a bit better that the security is there for you. I know we're in Tabernash, the place that barely has any crime, but still. You're a girl and alone."

I raised an eyebrow and just shook my head. "I'll be fine. I've got all the shutters down and it's locked tight. There was something outside when it got dark, but because I'm blind as a bat, all I saw was a flash of grey. I think it might have been some kind of bobcat. Or something."

It was quiet for so long, I thought the call had dropped. I pulled the phone away from my ear to check that we were still talking.

"Jasper?"

"Yeah! Sorry. I got distracted for just a second with this video game." Jasper couldn't lie very well but I let it go. "A bobcat? Well, those guys tend to stay away from people so you should be fine," he teased. "Call me in the morning before you head over?"

"Oh. Yeah. Sure, I will. Good night!"

"Night." He sounded distracted as he hung up.

I shrugged. Guys were weird. Really weird. I settled more under the covers after plugging my phone in before I clapped to turn off the remaining lights in my room.

Jasper

Seth was next to me as I hung up with Becca. He'd heard the last part of the conversation when I'd gone to get him. Learning that Becca's stepdad was a survivalist who believed in the supernatural had gotten both of our attention. Did Becca believe like he did? The community in large tried to keep our existence a secret because the Venandi would find us faster if humans were crying shifter. If humans learned about us, they'd learn about other beings and that could be dangerous for everyone involved.

Then she'd said there'd been something outside of her cabin. I'd felt myself go pale and Seth had me sit before holding the phone and putting it on speaker. He'd gestured with his hand to keep talking, but he'd mouthed to end the call as soon as possible. My abruptness had probably bothered Becca, but I'd have to make it up to her later. She was quickly becoming a friend, plus, she was just a nice girl.

My fox hissed at me.

"I thought we'd have scared off that asshole when you guys marked the cabin with your scents."

Seth placed my phone on the counter next to me. His eyes were stormy.

"I did too. That means this shifter isn't just passing through. He knows he's trespassing in our territory." Seth started to pace. "Damn it. What would happen if we weren't here? We've managed to keep this territory Venandi free because we've taken care of problems without attracting attention, but this shifter could fuck everything up."

"Not to mention, Becca could be in danger." My voice was dry as I pointed that out. "Shouldn't that be our number one priority?"

Seth growled; his tiger was fighting for control. "You know what I mean. I'll send Axel out to patrol around her house tonight to make sure the shifter leaves her alone. We'll figure out what to do with her being alone the rest of the summer tomorrow." He took his hair tie out and ran his hands several times through his hair. He always did that when he was pissed. He just messed up his curls.

My fox brushed against me as I stood. I wrapped my arms around Seth's middle, holding him tightly to my own. He was a few inches taller than me, so I rested my head under his chin. He was stiff for several heart beats before his arms encased me. He was still growling silently but I could feel the vibrations under my cheek.

My fox laid down as I relaxed within Seth's arms. He was our alpha, the guy in charge, but he was still just one man. We were all family and touch helped when we were upset. Seth finally relaxed. He called out for Axel as he stayed in our embrace.

Axel walked into the family room, saw that we were hugging, and walked over and wrapped an arm around Seth's shoulders. Axel liked to act gruff but he was one of the most protective shifters I knew. He beat Seth in that category.

"What's up?" His brows were furrowed. "Seth?"

Seth sighed as he rubbed his chin along the top of my hair as he calmed down more.

"That shifter isn't here accidently. He knows he's in our territory. He was seen briefly by Becca. I need you to go out tonight and make sure the shifter doesn't do anything. Don't engage if you see him, except to scare him off."

Axel stiffened next to us. "Is Becca alright?"

"She's fine for now. She went to bed. Her stepfather is a survivalist so the house has adequate protection," I mumbled as I looked over at him. "I don't like it, though."

Axel nodded as he stepped away. "I'll shift and head over." He tossed his phone at Seth, who caught it without blinking. "Don't let Cody touch my phone. The lil' prick figured out my pin last time and posted a bunch of shit. It was a nightmare to remove." He pulled his shirt over his head, tossing it onto the back of one of the chairs.

My eyes roamed over the planes of muscle. He had an impressive chest with a spattering of light brown hair down his six pack of abs that led downwards and disappeared under his pants. His hands started to push down said pants when he cleared his throat, making me look up to meet his eyes and laughed.

"Eyes up here. Don't objectify me, man." His teasing made all three of us laugh.

Seth let me go and my fox was purring happily as I stepped back. I winked over at Axel. "I am allowed to objectify you when you strip in front of me."

All three of us laughed as Axel finished removing his clothes. There was a groan of pain as he called on his bear as he shifted. Seconds later, a large brown colored bear stood in his place. He shook out his fur with a grunt before he stretched. He glanced at us as he lumbered over, pressing his face into my stomach roughly.

"Ow." I laughed as his cold nose moved up under my shirt. "I get it! I get it!" Laughing, I stepped away. "No more ogling you when you're about to shift."

He snuffed against my stomach before moving toward the front door. Seth followed him so he could open it.

"Thanks, Axel." Axel squeezed himself out of the door with a shove from Seth. "If you get in trouble, let us know."

Will do. His voice echoed through our heads from the mind link we all shared as animals while at least one of us was shifted. I watched as he ran through the night into the forest moving toward Becca's house.

I met Seth's eyes. "I'll see what I can do about researching any sightings in this area."

He nodded at me as he rubbed the back of his neck. "Thanks."

"Go to bed, Seth. You've been up for almost two days. Axel will let us know if something happens." I softened my voice so the order came out more like a request. He just nodded again as he lumbered up the stairs on the other side of the room. I turned to my laptop on the counter as I cracked my knuckles. Time to get to work.

CHAPTER 5

Becca

The sound of birds woke me. The sun was just coming up as it started to brighten my room. My mind was fuzzy for a second as I tried to remember where I was.

The cabin. Tabernash. Right. I sat up, stifling a yawn.

The shutters had retracted in my room and the light was that morning glow that made me feel warm. I stretched my arms out before pulling them behind my head. I cracked my back and moaned. Oh man, that felt good.

My phone alarm went off. My arms felt heavy with sleep but I managed to grab it and turn it off after a few more seconds. Oh man, that had been a really good sleep. This mattress was the greatest thing. Thoughts of going back to sleep filtered through my head but I remembered that I promised to visit the guys place today.

"Ugh." I threw off the comforter, swung my legs over the bed, and kept my phone in my hand. "Coffee. Tea. CAFFEINE."

Stumbling through the hallway to the kitchen would have been hilarious if anyone had seen it. I filled the electric tea kettle, turned it on, grabbed a mug, and dug through the cabinet for the loose leaf black tea I'd bought yesterday. It wasn't coffee, but it had enough caffeine in it to give me that jolt I needed.

As soon as the kettle went off, I grabbed it, poured the water into the mug over the tea infuser, and grabbed a packet of sugar. You could add milk to black tea, but I just wasn't feeling it this morning. As I waited for the tea to steep, I looked at my phone.

There was a text from Jasper saying good morning. A few texts in the family group chat from Mom and the twins. Mom wanted me to know she was going to dye Milly's hair blue if she didn't start behaving and I snickered. Milly was being a brat, apparently. She hated the color blue so if Mom was threatening that, she'd have done something bad.

I sent a quick text off to Jasper saying morning before I turned back to my tea. The first sip was like setting my mouth on fire but I didn't care. It was so good. I leaned my hips against the counter as I held the mug in both hands before blowing on the steam. I started to think about my plans for the morning.

I wanted to work more on the painting I'd started last night. Right now, it looked like a bunch of weird shapes with no definition yet, besides the outline of the eyes. The fox just wouldn't leave me. I was going to get messy, no way around it, I always did. I'd just have to take my shower before going over to Jasper's place.

I finished the tea and was putting my mug in the sink when Jasper sent a new text.

Hey! Why don't I come pick you up today? I know we'd planned for you to just call me to get directions, but this way you won't have to worry about finding the house?

Why not? Sure. What time?

How about noon?

Works for me. See you in a few hours.

It was only a little after eight in the morning, so I had time to work on the painting before I had to get ready. My stomach gurgled just as I was about to leave the kitchen. I grabbed a donut and stuffed it in my mouth before I grabbed my brushes. The light from the wall of windows was invigorating to me.

Soon, time just faded away. The fox was starting to come to life. I ended up using my fingers to brush the grass out that it was laying on. I used the corner of the sheet on some of the trees to blot the colors to blend them a little differently. I hadn't decided on if I wanted the scene to be morning or late evening. Because the fox was so animated, I was thinking morning to give off that kind of energy.

I was chewing on the blunt end of my brush, contemplating the colors when a knock on the deck door spooked me. The brush fell to the ground as I jerked my head up as my heart started to pound.

Jasper stood at the door with his fist knocking softer now that he had my attention. He grinned at me. My heart slowed as I laughed.

"Hey!" I opened the door, stepping back to let him inside. "Why are you here so early?"

Jasper's eyes crinkled in amusement. "Early? It's half an hour past noon. When you didn't answer the front door, I thought this might be the best way to get your attention since you're ignoring your phone."

My eyes widened as I really looked outside. The light had changed and the sun was high in the sky.

"Oh, crap! I lost track of time! I'm sorry!" I brushed my hands down the front of my pjs when I remembered they were covered in paint as I looked down. "Oh, crap."

Jasper's shoulders shook as he bit his lip to stop from laughing. It was sweet that he was trying not to embarrass me anymore than I already was but I just shook a finger at him.

"Go ahead. Laugh it up," I laughed. "Sorry. This happens a lot when I get distracted."

"I can see that." His teeth flashed as he grinned at me.

"Um. So, give me, ten minutes?" That would be enough time to try to scrub off the paint without a shower and get dressed. "Let me just clean my brushes."

Jasper shooed me with his hands. "Go get ready. Tell me how to clean your brushes and I can do it for you."

"That would be a lot of help." I usually wouldn't trust any of my supplies with anyone, but Jasper wasn't another artist who'd try to mess with my stuff. I told him quickly how to clean the brushes with warm soap water. "Don't forget to clean between the bristles. Thanks, Jasper!" I rushed from the room through the hall to my room.

"Sure!" Jasper's voice followed me as I closed my bedroom door.

My clothes flew off as I went into the bathroom. I turned on the hot water in the sink. As I waited for the water to heat, I soaped up my hands. It took about two minutes of hard scrubbing to get most of the paint off my hands and arms. I dried my hands with the hand towel as I brushed my hair out of its braid before putting it back into the braid again. My teeth were brushed for thirty seconds before I went back into my room to grab an old Hendricks shirt and jeans. I ran back into the living room with a little under a minute to spare.

"Ta-da! I did it!" I was a little breathless but I bowed to Jasper. "Ready!"

When I straightened, I noticed that Jasper was looking at the painting with a strange expression on his face. I stepped up beside him.

"It's not finished. It looks bad right now, but I'm hoping it'll come out the way I see it in my head when it's done."

I looked up into his face to see that his expression had changed to a look of soft surprise or awe. I couldn't tell which.

"You decided to paint a fox?" He finally looked at me, his eyes swirled in the light.

I nodded. "Yeah. I got the idea yesterday. I drew it but when you guys left, I had the urge to paint it, and flush out more of the details. The eyes are what keep bringing me back to it, though, and I haven't even really started on them."

"That's..." He seemed at loss for words. "...can I see it when it's done?"

"Yeah. Of course." I grinned at him and pushed my shoulder against his arm. "Didn't know you liked foxes so much."

That seemed to snap him out of whatever he had been thinking about. He grinned down at me.

"Yeah, you could say that." He stepped back as he placed his hands in his front pockets. "Ready to head out?"

"Yup." I grabbed my drawing pad and pencil case. "Let's hit the road."

Jasper watched as I set the security system. He nodded at me as we walked out the door. He waited as I locked the door and put the key in my back pocket.

"So, Cody is in charge of cooking today. As long as he stays away from eggs, it should be pretty good. The guy can cook practically everything, except eggs. He somehow manages to always get the eggshells in them, no matter how hard he tries."

Jasper opened up the passenger door for me. I had to grab the handle on the side to get up into the large SUV. He closed the door for me before running around the front to get into the driver's seat.

"So, stay away from any eggs at your place."

We both laughed as he started the SUV.

The guys' house was impressive. As Jasper pulled up in front of it, I had to stare. The house was situated right up against the forest. It was a three story log house with an attached two car garage. There was a wraparound deck on the second floor that looked like it went around the whole house.

"Wow. This place is beautiful." The awe was clear as I stared up at the house as we got out of the SUV.

"It's pretty awesome, right? When Seth put all our names on the title, I'll admit, I got a little teary eyed."

"Did you all grow up together?" I was curious about them since they all seemed so close.

Jasper grabbed my drawing pad and pencil case from me, carrying them under one arm while taking my hand in his other. I fought to hold back the blush that was threatening to overtake my face. My heart sped up, but it didn't have anything to do with anxiety.

"Yup. Our families are all spread out, except for Seth and Cody's. It's just Seth and his brother now. We played together when we were little before our families spread out. I stayed with Seth because I wanted to go to school here. Axel joined us in middle school from Montana. Cody," he paused for a moment in silence, "Cody just fit in with us, so we adopted him, so to speak, when he was sixteen."

Jasper opened the front door, holding it open for me. My hand felt a little cold after he'd been holding it but I ignored that as I stepped in. The downstairs was one big room with the kitchen toward the back of the house. Furniture sectioned parts of the room off. A large circular staircase on the right side led up to the second story.

"So, our bedrooms are on the second floor with the game room. The third floor is storage with two guest rooms." Jasper started walking to the dining room table that was located off of the kitchen in the back. "We usually spend most of our time in the game room or the pool outside during the summer." He set my things on the table gently.

"This place is beautiful." My eyes roamed over the artwork on the walls, drinking in the different styles. "It feels like a home."

Jasper grinned. "Glad you like it."

I was about to reply when there was a crash upstairs followed by cursing.

"Damnit, Cody! I'm exhausted!" Axel's deep voice echoed down the stairs. "I'm going to kill you!"

Cody's laugh came closer, we watched him as he ran down the stairs. He spotted us as he jumped off the last two steps. "Becca! Save me!" His face was lit up in laughter, his grey eyes sparked in amusement as he ran toward me. "Don't let him get me!"

I stumbled slightly when Cody grabbed my shoulders as he came to stand behind me, using me as a shield. His body was warm against my back and his hands clung to my shoulders tightly. My throat started to close.

"It was just a prank!"

"A prank!?"

Axel came down the stairs just then and I fought the laughter that bubbled up. He was soaking wet. His hair was drenched and his white muscle shirt was clinging to him. His sweat pants were wet around his hips but dry at the bottoms.

My mouth went dry as his appearance distracted me from my anxiety. Axel's shirt was wet enough that the outlines of the muscles of his chest and stomach were clearly defined. I had to blink a few times and internally slap myself. *This was the guy your best friend likes. Stop staring! Remember Felicity!*

"You are a fucking ass! You knew I was up all night pat—!" He stumbled over his words as he finally noticed that Cody was standing behind me. "You ass."

"It's not my fault that you sleep like a hibernating bear when I try to wake you up, when it's *time* to wake up!"

Cody pressed into my back and I went rigid. My heart raced and I tried to focus on breathing but it started coming out in short breaths. Too much. Too close.

Jasper got in front of Axel as he looked down at me in concern. I clutched my chest as I felt my throat close. Stop it, Becca. Deep breaths. They were close. Too close.

"Cody, back up. Stop touching her. Jasper, step back."

Axel pulled Jasper back and grabbed Cody's hands off my shoulders. Then he gently took my hand and led me across the room from them as I started to gasp for air. It helped when I realized they didn't follow. Axel stepped away from me but he bent his knees so I could see his eyes. They were furrowed in concern and the color of chocolate helped me focus. My breath was easier to catch now that my heart had calmed down. He'd led us to the corner of the room near the kitchen. He'd turned me so I didn't see the other two.

"There you go," Axel mumbled softly. "Felicity told me what to do if I was ever with you and you had an attack. You doing better?"

I nodded. I was a little surprised that I'd come up in conversation when he was with Felicity. I'd have to talk to her about it.

"Thanks. Sorry." I felt the blush I'd been fighting outside spread across my face. "I just have a hard time with new people and crowding," I whispered as I felt shame at it. Cody hadn't done anything on purpose. He'd been including me in his playfulness.

"Hey. Don't apologize. There's nothing to be sorry about." Axel offered me a sweet smile as he straightened up. "Let me get you a glass of water." He walked into the kitchen.

My heart rate slowed to normal as the adrenaline faded as I took deep slow breaths. I turned slowly to face the other two that had come closer but were still a safe distance away.

"Cody, I'm really so—."

He interrupted me, looking ashamed. "Don't say you're sorry. I'm the one who should apologize. I know I have a personal space issue with people I like."

I didn't like seeing him look so sad. Cody was nothing but nice to me yesterday. I smiled at him.

"Don't be sorry. This is just me and my stupid anxiety. You couldn't have known because I didn't tell you, right?" I stepped forward and touched his right arm hesitantly, not sure if it would be welcome.

He grabbed my hand in both of his and squeezed them. His grey eyes were earnest as he looked down at me. "You're okay, though?"

I grinned. "Yup. Axel was pretty awesome. That's probably one of the shortest anxiety attacks I've ever had."

"Felicity just mentioned the signs to look out for," Axel grumbled gruffly as he came back over to us carrying two glasses of water. He handed me the first glass of ice water. "Here you go."

"Thanks." I pulled my hands from Cody's gently as I took the water from Axel. The first sip felt good going down my throat.

"And, you." Axel turned to Cody and before anyone blinked, poured the other glass of ice water on top of Cody's head.

"Shit! That's cold!" Cody yelped as he jumped away. He flicked some of the water at all of us and I burst out laughing.

"You deserved it." Axel crossed his arms at him, smirking.

Jasper wiped his face slowly as he narrowed his eyes at both of them. "You're both idiots." He turned to me. "Would you like to go upstairs?"

I nodded at him but looked between Axel and Cody. "They're not going to try to kill each other, are they?"

All three of them laughed. A grin spread across my face.

"Come on." Jasper went to the table to grab my things, came

back to me and took my free hand, squeezing it gently. "Seth probably woke up with all the yelling."

"Is that bad?" I asked Jasper as we went up the circular staircase.

"Nah. He slept through the night, so it's fine."

Once we got to the top of the staircase, my eyes widened again and a sound of appreciation left my mouth at the sight. To the left of the area was a large room with comfy looking couches, a large TV, and next to the TV were all types of gaming consoles. But what got me was the view.

A French door led out onto the upstairs deck. Jasper stood back as I went to the French doors, opened them, and stepped through. The view was breathtaking from above the ground. I could only imagine what it looked like with snow. It was instantly relaxing and I could see myself painting out here, drawing, or even sculpting.

"This is my favorite place in the house." The low voice sent shudders up my spine that had nothing to do with anxiety.

I looked over my shoulder and up to meet Seth's eyes. My tongue swiped my lower lip automatically as I noticed that his curls were loose around his shoulders, he was shirtless, and his sweats were basically falling off of his hips. I soaked in that his muscles were perfectly symmetrical. He had a little red hair along his chest but not much. My eyes snagged on a piercing in his right nipple. It was a gold loop. Holy crap. That was hot.

Seth cleared his throat and that had me yanking my gaze back up to his face. He was smirking at me with the side of his lips twitching. I flushed again and looked back over the deck.

"It's relaxing. I love it up here because there's not much noise." I felt him shift behind me before he walked past to lean his forearms on the railing. He gazed out over the mountain. "The city is too loud. Too many people in one place."

"Yet, he loves to go dancing." Jasper came onto the deck to

lean next to Seth but he faced me with his elbows leaning backward.

Seth just shook his head at Jasper. "Shut up." His tone was soft with no heat in it. His shoulders relaxed a little more before he turned around to face me, copying Jasper's pose. "So, Becca, this is it. Our humble abode."

"Well, I haven't shown her the pool, but yeah, pretty much."

I snorted. "Humble. That's a joke, right?" My hands ran over the smooth wood of what had to be a handcrafted wood chair.

Jasper grinned. "Told you she'd fit in." He gestured inside. "I put your stuff on one of the couches. I figured we could all play some video games or you can work on your art?"

"Do you have Smash Bros?" I hadn't played that in a long time.

They both laughed. "Oh yeah."

"You're all going down. Greninja is mine." I went back inside, and sat on the corner of the larger couch after grabbing my things.

"Hey, guys! Hurry up! Smash Bros tourney!" Jasper came in with Seth laughing at something he'd said. He plopped down next to me but wasn't touching me, which after the anxiety attack just a bit ago, I was thankful for.

Seth turned on one of the gaming consoles before tossing two controllers at Jasper, who caught them easily. He handed one to me in a flourish.

"Let's see how badly we kick your ass." He winked at me.

"Never tell me the odds." I kept my face blank as I took the controller and faced the TV.

Seth looked over at me and groaned as Jasper gave a shout of delight.

"You're a Star Wars nerd, too?" Seth sighed. "Now there's two of them in my house."

"You love me and you know it." Jasper nudged Seth as he sat next to him.

Just as the intro to the game started, Cody and Axel entered from the long hallway in the center of the room. Axel had changed into a new tank and jeans. Cody just grinned at me before sitting on the floor between Jasper and I. Axel took the spot next to Seth. They both grabbed controllers from Seth.

The next hour flew by as we all played against each other. Cody was relentless but I managed to beat him a few times while he decimated everyone else. By the end of the hour, the other guys had given up and it was just Cody and I.

He was playing Link while I was Greninja. Both of our health bars were low. I was just about to throw a combo to win when Cody tipped his head back to look up at me from the ground and grinned at me.

"You're pretty hot, you know that?"

My controller fell from my hands as my mouth dropped open in surprise. "What?!"

He laughed as Link gave the last punch and the game ended. Cody punched his hand into the air in victory. I gaped at him.

"You cheated!"

He shook his head at me as he tilted his face to look up at me from under his eyelashes. He had really pretty eyelashes. "No, I used the truth to my advantage."

I went to reply when Jasper smacked Cody on top of the head. "You're so rude."

"Ow!" Cody rubbed his head. "What? I was being truthful!"

I just laughed as Jasper smacked him again. "It's ok, Jasper. I'll win next time."

Cody was just trying to be sweet to make up for when I had my anxiety attack, I knew that. But it was a nice compliment, nonetheless.

Seth and Axel looked over at us and shook their heads before going back to whatever soft conversation they were having.

My stomach grumbled just then and all of their eyes looked at me. It hadn't even been that loud.

"I'm hungry, too." Seth stood. "How about we order pizza? I can go pick it up. Cody can cook next time."

"Can I go with you? I'd like to grab a hot drink at Rocky Mountain Roastery Café? There's a pizza shop not far."

Seth looked surprised but nodded. "Sure. I don't see why not."

"Great!" I stood and handed the controller to Jasper. "I'll meet you at the SUV!" I left the room quickly, going down the stairs before anyone could say anything.

Axel

I watched Becca basically run from the game room. There was a tick in my eye, but I took a deep breath. Cody hadn't lied when he told her he thought she was hot, but he really needed to learn timing. She probably didn't believe him.

I'd surprised myself when I wanted to growl at him. She was Felicity's best friend. It was the only reason I could think of as to why I felt protective of her.

Last night had my bear in a rage as we went around her house. Whoever the shifter was, he'd marked over where we'd put ours. He'd even marked the front door with his urine. My bear had fought against me for a few minutes. It had wanted to find the shifter and deal with it, but the job had been to patrol and protect her, not to find him.

We'd always been over protective of those weaker than us. It drew me to Felicity. She was so tiny, but so fierce, she could easily tip over with just a slight push of my hand. There was something about her that drew me to her, but my bear was never comfortable around her.

"Meat lovers?" Seth's question interrupted my thoughts.

He was asking all of us. I nodded. "Get two extra-large for me, please." I rolled my neck around my shoulders.

"I want extra pepperoni and banana peppers." Cody gave his favorite.

"Meat lovers." Jasper was looking at the staircase. "I'm going to go check around her house again while you're gone."

Seth nodded. "We'll be gone about an hour. Be back before we are." He started toward the stairs before stopping. "Cody," he glanced back, "I need you to remember that she's vulnerable right now." He went down the stairs.

Cody's shoulders slumped as he put his elbows on his knees, burying his hands in his hair. "Why do I keep messing up?"

Jasper rubbed his head as he passed him but he looked at me. "You'll make sure he's ok?"

I nodded and sat next to Cody, wrapping an arm around his shoulder putting his head on my chest. "Hey. You didn't know that she has anxiety with new people or crowds. I wouldn't have known if Felicity hadn't told me." I placed my chin on his head. "And you knew she'd be shocked if you told her she was cute. That was a little bit of cheating."

Cody huffed. "I wasn't doing it all that much to win."

I moved and flicked his nose gently.

"Fine. I did it to win. But I wasn't lying! She's hot. Not cute, by the way." He leaned into my chest more as he relaxed.

I blinked a little shocked. "What? You actually think she's hot?"

He moved his head to look up at me. "You don't? She's just the right amount of fluff. My wolf likes her."

"I mean, she's cute and my bear likes her, but not *that* way. I know Jasper likes her as a friend. Seth? Well, who knows what Seth thinks if he doesn't tell us."

Cody just shrugged but didn't talk for a few minutes. "I'll be more conscious of what I do."

I grinned and nudged the top of his head with my cheek. "Alright."

CHAPTER 6

Becca

The ride into town was quiet. Seth had put on a CD that played what sounded like classical music. I thought it might have been awkward since I hadn't spent much time with him, but it was surprisingly comfortable. Seth had this quiet strength to him.

"How old are you?" I popped the question out randomly.

Seth turned left onto the road before he looked over at me with his right eyebrow up. "I'm twenty-five."

"Huh." He acted older but looked it. "I was going to guess maybe thirty." I kept my tone light and looked at him from the corner of my eye.

His lips twitched. "Nope. Not that old, yet." He glanced at me for a second before focusing on driving again. "You're twenty-two? Started college late?"

"How'd you know that?"

Seth shrugs. "I Googled."

My eyes narrowed. "Are you a stalker?" I grinned.

That got me a low laugh. "No, I'm just resourceful. Why did you start university late?"

I glanced out the window. The greenery was everywhere and

refreshing. "I went to a community college to get my generals. It was cheaper that way. But I did it online."

"I finished my Bachelors online, too. It was just easier since I was taking over the family business."

I turned toward him as I held the seat belt band at my chest. "Business?"

"Mm. Yes." The SUV stopped at a stop light. "I inherited the family business when I turned nineteen. You ever heard of Pots Grocery?"

I thought about it. There were a ton of grocery chains in Colorado, but Pots didn't ring a bell. "No. Sorry."

He shrugged as the light changed and we pulled forward. "It's not a big deal. Pots Grocery is mostly east coast. It's been in the family since the 1950's. I don't do much now that it's been a few years, but I still have meetings twice a month or for emergencies."

"Dang. That's impressive of your family." We pulled in front of a pizza store and parked a few spots down. "But is that really what you want to do?" I unbuckled and jumped out of the SUV.

I met Seth at the front of it on the sidewalk. He looked a little confused.

"You know, no one's ever asked me that." We walked down the sidewalk past one store before going into the pizza place. He held open the door for me.

The smells that came from the kitchen made my mouth water. My stomach growled in agreement.

"We need garlic bread too." I placed my hands on the counter as I looked up at the bright menu overhead. "Oo, garlic knots? Even better."

"Garlic knots it is," Seth laughed as he pulled out his card when the cashier came forward. He ordered several extra-large pizzas, the garlic knots, and two gallons of sweet tea. My eyes widened at the amount that displayed on the register.

"Let me help pay." I dug in my pocket for my wallet but Seth placed his hand over my arm. It was warm and sent a tingle up it.

"This is our treat. Don't worry about it. Besides, most of this? We'll eat it all. You'll probably have to fight for two pieces," he chuckled.

"It'll be ready in about thirty to forty-five minutes. Would you like a soda while you wait?" The cashier smiled at Seth. She looked to be in her early thirties and was obviously flirting.

"No, but thanks. We'll be back to pick them up." Seth smiled at her politely and grabbed my hand to pull me out the door.

"She was totally flirting with you." We started to walk down the sidewalk toward the café. His hand still held mine and I looked down at it, surprised that I wasn't having an attack.

"Yeah. Well, I was with you. It's rude for someone to flirt with another person if they're obviously with someone else." He just brushed it off.

My brows went up in surprise, but we'd gotten to the café and went inside. I squeezed his hand gently before pulling it back. He glanced down at me but I ignored his look as I went to the counter.

"I'd like a cherry vanilla steamer and whatever this tall guy wants."

Seth snorted as he came to stand next to me. He ordered a macchiato. As we sat at a table near the counter, I sat back in the chair.

"Back to flirting. We're not really together, so why was there an issue?" It wasn't often that I ran into a guy with manners like Seth. I was honestly curious.

He shrugged. "She didn't know that." His answer was blunt and honest. I grinned at him.

"Seth, I like you. I hope we can be friends. I have a feeling you don't bullshit."

He settled back into his chair with his legs sprawled out

where they were on either side of my own chair. He was certainly confident with his body. I tended to curl in on myself in public but Seth just seemed to spread out in his own space with not a care in the world. Maybe I could learn from him to be that confident.

"I don't. Bullshit that is." His azure eyes seemed even clearer as the light came through the window. "I'd like that. I don't have many friends outside of the guys. It's a sausage fest with them already."

I choked on my laughter as our drinks were finished. Seth stood before I could get up and grabbed them. He set mine in front of me as he settled back in his chair again, sipping his macchiato.

"Some men would like that. Just saying." I took a sip of my steamer and sighed happily. Nostalgia flooded my senses for a brief moment again.

Seth shook his head at me with curved lips as he sipped his own drink. "I'm not saying it's a bad thing. It's just nice to have someone..." He struggled for the right word.

"With boobs?" I hid my smirk behind my cup.

Seth threw his head back in a deep laugh. It sent a pleasant shiver down my back and I noticed that others in the café glanced over at him. His laughter was contagious because others were soon smiling before going back to their conversation.

"You say *I'm* blunt." His laughter trickled off as he shook his head. "But yes. Having a girl around is a welcome change." He glanced out the window. "I had a question. Your stepdad."

Oh boy. Here it comes. "Okay."

"You told Jasper that he believes in things not human." He was trying to be tactful and kept his voice low.

"Yeah?"

"What are your thoughts?" His stare was direct and pointed. It made me shift in my seat. Having his direct attention was a little overwhelming. He was a beautiful man and anyone would squirm if he looked at them directly.

"My thoughts? About my stepdad? I love him and my siblings." I sighed. "If you mean if I believe as he does? I don't not believe. I mean, it's a big universe."

His eyes narrowed before he nodded once at me. "Not a bad way to look at it." He stood just as I was about to ask him his opinion. He'd finished his macchiato and threw it in the recycling can. "We should head back to get the pizzas." He held out his hand to me.

I took it without thinking. He helped pull me up and threaded his fingers between mine. He was very touchy; it was kind of cute. My anxiety wasn't flaring up, so I was going with it. Touch was comforting and I didn't get to enjoy it as often as some. My drink wasn't done, so I took it with us as we started down the sidewalk again.

"About earlier, with Cody." Seth looked down at me. "He's very affectionate and sometimes doesn't think before he does things."

I shook my head. "He's a sweet guy. I'll get him back for cheating later." I finished my steamer and threw the cup in the trash can outside of the restaurant.

Seth grinned as he held open the door to the pizza place again but he kept our hands together as we entered and went up to the counter again. The same cashier was there, but her smile had turned cold, professional, and was no longer flirty. I hoped she hadn't made the food.

She turned around from the counter and opened a warming oven and pulled out several large pizza boxes and a smaller box that was the garlic knots. She placed them on the counter next to the register and pointed to a display fridge.

"You can get your tea from there. This is everything. Did you want to look at them?"

Seth shook his head and let go of my hand. "No, it smells

fantastic. Thanks." He looked at me as he picked up the boxes. "Would you grab the teas?"

"Yup!" I pushed open the door for him. "I'll be right there. You can get the car door?"

"Yeah. The back will open for me with my foot." He glanced back at me briefly before walking through the door.

I went to the fridge and had just pulled out the two gallons when the cashier spoke.

"You know, the second he realizes you're not worth his time, he'll dump you."

My heart pinged in pain as I gaped at her in shock. "Excuse me?" I might not have paid for the food, but I was still a customer. Not to mention, you don't say that kind of shit to people. Period.

My shoulders squared back and I walked out of the restaurant. Seth had just closed the back and met me at the passenger side. He took the tea and his eyes furrowed. "Are you alright?"

I had an idea and it was so out of character, I could already hear Felicity screaming in celebration for stepping out of my comfort zone. I looked up into Seth's eyes.

"Is that cashier watching us?"

He looked confused but looked up before looking down at me. "Yeah?"

I gulped but took the plunge. "Would you kiss me? I promise I'll explain once we get going."

His eyes widened slightly but I could have sworn they darkened a little before his lips curved. "Sure." I didn't have time to change my mind because he tilted my chin up with his index finger and slowly lowered his face. Just before his lips met mine, he grinned wickedly. Then his lips were on mine and all thought fled.

His lips were hot as he moved them along mine. My mouth opened to his instinctively and my tongue slipped out to lick at his lower lip. Seth made a noise deep in his chest that sounded like a rumble and my hands smoothed against his shirt. The heat from him was almost burning.

Seth nipped at my lips, dragging my lower lip gently between his teeth. A moan I couldn't stop came from me as I felt Seth's other hand hold the back of my head and tilted my head up more. That gave him easier access to my mouth as his tongue plunged into mine and our tongues danced with each other.

Seth had just moved his hand that was under my chin to my waist when a passing car honked next to us. That noise jolted both of us. I started to jerk back, but Seth kept me close holding the back of my head gently.

"Remember, you're still messing with the cashier." Seth kept his voice soft as he pulled up slowly before stepping back from me and the heat, he'd generated within me, sizzled out. "Come on, babe. In the car." His hand brushed my shoulder as he walked around the front of the SUV and got into the vehicle.

My throat constricted, but I gulped in a deep breath. Holy crap. That just happened and I was the one who asked for it. I swallowed as I got into the SUV and buckled in. I looked up just as we were pulling out of the parking spot to find the cashier glaring at me. The reason for the kiss flashed through my head and I grinned at her and flipped her off with both hands.

Seth burst out laughing as we turned onto the main road. I grinned over at him in triumph.

"Thanks for that."

"I can honestly say it was my pleasure. What did she do to earn that lovely display?" Amusement made his tone light.

I shook my head as I leaned back in the seat and relaxed. "It's not a big deal. That display was more than enough to teach her a lesson about civility." I sniffed and nearly moaned. "Oh man, that pizza smells so good. I can't wait to eat."

Seth looked at me out of the corner of his eye as he smiled.

"Make sure to grab the pieces you want before any of us start for ours. That way you have food."

"Alright. You know I'm not sharing the garlic knots, right?"

Ignoring how that kiss made me feel was probably the wisest choice for the time being.

Cody

After Axel left the game room to take a shower, I stayed sitting on the ground against the couch and stared at the TV for a long time.

First, I scared Becca downstairs within the first five minutes and then, I messed up by flirting with her to win the game. I rubbed my hands over my face before blowing out a breath. My wolf was pacing and restless. It wanted to get out and run but we wouldn't be able to do that until tonight.

I thought Becca was hot. Unlike Axel, I liked bigger girls. Plus, she was sweet. My wolf didn't usually trust strangers, but the second we'd met her, he'd wanted to roll on his back and give her his belly. I'd gone swimming yesterday to stop myself from hanging all over her.

Now this shifter around her house had all of us on edge. Jasper wanted to protect his friend, Axel was doing it because of her best friend, and Seth, well, Seth was going after this shifter because this was our territory and most shifters knew that. This one was either stupid or knew and was fucking with us. My wolf raised its lips in a snarl as it paced faster.

I stood and walked outside onto the deck. They'd left almost an hour ago, they would be back with food soon.

I sighed and stretched my arms over my head. I was yawning when I noticed Jasper in his fox form running out of the forest to the house. I waved at him as he transformed in the yard. My eyes roamed over his naked body in appreciation.

Jasper looked up at me and smirked. "Enjoying yourself?"

I grinned down at him. "Oh, most definitely."

Jasper flipped me off as I laughed. Tires on gravel brought my attention to the front of the house. "Seth's back."

Jasper ran inside and it was only a few seconds later that he was up the stairs and running down the hallway to his room.

"I love to watch you go." I made sure to yell after him.

His laughter could be heard through his closed door.

The front door opened, followed by Seth's voice, "Food time, you lazy assholes!" Becca's giggle made my wolf and I both preen. That was all the push I needed to get me to go downstairs.

Seth already had the pizzas opened out on the large dining table with plates next to them. Becca was putting a third piece of pizza on her plate and she was holding another box that with a quick sniff revealed that she held garlic bread.

"Ok, I grabbed what I'll eat. Let the beasts loose!" she joked at Seth as she walked to the other side of the table.

I watched, a little in awe, as Seth grinned at her as he piled his plate with pizza. He sat next to her and poured both of them a glass of what looked like tea each. He was almost touching her. My wolf stretched out happily as we watched them. Maybe Seth liked her too. That was a good thing.

She could be the one.

Becca

The banter between Seth and I had continued to improve during the drive back to the guys' house and was still going strong now that we were eating. Cody had popped downstairs within a minute of setting up the food. Jasper and Axel had come downstairs after him. It looked like Jasper had taken a shower with his hair still wet and slicked back. Axel looked a bit ruffled, like he'd taken a nap while we were gone.

Cody seemed a little more subdued than he had been earlier. I think he felt bad about cheating. He was picking at the toppings of his fourth slice of pizza. He'd sat across the table from me. Jasper was next to me while Axel had sat on the other side of Seth.

Deciding that a little peace offering was needed, I picked up one of the garlic knots, placed it on a napkin, and pushed it across the table toward Cody. His nose twitched cutely before he looked up at the knot first then to me.

"Peace offering? We're good, Cody." My tone was teasing but soft.

His grey eyes widened as he looked down at the garlic knot before shooting to look up at me again. He grinned widely at me before grabbing the food and stuffed it in his mouth in one go. The other guys moaned at him.

"Wait, wait." Jasper's elbow nudged my side. "Those were yours. You were hoarding them! But he gets one?" He reached for the knots.

I pulled the box to my chest and whacked his hand playfully. "He gets one because he's cute when he thinks he's in trouble and I don't want him to starve."

Jasper's eyes widened for a second before they narrowed on me. "You'll feed the brat, but not your friend?" He huffed. "That's rude!" He looked over my shoulder at Seth. "This is war. Help me out, mate."

I was laughing when I felt Seth's hands go around my waist. Before I could panic, I felt myself being lifted up and in his lap. My laugh turned into a squeak as my eyes yanked up to look at him.

"What...?" My stomach flipped and I don't think it was because of anxiety.

Seth was looking at his pizza, his arms on either side of me on the table. He took a bite of his slice while looking nonchalantly over at Jasper.

"If it's war, I'm on her side."

When he spoke, I could feel the vibrations in his chest. I wanted to lean into his chest, but that wasn't something a friend did with a hot guy friend. Right? I looked over at Jasper and his mouth had dropped in a little O.

"Ok, that's seriously cheating. We're supposed to be on the same side, Seth!" He threw one of his used napkins at Seth. "I want a garlic knot!"

I had to bite my lip from laughing at how exasperated he sounded.

"You didn't order them. Becca did. If you want one, perhaps you should try asking nicely." He took another bite of his pizza. "Like this." He looked down at me. "Becca, can I have one of your garlic knots, please?" His eyes glinted with a hidden message.

I wasn't sure what he wanted me to do, but I was going to go with it. This was fun. I took one, and as I took it out of the box, Jasper groaned in defeat. I didn't hand it to Seth, though. I put it up to his lips with my own smirk and a raised eyebrow. Two could play this game.

It backfired spectacularly.

Seth's eyes met mine again. They'd darkened and he opened his mouth to take a bite from the garlic knot. He bit it in half but his lips touched my fingers, which sent a zing through me. He smirked as he chewed. My groan of defeat joined Jasper's.

"Fine. I wave the flag." I knew I was blushing bright red, but I grabbed a clean napkin and waved it in the air.

Seth swallowed and laughed. He brought his hands back to my waist, squeezed once before lifting me off of his lap back into my seat. I couldn't believe he was able to easily pick me up like that.

I took a sip of my tea trying to get my blush under control. I looked up and caught Cody watching me. He stuck his tongue out at me and I lost it again.

"Can I have a garlic knot, please?" Jasper was overly dramatic as he asked the question. He laid his arms on the table and stretched out his hands. He clenched them open and closed a few times. "I need the garlicky, buttery goodness in my tummy!"

That did it. I choked on the tea as I had started to sip it and started to laugh in the midst of choking on the liquid as it tried to go down. I slapped at my chest as I tried to catch my breath, for once not because I was having an anxiety attack. Seth and Jasper reached out at the same time, slapping my back. That helped and as I took a grateful breath of air, I pointed at Jasper accusingly.

"That was a set up!"

He laughed at me as Seth joined him. I glared between the two but it had no real heat. This was probably the most fun I'd had in a long time. Sans Felicity.

Axel had been quiet while he ate and just watched us throughout dinner. I leaned back in my chair as the others started to talk about what they were going to do tomorrow. He was staring at his phone with his eyes down.

I stood, picked up my plate, grabbed Jasper, Seth, and Cody's since they were done. They thanked me as they kept talking. When I went to Axel, I sat on the chair next to him.

"You okay?" I kept my voice low and soft so that we didn't attract the others' attention.

He offered me a strained smile before he glanced down and shrugged as he put his phone in his back pocket. "I knew I wouldn't get to talk to Felicity much, but I haven't heard from her at all."

I blinked in surprise. She'd sent me a text earlier. I'd have to ask her what was up with her not talking to Axel. I touched his hand gently.

"I'm sure she's just busy. I know her family is overbearing with her for some reason. Especially this summer." I tried to offer the explanation, but I knew it didn't help much when he just nodded slightly. An idea popped up into my head.

"Hey. Would you let me draw you? I could send it to Felicity to tease her?" I grinned at him. "Like the pose of 'paint me like one of your French girls'?"

He turned to look at me full on. "Really? You think she'd like that?" He was pretty cute with how awkward he was about her for such a large man.

"Yeah! Of course!" I looked around, forgetting where I'd left my drawing pad. "We can start now if you'd like?"

"Wait. Wait!" Cody stood from his chair. He placed his hands on the table top as he leaned forward. "I want to be drawn too!"

Jasper and Seth looked over at me now. Seth's lips were twitching as he fought a grin while Jasper just smirked.

"We do too!"

I groaned but laughed after. "Ok, I'll draw all of you at some point this summer. Deal?"

Cody walked around the table to stand in front of me. He knelt on one knee and offered his hand. "I vow to be the best model of the four of us!"

Jasper walked from behind me and knelt next to Cody, copying his pose. "I, Jasper, with the body of a God, will be the best model you've ever had."

I laughed so hard, my sides started to hurt after a bit. Axel stood and went behind the two and smacked them on top of their heads, which just made me laugh more, although at that point, it was more of a rasping gasp.

"She offered to draw me first. So, I am the best."

I didn't hear Seth get up but felt him at my back. "Alright, enough shenanigans. Cody and Jasper, it's your night for kitchen duty, so put away the pizzas and clean the dishes, please." Seth put his hands on my shoulders as Cody and Jasper grumbled but got up to start clearing off the table. "Becca, why don't you go relax wherever you're comfortable? Axel will go with you if you need anything."

I tilted my head back to look up at him. He really was tall. "What about you?"

His hands moved to either side of my cheeks and smushed them together. "I need a shower." He smushed my cheeks to make my lips pucker like a fish as he laughed at me. I batted his hands away. Seth chuckled as he walked around me to go upstairs.

I rubbed my cheeks when I looked at Axel. He was trying not to laugh, but I could tell he was going to lose. I scowled at him, shaking my head. "Oh, go ahead. It was kinda funny."

Axel laughed under his breath as he held his hand out to me. "Come on. Your drawing stuff is upstairs."

With his hand in mine, I followed him up the winding stair case. He seemed more at ease after talking with me about Felicity. I was hoping that while I drew him, that I could get him to talk about her and their relationship. Any juicy gossip I could get to Felicity was my duty as a best friend after all.

He let my hand go as he grabbed my art supplies from the entertainment center where it rested next to the Xbox One.

"Why don't we go outside on the deck? I saw a nice chaise lounge that would be perfect for this!" I started to get excited to draw him. I was going to use graphite. That would be perfect to get the details I wanted.

I almost ran into the closed deck door because I wasn't paying attention, but Axel pushed it open just as I looked up.

"Felicity wasn't kidding." He laughed softly as he held his hand over his eyes as he adjusted to the sunlight.

"Wasn't kidding about what?" I put my supplies on a small table that was near the chaise lounge. It might be better to move the chaise than the table.

"That you space out when you start thinking about art." His light teasing brought a slight flush to my cheeks but he grinned at me. "I am a little jealous, to be honest."

"Why? I'm a scatter-brain about it." I went to the chaise to change the angle of the back so that it was lifted just about half a foot up. "Would you mind moving the chaise lounge a little to the left? I want the sun directly on your face."

He moved around me, his body brushing my side. He was so warm.

"Here?"

He moved the chaise lounge to the left. I gestured with my hand a little to the right until it was exactly where it needed to be.

"That's perfect right there. So now, just lay down on your side with your arms above your head, tilt your chin, and if you're comfortable, you can take your shirt off. If you aren't, you can leave it on." I stepped back as I watched him lift his shirt over his head and throw it on the ground without missing a beat.

My mouth went dry as I watched him get into position. The spattering of hair that trailed down his abs into his pants was tantalizing. He laid as I instructed and even tilted his head back just right and closed his eyes. His lips looked like they were pouting from this angle.

"Back to you spacing out about art," he murmured softly as I pulled up a chair to the table. "I wish I could be so passionate about something that I lose all sense."

I grabbed my 9H graphite pencil to get a soft sketch to

begin with. I started at the top first. "That's not football? Felicity says you're one of the school's best, like, that they've had in years."

He grimaced for a brief second. "I might be good at it, but it's not something I want to do forever." He had a line between his eyes that I made sure to add to the sketch. It made him look mournful and it was perfect.

"If you don't want to do it forever," I wondered briefly if he and Seth ever talked about their futures together, "what do you want to do?"

He was silent for so long, I thought he'd fallen asleep as I continued to sketch him. I was making great progress when he spoke.

"I want to work outdoors."

"Outdoors?" I paused for a second. "Like landscaping?"

"Maybe? I do take care of the gardens where we live."

My heart fluttered for a second. This big man who probably could easily squeeze someone to death, gardened and enjoyed it. He really was a teddy bear.

"There are classes at school you could take."

"I guess."

He was quiet after that. He didn't move or talk again until I finished the initial sketch a little over an hour later. It was probably a good idea we didn't speak when I started to really get into drawing his physique. My cheeks stayed red as I worked on his chest and arms. He had really defined arms that I wondered what they felt like if I were to trace them with my fingers.

I had to shake my head to clear my thoughts a few times. I'd seen plenty of naked men, and women, models. But I'd never responded this way and I was starting to feel guilty because he was Felicity's maybe boyfriend. Girl code superseded the hot factor.

Right?

"Hey! Are you almost done?" Cody popped his head out the door. "Is it our turn yet?"

I looked up from my sketch to smile at him. "I don't mind drawing you guys, but I think my hands are going to need a break. I'm almost done with Axel."

Cody walked over and looked over my shoulder at the sketch. His eyes widened. "Holy shit. I didn't know that you were that good! It looks like he could move any second." He cleared his throat. "And it's hot."

I raised my right eyebrow at him. He thought his friend was hot? That... was intriguing to think about. Maybe later tonight when I was alone and not surrounded by hot guys.

"You know I can hear you," Axel's grumble was rough. He'd been asleep for the past twenty minutes.

"You know you're hot. I'm just pointing it out." Cody shrugged as Axel opened his eyes to squint at him. "Besides, you're the one shirtless here. Not me." He grinned widely.

I shook my head, biting my lip to stop the giggle that wanted to come out. Cody seemed to bring this energy with him wherever he went. It brightened the area and people smiled.

Axel swung his legs over the side of the lounge and stood. As he stretched, my eyes traced his muscles. I yanked my eyes away after a second, only to turn and see Cody was watching Axel like I was.

Axel walked over to stand in front of us. He put his hand against Cody's forehead, pushing him back playfully.

"You're staring again." He tilted his head to the side as he looked down at me. "Can I see what you've done?"

I handed him the drawing pad silently. My palms were damp as I waited to hear what he thought. His eyes had widened for a second before they narrowed as he looked over the sketch. I started to pull at a loose thread on my shirt.

"I can't believe this is me. I was thinking you were going to draw a funny picture with that pose, but this..." Axel's voice was soft as he lifted his gaze from the sketch. "This is really good. You'll definitely impress during your internship."

My smile was so big, my cheeks hurt a little as I looked up at him. "You think so?"

"Can I get a copy of that? Purely for science purposes." Cody looked around Axel's shoulder to look at the sketch with a roguish grin.

Axel snorted before he handed me the drawing pad back. "I would like a copy, if that's alright."

"Of course! I can get you one tomorrow, if we are hanging out." I closed the cover on the book.

"Why are you both ignoring me?" Cody demanded as he walked around Axel.

I walked back inside as Axel replied and I couldn't help laughing.

"Because it's easier."

CHAPTER 7

Becca

Several hours later, the sun was setting as we all hung out in the game room. I was lying against the end of the right side of the couch and my legs were in Cody's lap. When we'd all started playing another game, he'd sat next to me after he'd asked if he could move my legs, I hadn't known he was just going to move them so he could sit and put them back where they were.

He'd been pretty sweet. He'd asked if it was ok and was worried that I was uncomfortable. I'd touched his hand closest to me and squeezed it.

"I'll let you know if I am moving forward. Deal?"

Jasper got up from where he was sitting in the chair near me. He started turning on the lights around the room as the sky darkened in the distance. After he finished, he sat on the chair again.

"Thanks," I whispered softly.

He winked at me before picking up his controller. "Always, Becca. I got your back."

"Alright," Seth, who was sitting on the other side of the couch, "I think we should play a board game. Anyone in for Monopoly?"

Cody and Jasper moaned at the same time. "No. No Monopoly. You cheat at it."

"How can you cheat at Monopoly?" I glanced between them.

Seth grins and winks at me. "It's just skills."

"Let's play Exploding Kittens." Cody threw his hands in the air. "Let's play! You know Becca will love it!"

I blinked. I'd heard of the game but never seen it before. I shrugged as they looked at me. "Sure!" Oh, I would regret agreeing to play this game.

Somehow, Seth always knew when the exploding kitten card was at the top. All of us kept getting the card but him. I was able to skip my turn with the action card twice, but otherwise, Seth won the game every single time. His smirk grew with each win. Axel, Jasper, and Cody were all sore losers. They yelled, threw their cards, and threatened bodily harm at Seth, but that just made Seth gloat even more.

It was two hours later when Jasper glanced at his watch. "It's getting late. Becca, why don't I give you a ride home?"

"OR," Cody spoke loudly before I could reply, "she could stay the night here. We have clothes that will fit her and we can just wash her clothes in the laundry for tomorrow."

My chest squeezed tightly for a few moments before I took a deep breath. The guys were looking at me to gauge my reaction to the suggestion. My cheeks went red as I ducked my head.

"Um, maybe next week?" I didn't want to tell them that I was wary about the idea. I'd only known them for two days now, minus Axel and Jasper, and I was comfortable around them, but I wasn't that comfortable yet.

Jasper wrapped his arm around my shoulder from my left. "No problem, Becs. We'll plan a sleepover like kids do later." He ruffled his hand through my hair as I relaxed against him.

"Let's get you home." He glanced over at Cody. "Come on.

After I drop off Becca, I need to go grocery shopping. You can help me carry everything."

Cody punched his right arm into the air. "Food! I want Oreos."

Jasper shook his head as he headed downstairs first with Cody behind him. "We'll meet you at the car!"

I turned to Axel and Seth taking a deep breath as I fortified myself. "Thank you. Both of you, for today."

Seth walked in front of me and placed his hands on my shoulders. "It's been my pleasure." His smirk grew as my face went red, yet again, remembering our kiss. "I'll be happy to do that again with you anytime." He leaned forward as he whispered this in my ear.

I giggled as I wrapped my arms around his waist in a tight hug without thinking about it. "Thanks, Seth." His body was hard but I felt like I could sink into him and stay for days. "Um, I guess I'll see you later?" I brushed some of the stray hair that had gotten out of my braid out of my face as I stepped back.

Seth tucked more hair behind my other ear. "You will. Let me give you my number." He held out his hand for my phone. It took him only a minute to put in his information in my phone before giving it back. "I know you have Jasper's, but now, you have mine. Text me when you're home." He squeezed my left shoulder before he left the game room down the hallway to the bedrooms.

I turned to Axel and smiled. "I'll make you a copy tonight. I'll talk to Felicity, too."

"Thanks, Becca." He approached me slowly. It was really sweet when he hugged me cautiously so I didn't freak out. "I'll see you soon. You have my number?"

I shook my head. "No." My phone was taken from my hand a second later as Axel put in his number. Before he handed it back, he saw something that made him snort and shake his head. "What?"

"Nothing. You'll see later." He gave my phone back to me. "Let's get you to the SUV before Cody perishes from his undying hunger for Oreos." He took my art supplies, not letting me carry them down.

Axel wasn't playing, either. When we got to the SUV, Cody was annoying Jasper on purpose about Oreos. I could only vaguely see their shadows even with the bright outdoor light.

"We need at least five boxes. I want Oreo ice cream too. We can make shakes?" He was talking a mile a minute.

Jasper noticed us. "Oh, thank God." He moved to the driver's door. "Cody, be a gentleman and open the door for Becca."

It looked like Cody saluted him before offering his hand to mine, which was easy to see since he basically put it in my face. "M'lady?"

My lips twitched in amusement. Axel shook his head next to me as he said goodbye, handed my things to Cody before leaving me to their care.

"I'll ride in the back seat. That way you won't have to change out seats when you drop me off."

Cody opened the passenger door. "Nope. You get the front seat."

Instead of arguing, I just got in. I buckled my seat belt as Cody got in behind me. He had my art supplies next to him.

"Alright. It's going to get dark." Jasper apologized as the inside light turned off automatically.

"It's ok, I promise. I'm used to this."

As the SUV pulled away, the light from the outside of the house faded and I was plunged into darkness. The lights where the digital clock was were super fuzzy, but still there. A yawn slipped out after a few minutes.

"Tired?" Cody asked softly.

"I'm not used to so much activity, I guess. I had a lot of fun yesterday and today. I'm sure I didn't have this much fun in a whole semester at school."

"Well, we are a bunch of fun guys." The sarcasm was thick as Jasper chuckled. "SOME of us could drive a saint mad."

I bit my lip hiding my laugh as Cody gave an indignant denial.

"How long have you all been friends?"

Silence greeted my question for several long moments. Beginning to become uncomfortable, I had just started to apologize when Jasper spoke.

"I've known Seth since I was a toddler. Axel since I was about ten. Cody joined our group almost four years ago permanently, but we've known each other in passing since we were little."

Sounds of shifting came from behind me. "My family moved around a lot, but we always came back in the summers." There was pain in his voice that I found myself reaching my hand back blindly to him.

His hand engulfed mine, squeezing it tightly. He whispered a soft, "thank you." I held his hand the rest of the way back to my house. It was a short ride, give or take fifteen more minutes. The lights on the outside were on as Jasper pulled up right in front of the front door. He flipped the inside lights on as he turned toward me. His eyes narrowed in on Cody's hand in mine, but he just smiled softly.

"I'll walk you inside. Cody, hand me her art stuff?"

Cody squeezed my hand one last time before he released it. He passed my art supplies over the console to Jasper. Waving good bye to Cody, I closed the passenger door. Jasper was at my side in a few seconds, holding my hand in his arm. I could just see the outline of his face until we got right under the light. His eyes were gentle.

"I'm not leaving until I get a text saying everything's alright and you're all locked in." Jasper was stern as he took the key I pulled out to unlock the door. "Deal?"

My lips curved in a smile as I looked up into his eyes. "Deal. Thanks, Jasper. Today was special." I stood on my toes to kiss his cheek before taking my stuff and closing the door.

Resetting the security system was done within seconds. All the security shutters were already down. I texted Jasper it was all good.

Text you tomorrow!

Leaving my art supplies and pad on the kitchen island, I went to my bathroom to start a bath. I was deciding on what I was going to put in the bath when my phone rang. It was Felicity.

"Hey!" Answering it quickly, I shut off the water for now.

"Hiya, chicka." She was tired but her tone lightened as we began to talk. "I miss your face and it's only been a few days!"

Leaning my hip against the sink, my chuckle was soft. "Sounds like you've been busy. What's going on?"

She blew a raspberry in my ear. "You always know. Don't you?"

"Mhm. You haven't talked to Axel since leaving the dorms, huh?"

There was the sound of moving in the background before a soft grunt from Felicity. "No. It's hard to explain. This family thing is intense. Honestly, I wouldn't even be allowed to talk to you if I hadn't had Wyn's support convincing my parents to let me keep my phone during the summer. I want to talk to him, but if my parents ever found out that I was thinking of dating a boy they didn't pick? All hell would break loose."

A cold feeling washed over me. "But you said that you'd talk to him during the summer to see how it went. I remember you said that to me, too. Are you going to break it off before anything even happens?"

She sighs deeply. "I don't know, Bec. It's only the first few days into this family thing. I'll have a better answer by next week. Okay?"

"Alright. I just want you happy Felicity. Axel, too."

I heard the grin in her voice. "So, tell me how the barbeque went? How'd today go? Are his friends as hot as Jasper?"

"They're all pretty damn hot." Finally saying it out loud felt great. "They're all really fun, nice, and smart, too. You'd like them."

"You're comfortable with them. That's awesome, Becca!" Felicity sounded excited for me. "I knew you could beat your anxiety. Are you focusing on your breathing when it starts?"

"Yes, Moooommm," I drawled out the word.

She giggled softly before she sombered. "I love ya, girly. I know I said we'd video chat tonight, but I'm beat. Can we video chat in a few days?"

"Yeah, that's fine." Thoughts of what this family gathering was all about raced through my head, but I kept my questions to myself. She'd tell me when she was ready. "I'm going to take a bath before bed. I'll text you tomorrow. Get some sleep, ok?"

"Yup. You too, sweetie."

After hanging up, I stared down at the phone for a few seconds. I debated on telling Axel what she told me, but after arguing with myself for several long minutes, I decided to wait on telling him the whole truth.

The bathtub didn't have much water in it yet, so I just turned the water back on to as hot as it would get, since it took a bit to heat up properly. My cellphone was laid on the corner of the tub in case I needed it. After it was ready, I threw in a large lavender bath bomb. Sinking into the hot water felt amazing.

Thirty minutes later, my skin was prune-like as the water cooled down. Stepping out of the tub as it drained, I jumped in the shower for a quick thirty second rinse. My teeth were chattering by the time I was done.

Just as I wrapped my towel around me, my phone dinged. My eyes furrowed briefly as the contact name read: 'Boyfriend'.

Hey. Jasper said you got home safe. Just wanted to tell you good night and thanks for going to get the pizzas with me today.

Laughter bubbled out of me as I figured out that Seth had put himself as 'Boyfriend' for his contact name.

Sure. It was fun. **Boyfriend**.

Turning off the bathroom light, I climbed into bed. I was too tired to put on pjs, plus I was alone, so it didn't seem like a big deal. Seth sent a reply.

I thought it was quite clever. Are you all ready for bed or staying up?

I bit my lip thinking about how to reply. I wondered what his reaction would be if he knew I was naked? As soon as the thought went in my head, I threw it out the window. We might have shared a mind shattering kiss, but we didn't know each other. Plus, he probably had super models vying for his attention.

I just got done with a bath. Now in bed. About to turn off the lights to sleep. Are you going to bed?

My mouth opened in a large yawn as I settled under the covers. I clapped my hands to turn off the lights before picking up my phone again.

Yeah. I'm already in bed. Just wanted to check on you. Have a good sleep, ok? Remember, you need anything, you call us.

Thanks, boyfriend. Good night.

I snickered softly to myself as I plugged in the phone before turning off its flashlight and screen. It took barely three minutes to sink into my dreams.

Seth

My sigh was silent in the room. Thoughts of the day flew through my mind. My tiger had responded to Becca the second he'd met her yesterday. He'd chuffed and wanted me to puff out my chest to get her to notice us. That didn't happen.

The girl needed our help. She had no idea what kind of danger a random shifter could pose to a human. I was still curious about her stepfather. It looked like, based on the security he'd installed at just a vacation house, he might know more than he's telling his family. I'd bet my tail on it.

But sleep was eluding me as my mind ran through different scenarios. If we didn't find this shifter soon, we'd need to get Becca to come stay with us or have her leave for her house in the city.

Cody was on guard duty tonight while Axel searched for the asshole further out. Jasper would be back soon with the groceries. He'd texted a little while ago letting me know he'd take care of it so I could sleep. Jasper was always worried I was doing too much. He was probably right, but I was the alpha of our group.

On top of that, I have the family business to oversee, my younger brother, and trying to find a tiger mate so that our species didn't die out, since we were the last.

My phone dinged with the last message from Becca saying good night. Her sense of humor was refreshing. Even with her anxiety and blindness at night, she was still filled with life. Her artwork she let us see today of Axel had been breathtaking. She was comfortable with us, that much was easy to see as long as we didn't startle her.

My tiger had enjoyed the kiss we'd shared to mess with the rude cashier. I'd heard her from outside, but hadn't been able to do anything about it. When Becca had asked me to kiss her, I'd had to fight back my growl of approval. She wasn't a pushover, regardless of her anxiety.

That kiss. It was everything a first kiss should be and not be. It was hard to stop. I'd had to remind myself she was a human. I had a duty to my species and family. It just couldn't happen. Even if I liked the way she smiled when she was excited, the way her cheeks turned red when she was embarrassed, or that even her scent made my tiger and I just relax.

My tiger only reacted that way to the guys. Now that Axel was in love with a human, there was a missing piece in our family. Understandably, Axel wanted to get to know Felicity more before he revealed what he was, so he kept distance from us sexually in respect to her. It wasn't common for humans to join packs, but it wasn't uncommon. She'd have to be open to being with the rest of us. Plus, I had to find a mate, preferably another cat species. It wasn't what we wanted, but it was what would happen.

My phone went off again. This time, it was Jasper.

I stopped back at Becca's to check on Cody. He's set for the night with some food while he stands guard. I'll be home in about twenty minutes. Do you want to have some dessert? ;)

I snorted.

You mean dessert or "dessert"?

Maybe both.

My cock hardened. I hadn't gotten to be with my fox for a few weeks because of his school schedule.

Hurry home.

My tiger stretched as he started to pace, flicking his tail every few seconds in anticipation. My lips twitched at how eager he felt. I was feeling that same anticipation. Maybe a romp with our fox would help us get our focus away from Becca.

My feet swung over the side of the bed after removing the blanket. I pulled on a set of boxers before going downstairs. We didn't need lights on because our animal senses were enhanced, but I still turned on the kitchen light so we could unload the groceries quickly. Even though Jasper said he'd take care of it, we wanted to take care of our fox in bed quickly.

The sound of the SUV pulling up in front of the house ten minutes later had me moving outside to meet Jasper. His eyes brightened as they met mine. His arms were full of groceries.

"Hey." His voice was deep. "There's a few more in the backseat. The keys are on the hood. Lock it up while I start unloading the bags." As he passed by me, he smirked.

That was all I needed to race to grab the rest of the bags before locking it up. Jasper was almost through most of the bags already. The bags I carried thunked on the counter as I wrapped my arms around his waist, pulling his back against my front. My cock already hard.

Jasper purred as he put up the cold foods. "Hey, pussycat," his ass wiggled against my jeans, "almost done with the groceries. Then I'm all yours."

"Let me help. Make it faster."

It was quiet as we unloaded the rest of the food besides the crinkling of the bags or the sounds of food being put in its place in the cupboards. Five minutes later, it was done. I didn't wait for Jasper to say anything before I picked him up, slinging him over my right shoulder. I ran up the stairs as I rushed down the hallway to my room at the end of the hallway. Jasper was laughing the whole time until he was thrown onto his back on my bed.

I knew my eyes flashed in the dark. The time it took to remove my boxers felt like an eternity as I watched him shimming out of his own clothes. When he laid back with his left arm above his head while his right hand stroked his cock, my own jerked in response. My tongue slowly licked my lips as I zeroed in on his cock.

It was a thing of beauty. His veins throbbed in response to his arousal as I approached slowly. The bed dipped as I crawled onto it. My hands laid on either side of his shoulders as my legs boxed in his own. Jasper's emerald eyes darkened as we stared at each other silently for several heart beats.

"Where's the lube?" Jasper whispered softly.

"Here." I reached out to the nightstand, pulling out the lube that was within the single drawer. "First, I want to taste you."

His loud moan had me answering with a low growl. The lube was forgotten temporarily next to him on the pillow as my lips met his slowly. As they touched, my tiger pushed forward, wanting to rub ourselves all over Jasper's body to claim him as ours again.

His chest tribal tattoo ran from his left pectoral in swirls of black across to his lower right ribs. It was easy to bite and suck as I followed its path. I bit just hard enough to cause a mark to appear. No hard marking would happen until I was riding him. He didn't seem to care. Every time my lips left his skin, Jasper made a small mew of protest.

As my tongue dipped along his belly button, his hips moved restlessly knowing that I was only a few inches away from his cock. His nails dug into the sheets as a ripping sound of fabric echoed through the room. A harder nip on the side of his right hip brought out a loud moan.

"Why are you teasing me?" The need in his voice was something I could roll around in all night like it was nip.

"I'm a cat and you're like a mouse." My smug tone had him growling loudly at me. He tried to sit up but my right hand pressed him down firmly. "Stay." Snapping my teeth at him, I went back to kissing down his stomach.

Finally, as I reached the base of his cock, my tongue slowly took a long lick from the base of his shaft to the tip before my lips curved around his head. Jasper didn't move but his body vibrated under my hands. As my mouth moved down his length, I started a low hum in the back of my throat that had Jasper whimpering.

I cupped his balls, pulling just enough that it had his cock already twitching within my mouth. Taking that as a sign, I drew my cheeks in as I sucked with force, moving up and down. He had already leaked a little of his cum, he tasted salty and I wanted more but I'd have to come back next time to finish him with my mouth. My tiger and I needed inside of him right now.

As I pulled back releasing his cock with a short pop, my laughter came from deep within my chest as he gave me the dirtiest glare.

"Asshole!"

Narrowing my eyes at him, he stopped as he had started to reach for me. His lower lip jutted out, he looked so frustrated. My tiger growled at me. He wanted to be inside the fox, but he also didn't like our fox becoming upset with my teasing.

"Alright, alright." My chuckle was soft. I grabbed the bottle of lube and squirted a generous amount onto my palm before handing it to him. "Get yourself ready for me, kit."

Jasper flashed his grin at me, letting his fangs show as he spread his legs wide, his knees pulled up, as he gave me the show I wanted as I stroked my own shaft with the lube. Soft panting came from him as he used two fingers to get himself ready. The sight of his open mouth with his pouty lips had me gritting my teeth as I fought to keep control. I could only give him another minute before roughly barking at him to stop.

"Get on your knees, fox."

Jasper rushed to obey, popping his ass up in anticipation, even giving it a wiggle at me. I laughed low before slapping his right cheek. He just wiggled more eagerly before looking over his shoulder at me.

"I need you, Seth." His tone was rough, filled with need.

"You have me, baby. It's been too long." The need to protect him was almost as fierce as the need to mount him to brand him as mine again.

I held my cock while slowly pressing the head past the first ring of muscles. Jasper bunched the sheets in his hands as he began to purr loudly which made his muscles vibrate around my cock. I snapped, not being able to control it any longer.

One hard thrust had me buried inside of him. We both let out low moans. This. Being connected physically kept us all grounded as a family. My pack. My lovers. I'd never be able to move forward from my past without them.

My hands gripped Jasper's hips, digging my nails into his skin as my own hips slammed into him, again and again. The only sound in the room for a long while was our panting, the slapping of our skin together, and sometimes, the soft creak of the bed.

My cock hit Jasper's prostate every time, making my fox slowly start to writhe underneath my hands. I was getting close, too. I needed to mark him before either of us came.

I stilled for a moment, much to the chagrin of Jasper. Pressing kisses along his back, I moved forward so I was laying across his back. My kisses turned to nips along his neck from his shoulders.

Jasper moved backward, trying to fuck himself on my cock but my snarl made him freeze. His panting had become louder as his arms shivered. I knew how close he was, but making him wait was icing on the cake as I took my time to leave small hickeys on his upper body.

"For fox's sake, Seth, please!" Jasper turned his head to look at me as he begged.

My elongated teeth pierced into Jasper's left shoulder, replenishing my mark that was permanently part of him already. My hips slammed into him harder and faster than before. His cry as he came was ecstasy to our ears as we spilled our seed inside of him shortly after.

"Fuck." Jasper collapsed onto his stomach as he groaned.

"Seth, you're a fucking beast." His voice was muffled in the pillow. "I fucking love you."

Pulling out of him, I stroked his back with my hand gently running up and down. His habit of using the word 'fuck' during sex was adorable.

"Roll over. I have some wet wipes in the drawer. I have a feeling you wouldn't make it to the shower." My tone was soft as he slowly rolled onto his back.

The top sheet was soaked through. It made my chest puff out in pride. It'd be uncomfortable to sleep on, though. "Jasp, let's remove the sheet so we can sleep on top of the comforter tonight. I'll wash everything in the morning."

"I can't move my legs." His twitching lips gave him away.

Snorting as I handed him the wet wipes, I pushed him gently off the bed. Removing the top sheet and placing the comforter back onto the bed took less than a minute. Jasper was curled up in the middle of the bed before I could turn around to pick him up. He'd cleaned himself up before throwing the used wipes in my trash bin next to the nightstand.

"Bed hog."

Warmth flooded me. My tiger wanted to cuddle now that we were both satisfied. Quickly using a clean wipe, I was laying in the bed wrapping my arms around Jasper's front, pulling him back into my chest. He was purring softly as he slowly drifted off.

"Good night, kit." I kissed the back of his neck before falling asleep myself.

CHAPTER 8

Becca

A few weeks passed. My art was finally flowing out in the different mediums. I'd even made a few cute creatures out of polymer clay. They weren't professional looking, by any means, but they gave me enough confidence in this medium that I wanted to continue with it. The twins would like the little creatures for Christmas.

I spent most of the days alone as I worked. One of the guys usually texted me throughout the day, I'd even video chatted with Cody a few times after he got my number from Jasper. They weren't pushy, but every other day, I'd find myself at their house to have some kind of meal and a few hours of video game play or board games.

I'd started to notice that they liked to touch. Not just me, but brief hand touches, shoulder brushes, or hugs with each other. They didn't seem to care that I'd seen the displays of affections.

If I were honest with myself, I was a little envious with how comfortable they seemed. Plus, deep down, it fed fantasies kept hidden.

A few days later, I woke up in the morning to my text message alerts going off every few minutes. I dragged myself out of bed, hopping quickly doing the potty dance. Bathroom first before checking the messages. It took a little over ten minutes to finish in the bathroom since I wasn't taking a shower. The cool water on my face was what really woke me up.

The security screens were already up, so it had to be past seven when they were automatically set to raise. My phone had fallen to the floor in my haste to not pee myself. My breath came out in a relieved sigh as I turned it over to find no damage to it.

My relief was short as I started to go through the messages even as another one came in. Sheesh. What was going on? The first few were from Mom asking if I was okay, that she saw the news.

What news? I headed out to the living room to turn on the TV as I kept going through the other messages after sending a quick text to Mom letting her know that I was fine, that I had just woken up.

The other texts were from Jasper, Felicity, and a few art colleagues from school. Most of them asked if I was alright, they saw the news, etc. Only Jasper's texts were different.

Call me when you wake up.
Are you up yet?
Woman. WAKE UP!

Obviously, something was up, but Jasper's texts made me snort happily as I looked for the local news station. What came on made my knees go weak. Luckily, I was standing next to the ottoman, so I sank down onto it, staring in utter revulsion at the scene on the screen.

My phone was forgotten momentarily as the volume went up so I could listen to what was going on as I tried to make sense of the pictures flashing across the screen.

"...these pictures were sent into the station early this morning, right before the sheriff's department appeared at the scene. They've asked us not to share these with the public until they figure out what's happened, but we felt it was our duty to show those in the area of Tabernash so that they can take the proper precautions." The anchor stared straight into the camera as it went back to her briefly. "The pictures you see have been authenticated. Law enforcement has said no comment as of now, but as our viewers can see, this appears to be a male body in pieces. We have reached out to experts to review more of the pictures to see if they can tell what caused the damage but it was clearly violent."

The pictures appeared on the screen again. My blood froze as I saw what was a man's forearm laying on the forest floor. The fingers were curled and were covered in mud that was mixed with the blood that was soaked around the arm. He'd had to have been terrified. What the hell had happened?

"This occurred in Tabernash, up higher in the country to the north east of the town in the woods." The news displayed a map showing the approximate location of the attack. It was only a few miles from my house. "This attack comes a week after a woman near Winter Park was attacked on a hike near her home by some kind of animal. We have no information if this is related to that incident or not at this time."

The loud blare of my phone ringing made me jump. I realized that the news had started an anxiety attack without noticing yet, but the phone brought me back to the present. My heart rate had already sped up in the oncoming attack. I took two slow deep breaths as I answered the phone without looking at who was calling. The edges of my vision were turning black as I fought against the grip.

"Hello?" My voice was a little rough.

"Damnit, woman." Jasper's voice was a welcome distraction to pull me from the anxiety except his was strained. "Why didn't you text me? I know you're awake!"

"How'd you know I was awake?" My voice was breathless as my body began to shake all over.

Jasper was quiet for a second before clearing his throat. "I just do. You've heard what happened?" He didn't wait for my reply. "We're going to come get you, you're going to stay with us. Pack your stuff, whatever you don't get done by the time we're there, we'll help."

The sudden command was just what I needed as the blackness dissipated slowly as I continued to breathe deeply. My body was still shaking, but my heart rate was slowing down. Progress.

"What? I'm not staying at your house. My house has the security, remember? Yours doesn't." A soft sound made my eyes narrow. "Jasper, did you just scoff at me?"

My answer was a loud sigh before a scuffling came over the line. Seth's deep voice came on and damnit, my toes literally curled into the rug.

"Becca, we're just worried. If you aren't comfortable staying with us, we can come stay at your place. I'd," a loud noise followed by some grumbling, "WE'D feel better if we were with you. Our house is a little further from the body location, so we thought it'd be better to stay here."

This time when my heart sped up, it wasn't because of anxiety. It was because these four men cared about someone, they barely knew, who was alone. Scraping my finger against the ottoman's leather, I went over my options for a few more moments.

"Becs?" His tone softened.

"I'm thinking." I paused again. "What if I call Gary? See if he thinks it's better to stay in this house or yours? I'll call you back right after."

"That's fine. If we don't hear from you in thirty minutes, though, we'll be on our way to you, regardless. Deal?"

I felt his protectiveness even through the phone. My smile could be heard as I agreed before hanging up.

Gary's phone rang once before he answered.

"Becca. Thank goodness. Your mother was just about to get into the car. Are you alright?"

"Gary! Give me the phone this second!" Mom spoke over him.

The phone had to have been handed to Mom because the next voice on the line was hers.

"Becca Rosemary Lanore how dare you not call me! Instead I get a text?"

A throb started over my right eye. Oh, parents.

"Mom, I'm fine. You were the first person I responded to, but I had a lot of messages to catch up on."

She blew out a loud breath. "I guess that's alright. Look, I want you to pack up and go home. We'll leave later today and be home in two days with the twins."

"Now, Ginny..." I could hear Gary trying to calm Mom down.

"Mom, I'm fine. I wanted to ask Gary about the security on the house. Those guys I made friends with? Want me to go to their house and stay with them, but.."

"Oh! The four boys?" She was way too excited. "That sounds lovelllyy! I love you, sweetie. Here's Gary back."

I didn't even get to finish before she fluttered off. I knew if I laughed, she'd know, though, so I kept quiet until Gary came back on the phone.

"Sorry about that, kiddo." Amusement and love laced his tone. "You know your mom."

"I do. I love you, guys. But I'd like to stay up here. The guys, that I'm sure Mom told you about, want me to come stay with them..." I continued with information about them, any answers I could give about their house, and location to Gary.

He hummed and hawed through the information. I could hear paper rustling, like he was looking through some things. After I'd answered the last question, he tsked.

"From what you've described, their house may not be the best location if there really is some kind of... thing that's out there killing people. Our house is equipped to handle pretty much anything. I'll give you a code to input into the system to voice activate the commands. I'll send you some information via email about some hidden features, too. If you insist on staying there to work on your art, you need to be hyper aware of everything around you. I'm not okay with letting you stay there, but you're also an adult. I can't force you to go home. If you can get the guys to stay with you, then it should be fine. Find out if they know how to handle a gun or if they even have one. If they don't stay with you, I'm agreeing with your mom and we'll all be home in two days. Sound fair?"

"Yes, definitely. Thanks, Gary."

"Love you, kiddo. Follow the email instructions to the letter, promise?"

"Promise."

"Alright, get back to your art after the house is set up. I'll call you in the evening to make sure you've got it all set up."

"Okay. Talk to you soon, lots of love to everyone."

Hanging up, I noticed that I'd finally stopped shaking all over. There was a plan now. It would be okay, plus, I'd get to hang out a whole lot more with the guys if we were all staying in the same place.

I called Seth's phone this time. I had just barely beat the thirty minute mark.

"Pretty close, Becs."

There went my toes with a tingle up my spine.

"Sorry? But, um, Gary agreed that staying here would be better for me. You guys are welcome to come stay. You'll have to pair up, but there's plenty of room. We'll have to go grocery shopping, though."

A car door slammed. "We got it handled. We're already in the SUV with food and our stuff. We'll be there in ten."

"So, you were going to come over anyway, weren't you?"

"Yup."

My laugh burst out and I had to hold the phone away from my ear.

"See you in a few." I hung up shaking my head.

These guys were silly. A little, or a lot, depending on how you looked at it, bossy. I didn't mind. It had been a long time since I'd been comfortable so fast with someone not family. Even with Felicity, it took a little longer to be comfortable with her.

Speaking of Felicity, I sent her a quick text.

I'm fine. Was asleep when you sent texts. I'm staying in the house unless I absolutely have to go out. Axel and his friends are staying too.

The email from Gary came through a few seconds later. I'd look at it after I got the guys settled in. My stomach growled. And breakfast. Right after breakfast.

The weather was still beautiful outside. The temperature gauge over the sink read that it was only sixty-two degrees out. It was a little warm for it, but I wanted some cream of rice. I wasn't a big cream of wheat fan, but give me real cream of rice? I'd do anything for it. Well, within reason. I pulled the ingredients together before tossing them into the pot together.

Just as I turned on the burner on the stove for the pot, there was a knock on the door.

"Who is it?" I put the burner on medium after placing the pot over it.

"Your knights in shining armor, fair maiden! We are here to lay at your feet in servitude!" Cody called out.

What started as a snicker had transformed into a full chortle with snorting as I opened the door to find Cody on one knee in front of the door with his opposite arm thrown upward in a dramatic fashion. I laughed so hard, my sides started to ache.

Cody's eyes twinkled wickedly as he grabbed my right hand. "Fair maiden! Say you'll accept us as your servants to forever protect you!" He kissed my fingers, which, even though I still couldn't stop laughing, gave a pleasant feeling up my arm to my chest. He wiggled his eyebrows at me. "Yes?"

The other guys were leaning against the front of the SUV, watching the scene. Jasper was shaking his head with a large smile. Seth just stared at me, but I could see the tiny smile he was fighting to keep off his face. Axel had his hand over his face, as if he were embarrassed on Cody's behalf.

"Yes, fine." Those were the only two words I could form as I tried to stop laughing. His next words didn't help, they set me off again.

"Huzzah, sweet maiden! We are now your servants. Protectors. Sex slaves. Food bringers. Clothing washers!"

"Oh my God!" That was it, I was going to pee myself if I laughed any harder.

Seth took pity on me.

"Cody! Stop galavanting. Come grab your stuff."

Cody's shoulders slumped as he stood. "No fun."

I felt a little bad. He looked like a kicked puppy. He'd just turned around to go help the others but I placed my hand on the middle of his back, making him look back at me.

"Thanks, Cody. You're wonderful." I had to stand on my tip toes, but at least I was able to kiss his cheek. Unlike with Seth or Axel, I'd probably only get their throat, possibly their chins if I jumped a little. Cody's cheeks flushed red as he grinned widely at me before running to the SUV.

Jasper, with Axel, went to help Cody grab things out of the back of the SUV. That left Seth leaning against the hood of the SUV, looking back at me. I swear his eyes looked like they had something moving within them, but it was probably just my stupid eyesight issues. He tilted his head as I walked over to stand in front of him, my eyes trailed his hair that he left down. It shone in the morning light. His smile spread slowly.

"Hey, girlfriend." There it was again. The voice that just danced over your whole body.

"Morning, boyfriend." My smile matched his before we both snickered. "It's really sweet of you guys to come stay with me. You know you don't have to."

The bang of the trunk closing had Seth standing straight. His hand reached out to ruffle my hair into a mess, he ignored my 'Hey!'.

"Yes, we did. So, don't feel guilty or whatever girly feelings you have about it. We couldn't let a woman be alone when there's some kind of... thing... out there killing people."

He'd called the killer a thing like Gary had. It had to be either a rabid predator animal or a psycho axe murderer. I just hoped that whatever it was, the cops caught it before someone else suffered the same fate as the guy from the pictures.

"We brought sustenance!" Axel came around the other side of the SUV to stand next to me. His grin was infectious.

"You mean it'll last maybe two meals before you've finished it?" I'd had to tilt my face all the way up to look up at him since he was so close.

"Oh, the small female has jokes." He threw three of the four bags he had in his arms at Seth, who caught them easily, even though I could tell they were heavy. Axel kept the last bag under his left arm.

"Small? Sir, you need your eyes checked." To prove the point, I moved my hands down my body. "This is all fluff and jiggle. Nothing small about it."

There were growls from all the guys as Cody and Jasper rounded the other side of the SUV to stand with Seth. They were all logged down with their luggage. Glancing between them, my eyes furrowed in confusion.

"Uh, you all just growled. You growled at me. I know it's early, but I have breakfast on the stov... EEP!"

Axel cut me off as he bent down before swinging me up over his right shoulder in a fireman hold. My mouth hung open in shock as I looked up to meet the other guys' amused faces. They weren't growling anymore, they were laughing at me!

"What are you doing, Axel? Put me down! You're going to hurt yourself!" I vehemently tried to ignore the fact that my face was level with his very generous and plump ass.

"Oh, hush. You have cushion for the pushin'. You barely weigh a thing to me." His voice grumbled over to me. He jerked the shoulder he had me on, making me bounce a few times. "See? Light as a feather."

"Oof!" My right eye began to twitch slightly as I glared at the other guys from upside down. They just laughed as Axel walked us inside. He dropped the bag he carried next to the door. It fell with a loud thunk before he moved to the kitchen. "Um, we're inside, can you let me down now?"

Axel sniffed at something. I assumed it was the cream of rice that was on the stove.

"Mmm. Homemade? My favorite. Just need to add some cinnamon." He started moving around the kitchen, still with me hanging over his shoulder like a swinging monkey.

I just shook my head. Sure, I was acting like it was a hassle and it was slightly annoying, but there were no signs of panicking.

The front door closed as I heard the rest of the guys come inside. They were talking softly enough I couldn't hear anything except snippets.

"Where's your rosemary?" Axel opened an upper cabinet.

"Oh, heck no! You're not going to add that to my cream of rice! Put me down!" That would ruin the sugary beauty of it. "Plus, cinnamon and rosemary? How does that even work?!"

"You can't stop me, might as well go with it."

My annoyance spiked a little more. "Jasper! Cody! Seth? Come on! A little help here! He's going to mess breakfast up!"

A few seconds later, the other three were looking down at me as they sat at the island bar stools. Cody shot a sympathetic look, but he shrugged his shoulders. Jasper winked at me as Seth sat there with his cheek resting on his palm.

"No one? Really? Axel, if you dare put rosemary into that, it's blasphemy!"

My body went up and down a few times again as he laughed in response. "It'll be good, I promise!"

"No! That's it! You asked for it!" What was I doing? I was going to do it, but oh my God, Felicity was going to kill me.

"Didn't we just go over this? You can't." Now all four of them were chuckling softly.

The loud smack sound seemed to echo in the room as it went quiet. I felt the three guys eyes on me as Axel stiffened slightly.

"Did... you... just smack... my ass?" I could hear the wonderment in his tone. "Really?"

"I did! I'll do it again! I'll even bite if you don't let me down!" Flinging my hands out like a bird, I waved them up and down.

"Ooh. If she's biting, let me take her, Axel!" Cody bounced up from the barstool excitedly. "She can bite me!"

Axel was silent but I started bouncing again. He was laughing at me! I let out a loud growl of my own as I pulled my hand up to smack his ass again. Just before I landed the smack, I found my world moving again before I found myself upright again, but being held up like a princess. My head felt wobbly as the blood rushed down again.

"Wow. Trippy," mumbling the words, I looked up into Seth's face. "Hi."

His azure eyes seemed brighter, like they were drawing me in. I had a strange urge to run my fingers up his cheeks into his hair.

"Ahem."

I froze just as my fingers were about to touch Seth's cheek.

Glancing over to the island, Jasper had coughed into his hand to jerk me out of the weird situation I'd almost found myself in.

Clearing my throat, "Thanks, uh, Seth. You can put me down." I knew without looking again that the others were probably enjoying this way too much.

Seth didn't say a word but he slowly put me down and I felt his hard body the whole way down. Oh. My. God. These men weren't real. There's no way that they all had perfect bodies but I could attest after the full on body feel that Seth, at least, was real in every way.

Turning my attention back to the stove, I screeched just in time to see Axel had found the rosemary. It took a small hop but I grabbed the bottle from his hand, throwing in back into a lower cabinet.

"Don't you dare!! Rosemary does not go in cream of rice! Out! All of you! Out of my kitchen!"

"But Axel is a really good cook." Cody was rubbing his ears with a distressed look on his face. Jasper had a similar face.

"I make my cream of rice sweet. Not savory." Cody stared at me as his eyes widened, making him look like a puppy again. "Oh, fine! How about we meet in the middle? I'll not season it, we leave it plain and we put whatever we want in our own bowls." They all nodded as I looked around at them.

I narrowed my eyes at Axel as I pointed my finger at him. "You're going to pay for that, just be warned."

His white teeth flashed against his dark skin. "I look forward to it, small woman."

"Ugh." I couldn't keep up the façade as I shook my head smiling. "Out of the kitchen. If you want to help, you guys take your things to the two other bedrooms. The master bedroom has one bed, the twins have a bunk bed. Seth and Axel, you guys might be more comfortable in the master bedroom because of, uh, well, how large you guys are."

"Yeah, they definitely are large," Cody snarked as he jumped from the bar stool to grab his bags. He dodged a head smack from Jasper, which just led to a mini wrestling match between the two.

Seth sighed but looked over at the two fondly. "Cody just likes to make jokes." He turned his attention to me. "We'll put our bags in the rooms and come out to have breakfast with you before we unload the groceries. There's nothing that won't keep for a bit." He jerked his head at Jasper to go with him before leaving the kitchen.

A large hand rested on my shoulder as Axel came to stand next to me. "I didn't really upset you with that, did I?"

I had to remind myself that this was the guy that Felicity liked but still had to talk with. Therefore, he was off limits to kisses on the cheek or big hugs. Instead, I patted his hand, squeezing it gently.

"No, in fact, it was the first time it's ever happened to me. It was kinda fun."

He flashed his pearly whites again before following the others. I could hear them talking, or arguing, couldn't really tell from here, before the bedroom doors opened. It was a good thing I'd aired out the other rooms within the first few days.

The rice was ready at that point. The pot was moved to the side so that it could start to cool off slightly before it was served. The cinnamon and brown sugar I wanted were already on the countertop, but for the guys, I pulled out other spices, herbs, and even hot sauce, in case they wanted savory. Just thinking about cream of rice as savory made me gag a little. This is probably one of the reasons I was a big girl. Sweets were my weakness.

The bowls were spread around the island with spoons next to them. I put down the mix-ins, along with napkins. I was just contemplating what drinks to put out when the four came back into the living room. Someone's stomach growled loudly, and for once, it wasn't mine.

"I call dibs sitting next to Becca!" Cody rushed forward. "Can I help with anything?"

"Actually, if you could grab the pot with the hotplate holders next to it? If you'll put it in the middle of the island, that would be great." I glanced at the other three as they settled around the island. They'd grabbed two of the chairs from the deck to set next to them. "What do you guys want to drink? I have orange juice, milk, or bottled water." I bit my lower lip to not giggle at the huge height difference the chairs made as Seth and Axel sat in them.

"Water," they said it all at once, including Cody.

"Ookkayy. Water it is." They were so weird and I really liked them for it.

Cody placed the pot onto the island. I wasn't worried about it being too hot for it, the marble was able to withstand high temperatures. He'd even grabbed the big spoon for serving. I placed five bottles of water next to the mix-ins, making sure to take one for myself. I settled next to Jasper as Cody sat on my other side. We were all on one side but it was only a little crowded, it felt like home.

"Ok, time to eat! I'm starved!" Jasper grabbed the serving ladle and started to dole out the rice to everyone. He gave another wink at me as he topped my bowl up. "Thanks for breakfast, lovie."

Bumping our shoulders together, we all began grabbing the mix-ins. Mine was ready before the others. I watched curiously at their choices. Axel did the rosemary, cinnamon, and granola. No judgement (lies, I was judging). Seth grabbed the regular sugar with butter. Jasper added a little salt, the brown sugar, and just a bit of butter. Cody was the one we all stared at with horror.

He put hot sauce, sugar, butter, and garlic powder. When had I put garlic powder with the other stuff? I must have just grabbed it with everything else and just didn't notice. He mixed it all together as he hummed under his breath before taking a taste. His face screwed up in concentration before he grabbed more garlic. The next taste seemed to be what he was looking for because he put the mix-ins back in the middle of the island. He finally noticed we were all looking at him.

"What? It has to be just right." He took a large spoonful, and gave an exaggerated moan. "So good."

"No one is going to kiss you when you have that on your breath," Axel rumbled from the far side as we went back to our bowls.

"You wound me, Axel! I am a great kisser! As you well know."

Anndd I choked on my food. The spoon clanged as it hit the surface. I had to hit my chest, coughing for several seconds. Jasper grabbed my water to open it. I took it sipping the water as I got over swallowing my food wrong like an idiot.

"Sorry." I had to clear my throat a few times before I stopped sounding like a strangled frog. "That just caught me off guard, is all." I smiled my thanks up at Jasper, whose eyes were furrowed in concern. "I'm good!"

I looked to my left at Cody, whose ear tips were bright red as he focused on his food. He avoided my questioning look. He just continued to stuff his food into his mouth, which made his cheeks start to puff out like chipmunks when they stuff theirs with nuts.

Since he wasn't looking at me, my camera took a picture with a click-snick sound. Cody finally looked over at me with his cheeks near bursting, he wasn't even swallowing, just stuffing. I had to draw this. I took another picture before he swallowed. It looked painful, but as soon as he was done, he tried to grab my phone.

"Oh no! These were perfect! You wanted me to draw you!" I leaned over in the stool away from his reaching hands. "Don't you dare!"

Everyone was laughing again as they watched me wiggle out of

Cody's reach. Hands around my waist lifted me off the stool and into Jasper's lap. Stiffening, I looked up at him. His eyes were crinkled as he grinned.

"Want some help keeping your phone away from the scavenger?"

"I am not a scavenger, you beast!" Cody's outraged howl had me doubling over at the ridiculousness of this situation.

"Yes, you are." Jasper sounded bored, causing Cody to get even more agitated. Jasper curled himself around me so it felt like we were cocooned together. "I have the fair maiden now, Cody!" He laughed in a mock evil voice.

"Dear Lord." Seth's exasperated tone made both of the two men freeze in their antics. "Let her finish her breakfast. Cody, leave her phone alone. Jasper, pass her to me with her food."

"Wait. What?"

Jasper didn't even hesitate to move me to Seth's lap, who sat next to him in the chair.

These men picked me up so easily, it was insane!

Seth's left arm wrapped around me, pulling me up against his chest as I sat sideways on his lap. Jasper pushed my food next to Seth's.

"Eat," Seth mumbled softly as I felt his chin brush the back of my hair.

"Right." It came out as a squeak. I could eat while sitting in one of the hottest guy's lap as he held me like I was something precious.

No, I couldn't. My focus was lost at the feeling of where our bodies touched. As I tried to eat, my spoon kept missing the bowl altogether.

"You alright there? Need some help?" Seth had moved so he could whisper that in my right ear. His lips touched my sensitive outer skin.

My body visibly shuddered, which just made me blush harder

because I knew he felt it. I was coming undone by these guys and it just wasn't fair.

I liked it, though. I wouldn't say it out loud. There was no way they were serious with their teasing.

"I'm good."

With effort, I finished my food, except I didn't taste it. My mind was going everywhere as I contemplated why Seth was holding me when he could have just switched seats. That would have just as easily stopped Cody from trying to take my phone. Did he want me in his lap? Maybe he did like me?

Nah, there was no way.

Axel

I'd found the body before anyone else in the early morning just as the hint of the sun began to lighten the sky. I'd been tracking this rogue's scent all over the mountain for a good portion of the night. I'd been just about to turn around to go home in defeat when the wind had shifted just so with the scent of fresh blood.

The body was torn to pieces. The head was missing, as well as the lower stomach. My bear had snarled silently as we canvassed the forest around us. It was a small clearing. I'd sniffed just enough to know that the man had been alive as this sicko had dragged him here before eating him alive. It looked messy, except it wasn't. The body parts had been arranged in such a way that the rogue would have had to do it, probably when the human had still been alive before his head was ripped clear off. It wasn't any way that I would wish on anyone to die.

I backed away after sniffing out all the scents around the body. I moved to a large tree about a hundred feet from the scene before climbing it to a tall branch that would hold our weight. I transformed back, ignoring the rough bark under my ass. We'd all put our cellphones around our necks in a little bag so that we could stay in contact for long distances once we'd realized the situation was more dire than we'd first thought.

Seth was guarding Becca tonight, but he would be in his human form since his senses were twice as powerful as ours in human form. The benefits of being an alpha, he shared some of our powers that boosted his.

"Yeah?" he answered before the first ring even finished.

"I found a body."

"How close?"

I tipped my nose back so that I could take a deep breath in.

"I can vaguely smell you. Possibly fifteen miles from your location. I'll send you the coordinates after we hang up. What do you want me to do?"

"This asshole is getting bolder. First, the dead animals he's been shredding around the forest for us to find, marking everywhere as if this were his territory, that hiker, and now this." Seth was perfectly controlled, which meant he was ready to shift and destroy something. "This is too close to home. I can't figure out what this asshole's goal is. Come home."

We'd proceeded from there. Seth was worried about how close this asshole was to our house, but more importantly, to Becca's. This rogue had been around for months. His scent was all over Becca's garage, it was old. Something had set him off. Us? Or Becca being back at the house? It could be a coincidence, but I doubted it.

After I'd gotten back to the house, Jasper was put in charge of getting ahold of Becca, we didn't want to bombard her with messages. Cody was sent to watch over her until we could bring her here. He'd run out of the house faster than I'd ever seen him move. He seemed to really like Becca. They all did. I felt fondness for her. I was protective of her, too. But that was just because she was Felicity's best friend.

"FUCK!" Jasper had thrown the remote on the floor as I'd come out of the bathroom.

"Jasp? What's up?"

He had the news on. The scene from the woods was splashed across the screen. "What the hell?" How did someone get those pictures? We'd sent an anonymous call to the cops where to find the body, but that had only been an hour ago.

That's when it hit me. "The fucker took the pictures himself."

Jasper turned toward the tv as he rubbed his chin. "You think? That would mean he can't be a rabid rogue. This is too intelligent for that."

I wrapped my arms over his shoulders to pull him into my chest. We both needed the touch. My bear even calmed down as he felt our pack member. I really liked Felicity. It just hurt that I had to step back from the others while I pursued her. They understood, but it still sucked. We craved touch. I knew that Cody missed me and my bear especially. He'd been the most hurt when I'd told them I wanted Felicity. He'd understood, but that didn't stop the hurt I caused him because of it.

Jasper sunk into my arms. His fox purred loudly as he tipped his neck to the side for me. My bear wanted to bite him. I nuzzled his neck, rubbing my scruff roughly along it. It was the only thing I could do. Any thoughts of sex, or touches that led to it, always made me feel guilty.

It'd hurt Felicity if I did. She'd be introduced eventually to the pack. I wanted her to accept all of us as hers, but she was human. That's why I was taking so long courting her. I wasn't about to spook her until there was enough trust between us.

Plus, there was Becca now. Having her thrown in could make Felicity's acceptance harder.

Jasper whimpered softly. My heart broke a little. My arms tightened around him.

"I'm sorry, Jasp," I whispered softly against his neck.

He sighed. "It's ok. I know why. I understand, too. I just miss you." His voice was just as soft as mine. My bear raged inside of me, angry that I'd hurt our pack again. He didn't like Felicity, didn't understand that when I was around her, I was deliriously happy. I didn't understand it myself, either. It was just a pull I felt that compelled me to her.

My bear demanded I do something to comfort our fox since I started this. It wouldn't ease my guilt, but if it gave him what he needed, albeit small, from me, I'd do it. I pressed a kiss to his neck, making a slow but long lick up it to his ear. Jasper's body responded beautifully, but I had to pull back before going further. I pressed a small kiss to his forehead as I went to pick up the thrown remote.

"So, we're dealing with a rogue, but he's not rabid. Why would he draw attention to himself this way? It only takes two of this kind of report to find its way into the Venandi's hands before they swarm this area. He's put himself, and us, in danger." Jasper had turned his back to look out toward the deck. "It just doesn't make sense. If he was rabid, he wouldn't care about bringing the Venandi here."

My bear pushed against my skin.

"Maybe that's his goal. He wants our territory? Bring the Venandis here to find any shifters in the vicinity and kill them while he hides somewhere."

Something about that logic still didn't sit right with us.

"We won't know until we capture this shitface. Jasper, call Becca again. Get her here," Seth announced as he walked up the stairs to join us.

That conversation with her is how we all ended up moving in temporarily to her place. My bear had enjoyed himself when we'd carried her over our shoulder for a bit. We'd even secretly enjoyed her fierce little act when she'd smacked our ass. Even thoughts of Felicity couldn't make me feel bad about it. Becca was a little firecracker once she got over her anxiety around us.

Her body image needed work. She was stunning in her own way. Her personality just made her even more so. Sure, to humans she might be considered over the average weight, but I didn't think she was. She was plump, soft, and I knew the other three enjoyed touching her, as well as holding her. Shifter women were like the men, no softness to them at all. It was something I knew we all enjoyed about the human women we'd slept with together in the past.

She'd somehow managed to make the day seem a little brighter as she messed with Cody. When he'd casually mentioned kissing me, it'd shocked Becca but she hadn't said anything about it. My fists had clenched because those of us that were pack had felt the pain Cody hid behind his silly actions after speaking about kissing. My bear was restless again. I'd have to do something about this situation with Felicity soon. I couldn't take hurting my family much longer. Just the brief taste of Jasper earlier had left me wanting with a raging hard on that I'd had to beat off in the shower right before we'd left for Becca's. No one had mentioned I'd taken one just a little earlier.

A cell phone went off as we cleaned up breakfast. Becca pulled hers from her jeans. She offered us an apologetic smile as she answered.

"Hey, Gary."

We all went back to cleaning up. We could easily hear the conversation.

"Hey, kid. You got my email instructions? Is it a good time to walk you through activating the voice activation on the system?"

My bear hunched at the voice on the other line. He'd started to prowl angrily. He didn't do well with other men that were unknown to us.

"Yeah, sorry I'm a little late. The guys got here. We just finished breakfast."

Becca's voice softened as she spoke with Gary. It was obvious she loved her stepfather.

"Don't worry about it. Let's get started. It'll take a few minutes. Go to the security panel...."

I tuned out the conversation as I finished cleaning the dishes. Seth came to stand next to me as he grabbed another towel to help dry them.

"I think there's more to this Gary than meets the eye." He made sure to keep quiet, barely whispering at all so that Becca didn't hear us.

"I agree. Even if he's one of those apocalyptic preparers, this house is extreme. There's got to be more to his story. Becca seems open minded, but I don't think she really believes in it all."

"She believes that he believes in it. That's all she needs to trust him. She's got a good soul."

A loud beeping went throughout the house that had all of us clutching our ears. It lasted for about thirty seconds before shutting off.

"Sorry, guys! I had to reset it for the voice activation!"

Cody came into the kitchen to grab what remained of his bottle of water. "Don't worry about it, maiden. You just do your thing." He turned his back on me pointedly.

My lip lifted in a silent growl. Seth slapped my back before squeezing my shoulder. "You kind of asked for it, bear." I could hear his tiger in his snicker.

"I'll teach the pup some manners later." I pinched Cody's ass as I walked around him to go help Becca.

CHAPTER 9

Becca

The day passed quickly as Gary walked me through setting up the security system to react to voice commands, but he also had me activate a few extra features I hadn't known were even installed. On top of the bullet resistant glass and security shutters, he had me activate a high frequency alert that would blare inside. I couldn't hear anything, but Gary had said that the high frequency would knock down, temporarily, anything that could hear it.

I doubted we'd have to use that at all. I turned it on so Gary felt better about me being in the house without the rest of the family. I could hear Mom in the background giving the twins a hard time during part of our call. I missed them. I wasn't going home, I had to get my portfolio filled with more if I was going to hit my goal. I wouldn't be able to do that if we all went back home.

The last feature was weird, even for Gary. He had me move to my bathroom to find a hidden panel that was located next to the light switch. I'd had to press hard on the wall to get it to reveal the panel.

"This is in case there's a break-in. It operates on its own system, so if someone manages to cut the power, this will still work. It runs off of a different power line that's hidden. You'll get in here, press the red button first. That will activate a lockdown of the two doors. If the doors are somehow gone, security bars and security screens will descend as a last resort. The orange button is the second one you push. It will send an alert to me and to a friend who will be able to get to you within a day. I know it's a long time, but it'll be ok if you stay in there. The white button at the bottom will allow you to get out of the room if the threat is gone. If you ever have to use this, you get into the bathtub and lay down as flat as you can, alright?"

"Ok." This was a lot. "Red button, orange button next, and only press the white button when it's safe. How will I know your friend is who he says he is?"

"That's my smart girl. He'll tell you a poem. The one I recited to your mother at our wedding. You remember it?"

Oh, did I. It'd been beautiful.

"I remember."

"Good. That should do it. You can key the men to the voice activation, but not for this room, alright?"

"Why not them? If there's an attack here, they need to be safe too."

"Trust me. If they are who I think they are, your 'guys' can take care of themselves."

What?

"Now, I've got to go help your mom before she burns down the house. Call me at any time of day or night, got it, kid? I'm only letting you stay there since you have those guys with you. Night, kiddo."

He hung up before I could ask him what he'd meant by if the guys were who he thought they were. That was such a strange thing to say. Did he know them? I'd have to ask them.

"Knock knock." Cody stood in the bathroom doorway that

led to the twin's room where he was staying. "You're all done with your stepdad?"

"Mmm. Yeah. All done." I hid the phone in my back pocket. "And it's locked so you can't get at those pictures. You guys went outside for a bit, did you go swimming again?"

Cody's grey eyes caught my attention as he stepped into the bathroom, coming to stand in front of me with barely an inch of space between us. "Something like that. We didn't want to interrupt when you activated that high frequency alert. I'm a little sensitive to noise."

"Oh! I didn't even think to ask. I'd noticed before that you didn't like super loud noise, I'm sorry, Cody! Are you okay?"

My hands were touching his ears as I stood on my toes to look at both of them from side to side. "Do they hurt? I don't know much about ears, but I'm sure there's a doctor in town somewhere."

He covered my hands over his ears, keeping them there. His expression was one I hadn't seen on him before. His lips were turned up that, if it was a woman, I'd say a pout, but not on Cody. I'd seen him pout before. His eyes seemed brighter as he bent his head so that we were nose to nose.

"I don't need a doctor, Becca." My heart started to thunder within my chest. "I have you."

He titled his head just so before he slowly pressed forward. He was going to kiss me! My eyelids closed in anticipation automatically. But the kiss never came. He'd let go of my hands, letting them rest against his chest. My brows drew together as I slowly opened my eyes. He was still looking at me but as my eyes were opened all the way, he grinned wickedly before stepping back as my hands fell from him.

"What..?"

"Thanks, dove." Cody held up my phone in his right hand. He

turned as he ran out of the bathroom. I heard the bedroom door open before his feet pounded against the floor.

THAT. LITTLE. ASSHOLE! He'd tricked me! I fell for it! To think, I'd wanted him to kiss me. Just as I was about to storm after him, my last thought made me pause.

I hadn't thought about it all that much, but I was attracted to all four of them, even if Axel was off the market. Although who knew what Felicity planned to do at this point. I'd been flirting with the other three guys. It came out so naturally, half the time I didn't even notice it was what I was doing. The other half, they had me so wound up, I didn't know what way was up and what way was down.

That wasn't really natural was it? At least to the rest of the world. They'd call me a slut, or a whore, if I said I liked them all that way. As I sank onto the edge of the bed, I rubbed my hands over my face. If a guy slept with multiple chicks, or guys, at once, he was a pimp. He'd get a high five or a slap on the back. If a girl did the same thing? She's always labeled a slut, a whore, or a prostitute. It was pretty fucked up as I thought more of it. If the parties were consenting, why should it matter who you loved or slept with?

I made a note to myself to do more research about it later tonight after everyone was in bed. I'm sure I couldn't be the only one out there who'd experienced these kinds of feelings for multiple people. I liked them all and I wouldn't mind sleeping with any of them. A soft giggle escaped at that thought. I'd have never even thought about sleeping with someone I barely knew a few months ago.

"Hey, Becca!" Seth's voice filtered in from the living room. "Someone has your cell phone to give back to you."

I couldn't hear the words but I could hear Cody grumbling. I grinned. Seth, my hero. As I got there, I wished I could take a picture. Seth was sitting on Cody's ass on the couch. Cody was trying to get free but Seth looked like he was pretty unmovable. He held up my phone in his hand.

"I believe this is yours?" He crossed his right leg over his left as he leaned back onto the couch. Cody grunted.

"Becs, I'm sorry! Help me! This big oaf won't let me up! I'm dying!" Cody flailed his arms out.

"Nope. You tricked me. I'm on Seth's side."

Seth handed my phone back but placed his other hand over mine. "Do I get a reward, girlfriend?"

"'Girlfriend'? What's with that? You guys said something like that earlier." Cody glared at us over his shoulder.

"Didn't you know? That's what Seth said I am." The struggle was real to keep a straight face as I turned to face Seth again. "What would you like?"

Seth's body moved up for a second as Cody tried to buck him off again. It just caused Seth to grin wider. He tugged on my hand so I was leaning against his chest. He was so warm.

"How about a kiss as a reward for your chivalrous boyfriend?" His eyes hooded over as he looked at my lips.

My tongue came out to lick my lips nervously. I felt a small thrill as his lips parted as his eyes flared with heat. He wanted to kiss me, there was no way he was acting. Perfect revenge and a kiss from Seth? No way was I going to say no to that.

"Sure." I tried to sound cocky but it fell flat. I sounded breathless.

"What? No! No kissing while you're sitting on me!"

Cody's shocked voice faded into the background as Seth kept his eyes on mine as he closed the distance between us. Mine closed shut just as our lips touched. If I hadn't already been leaning against his chest, I'd have lost function in my legs at this point.

His lips were hot, like last time. His tongue swept across my lips twice, seeking entrance. Mine parted in utter surrender as he deepened the kiss. It felt like I was falling as his tongue drew mine into a dance. I could feel his hands move from holding mine as they moved up my arms in a soft caress. My phone fell to the floor as his shirt was gripped tightly in my hands.

The kiss turned hard. My thoughts were jumbled as the urgency between us seemed to pick up. His rumble was back as his arms pulled me straight against him. My hips moved on their own to press against his where I felt a notably large hard on.

He wanted me. He really wanted me. This time, I moved my hips on purpose to grind against him. His low growl was my reward. We pulled back slightly from the kiss.

I couldn't keep the smile off my face. When our eyes met again, his were a deeper blue. There was another flash like something within his eyes moved but I brushed it off again. It was the lighting or the sexual tension. Had to be.

"Are you assholes done making out practically on top of me?" Cody demanded, annoyance laced his tone.

Breaking eye contact with Seth physically hurt as I looked over to Cody. He was glaring at Seth before looking at me. His face softened somewhat, but he still looked upset. I tried to ignore the pang for upsetting him. Served him right for not kissing me when he'd had the chance.

Seth suddenly bounced on Cody's ass with his own twice, making them both bounce on the couch. "Stop pouting. I'm done." Seth looked at me from the corner of his eyes with a look that said for the moment.

"Can I get up now?"

That's when Seth laid across the couch. He covered Cody with his front while he used Cody's head as a pillow.

"Nope." He smirked at me as Cody struggled with no avail. "He's quite comfy."

I shook my head. "You guys." I glanced at my art supplies that someone had moved next to the TV. They'd folded up the sheet before placing it under my painting that I was working on. I'd finished the fox two days ago. I'd hang it up in my room later until it was time to leave for the summer.

"Jasper and Axel are out in the back if you want to say hi to them. Axel is barbecuing some chicken for dinner." Seth wiggled more on top of Cody, who looked to have given up. His face was turned toward the couch.

"I'll go see if I can help."

But before I did that, I picked my phone off the floor, took a quick picture before rushing out the back door before either of them could say anything.

Cody

I was kicking myself for chickening out with kissing her. Our lips had been so close when I'd frozen in panic. My thoughts had betrayed me as my inner demons had reared their ugly faces.

What if she was disgusted with me? What would happen when she learned what kind of coward I was? Always running, always goofing, but never serious about anything. What if she left if I touched her that way? What if she hated me for taking advantage of the situation?

The demons laughed inside my head as my wolf bared his teeth as they circled us. Useless. That's what I was. Everyone should just stay away from me.

I'd jerked back, grabbed her phone, and ran for it. Using the phone as a way to make her think I hadn't wanted to actually kiss her when I ached to. I'd literally ran into Seth as he was coming back inside from the deck. My nose still hurt from it. He'd taken one sniff of the terror coming off of me before he had me on the couch face down before sitting on my ass.

"Deep breaths, baby. No one is going to leave you. I'm right here." He'd stroked my hair down my rigid back until I'd relaxed. He was heavy but being a shifter came with perks where it didn't actually hurt. I stayed where I was because he was Alpha.

Then he'd continued my 'joke' by giving her back her phone. He made out with her while I watched. I thanked the moon that I was laying on my stomach so she wouldn't see how hot the scene made me. I'd bucked a few times to continue the charade. I wanted to be kissing her, though. I bet her lips were just as soft and plump as they looked.

She was outside now. Seth was laying across my body with his. I felt his cock pressing through our jeans against my ass. My wolf wanted him to bury himself deep within us, but there wasn't time for it. We whimpered quietly.

"We all love you, Cody. You never have to worry about those demons. We're here. We'll protect you forever. Becca likes you. You can smell her lust for you and the others." Seth deepened his voice as he whispered into my ear. "You know I'll be with you as long as we're alive. Your wolf is mine."

Fuck yes. We were.

I pressed my ass up against his cock. Just the friction of it had me almost bursting. Seth bit down on my ear, pulling it between his teeth as his hands pulled my arms above my head over the couches arm rest. I gasped as he ground against me. It wasn't long before I was panting as Seth ground his cock against my ass. His lips moved from my ear to the back of my neck. He moved my hair gently to the side even as he continued to rock us roughly into the couch before he bit so hard into my neck, I started to howl as I came. His hand covered my mouth and I bit down to muffle my cry against his hand.

He hissed softly as his thrusts turned short, the friction still driving me mad. He kept his teeth in my neck as he grunted softly before I felt him shudder as he reached his own release.

"Damn, pup." His voice was gruff as he sat back slowly. "I didn't hurt you?" His hands were gentle as he got off of me to help me sit up before kneeling in front of me. He brushed his thumb against my lips.

"Yeah." My eyes closed. "I'm okay now. Thanks." His lips pressed against mine roughly for several seconds before he stood.

"Let's get some new clothes. It sounds like the chicken is ready."

"She didn't see us, did she?" I let him pull me up, keeping our hands laced together.

"No, Axel and Jasper kept her attention so we could finish what we started." He looked at me smugly. "I doubt she'd have minded seeing though. Just a hunch."

I shook my head as we separated to grab clothes. I kept my voice the same level, knowing that he could hear me in the other room.

"She'd make a great mate for all of us."

The rustling of clothes from the other room paused. "She's human."

"So is Felicity."

"Axel won't want to change her. Not when we all don't feel the same pull to her as he does."

"Our animals all feel that pull with Becca. Axel does too, except he ignores it because of Felicity." I pulled on an AC/DC shirt that had seen better days before grabbing my brush. "You could change her," I said this much more softly.

Seth appeared in the doorway. "I can't. Neither can the rest of us. You know the chances of her dying are almost a hundred percent. We can't attempt to change her for our own selfish reasons. It's more than likely after this summer is over, after we've taken care of this rogue, we'll never see her again."

My wolf and I whimpered softly. I stepped into Seth's arms as he held me close.

"I know, pup. It sucks." His lips pressed into my temple. "We'll take care of this idiot so we can enjoy the rest of our summer, yeah?"

He felt my nod but squeezed me tightly once more before stepping back.

"Let's go eat. After, we'll play whatever game you want. I want you to stay tonight while me and the other two go searching for the rogue. You'll be in charge of making sure nothing happens to Becca, got it?"

I opened my mouth to argue but his stance meant that this was an order not a request. Besides, getting to be inside with Becca instead of standing guard outside? Sounded a lot better to me. None of us would get any sleep tonight but we'd handle it.

CHAPTER 10

Jasper

"A rhino?"

Axel groaned as he circled the pointed thing, he'd drawn on top of some kind of animal. I had an idea what it was but this was so much more fun to mess with him.

"What? It's a MwahMwah cat with a horn?"

This time, he glared at me as he stepped away from the large drawing pad to cross his arms. Looks like he caught on after all.

"Ten seconds!" Cody gave us the remaining time.

"Um." I rubbed my neck as I looked at the strange drawing helplessly. Becca giggled next to me. I finally let myself grin. "Oh! I know!"

"Four...three... two..."

"A unicorn!" I answered.

It came out just milliseconds before Cody yelled, "Time!"

Axel threw his head back as he swung his arms downward. "You're an ass. You know that? You knew exactly what it was but made me dance around like an idiot for your own amusement!"

"Not for my own amusement. For everyone's! I'm a giver, remember?"

Becca giggled harder, leaning in to me as she covered her

mouth. She was trying so hard not to hurt Axel's feelings, but she didn't have to. He was well aware of what I'd been doing. Seth and Cody just laughed their asses off when Axel threw his marker at me. I easily caught it before it hit Becca.

He sat next to me on the couch before leaning against me to whisper in my ear, "You're in for it." He stayed leaning against me as I fought to contain my fox's purr.

We'd missed his affection. I winked at him as we watched Becca stand for her team. She was paired up with Seth since Cody had volunteered to be the referee. Cody handed her the card with what she'd have to draw for Seth. Her brows pinched together for a second as she pursed her lips. I doubted she even noticed she did that when she thought about something. She handed the card back to Cody and stood in front of the pad. She'd grabbed a purple marker.

"Ready?" Cody looked for her nod. "Go!"

I sat back leaning against Axel's shoulder, as we watched her work. She'd faced the pad with her back to us. We were all watching her ass as she moved. I didn't even have to look at my pack to know that we were all doing it. My fox sent me an image of biting her cute butt and I ground my teeth together to stop the moan the image produced. My fox chuffed in amusement before curling up to enjoy the rest of the game.

She turned around all too soon with a shit eating grin, jolting us all to pay attention to what she'd drawn. My mouth dropped. If there was a cricket nearby it chirped. She'd drawn a rough caricature of what looked vaguely of Axel but his body was a stuffed animal with a large red bow tied around his neck. Axel groaned, as if in pain, next to me, setting Becca off again.

"One minute," Cody's voice sounded choked as he physically looked like he was holding back from laughing.

"Teddy bear," Seth said calmly but his foot was tapping, which meant he was doing his best to keep a straight face.

"Time at fifty-seven seconds left." Cody lost it, falling off the couch's arm rest onto the ground laughing so hard, he'd begun to cry. "Team Seth wins!"

Becca was bent over clutching her stomach as she gasped for air in between her laughs.

"She got you." I bit my lip to stop from joining the others. "She got you good."

Axel was leaning back into the couch. His deep rumbles in his chest turned into a loud belly laugh. I couldn't hold it back any longer.

"Damn. That was good. But why a teddy bear?" After we'd all settled down, Axel asked the question.

She shrugged. "That's what you remind me of. You're this big, gruff, sometimes scary looking guy, but, in reality, you're a big softy."

She'd hit the nail on the head. Well, for the most part. Axel was a big softy with those close to him. Otherwise, he really was unapproachable. We glanced between each other with smiles. I noticed that Cody stared at Becca with longing.

"Don't you dare tell anyone that," Axel roared playfully, with mock anger.

"Or what?" Becca jutted out her hip, placing a hand on it. "You'll carry me around like a sack of potatoes again?"

"Becca 3. Axel 1. Checkmate," Cody interjected.

She beamed at him. "Damn straight."

"Alright, alright." Seth stood up. "It's pretty late. Why don't we all head to bed?"

Axel and I straightened. We had to wait until Becca slept before we went hunting.

"Aw. You're right." Becca glanced at her phone. "I've got a few things I need to do tomorrow in the morning." She picked up the markers, putting them in the small basket for them, that we'd haphazardly put down.

"I'll clean up," Cody offered.

"Thanks." Becca handed him the basket. "Good night guys! I'm really happy you're here."

She went over to Axel and hugged him tight but only briefly. I'd never seen such a look of confusion on his face as she stepped away. I had my arms up for a hug as soon as she looked at me. Her lips quirked as I pulled her into me tightly. I even lifted her from the ground for a second before placing a kiss on her cheek. She fit so perfectly. If only she weren't a human.

It was all too soon she was in Seth's arms. Anyone could see that he felt the same pull as Cody and I did with her. He pressed a kiss behind her right ear whispering good night to her with his sex-me-up voice that my fox always rolled over onto his back for him for. Cody pulled her away from Seth, wrapping his left arm around her shoulders while his right arm held her head into his chest.

"It's okay, fair maiden. I'll protect you from this ogre." He proceeded to pull her back through the room and down the hall.

I shook my head, smiling at his antics. After his freak out earlier, I'd been worried he'd be out of sorts for a while but Seth had done what Cody had needed. It'd been hard to hear them while we'd been on the deck. I'd had to do my best to hide my hard on. Axel had been lucky, he'd been facing the grill the whole time. He hadn't had to distract Becca from noticing the uncomfortable state we were both in. I'd enjoyed that he'd still been affected by our pack like that.

Seth waited until we heard Cody close Becca's door after saying good night. We all kept our voices low so Becca wouldn't be able to hear us. Cody nodded to us as he came back into the room.

"Alright. You all know the plan. Cody is protecting Becca. We'll stay within earshot of each other as we hunt this fucker. Axel, you have the freshest scent, we'll follow you. We need to find him in the next few days or I can guarantee we'll have to leave the area because the Venandi will be swarming our territory. We don't have enough backup to deal with them, since they come in hoards, right now. We maybe have a week before that happens if he does something again."

We all nodded in understanding. The Venandi weren't as deadly as they liked to think when they were on their own. They came in groups when they went hunting. Overwhelming numbers can take down a shifter if they couldn't get away fast enough. With the advancement of technology, the Venandi were winning this war that we'd never asked for.

We knew that the majority of the Venandi in the states resided in Texas. They'd taken that state over thirty years ago. The survivors of the packs, if there were any at all, from Texas had moved to Canada seeking sanctuary. Texas was too big of a place to narrow down exactly where their main headquarters were kept.

The only places they'd been unable to infiltrate were Canada and Alaska. The packs there had formed together with each other, making it difficult for The Venandi to gain any traction. They were winning here because most of the shifters here were stuck in the old ways by sticking to their own species.

With Seth, we'd been working on slowly gaining surrounding packs' trust for alliances, but it was hard won and slow. It wouldn't help us in this situation right now.

"Here are the bags for your cells. I'll put them on when you shift." Cody waved the necklaces for our cells in his hands weakly. "Becca was tired, so hopefully it doesn't take long for her to fall asleep."

Seth nodded. We'd all keep our ears focused on her breathing so we could move out as soon as possible. My fox was ready to hunt, he was craving the feel of fresh blood between our teeth as we defended our family.

I was the first to strip my clothes off. Shifters were never shy while naked, like all the romance novels say, we got used to it at a young age. Transforming in clothes can hurt. I enjoyed the looks that my pack gave me, though. I shook my ass at them before letting my fox take form.

Seth and Axel would have to wait until we were outside. They'd probably crush something if they transformed in here. My fox wasn't small, more like the size of a black lab, but we were the smallest in the pack. We rubbed our face along Seth's leg.

"You guys be careful." Cody knelt in front of me with my phone he'd grabbed from my pants pocket. "Here." He placed the necklace over my head. He kissed my nose playfully. "Don't take all the fun, yeah?"

You're gonna get spanked later. My tail flipped out at him.

Cody smirked. *By who? I usually do the spanking with you.*

We all groaned in the mind link.

Focus, you two. Play time when we aren't working. Seth admonished us but we all could feel his love through the link.

Her breathing's evened out. Sounds like we're good to go. Axel had moved his head to the side slightly.

Agreed. Let's go. We'll be in touch. Seth went over to the control panel. He'd studied the email that Gary had sent Becca. She'd been more than happy to have help going over everything. He was able to retract the security screens and unlock the front door on a thirty second timer without the alarm going off.

I was the first out, snaking through Seth's legs as soon as the door was opened. My right ear twitched as my nose took in the scents in the immediate area. The rogue's scent was faint. He hadn't been back since that first night Axel had come to guard the house when Becca had mentioned seeing something.

Speaking of, Axel came to stand next to me in his bear form. He was huge, even bigger than Seth. His bear had to weigh close to eight hundred pounds. His dark hair matched his skin tone.

One of his paws could easily smack my head right off my shoulders.

I'd never do that. His nose nudged my face.

Sorry, didn't know that I was projecting.

You always project the first hour or so after a shift. Seth moved silently to stand in front of us.

He was sleek, dangerous, jaw dropping. Even when he ran, he made no noise. His tiger eyes, unlike normal tigers, were his azure blue that gleamed in the light.

Let's get moving. Cody, you all set?

The door clicked shut behind us. *You're good. Be safe. Love you guys.*

Axel, lead on.

Seth

We stayed silent as we moved out in a triangle formation. I could see glimpses of Jasper to the far right. Axel kept to the front of the group. We were approximately a quarter mile apart. He led us north for some time before abruptly turning west.

Fresh scent.

My tiger wanted to let loose a growl but I held back. The rogue could be close, we didn't want to alert him if he was. Jasper was there just as I'd arrived. Axel gestured in front of him.

The scent had to be less than an hour old. My nose twitched at the unpleasant sour smell that accompanied it. It was the first sign that this shifter was starting to lose his mind. Underneath the sour smell was the musk of some kind of wolf. The wind shifted, causing me to sneeze as it blew the scent straight upward.

Ugh. I'll be tasting that for days.

They chuckled.

Let's see where this leads. When we do find him, we take him down, no matter what. You have permission to let loose.

The link was silent as they fell behind me as we started to follow the fresh trail. With what I just told them to do, they were shocked. I didn't blame them. A shifter had to be in control of their animal at all times. It was a partnership, but our animals were still that. Wild. If we gave control, even briefly, the destruction could be devastating. I wasn't worried about my pack. They'd listen to me when I'd give the order to stop.

So, are we going to talk about the pull we all have to Becca? Jasper decided to start this conversation in the middle of tracking the rogue.

Really? Now? Axel huffed. *It's not the most ideal of times.*

I kept silent as my senses swept out in front of us.

I think it's a great time. Jasper wasn't as snarky as Cody, but he sure loved to pull on Axel's leg just as much as Cody did.

Sure. Okay? There's a pull. She could possibly be a mate for the pack. But I'm in love with Felicity. Remember? I could feel Axel roll his eyes in his response, even if he was putting up a front.

You're so full of it, Axel. Tell us what it is about Felicity that you love so much? She has no pull to any of us. Don't you find that just a little strange that you're experiencing a human emotion for her when your animal doesn't?

Axel growled softly before stopping in his tracks to face Jasper. *You were fine with it before you met Becca.*

I stopped, my tail flicked in annoyance. We didn't have time for this.

We wanted you happy. Obviously, we should have just been honest. We don't like her or feel any kind of attraction toward her. AT ALL. Not even for a one night stand.

Axel's shock, followed quickly by the feeling of betrayal flooded our mind link.

ENOUGH. This is not the time to discuss this, Jasper. I snapped out as I swung my face into Jasper's. *Focus on the job at hand.* I moved to stand in front of Axel. *We will talk about this when we finish.*

I didn't wait for any reply since I knew they wouldn't contradict my orders as I went back to searching for the damn rogue.

It was a long night as we searched, covering miles of forest. His scent just disappeared abruptly at about five miles from where we'd found it. We searched for over an hour, even went so far as to climb into trees to see if he'd been smart enough to use them to disappear with, but it had just vanished.

Let's head back. My fur stood on end as anger filled me. We had been on his trail and lost him. My tiger snarled in outrage.

We'll go over the map to see the areas we've gone over. We'll try to narrow it down further. We'll sleep a few hours. We're going to have to start going out during the day in shifts starting tomorrow. No one goes out alone.

The trip back to Becca's home was silent as we all mulled over our own thoughts.

CHAPTER 11

Becca

I'd slept in a lot later than normal. It was nearing eleven when I'd dragged my butt out of bed. Yesterday must have taken a lot more out of me mentally than I'd realized. I had to admit, though, it was the first night that I'd truly been able to relax into sleep within seconds after my head hit the pillow.

Today was a special one. It was the anniversary of Dad's death. It was always bittersweet, but at least this year, I could do what I wanted in honor of his memory at one of his favorite places. I'd been planning it for the past six months when I'd found out that I'd have the cabin to myself this time.

Cody was in the kitchen, swinging his hips to and fro at the stove with earbuds in his ears. He was such a silly, sweet guy. The prank he pulled yesterday was just like him, but I still thought he'd been about to kiss me. He'd chickened out. I don't know if it was because he was shy or what. I just knew that I was really starting to like these guys in a romantic way.

I'd fallen asleep faster than planned last night. I hadn't done any research into multiple partners. It was on my to do list today.

A wicked idea popped in my head as I moved into the kitchen when Cody didn't make any sign that he'd seen or heard me.

He was still moving his hips to whatever song he was listening to as he was cooking something that smelled heavenly in a frying pan. It was time to be the one to tease him first.

I was going to be bold! No anxiety or social awkwardness would stop me! At least that's what I kept repeatedly telling myself as I moved toward him.

My arms wrapped around his middle while I pushed my cold hands under his shirt as my hips matched his movements. An internal shiver shook me as my hands felt his hard muscles. Cody stopped for a millisecond before he continued his movements. He looked over his shoulder down at me with a big smile as he pulled out one of the earbuds.

"Well, well. My fair maiden decided to join the world of the living. I hope you're hungry! The guys are sleeping still, too." His right hand held a spatula. His left hand went to hold my hands to his stomach firmly. "Mmm. Such cold hands. Were you trying to sneak up on me?" He bumped his butt back into my stomach playfully.

"It didn't work. Did it?" We were still moving to whatever beat he was listening to.

"Not at all. But you get points for trying!" Cody sang out merrily. "I hope you like fajitas. Not the breakfast of champions, but it is the lunch of winners."

"Lunch of winners?" I had to tug my hands a few times to get him to let go of them. "I'll take it. What can I do to help?

"You can sit your pretty butt on a stool and watch me." He faced me. My eyes roamed down his chest. He was wearing a very tight tank top that said, 'I know I'm pretty. My best asset is up here'. There was an arrow that pointed downward instead of up. It had my lips twitching as I fought not to smile.

"That's a terrible shirt."

"What? How can you not like my shirt? It's so accurate!" He

put the spatula down on a napkin on the counter as he hooked his thumbs on his sweatpants. "Don't you want to see it?"

"Oh. My. God." I slapped my hand over my eyes as he started to pull his pants down. The urge to peek was overwhelming.

"Come on. You know you want to." Cody's voice had smoothed out as it danced across my body. He sounded closer as well.

"You win!" Keeping my eyes shut, I searched for the napkin holder on the island to wave one in surrender.

Cody's chuckle sounded just to the left of me. His body heat felt searing as he hugged me. "That's right. I win. You can open your eyes, starlight. I'll behave."

My eyes squinted at him as he stepped back to go back to the stove.

"I'm going to get you one day, you know that?"

"You can try." His back was to me, but amusement was clear in his voice.

Tilting my head, I looked at his back more closely than before. There were scars, so faded that I wouldn't have noticed except I was squinting at him. They were jagged. Something sharp and nasty had to have made them. The scars trailed from the back of his arms in some kind of pattern and continued under the shirt. Those looked like they'd been given intentionally.

There was more to Cody than meets the eyes. His scars were personal and I wouldn't ask him about them. One day, maybe, he'd talk to me about them when he opened himself up more to me. If there was a 'one day' in the future after summer, that is.

The thought of summer ending made me look out the window. What would happen after summer? Would everything go back to the way it'd been before? Would I take a step backward in my social anxiety? These guys had done wonders for it in a few short weeks in making me relax. Would I only get to see Axel and

Jasper when Felicity hung out with Axel? Cody didn't even go to our school. Seth worked.

An ache in my heart had me rubbing my chest. I hoped we'd all still be friends, even if it meant that these feelings that were blooming within me had to wilt to keep in contact with them.

When we were back in the city, there'd be hundreds of better looking, gorgeous skinny women who'd throw themselves at the guys' feet. There'd be no way I could compete with that. I was the only woman they had around here, maybe that's why they flirted the way they did. Because I was the only one around?

My thoughts had taken a dark turn. That blackness on the edges of my eyes had creeped in while I'd been musing to myself. I closed my eyes with a deep breath.

The guys weren't like that. Least of all Jasper. He'd already showed that he wanted to be friends during school.

I wasn't going to let my insecurities win.

"Hey, Becca," Cody's soft voice got my attention, "you alright? Lunch is ready."

I opened my eyes to find him peering at me from the side of the island where he'd moved again to be next to me. There was a steaming plate of tortillas with the skillet in front of me. He'd even put out the plates and utensils while I'd been mentally talking to myself.

"I'm good. It smells so yummy, Cody. Thank you!" To show him that I was, I started piling my plate with two tortillas filled with the fajita fixings. The first bite was hot, but so worth the slight burn. "How are you all such good cooks?" I mumbled around the food in my mouth except it came out sounding more like, "Puw aw yoo ah gedook?"

He moved to sit next to me, filling up his tortillas. "Seth made us all take a few cooking classes. He was tired of all the burnt toast." He actually took the time to blow on his food, unlike me, before taking a bite. "Plus, I like cooking."

"Huh. He really takes care of everyone, doesn't he?"

We both were quiet in a comfortable silence for a few minutes as we ate.

"Yeah. He's like our Daddy."

This was the second time that Cody had made me choke on my food within forty-eight hours. He was busy laughing his ass off as I attempted to slap my chest as I coughed. A large hand patted the middle of my back as I stopped dying from another Cody innuendo.

When I looked upward, Seth was the one who had been patting my back and now stood behind me. I resisted the urge to lean back into him. His eyes swirled with emotions as he graced me with a soft smile.

"We have to start watching to make sure you don't choke to death at every meal, hmm?" His hands came to rest on my shoulders as I looked up at him.

"It's not my fault that he's a pervert and he says those... those things!"

Cody howled louder. I looked over to him to see him slapping his knee as his left hand on the island seemed to keep him from falling over.

Seth's hands squeezed my shoulders before he pulled up the last stool on the other side of Cody. He filled his plate with the remaining food.

"You'll learn, Becca, that he may be the most outspoken pervert, but the rest of us are just as perverted. Just in other ways, ones that are more subtle. After all, I am the Daddy who taught him everything he knows." He gave me an exaggerated wink as he bit into his food.

My mouth gaped as Cody finally laughed so hard, he fell onto the floor on his back. He clutched his stomach.

"Her face! Her face!"

I'd show them. I could get a reaction from them, too. My

thoughts whirled as I searched for a way to get back at them both.

For now, I just finished my food as I mused over what I could do. Stupid boys.

After we finished lunch, brunch, or whatever you wanted to call it since it was Seth and I's first meal of the day, I was cleaning the dishes after shooing both of them away.

"What about Jasper and Axel?"

"Jasper will be up momentarily. We have an errand to do in town." He gestured between Cody and himself. "Axel will be up soon, no doubt. He'll be hungry as a bear when he does. I was going to make some food for him before we head out."

"Can I come with?" I'd moved to drying the dishes now. I had what I needed but I wouldn't mind picking up a few more things I know that Dad liked. I was debating on inviting the guys with me.

"Nope!" Cody answered cheerily. "We're doing something special. You'll have to wait."

I didn't miss the look Seth shot him but he stayed quiet. Obviously, it wasn't special. They wanted a guys day. That was still a thing, right?

"Righttt." I shrugged. There was no reason for the heartache I felt. I hadn't even told them, or asked them, about spending my Dad's anniversary with me. "I'll babysit Axel for you if you guys want to head out before he wakes up. I'll get some food for him!" If they weren't going to tell me what they were going to do, I'd keep mum on what I'd planned for today, too.

"You sure?" Seth came to stand next to me as he leaned against the counter.

His biceps bulged as he crossed his arms. An image of me licking them popped through before I found myself shaking my head as red tinted my cheeks. How were these guys so flipping ripped? It had to be against some kind of universal law.

"I'm sure. I've got to work on some art. I was planning to spend some time outside for it." Which I was, I just didn't elaborate where.

"Sounds good." Seth ruffled my hair making most of it to fall out of the loose ponytail. He just grinned as I glared at him. "Cody, wake up Jasper, please."

"Righto, boss man."

He just shook his head as he watched Cody leave the room to the room he shared with Jasper. "Do you need anything from town?"

"That's sweet. I'm good." A little tension that I'd been holding relaxed. They didn't know what today was and how could they?

"Call me if you change your mind?" Seth didn't move from his spot.

"I'll call you." I laughed. "I'm going to make food for Axel, now. Go get yourself ready for your guys trip."

I could feel his eyes on me as I moved around the kitchen but he left shortly after. About ten minutes later, Jasper was at the island, sipping some coffee as Seth was putting a few things in the backpack on the couch.

There was a loud crash from the master bedroom followed by Cody's voice in a yelp. I set down the knife I'd been using to spread mayo on one of the many sandwiches I was making in concern.

"Uh, guys?"

I winced as there was another sound that reminded me of when you ran into someone.

"It's alright." Jasper yawned. "Cody lost in the draw to be the one to wake up Axel. He was up late, so when he gets woken up suddenly, he's a grouch. And you know that Cody enjoys messing with all of us."

"Ah... huh."

Thankfully, there were no more loud noises. After a few more minutes, Cody came out into the living room. His hair was everywhere but he looked okay.

"Good job, slick," Jasper snickered into his mug.

"Totally worth it." Cody flipped Jasper off as he started to put his hair in a braid. "Um, but if we could leave before he gets out here?"

"Let's head out, boys." Seth's voice rumbled through the room. "Jasper, you'll be driving."

Jasper gulped down the rest of the coffee as he grabbed the keys that they'd placed near the door on a small entrance table. "Sure thing." He looked over at me, his emerald eyes soft. "See you in a little bit. Lock up behind us."

I'd been about to reply when Cody popped up next to me, crushing me in a hug.

"Eep." I'd barely been able to squeak out as he swung me around once. I clung to his arms. He was a lot stronger than he looked.

"We'll be back soon. Okay?" He placed a chaste kiss on my forehead before he rushed out the door following Jasper.

"He makes me so dizzy." My lips curved up as I rubbed the back of my neck. "Such a dork."

"Mmm. He is." Now it was Seth's turn as he walked up to me before he left. "Axel will be out in a few minutes. Call us if you need anything," he repeated himself. "We should only be gone for a few hours. Do you feel like some takeout for later?"

"Yeah." I was hoping he'd hug me.

 If I only had this summer to be close to them, I decided I wanted to take full advantage.

He didn't disappoint. I was pulled tightly into his arms, surrounded by his warm body and scent. He pressed his lips to the top of my head for several moments. My limbs were becoming puddy just as he stepped back.

"Can't wait to see what you create today!" The door shut behind him.

"Lock door." The voice command worked right away as I heard the snick of the door lock. That was pretty neat.

A yawn came out of nowhere while I started to work on the sandwiches again. I was making two for Axel now, with several for later. I wanted to have a picnic at Dad's spot. The sandwiches got wrapped up and placed in the fridge. Potato salad from lunch yesterday would go in too. I had bought a can of honey mustard Pringles, Dad's favorite, for the occasion too. I'd hidden it in the cooler that was hidden in the island's lower cabinets when the guys had said they were coming to stay with me. It was a good thing, too. These guys ate more than I did.

I was trying to pull the cooler out, as it'd somehow managed to get stuck in just the right position that made it hard to maneuver. My arms strained as a grunt came out.

"What are you doing?" Axel's roughened voice came from the other side of the island. His steps came around the corner.

Just as he came around, I'd given one last tug that achieved moving the cooler out but sent me flying backwards. My head smacked against the cabinets under the sink.

"Ow." My head spun for a second in a daze.

"Becca!" Huge calloused hands framed my face as my eyes came back into focus. "What the heck are you doing, you crazy cub?"

Oh. My mouth went dry as I looked up into Axel's warm chocolatey eyes. His brows were furrowed in concern. He hadn't shaved again this morning, his scruff was looking more filled in, it just highlighted his sharp cheekbones more clearly. He was shirtless, the heat that he produced was coming out in waves. Not to mention as I looked lower, the pants he was wearing looked like they could fall off at any second. I'd drawn him shirtless, but being this close was overwhelming.

"Cub?" His tone roughened as he tipped my chin up to look at his face again. His eyes were bouncing between both of mine. "How hard did you hit your head?"

"Not that hard?" I swallowed a few times to get rid of my dry mouth. "I'm good."

He narrowed his eyes at me but backed up a little. His hands fell from my face, leaving me feeling a little lost for a few brief seconds.

I REALLY needed to do that research as soon as I could. I reminded myself firmly that he was Felicity's. He was off limits! Even if she was taking forever to talk to him. Second thing to do tonight, tell Felicity to talk to him.

"You're not dressed."

Axel grabbed my hand to help me get on my feet. "No, I'm not." He noticed the cooler that was haphazardly on the ground in front of us and picked it up. "Going somewhere?"

Perfect distraction! He handed it over to me as he eyed it warily.

"I was thinking a picnic. Would you be up for that?" I moved to the fridge, pulling out the food for him to eat here. "Here. Seth said you'd be hungry when you woke up." I handed him the plate. "Do you want anything to drink? Milk?"

He'd taken the plate gingerly while still watching me. One of the sandwiches was half gone with his first bite. "Where?" He finished the first one.

I'd started to fidget under his stare. "About a two mile hike up the mountain at a small clearing along the creek."

He didn't look away from me as he finished the food. He placed the plate in the sink before he crossed his arms. "Why?"

"Why?"

"Why do you want to go for a picnic into the forest that could potentially put you in danger?"

Curling my shoulders inward, I rubbed my arms. "Today is

special. It's really one of the two reasons I came up here on my own."

Axel's stance softened along with his voice. "What's the occasion?"

"Today is the anniversary of my dad's death. The place I want to go is one of my dad's favorite places that we used to spend hours at daily when we'd be up here together before he passed." It'd been over ten years, but talking about him still made my heart ache. "You don't have to go with me."

He snorted loudly as he uncrossed his arms. "You're joking, right? You've asked me to go someplace special to you. Not to mention we're having a picnic. Who could say no to that?"

I perked up. "Really? You'll go? You're not going to try to stop me?"

He shook his head, some of his hair getting in his face. "No. Seth might have, only because he's a maniac for safety. I am too, but this is obviously important to you. So, I'm going along to make sure nothing happens and share a nice picnic with my friend."

The large smile almost felt painful with how happy I was. "We're friends?"

His right eyebrow went up. "You didn't think we were? " He shook his head at me. "Why are girls so weird?" His tone was light as he teased me. "Let me go get dressed. We'll go whenever you want to." He headed out of the kitchen to go back to the master bedroom.

"Axel?" He stopped but didn't look back. "Thank you." He nodded once before leaving.

It wouldn't be that long of a hike, but I needed to be wearing the right type of clothes and shoes. The cold food could stay in the fridge until right before we left. We needed a blanket for the picnic, along with the candle I'd made a few months ago of my Dad's favorite scent, which was a mixture of citruses. It was a little too fruity for me, but I remembered Dad always loved the smells. He used to spray the aerosols with these smells and say that it gave energy to small people.

The house had a small linen closet outside of the master bedroom at the end of the hall. There was a heavy quilt that Mom's grandma had made specifically for picnics. It was colorful and we'd sprayed it with Scotchgard a while back to help with preventing further stains when Mom inherited from her grandma.

I'd just hung the quilt over my arm when I heard a soft grunt from the master bedroom. That's when I'd noticed the door hadn't closed all the way. I moved over slowly to peer in about to ask Axel if he was okay when the sight of him pulling on tight briefs left me speechless. I'd gotten a quick glance of his, uh, soft member and felt my whole body burn red. Holy shit. I held my breath. He looked to be the size of an average man when they were hard. I might not have had much sexual experience, but I still watched porn just like everyone else.

Axel shifted slightly so that I was now looking at him from the side. He was beautiful. I wanted to draw him again as the light shone on him at this angle. I was still focused on him, dazed, when he turned again to grab the shirt he was going to wear. I had to shake my head roughly. I was not a peeping tom! He was my friend! I rushed down the hallway to the living room.

I was holding my hands to my cheeks as I focused on trying to cool my body down when I heard him leave the bedroom and walk down the hallway.

"Hey."

I turned to look at him with a forced smile. "Hey. Um. I'm going to go get changed. I'll be done in a few minutes. Would you mind putting this stuff at the bottom of the basket?" I pointed out the candle, lighter, the bear spray, and quilt before gesturing to the basket.

Axel chuckled as he picked up the bear spray. He held it up with a twinkle in his eyes. "You know how to use this stuff?"

"Yes. Well, at least I've read the instructions."

He shook his head as he continued to chuckle at it. "Go ahead and get changed. I'll have everything ready when you get back. Are you taking any of your drawing pads?"

"Oh, um. The small one with just some charcoal pencils." I pointed at them on the ottoman.

"Awesome. I'll put those on top of the cooler so that they don't get crushed by everything in here."

Nodding my thanks, I practically ran back to my room, shutting the door roughly. "Oh God. What were you thinking, Becca? He's your best friend's boyfriend! Staring at him while he's getting dressed is a big no no!" I covered my face as I groaned. "I gotta do that research tonight!"

I glanced at the time on my phone. I did say it would take a few minutes. It would actually take barely a minute to change since I'd already put out the clothes and shoes last night.

If I was quick, I could take care of myself. If I hurried, he'd never know. I wouldn't think about Axel, no. I'd just think about Tom Hiddleston naked. Yeah, that always worked. My trusty little vibrator was in the back of the drawer, but it was raring to go as soon as I pulled down my pants and underwear. Just a minute, that's all I needed.

Axel

Becca was acting strange ever since I'd helped her up from the floor. Shaking my head, my lips kept the smile I'd had on my face since finding the bear spray. The little human really was prepared. I knew it wasn't a good idea to leave the house, but the others were out hunting in daylight.

Plus, I'd be with her. She'd have gone alone if I hadn't said I'd go with her. She was just that stubborn.

I was grabbing the food she'd put together for the picnic when I heard a buzzing noise come from her room. What the hell was that? I hurriedly set the covered food down and quickly moved to her room. I was just about to knock when I heard it.

She moaned. It was soft, muffled by something. But I clearly heard it. It clicked.

The buzzing was a vibrator. I'd never gotten so hard so fast before. My cock throbbed as I shamelessly pressed my ear against the door. I didn't need to, I could hear like I was in the room with her, but I needed to lean against something. Her breathy pants started to pick up as the buzzing noise went low before going back up to high.

"Ah..." she barely whispered. "Ah... Ax...el..."

Oh. Fuck. I unzipped my pants slowly before pulling out my cock. I started to stroke it after wiping the precum with my thumb. My bear was rumbling in pleasure at the sound of her voice. My strokes matched her pants, picking up faster as hers did. My mind was blank except the woman on the other side of the door. What would she look like with her legs spread wide for me? Her cheeks would be flushed as my hands ran down her sides before pulling her legs over my shoulders. Gods, she'd be so wet as I slipped inside of her. She'd take me like she was made for me.

"Nnn!" Her moan was a little louder as there was a rustle of sheets. "Faster... go faster... Axel..!" She'd whispered this so softly, she barely got it out. I had to strain to hear it.

My cock was about to burst just listening to her. That's when she came. She had to be biting something to stop her cry. The pure ecstasy that couldn't be contained had me coming against the door. I was able to keep quiet by biting my lower lip until it bled on the inside but I came hard. I rested my forehead on the door as I panted after my release. Becca seemed to be in the same position. The sound of the vibrator turning off reminded me that I had just listened in on her and came all over the door.

Shit. I jerked my shirt over my head and wiped the door down just as I heard her walk into her bathroom. I threw my shirt in the hamper as I went into the room that I was sharing with Seth to grab a clean one. I looked at myself in the mirror in the master suite bathroom.

Shame washed over me. She was my friend. She wasn't Felicity, yet I just came all over her door while listening to her like a pervert. Turning the cool water on, I splashed it on my face. How was I going to look her, or Felicity for that matter, in the eye again? Plus, why had she said my name? Not once, but twice!

The sound of her closing her door prompted me to throw on the clean shirt before leaving the room. She froze as she met my eyes. Her cheeks flushed bright red, matching my vision of her on the bed. I gulped but forced a smile.

"Hey, you ready? I've got everything ready except for the food in the cooler. Just gotta get that done and we can head out." Acting like I heard nothing was a bit more difficult when I was face to face with her.

The food was just where I'd left it, but the fridge was still open. Becca was still behind me so I grabbed the fridge door just as she stepped next to the island.

"Am I missing anything?"

She took the food, averting her eyes from me. She was so cute.

"Um, no. Well, we need water, so grab a few bottles?" She rushed over to the picnic basket to finish getting it ready.

This was going to be an awkward hike if I didn't act like I hadn't listened in on her like an asshole. My bear was content, and he grumbled at me for being upset about what we'd done. For all he cared, she wanted us, just like she wanted the others.

Shaking out my shoulders, and clearing my thoughts, I grabbed four bottles from the lower shelf. These wouldn't fit in the picnic basket, so I grabbed my backpack where I'd left it next to the door last night. I shoved my phone inside with the bottles.

"I'll carry the stuff. You have a compass? Know how to use it?" I teased her.

That flash of fire in her eyes came back. Good.

"I know how to use a compass, but we're not going to need it. I've been there so many times, I could get there blind folded."

I cracked a grin at her. "Oh? Should we try that?"

She gave an exaggerated eye roll. "You know what? I was going to offer to help carry your backpack as a switch off with the basket. But for that? You get to carry it the whole way there!"

I was still laughing as we stepped out onto the deck. She gave the voice activation command for the security system to turn on within a few seconds after she'd closed the door. My eyes trailed down her body, checking to make sure she was wearing comfortable clothes and the right footwear for a hike. My bear rumbled happily taking in her curves while I ignored him.

"You have broken those boots in, right?"

"No. They're brand new out of the box."

"Sarcastic is not a nice look on you." My grin just kept getting bigger.

She flipped her hair over her shoulder before proceeding to ignore me as I followed her toward the small pond. This was the first time we'd actually spent time alone, minus when she'd drawn me for her portfolio.

"So, we just follow the little stream up about two miles. The clearing is only about ten feet from the water, but you'll know it when we get there."

As we walked further into the forest, I made sure to walk next to her. My senses spread out as I searched for anything out of the ordinary. The early afternoon light shined through the gaps in the trees making it easy to see a well-worn, but old, path that we were following.

"How long has he been gone?"

Becca sighed softly as she glanced upward to the sky. "A little over fourteen years now. I miss him. I know it's weird, but I have all these memories of him, even though I'd been so young when he'd passed. We spent a lot of time up here. I remember that the most."

"You were close. I envy that." My nose twitched at a faint unknown scent. I glanced to where it was coming from before dismissing it when I noticed a small hole in the ground. Must be a small rodent.

"Why? What about your parents?" I felt her gazing up at me as we continued our hike. The ground was starting to incline the further we walked.

Emotions swirled within me as thoughts raced through my mind. My family was all alive, but we weren't exactly what anyone would call close. My grandparents ruled with an iron fist up. I'd grown up in the mountains here. The family owned a very large piece of land in the backwoods that kept us segregated from most of society. My father ran a hunting business for rich folks that kept electricity on. All the cubs were homeschooled. Our parents never wanted us to leave because they were terrified of the outside world and the Venandi.

The only time I ever saw anyone, whether it was humans or shifters, was when my mom would sneak us out for playdates with the guys. When I turned eighteen, I left in the dead of winter in the middle of the night. I wanted to make something of myself. Contribute to the world somehow. With Seth working on uniting the shifters in the US, I knew I wanted to help. It'd been slow, oh so slow, work, but there was some progress. I never wanted what happened in Texas to happen anywhere else.

"My family overall…" I searched for the best way to tell her without giving too much away. "I grew up in what was, essentially, a compound. They weren't exactly the best parents. I left when I turned eighteen."

Becca stopped walking, making me pause to look back at her. Her large light blue eyes, that always made me think of water when it made ripples, held a deep pain in them. For me.

"That sucks. I really can't imagine not having the family I have now. Even when it was just my mom and me, she always made sure I knew I could come to her for anything." She shook her head, which made some of her hair become loose from her braid. "You have your brothers, though. You're happy with them. Plus, you and… Felicity? Has she reached out to you since we talked alone?"

Guilt gripped me briefly as I thought about earlier for a second. My bear huffed at me in annoyance. He'd enjoyed it so much that he kept pulling at me to forget Felicity and jump her best friend.

"No, not really. I know you said you'd talked to her. That she needed to tell me her feelings, but the only thing she's really done is say she needs to tell me in person. That it wasn't a text conversation." We started moving forward again. "Is that, like, a girl thing?"

Her laughter sounded like bells throughout the forest. "It depends. Usually, if a girl wants to talk to you face to face, it's either to tell you her feelings, or to break up with you. But guys do that, too. I know Felicity said she had a lot of things she was dealing with her family this summer, but she is going to be here next month, so that's good, right?"

My answer was a hum as I thought about it. Felicity hadn't started acting weird until after school ended. When we talked on the phone the few times since, she'd kept our conversations less than five minutes, and she always sounded so distant. Not at all like the girl I'd met and fallen for during the school year.

Maybe it was time to force her to talk to me rather than wait until she was here. These thoughts and feelings were confusing me about my family, and now, Becca.

CHAPTER 12

Becca

When I'd come down from my climax, I'd wanted to smack myself. My fantasy had quickly changed from Tom Hiddleston to me riding Axel. I hadn't even noticed until after I'd finally relaxed. What was worse, as soon as I'd cleaned up, gotten dressed, and left my room, Axel had been coming out of his room. My mind froze thinking that he'd have heard me. But he hadn't acted any different. He'd actually been in a good mood, which helped me fight against the embarrassment I'd felt. If he'd have heard me, that would have been such an awkward conversation. I'd probably have died.

We were finally almost there. Which was good because I was sweating like a fat kid chasing the ice cream truck. Axel looked like he'd just stepped outside. I was tempted to grab some paints and mess with him when he was asleep tonight. It really was unfair how fit these guys were. And that I still hadn't gotten to watch any of them work out shirtless, yet.

"We're here!" My announcement was soft as I led him to the clearing next to the small creek. It was small, but all of the rock furniture that I'd put together with my dad was still here. Some animals had knocked over some of the smaller rocks, or maybe the weather had, while it looked like some nests from various creatures were scattered around.

We'd started building this little 'playhouse' when I was two. Dad hauled the huge flat rocks from near the house when we'd stumbled across this place and I'd yelled that it was perfect for my own little house. We'd sectioned off small 'living' areas. There was a kitchen with a sink made by using an old bucket. There was a tiny couch and bed. I'd been able to actually use the little furniture when I was little. Dad would sit in the middle of all of it and we'd have a picnic together. Mom would come up here at least once with us during our trips.

Anytime we came up to the cabin, I'd come to visit, but it hurt too much to stay longer than a few minutes. This time, I wanted to stay for a while and try to connect with Dad on his anniversary. Having Axel here helped more than I thought it would have. I only felt like crying a little bit instead of breaking down.

"This," Axel smiled softly as he ran a hand over the small stature that was the fridge, "you did this with him?"

"Yeah. We did it gradually over a few years. We'd spend full days up here together playing house." I stepped into the middle of the play area. "We'd have a picnic right here. We'd watch the clouds through the tops of the trees, making up stories. One time, Dad played the big bad wolf as I played Little Red Riding Hood." Turning in a circle slowly, I let the memories roll over me. "Dad was everything to us."

Axel stood in front of me. He cupped my cheeks while his thumbs rubbed tears that I hadn't known were falling away. "You want to know one of the best things about being a teddy bear?"

"What?" My voice cracked.

"I'm a GREAT hugger." He bent his head until his forehead pressed to mine. "Can I hug you?"

My tears fell faster. For Dad. For his loss. For the kindness this man showed me. For the other three men who'd rocked my world before turning it upside down. I couldn't answer him, so I just wrapped my arms around his middle pressing my face into his chest as I cried. I felt him hold me around the waist tightly as his other arm held the middle of my back with his hand pressing the back of my head to his chest, patting gently.

"That's a good girl. Let it out." I felt his cheek rub along my hair. "No one but you and me are here." He started to sway me gently.

My heart cracked again. Thoughts about Dad fled as feelings that I had been trying so hard to keep back about him flew outward to join my other confused feelings about all of the men. Just being in his arms, I felt like I was home. Just like with the others. How was this fair?

How did I go years without caring one way or another about any guy to meet four all together and my uterus panted like a hussy for them? Why did Axel have to like Felicity? Why did she have to keep acting like she wanted him but was stringing him along? It was obviously stressing him out.

Not to mention, I was starting to suspect that the guys may not just be friends, based on some looks I'd caught out of the corner of my eye at times. I'd seen Jasper get his ass groped by Cody more than once. It was kind of a turn on when I started really imagining it.

But if these guys were together, in that way, would they even really care about me? I mean, I'm not stupid. I'd felt how Seth had reacted when we'd kissed again. What if they just wanted a fling? Would I be able to do that? These thoughts just kept going round and round in my head.

Before long, my tears had dried out. Axel slowly came to a stop from swaying. I looked up into his face, still in his arms. "Thanks, teddy bear." I'd had to clear my throat a few times to get that out but when I did, he kissed my forehead. My eyes closed as I cherished it.

"You're welcome. If you tell the other guys that this happened, that I called myself a teddy bear, I'll deny it ever happened." His dark eyes widened in mock fierceness. "Got it, cupcake?"

"'Cupcake'?" I pushed at his chest playfully. "Since when am I a cupcake?"

He shrugged as we both stepped back from each other. "Since now?"

"You're so weird." My smile let him know I said it teasingly. "Are you hungry?"

"Hell yes. You're a harsh hike mistress. Didn't let me stop for treats or anything."

Looking over my shoulder at him, my smile softened. "I guess that means I need to make up for it."

The quilt took seconds to set up in the middle of the play area. Axel placed two rocks at each corner of it so that it didn't blow away if a gust of wind happened through and we weren't sitting on it.

I sat the basket in the middle before sitting myself. The food was basic but that hadn't been the point of this venture. Passing out the sandwiches, I only took one, Axel handed me a water. While he began to eat, I placed the candle on top of the closed basket as I lit it.

"I won't leave this lit for very long." I closed my eyes as I started talking to Dad. "Hey, Dad. I know it's been sometime since I stayed here longer than a few seconds." The aroma from the candle wafted around me slowly. "I'm doing okay. I've made some wonderful new friends. My art's gotten better. Mom's doing great." I felt a single tear fall but this time, it was a happy tear. "I love you. I know you're always there."

A soft wind made the tendrils of my hair lift for a brief moment. When I opened my eyes again, Axel was watching me with an expression that I didn't know how to describe.

"Hey, Dad," Axel spoke gently as he kept eye contact with me,

"I'm Axel. A friend of Becca's. Promise that she really is doing great. My family is taking care of her, too." He blew out the candle.

As the smoke slowly dissipated, I held my breath as we looked at each other. Some chittering birds flew over our heads, breaking the moment. My cheeks flushed, yet again, as I started putting away the now empty food containers. My drawing pad fell open when I moved it slightly.

Axel picked it up before I could. It had fallen open on the picture of the girl I'd drawn the first day I'd gotten into town. Axel's brows furrowed together as I watched him trail a finger along the spine of the pad. "What's this?"

"Honestly, I just emptied my mind when I drew that. I let my hands do the work. It makes me feel grief, overwhelming confusion, and haunted nightmares all together." I took it from Axel. "It also gives me hope."

"Hope? How?" Axel leaned forward so that his hair fell over his eyes.

"She's crying out all of these feelings. When she's gotten it all out, the tears won't be black anymore. They'll clear and that's hope." I closed the drawing pad. "It's hope that keeps us going, even if it's the most dangerous feeling of all."

His hands slipped into the front pockets of his jeans as he rocked himself on the balls of his feet. "Now I'm even more confused."

"Hope can keep us moving forward. It's always teasing us with what's right in front of us, but it's only if we just keep moving forward. What happens if you reach the end of hope because it's just gone on for far too long?"

"Shit, cupcake, that's deep." Axel shuddered visibly, shaking his shoulders.

"I'm an artist, teddy bear, it's what we do. Deep emotion, heart string cutters. That's us."

Axel snorted as he stretched. "What's the plan? I could use a nap."

"Well, I wanted to get pictures of the area, it's going to take a while. You could do that while I draw?"

Axel had his shirt off before I finished talking. My mouth went dry, yet again.

"Don't mind if I do." He scrunched up his shirt using it as a pillow as he lay down on the quilt. His eyes closed as his chest moved up and down smoothly.

The bird calls in the background were soothing as I began to start with landscape photos for a full picture of the area. I wanted to get the basics first. I'd get closer to each piece after so I could get more details with zoomed in pictures. I planned to do a memorial piece for Dad. It would take a while with what I had planned, but I was planning on it being my best work. It was the least I could do for Dad.

Time faded away as I focused on getting pictures. The lighting was slowly changing but I took the pictures following the light so that I would be able to get the best angles. I only noticed that it had been at least an hour when my phone gave a notification that the battery was overheating because of having the camera going for so long. I'd taken close to two hundred pictures.

Sitting back from where I'd been kneeling, I stretched my back. Axel looked like he was still sleeping. Turning off the phone, I put it in my pocket to cool down. I figured I still had about ten minutes before I'd have to wake Axel to start the small trek back to the cabin.

I sat across from Axel, making sure I had a good view of his face and started to do a quick sketch of his top half of his body. There really wasn't a reason to do it, only that my fingers wanted to sketch out his features again.

I became so focused on the dip of his upper lip sometime later that I didn't notice that the forest had gone silent. I hadn't even noticed that Axel was on his feet until I looked up again. He wasn't smiling. No, his face had turned predatorial. I swear his eyes had gone several shades darker as he slowly moved his head to look toward the creek.

When I followed his gaze, I didn't see anything. But I did notice that all sound had disappeared. There were just the breaths from me. Axel gestured slowly with his left hand at me to be quiet as I'd opened my mouth to ask what was going on. The sudden sound of debris brought my eyes back toward where Axel was staring at so intensely.

Ice froze my blood as something straight from a horror movie stepped out of the cover of the trees. The thing had a lupine body including its muzzle, standing on all four legs. It had fur all over its body but in spots, it was short fur due to scarring that could barely be seen. It was huge. It had to come up to my shoulders if it were standing in front of me. The teeth were long, sharp, and covered in blood along its muzzle and nose, like it'd just finished a hunt. That wasn't the scariest thing about it, though.

Its eyes were white besides a slit of black for pupils and I could have sworn there was an intelligence in them that wasn't an animal. The sound it made at us made me want to run for my life.

"Becca," Axel kept his voice soft, "when I tell you, you run to the cabin. You don't look back. You don't stop. Activate the full security system. You call the others as soon as you're safe in the cabin."

"What?" Hissing softly, I kept my eyes on the wolf monster, "what are you going to do?" Surprisingly, I wasn't having an anxiety attack. I think the adrenaline of the situation was holding it back.

"Just do what I say." He moved slowly into a stance where his right leg was pulled back like he was about to start sprinting at the beast. "It's going to be alright."

I didn't have another second to tell him no when the monster took the decision from me. It snarled looking at Axel and bunched up like it was going to leap.

"Now! GO!"

I found myself running in the direction of the cabin, fueled by my terror, while keeping the creek within my sights. The sounds of snarls followed behind me. When the snarling started to fade, I tripped over a branch. I stumbled to my knees as my breaths started to come out in quick succession. I was not a runner. My hands dug into the sparse grass in front of me.

What was I doing? Axel told me to run, but how could he take on something like that monster? He had the bear spray but he hadn't even glanced at it when he looked like he was moving at that thing! He was sacrificing himself for me! I couldn't let him do that!

It might already be too late, but I had to do something. I fumbled in my pocket for my phone. Turning it on felt like time slowed down. As soon as I had a bar, I dialed Seth's number all the while my hands shook. He answered after three rings. I didn't let him get a word in.

"There's a monster wolf thing that's attacked us. Follow the creek from the backyard about two miles. You'll see it." The phone was back in my pocket not even a second later as I stood. I wasn't going to let Axel do this alone. I had to believe he was alive.

Running back to the clearing seemed to take less time than it had when I was running away. As I got closer, the snarling was back, except that it sounded like another animal had joined in. There was a roar followed by the quick sound of a yip that had to have been the wolf monster. Axel wasn't making any noise, maybe he'd gotten away.

As I came up to the clearing I hid behind a large tree and glanced around it, trying to get my bearings of what was happening. My heart felt like it stopped.

The monster was still there. It stood facing me but it was now fighting the biggest grizzly bear I'd ever seen. Even in documentaries. What the hell was a grizzly bear doing in Colorado? We only had black bears!

At least it was keeping the wolf monster busy. Scanning the clearing, I had to stifle a cry of remorse when I noticed Axel's pants, shoes, and socks all torn to pieces close to the now overturned picnic basket. Just as I started to back away to run, a logical observation held me in my tracks. His things were torn, there should be blood everywhere, but the only blood I could see was still around that monster's mouth.

What the hell?

The bear, with it's very deadly looking claws, slashed at the monster as it dove at him. It tried to avoid the claws but the bear got a hit in on its right shoulder, enough to expose muscle beneath its fur. It yipped again.

The wolf swung itself around from the left side of the bear. I had to slap my hand over my mouth to stifle my cry when it jumped on top of the grizzly, digging its teeth deep into the back of the neck of the bear. The bear bellowed as it shook its body trying to dislodge the wolf.

The monster just seemed to dig its teeth in deeper. Its own claws were trying to rip into the back of the bear. That's when the bear swung toward me, noticed me, and everything I knew changed.

The eyes of the bear that looked at me in panic were those of Axel's. There was no denying those beautiful brown eyes that pulled you in. Axel was the grizzly bear being attacked, and hurt, by this monster thing. No wonder his clothes were torn.

"Ram it against the tree sides!" In case he didn't hear me, I pointed repeatedly at the trees near him.

He seemed to understand because the wolf found its back that still hung off the bear, no, Axel's body, was suddenly bashed over and over again against the trees. It growled maliciously as I watched its mouth clamp down harder into the back of Axel's neck.

No. No. Whatever Axel was, I couldn't lose him. The bear spray! I was looking for it on the ground around the turned over basket, but a thought from another random documentary popped into my head as I looked for something to help with. Wolves didn't like fire (who did?). Sometimes bear spray didn't work on certain animals, wolves included.

Good thing I had the lighter and bear spray I'd brought along! Scrambling over the scattered rocks that used to be the little play area, I found the lighter next to my drawing supplies. I didn't see the bear spray in that area. I grabbed the lighter and started to search for the spray while keeping an eye on the fight.

Axel had started to weaken. He was starting to get slower as he attempted to get the monster off his back.

"Come on, Axel! Get him off of you!" The pleading in my voice carried over the clearing. We met eyes again. I breathed a sigh of relief when his hardened with determination.

That's when I saw the spray. It had gotten thrown across the clearing. It was sitting next to the creek. I'd have to go around the fighting pair to get to it. Squaring my shoulders, I ran. I stayed away from the fight as much as I could and had it in my hands within seconds.

Popping the top off, I was just in time to watch Axel finally throw the monster wolf off of him. He wobbled where he stood watching the monster get to its feet again, before shaking its fur out. Axel was hurt, he fell to his side. So was the monster, but it looked like it was ready again to tear into him. The wolf looked like it was grinning as it took a step toward Axel.

"Hey! Ugly!" I threw up my arms waving to get the monster's attention. "Look! Easy prey! Come on, you big ugly fuckface!"

Oh, it didn't like that at all. Exactly what I wanted. I flicked the lighter on, getting ready myself for the monster wolf to come at me. Axel was growling weakly as he started to try to get up again. The monster looked at him again, his tongue came out as if he were about to lick his lips. No more waiting. If I didn't move, Axel was going to get hurt more.

"LOOK OVER HERE, YOU FUCKFACE!! COME AT ME!" I sidestepped twice, putting a little more distance between Axel and I. I'd have to hope it was enough.

The wolf snarled as it snapped its teeth at me. It shifted and I knew it was getting ready to lunge. That was my cue. Just as I swung up my arms, with my right hand a little further out then the left that held the aerosol, it ran at me. I waited for the last second when I saw the blacks in its pupils before moving.

I pressed down on the aerosol can so that the spray hit the lighter and watched as my impromptu flamethrower came to life. The monster jumped right into the spray. The howl that erupted from it as it backed away hurriedly from me was filled with pain. I followed as close as I dared, keeping the spray on-going. It wouldn't last forever. I needed to get as much damage done to the monster as possible to get it to leave us alone.

The smell of burning skin and fur permeated the air. The wolf was trying to clear its eyes out with its paws as I followed, aiming for its face again. As I watched fire begin to lick around its fur, it was distracted enough that I quickly lowered the lighter so that the spray went directly into its eyes and nose.

The monster began rolling around trying to put out the fire along its fur before it began to sneeze in between snarls mixed with whimpers.

"Get out of here! Or I'll come at you again with more!" I'd moved back to stand where Axel still stood weakly. He grumbled at me, pressing his nose against my stomach as he tried to get me behind him but I stepped slightly away from him. "Get!"

The monster snarled in our direction but its eyes were swollen shut as well as its nose was running. It threw back its head and gave a huge howl that made me want to clamp my hands over my ears. It turned into the forest before disappearing into the trees.

Both Axel and I stood where we were, not moving and at the ready, at least as much as we could be, to see if the asshole returned. After giving it five minutes, I turned to look Axel in the eyes.

"You have a lot to explain, you know that?"

He moved his head once.

"What do we do? You're really hurt." The wounds still looked like they were bleeding. I held a hand over them, not touching so I didn't hurt him, but heat poured from the wounds. I was afraid he'd get an infection. Could he get an infection?

Axel moved his head so that his nose touched my hand and snuffed it gently. He looked over to the quilt before looking at his torn clothes.

It was time to see if Scotchgard was resistant to blood. When I grabbed the quilt that had survived the fight without a scratch, there was a grunt behind me. Spinning around, Axel was on his hands and knees on the ground, butt naked. The gulp that I took became stuck in my throat.

His whole back was covered in open bloody wounds. As I got closer, tears began to fall when I saw the back of his neck. Parts of the skin were loose, exposing muscle beneath. How he was still conscious was a wonder to me.

"Axel." His name came out choked. "What can I do?"

He was breathing heavily. His arms were shaking as he held himself from falling forward. "Did you call Seth?"

"Right before coming back here."

He huffed in a mix of a strangled laugh and moan of pain. "We'll talk about that soon. Do you still have your phone? Mine didn't survive my shift."

"Uh, yeah. It should be. Here." I gently placed the quilt under his chest and lower body. I made sure that my eyes were looking into his so I didn't embarrass him. "Lay down, slowly. I'll call them again. Okay?"

He nodded, knowing that I would wait to make sure he did it. He tried to hold in how this was hurting him but a small whimper fell from his lips just as he lay on his stomach.

"God, this hurts."

Understatement of the year.

Dozens of missed call notifications displayed on the phone screen as I unlocked it. All of them were from Seth. The last one was two minutes ago. I couldn't believe this whole thing had been less than fifteen minutes.

Seth's voice was strained the second he picked up. "Becca, we're two minutes out. What's happening?" Before I could get a word out, he continued, "Please, tell me you're unhurt."

"I'm fine." There wasn't a scratch on me but now that the immediate danger had passed, my whole body started to shake. I fought to keep the attack at bay until they were here. I had to protect Axel until they were here. "Please, hurry. Axel's really hurt." My throat felt like it was raw as I focused on not losing it.

"We're coming, baby. Hold on. Stay on the phone with me. Focus on my voice." My eyes closed briefly as his comforting purr rolled over me.

"I see them!" Jasper's voice shouted out through the phone, but I could also hear him.

The phone fell to the ground with a small thump as my anxiety finally rushed at me now that I knew we'd be safe with them here. When they came into the clearing, they found me curled on the ground next to Axel, who was cooing at me, even though he was in so much pain, as I silently sobbed out the fear and panic. I had his hand clutched to my chest.

"Shit," Cody's whisper was shocked as they came to stand around us. "Axel." He sounded close to tears himself.

I didn't look away from Axel's eyes. They were glazed over, yet he still kept his attention on me. I wanted to be strong for him, for the others, but after the adrenaline left me, I had nothing inside of me any longer except the fear, horror, and confusion that I'd pushed down during the fight.

Someone knelt next to my head. The scent of Seth drifted close just as his hand clutched my shoulder, squeezing gently.

"We're here. Axel's going to be okay, baby. He just needs to shift again to finish the healing process."

"W... hat?" Hiccups had now joined my silent sobs.

"I'll explain everything when we're back at the cabin. Can you let him go so Jasper and Cody can help him?"

I clutched tighter to Axel's hand. I'd let him out of my sight before when I'd run like a coward. I didn't want to let him out of my sight again.

He seemed to understand because his hand squeezed mine. "Cub, I'll be right behind you. Okay? I swear. Can you let Seth help you?" He managed a small smile.

"Okay." My death grip on his hand let go.

"Good girl," Seth mumbled as I felt myself lifted up into his arms. My face nestled into his chest. "We're not moving until they do."

I wanted to watch how they were going to help Axel, but Seth was so warm and safe that my muscles relaxed, from being clenched as I'd freaked out, which made my head heavy. The last thing I heard before I passed out was Seth's voice, humming to me gently.

CHAPTER 13

Jasper

When Seth had gotten the call from Becca, I'd felt the world tilt. The rogue had found them? Why were they in the woods to begin with? Axel knew better! Oh, dear Moon Goddess, please, protect my pack!

We were in the middle of the range near Winter Park. We'd picked his scent up, but it turned out that it was a false lead. How had it gotten around us when this trail was less than an hour old?

Seth stayed in his human form as he looked at both of us. Our leader was close to losing it, but he was keeping it together for us. Cody was literally vibrating next to me, wanting to run. I could see Seth calculating how fast we could get there.

"We run. Leave the SUV for now. We can get there faster on our feet. I'll keep trying to call her. Let's go."

We could still run faster than most, even in our human forms. Seth crashed through the forest, keeping pace with Cody and me as we bolted toward the cabin. I could smell the cuts that Seth received from the ground but I knew he wouldn't even notice them. Not when our pack was in danger.

We were still out of range to communicate with Axel. Terror filled my mind as I began to imagine all the scenarios that could be happening. I knew Axel was strong, he was almost as strong as Seth, but he'd be focusing on protecting Becca. My fox reached out soothing me, reminding me to trust in our bear. Minutes passed by as my desperation built.

The sound of Seth's phone as he tried again to reach Becca with no answer sped us along. The miles between the cabin and us flashed by. We still wouldn't be there for another fifteen minutes, at the earliest.

We can't be too late. Cody's voice filtered through our link.

I knew he was having flashbacks to what happened with his family. To the atrocity that no one should ever have to go through.

We won't be. Seth pushed through the link, lending Cody strength. *Focus on now, Cody. They need us. You are not helpless now.*

Right.

As we closed in on the cabin, the familiar link of Axel's joined us, albeit faint.

Axel? Tell me what's going on. Our alpha pushed out his awareness to reach out to him.

Rogue. He's powerful, boss. Axel's pain radiated through the link, making all of us growl. *Almost killed me, I can barely keep awake.* Through his pain, the feeling of awe pushed through. *I sent Becca off, but she came back. She knows. She... guys, she saved me. She drove the fucker away.*

Shock traveled through from all of us at his statement. She'd saved him? From the rogue? How? My fox bristled as it pushed to have us run faster, even though we were all running on a full out sprint. The cabin came into view as we passed it to follow the creek to our bear and woman.

Questions after we get them safely away. Seth interrupted the questions Cody and me sent toward Axel.

The phone barely rang before Seth was answering it. "Becca,

we're two minutes out. What's happening? Please, tell me you're unhurt."

Back to human forms. Keep aware, but if Axel's sure the rogue's gone, we don't need to scare Becca anymore then she's already been.

"We're coming, baby. Hold on. Stay on the phone with me. Focus on my voice." Seth, even though we all felt the anger that he was containing, spoke soothingly to our woman.

The change happened to me within one breath to the next. Cody followed right after.

Just as Seth spoke to Becca, letting her know we were almost there, the clearing came into sight.

"I see them!" The relief that rushed through me was only brief.

Becca dropped her phone as she curled up, clinging to one of Axel's hands. She'd begun to shake uncontrollably.

"Shit." Cody slowed as we walked into the clearing. "Axel." Tears filled his eyes, falling down his cheeks.

The clearing we stepped into had rocks of every size strewn everywhere. That was strange but could be filed away for later. There was a large picnic basket with various things strewn about, including Becca's art pad and pencils. They'd come up here for a picnic? Why wouldn't Axel stay near the cabin?

My fox hissed at me, reminding me to wait until later to find out what exactly happened after we got our loved ones to the safety of the cabin.

As I got closer, the sight of the injuries that covered Axel, including his neck basically being torn off, had me glancing around again. I knew the rogue was gone, based on the information Axel had given us, but I wanted to sink my teeth into the asshole and tear him apart.

Seth knelt behind Becca. "We're here. Axel's going to be okay, baby. He just needs to shift again to finish the healing process."

"W... hat?" She'd started to hiccup.

"I'll explain everything when we're back at the cabin. Can you let him go so Jasper and Cody can help him?"

Becca didn't reply but Axel spoke, his voice cords were damaged. "Cub, I'll be right behind you. Okay? I swear. Can you let Seth help you?" His smile was pained, but he was being strong for her.

"Okay." She let his hand go slowly so that Seth could pick her up.

"Good girl." Seth gestured to Cody and me. "We're not moving until they do." After a minute, he looked to Cody. "Shift."

Cody quickly shifted again, leaning his head against Axel's leg.

She's passed out. Axel, I'm going to lend you power so you can shift again to boost your healing power. I need you to transform back to human again so that Jasper can help you while Cody keeps watch for signs of any other attack. Seth didn't wait for Axel's reply to his command.

My fox shuddered at the amount of power he pushed out toward Axel. The grunt of pain from him as he changed to his bear and back again had my fox's ears pinned back.

FUCK, that was almost worse than getting the fucking wounds! Axel cursed some more through the link, but he was able to stand on his own. He leaned against me heavily as I wrapped an arm around his waist, avoiding the wounds higher up. They'd begun to close, even his neck looked better as skin began to knit together.

"Easy, big guy, I got you." Even with almost all his weight leaning into me, I didn't budge. I borrowed more strength from my fox, who gladly gave it to help our bear.

"Cody, I want you to watch from all angles. Go around us in a large circle as we head down." Seth began to walk toward the cabin.

Becca

Floating in a blissful peace, I was wrapped in warmth. I didn't want to move at all. Nothing could hurt me here, I was safe.

"...to wake up." That rough voice started to pull at me.

"She needs... leave her be." The other voice was familiar as well.

There was a tickling at the back of my mind as I started to rise from my floating peace. Something had happened, but what was it?

"There she is."

Jasper. That had been Jasper's voice. The other two had been Seth and Cody. There was just one voice missing. Axel. Why wasn't Axel telling them to let me sleep?

Axel.

The monster wolf.

The grizzly bear.

I came to in the next second, jerking upward so fast that the top of my head hit something so hard, I saw stars as I blinked my eyes open.

"Oooowwww. What was that?" My head was tender where I rubbed the spot that had hit something.

"That would be my chin."

As I looked to my left, I found Cody sitting on the ottoman leaning away from me, rubbing his chin.

"Damn, girl. If your head is this hard, you must have a mean left hook." His eyes sparked at me with a strained grin.

I found myself laying on the couch. Seth was near my feet. Jasper was leaning on the back of the couch looking over it to meet my eyes.

"What happened? Where's Axel?" I fired rapidly. "Where's that monster?"

"Woah. Take a breath." Jasper placed a gentle hand on the shoulder closest to him. "We'll explain everything. Have some water." He offered me a bottled water that had condensation running off of it.

The top twisted off and I had half of it finished in a few seconds. The fight went flying through my head all over again. Axel wasn't human. Odds were that none of these guys were. The hand holding the water clenched tightly, causing some of the cool water to spill into my lap, yet I barely noticed as I narrowed my eyes on each of them.

"Start explaining! What was that thing? Where's Axel? Is he okay?" I pointed at Seth, even as my head spun. "What are YOU?!"

Seth kept his face blank all the while as I started to lose it, mainly directing it at him, which I knew wasn't fair. He waited until I stopped firing my questions. My hands had started to shake again.

"First," he kept his voice low, trying to calm me down, "Axel was in the shower. He'll be here once he's put some clothes on. He's healing. He'll be fine by tomorrow morning, at the latest." He reached out slowly to my left foot. When he saw that I wouldn't jerk away, he wrapped his hand around my ankle, his thumb running circles gently. "Second and third are similar only in the explanation. Do you remember when I asked you if you believed as your stepfather does?"

I nodded warily at him. "Yes." I knew where this was going. It was as obvious as Axel being able to turn into a very large teddy bear with fangs and claws.

Seth running his thumb along my ankle was soothing. My shoulders pressed deeper into the couch's cushions.

"We are some of those other things that exist out there."

He made eye contact with me. This time, I finally let myself see what swirled within his eyes that I always played off as a trick of the light or that I hadn't seen it. Stunning azure eyes made me feel like I was drowning in my feelings before another stepped forward within them. His eyes darkened as whatever was there stared back at me. I sucked in a breath.

"It's true." My whisper sounded like a shout in my ears. "What are you guys? Werebears? Was that other thing a werewolf?" This time I asked the question without the panic that I had before. I met each of their eyes as they peered at me.

"Well," Axel walked into the room slowly, "you already know that I'm a grizzly." He really had just stepped out of the shower because he was wearing gym shorts only. Water droplets still glistened on his chest. He ran a hand through his damp hair. "We aren't werebears or wolves, like the movies or books like to call us. We are shifters." He walked over to the couch; his gaze fell to my feet to Seth. "Can I sit here?"

"Oh, yeah. Of course." As I shifted so that I could sit up, Axel just took my feet in both of his hands as he sat down next to Seth before putting my feet in his lap. Seth reached out again to my left foot and continued his caressing. I noticed that Axel leaned heavily into Seth's side.

"So, shifters."

Axel nodded at his friends. "We're all shifters. So was that thing that attacked us. He's a rogue, meaning he's not part of a pack of any kind. He's been trespassing on our territory. We thought he might be rabid with the way he attacked that human, but the thing we fought yesterday was not rabid. He was too smart for it."

Yesterday? How long had I been sleeping?

"It's early, hun, barely past five in the morning. You only slept about ten hours." Jasper squeezed my shoulder again. "You needed it."

"Alright. You're all shifters. That monster was also a shifter." I needed coffee for this conversation but I wasn't moving. "You said that you're a pack? Isn't that a wolf thing? But you're a bear? Does that make all of you bears? Axel, how are you okay after that fight? How are you healing so quickly?"

Axel chuckled. "As shifters, we have accelerated healing. We are faster, stronger, and have super hearing. Overall, we're better at everything than most humans." His chest puffed out a bit as he spoke. "The worst of my wounds was my neck. I'll be slow for the rest of the day as my internal injuries heal. I shifted back into my bear before back to human again. The change helps boost our healing powers." His big hand touched my cheek briefly. "We're all different animals, but we're all a pack."

If my eyes could show what was going on in my head, they'd be swirling. "Okay."

"It's a lot of information, guys. I think we need to just give the basics right now so we don't overload her," Jasper mumbled. He leaned over the couch to brush some of my hair from my face.

"I can do that," Cody jumped into the conversation. "Becca, the things that go bump in the night? Are real. Just like how there are bad humans, there are bad things that go bump in the night. Equally the same for good humans, etc. Our pack is unique because most shifters tend to stay within their own species. We formed our pack outside of different species because our bonds were stronger than blood. We're trying to find out why this rogue is hellbent on hurting humans and drawing unnecessary attention." He paused to take a deep breath. "I'm a Canadian Timber Wolf, Seth is a Siberian Tiger, and Jasper is a Sierra Nevada Red Fox. We'll tell you more about our pasts perhaps down the road."

I was beginning to get a headache. The animals they shifted into made sense, though. Especially Seth's. I kissed a tiger, twice. I'd been held by a wolf and a fox. I'd masturbated about a grizzly bear. Giggles started to come from me slowly, but it wasn't long until I was just laughing outright. Tears leaked from my eyes.

I felt their eyes on me as I cracked up.

"Guys, did we break her?" Cody warily asked. "Is there a reset button on her?"

Now I was snorting between laughs as I lay on the couch.

"Yeah, I think we broke her." Amusement laced Seth's voice. "Just give her a minute."

Minutes passed before I quieted. This was really happening. Everything Gary believed was true. Just wait until I talked to him.

"Back with us?" Jasper's face came into my vision as he looked down at me in concern.

"Yup." I let the 'p' make a pop. "How have you hidden from humans?" Gently tugging my feet out of Seth's grip and off Axel's lap, I sat up, crossing them under me.

"Most of the time, human's brains just give them a reason to ignore something they don't understand." Seth leaned forward as he rested his elbows on his knees. He was looking out the window. "Most of us just want to live our lives. We tend to live in areas where we can let our animals out without worrying about running into humans. That's why we have the vacation house here."

"We're not hidden from some humans." I could barely hear Cody as he whispered. "There are humans that know about us. They hunt us." He slouched forward.

Seth touched Cody's knee that was closest to him. "There are humans called 'the Venandi' who have made it their mission to find anything not human and exterminate them. That's why we all try to keep a low profile here. That rogue has put everyone that's a shifter within a thousand mile radius in danger."

My arms wrapped around my sides. "They want to hurt you guys?"

"No," Jasper came to sit on the couch's arm rest now that I had moved, "they want to kill us. All of us."

Silence filled the room for several heart beats.

"Let's move on. This is a topic we can discuss more of, later." Axel cleared his throat. "Becca, will you keep our secret?"

That was a stupid question and I let him see my face. Seth clapped his hand on Axel's shoulder.

"I'm assuming that's a yes by the death look she's giving you."

"Of course, I'll keep your secret! You being able to shift into cuddly animals doesn't change that you're my friends." I shrugged. "It honestly explains a lot. Like how you're able to pick me up like I'm a size zero."

My lips twitched up when they all turned to scoff at me.

"You're not heavy. Stop saying that you are." Cody straightened from where he'd almost curled in on himself to point at me. "You're a perfect fit for us."

Uh, what? Just as I began to ask him what he meant, Jasper cleared his throat.

"Becca, why don't you take a shower and a change of clothes? We didn't change you because we didn't want to upset you further."

Glancing down, I finally noticed I was still wearing my clothes from the picnic and they were covered in grime, dirt, and spatters of blood. "That is a great idea."

"I'll go turn on the shower for you." Cody bounced up. "Do you want a hot bath after you get the dirt off?"

My heart moved to my throat. "Yeah," I had to swallow, "thank you, Cody." He scrambled out of the room. I looked back at the other three. "Can I talk to Gary about this? I know you want it a secret, but…"

"He knows about us. I'm almost a hundred percent sure about it. So, go ahead." Seth stood to help Axel up. "Whatever you need, you tell us, Becca. We aren't leaving you. We'll protect you."

Jasper took my hand as he stood, too. "I'll make some coffee and breakfast." He looked worried as he looked at our hands together, like he was afraid I'd reject his touch.

Silly fox. I squeezed his hand before kissing his cheek. "Thank you. Nothing's changed."

Giving them a smile, I went to my bedroom. The bathroom door was open. Cody was filling the tub with hot water. He looked over to me. His grey eyes had darkened as they met mine. I realized that the mask he'd been holding in place that had been cracking apart during the conversation, had finally fallen off. What I glimpsed was something haunted and dark, but filled with passion.

"Here you go." He turned off the water. He'd lined up several different bath bombs on the counter so I could choose.

"You're sweet, Cody." My fingers kept busy as I pulled on a loose thread. Becoming shy all of a sudden, I kept my head down as I felt him walk up to me. His shoes came into my line of sight.

"Now you play docile?" His breathy laughter traveled along my neck. "I don't believe it for a minute."

His fingers touched at my chin gently, pulling my flaming face up to look at him. Now that I had stopped giving excuses, I knew what I saw within his eyes was his wolf.

"This is how I usually am."

"Not around us, you aren't." Cody cocked his right eyebrow up as he gave me a smirk.

My mouth opened to argue but I closed it. He was right. After that second meeting with them, I'd started to feel more comfortable around them than even Felicity.

Cody grinned. "See?" His thumb started to rub my lower lip.

That was dirty. All normal thoughts ran from my mind. Just the small caress had my knees starting to feel weak.

"Don't think you can win by batting your eyelashes. I remember the last time you tried this." I narrowed my eyes as I looked up at him. I wasn't going to fall for it this time. I don't think I'd be able to handle it if he pranked me again.

"I don't plan on it." His face came closer to mine. "Your bath is ready. Take your shower. I'll be in the living room with the others. Just say my name if you need anything. I'll hear it." His lips were just an inch from mine. He watched my reaction as he was about to brush them to mine.

Wait. The advanced hearing. I knew my whole body paled and Cody noticed because he jerked his head back from mine. If they could hear so well, did that mean Axel had heard me when I had used my vibrator?

"Becca?" Cody cupped my cheeks with his hands. "What is it?"

"Can you even hear if the door is closed?" I whispered in horror.

His brow furrowed but he nodded. "Yes. Why?"

"Oh God!" I moaned as everything turned red now.

"What?" Cody didn't let me go. "Becca?"

"Axel... heard me." I looked up at him fighting tears.

"Heard..." He looked confused for a moment before he realized what I meant. I wasn't expecting his reaction, though. A growl ripped from low in his chest, I could feel the rumble through mine. "He got to hear you?"

I tried to pull his hands away. "Don't say it so loud! I don't want the others to hear!" Whispering fervently at him, I tried to look anywhere but him. Why had I told him?!

"Becca." Authority wrapped around me. He squeezed my cheeks gently. "Look at me."

Not having a choice, I looked at him again. His expression was fierce but softened as we stared at each other.

"I'm going to kiss you," he announced. "I'm going to make you forget everything but my name. Alright?"

My head was nodding in consent as my eyes closed before his

words really made sense in my brain. He didn't give me another second to change my mind.

His lips were so soft, plump, and heated as they met mine. His tongue brushed along my lower lip as he pushed for entrance. My body melted into his. He moved his hand from my cheeks. I felt them stroking along my sides.

As his tongue took control, he walked us backward through the bathroom to the edge of the bed. My knees touched it before I was on my back. He grabbed my hands to pull above my head in one of his. The whole time our tongues danced. When he sucked on mine, I couldn't hold back the moan because it caused heat to pull between my legs within seconds.

"Oh." I was panting as Cody pulled his lips away to move to my left ear. At the feeling of his hot breath, shudders wracked my body. When he bit down on the lobe, I jerked on my hands in his hold. I wanted to touch him.

"Nuh-uh," he chuckled softly, "This is about you, baby. Just enjoy." He pressed tiny hot kisses down my neck.

"Cody," I whined out, forgetting about everything but him. "Please."

He was kissing my collarbone as he moved back up the other side of my neck. "Yes?"

"Kiss me." I could feel my body shuddering under his kisses.

"As my fair maiden requests." He claimed my lips again.

I bit his lower lip in retaliation for the teasing. It seemed to turn him on more as he pressed his lower body into mine. He was hard as he grated his hips to meet mine. Lightning hit me. My legs clenched together as I felt my pussy throb.

Cody's kiss got harder as I drowned in his taste. His hips moved against mine faster as our breathing became labored. He pulled back slightly to let my hands go. He ran his hands down my chest to my jeans.

"You're so damn beautiful." His fingers flicked the button

open before he dragged the zipper down on my jeans. Just as he started to tug them off and I lifted my hips to help, he groaned, as if in pain. He pressed his forehead into my stomach. "Fuck." I watched him take a deep breath before he looked up at me as he stood.

"What?" Sitting up, I reached out for his hand. He threaded our fingers together without thought.

"You need to take your bath, maiden. Before it gets cold." He winked at me saucily. "We'll continue this later, I promise." He kissed my fingers individually. "I'm going to help get food ready."

He let our hands separate. He left my room, closing the door softly. What was that about?

I felt like smacking myself. The other guys could probably hear everything we'd just done.

I moaned in embarrassment before throwing myself backward on the bed. I could have sworn I heard someone laughing, but it cut off abruptly.

CHAPTER 14

Seth

Listening to Becca verbally spar with Cody had us all relaxing. That had gone a lot better than any of us had been hoping for. I'd have to thank her stepfather for paving the way for us. Axel seemed to be the one who'd been the most worried. Jasper was in the kitchen starting on food. It would be protein filled for Axel, pure meat for the bear, to help his healing process along.

We all froze as Cody asked Becca what was wrong. I was off the couch moving toward the room when Becca answered him. She sounded mortified but my tiger flicked his tail when we figured out what she admitted to. I looked over my shoulder to meet Axel's gaze. His body was flushed as he rubbed the tops of his legs in embarrassment. He shrugged at me, but avoided my eyes. My tiger rolled on his back in amusement.

Becca had touched herself and Axel was there to listen to it? I needed to hear about it, but first, I relaxed against the wall to listen to what Cody was doing. When Cody took charge, it was hot. I enjoyed watching him dominate our fox. Now, he was making Becca submit to him. When her first breathy moan sounded, my cock jerked alive.

My head rested against the wall as I closed my eyes, imaging the scene as their pleasure sounded around us. Having superior hearing came in handy so many times. Axel huffed in the background, sounding uncomfortable. My lips twitched because I knew he was adjusting himself. The sound of a zipper had me sighing before I cleared my throat to make sure Cody knew he had to stop. It wouldn't be fair for her to go any further without knowing our wolves, not to mention the rest of our animals', intentions. I'd finally admitted to myself when we'd been running to them, hoping they were okay, that this girl was all of ours. It didn't matter that she was human any longer. My tiger wanted her as ours. I'd figure a different way to repopulate our species.

Cody appeared in the hall. He closed the door behind him as he walked toward me, his hips had a cocky sway in them. My lips twitched in amusement. He was preening. He stopped briefly as we heard Becca moan again, I laughed softly at the emotions that were behind it.

We didn't speak until we were back in the living room, sitting around Axel. Jasper brought over coffee. He grinned at Cody as we all received a mug.

"Damn, Cody," Jasper snorted. "That was hot."

Cody beamed. "She's the one." He looked at Axel. "You got to hear her pleasure herself and you didn't tell us? That's not cool!"

Axel moaned as he ran his hands through his hair. "It wasn't like that. I didn't mean to. I couldn't help it." His eyes pleaded at us. "I'm not a pervert."

"Never said you were." Jasper leaned against him, offering comfort. "None of us would have been able to turn away."

Axel visibly relaxed as Jasper pressed into him. "She mumbled my name. I couldn't leave, not after hearing it," he muttered.

My cock strained against my jeans. I wanted to hear her moaning my name as I mounted her. Her voice was quickly becoming an aphrodisiac after hearing the way she was when touched. My tiger sent me pictures of her laying underneath us, her hair in my fist as we pounded her into a mattress. It took all I had to hold my groan back. The others watched as I adjusted myself with my free hand as I tried to get comfortable again. They weren't doing any better.

"So," clearing my throat, "we need to make a plan. I want to speak with Becca's stepfather about what happened. We need all the help we can get if we're going to find this fucker."

"I think he's after Becca," Axel spoke softly as he looked toward the hall to her room. "When it came into the clearing, it only saw her. Even when I made myself a target, it tried to go after her."

A mug broke as it shattered into pieces to fall to the ground. Cody cleared his throat at me as I looked down. The coffee had caused burns on my hand, but it had already begun to heal. My body had gone cold in rage. Cody left for the kitchen but came back with a broom and dustpan.

"You okay, boss man?" He offered his throat to me as he knelt to clean up the mess I'd made.

That little movement had my teeth sinking into his throat, not breaking the skin yet. I hadn't realized the fury that overtaken me at the rogue going after our girl until that moment. Cody moaned lustily underneath my teeth, breaking the rage. I licked at his neck in apology as I pulled back.

"Damn, boss man," he winked at me as he swept up the pieces, "you tease."

Jasper replaced him as he used a towel to mop up the spilt coffee. He offered me his throat, letting me bite him to reassure myself that my pack was alright, so that I wouldn't burst into Becca's room and do it to her. Jasper loved when I sucked on his neck as I bit, so I teased him a little before sitting back. Jasper sighed happily as he moved away.

My eyes met Axel's. We hadn't touched or asserted our dominance with our bear in months. His eyes lightened before tilting his head to the right. That's all I needed. I straddled our bear, my left hand holding his neck gently, pressing close before biting into his neck, drawing blood this time. It had been too long to not mark him as ours. I took care to avoid the back of his neck, pressing harder. His cock brushed against mine. My right hand snuck under his shorts to grasp his large cock in it. I squeezed, making him know who was in charge as he growled roughly. My hand ran up and down his cock, not gently, but it was enough to have him whimpering with need, even as I held him still with my teeth.

A throat cleared behind us but I ignored it as my hand sped up, squeezing Axel's tip. He was groaning as I let his neck go gently. I lapped at the wound, still working his cock in my hand. It didn't take long before his cock gave in, his cum covered my hand and fingers. He looked up at me, his eyes filled with all the emotions he'd held back when he'd distanced himself from us all those months ago. I pressed our lips together in a chaste kiss, letting him know everything would be fine.

"Sorry to interrupt," Jasper croaked out. "Becca is about to leave her room from the sound of it."

Sighing, I sat back in my spot. My hand was still covered so I licked it clean, watching Axel's face. His lips parted. Even Cody moaned as he watched. My amusement showed as I looked at all of them.

"We are pack."

Becca

The quick shower was cold as I rushed to get the dirt and grime off of me. The bath was calling my name. Even after making out, almost going further, with Cody, I needed to decompress in the hot water. My teeth chattered together as I stepped out of the shower. I checked the water temperature in the tub, noting it was cooling a tiny bit. I unplugged the bath for four seconds to let some drain, asking my Mom for forgiveness in my head. I turned the hot water all the way on while I grabbed a lavender bath bomb.

Stepping into the tub, my body started to feel like jello. I flipped off the water as I laid back, sighing in happiness. My muscles started to relax in the hot bath. I didn't want to spend too much time in here, I still had questions and I needed to call Gary, but at the moment, I just wanted to stop thinking.

My lips were swollen from kissing Cody. He'd cockblocked himself, and me, which had been frustrating. At the same time, I was thankful he'd stopped. I wanted my first time with him when I wasn't all nasty. I didn't care about researching anymore. Not after all of this. I was going to follow my feelings and fuck society's opinions. It was my body, and my heart. I wasn't going to let anyone, including myself, stop my feelings anymore. Cody would never have kissed me like that, or said what he'd said, if he didn't feel something toward me.

The water had turned slightly cool by the time I pulled myself out of the bath. Soreness, that I hadn't noticed before, made my movements stiff at first, but they'd be worse if I hadn't taken that hot bath.

The morning had just started, yet I wanted to feel comfortable so I dug through my clothes until I pulled out a fuzzy onesie that had a hood as well. I grinned at it. The twins had gotten it for my birthday last year, it was my favorite thing to wear when I needed to feel wrapped up. It was dark red with a long tail in the back. The ears were fuzzy with eyes on top of the hood. It was supposed to represent a red panda. The twins had felt bad they hadn't been able to find a panda one, but figured a red panda was the next best thing. They'd gotten cookies for a straight week from me.

The best part of it, as I finished getting into it, was that the hands had gloves that made it look like I had paws. I slipped my phone into the front pocket before heading out. It would be entertaining to see the guys reactions to such a childish pajama set.

They were all talking quietly as I walked into the room. They all turned at the same time to smile at me. When their eyes widened, I bit my lip to stop the giggle I so wanted to let out.

"I call first cuddle dibs!" Cody sprang up but Jasper was faster.

He was in front of me in the blink of an eye. His emerald eyes sparked in mischief. "You are so friggin' cute." He swung me up into his arms as I gave a small squeak. The strength these guys had was still surprising me. He sat back on the couch with me in his lap, with my legs sprawled across Axel's legs while my padded feet pressed against Seth's leg.

"That's not fair!" Cody whined as he faced us on the ottoman. I smiled at him as he grinned wickedly at me. My face flooded.

"You got to make her a bath. It's my turn to spend a little time with her." Jasper ran his left hand down my back as his right arm held me in his lap. A sigh slipped out because that felt good.

"How do you keep getting cuter?" Seth drew my attention. "I want to eat you up." His expression was dark but I knew he was teasing.

"I wouldn't taste very good. I'm all—"

"Don't finish that sentence." Jasper pressed his index finger to my lips. "We all know how good you'll taste."

The implication of his words had me looking up at him in shock.

Jasper kissed my forehead as he removed his finger from my lips. "That's another discussion for another time, sweetie."

Seth cleared his throat. "That was my fault." He didn't look sorry. "I was hoping you'd call your stepfather now? Would you allow us to speak with him?"

Digging around in the pocket, I held up my phone. "I don't mind. I bet he'll be thrilled." I grinned. "I'm surrounded by four shifters. He'll probably shit his pants."

"Or something." Axel coughed.

"Let's just call him." Jasper moved slightly as he wrapped both arms around my waist. "We'll be quiet until it's our turn."

I found my head resting on his chest. I'd slept for a while earlier, but being surrounded by them and the warmth of my pajamas, I could have fallen asleep. Shaking my head once, I called Gary before I forgot what'd they'd ask me to do.

"Hello?" Gary's voice was muffled and sleep filled. I forgot that we were an hour ahead of Pacific time.

"Gary? I'm sorry to wake you up. Something's happened…" I trailed off.

"Becca?" I could hear him sitting up. "Are you alright? What happened? Wait." There was the sound of shuffling feet and a door closing. "Okay, I'm in the office. I didn't want to wake your mom up. What's going on?"

I wasn't sure where to start, so I winged. "Shifters are real. You were right. The guys are shifters. There's a rogue wolf shifter that tried to kill Axel." Word vomit continued to spew forth from me for several minutes as I tried to catch him up on everything that I knew.

Taking a breath once I was done, I waited to hear what he had to say.

"I assume the guys are next to you?"

"Yes," Seth spoke. "We can hear you, as you can hear us."

I blinked at Seth but he just smiled at me.

"Good. Becca, first, I'm relieved you're alright. Second, I can't believe you attacked the rogue on your own!" His words were stiff but I heard the underlining pride in his voice. "Third, I knew your new friends were shifters. It was easy to tell by the way you described what was going on."

"How?!"

He sighed. "I'm an ex-Venandi."

Seth nodded as he stared at the phone. "I had a feeling it was something like that. Are you part of the rebellion I've heard rumors about?"

"Yes." Gary huffed softly. "I wish I could have told you, Becca. But your mother doesn't know either. The twins know because I'm training them. Their biological mother was a Venandi, too."

I slumped into Jasper's arms even more. He squeezed me tightly in response.

"What does all of this mean?"

"It means that this discussion would be better in person. Seth, I assume you're the Alpha of the group?"

"I am." Seth squeezed my padded feet. "We wanted to discuss with you about why the rogue is fixated on this area and wanted to kill Becca."

I froze. What? Jasper stroked my arm.

"That rogue needs to be taken down. I know who it is, I can tell you where he's most likely hiding now that you've flushed him out. Had I known he was still alive and in the state, I never would have let you go there, Becca." Gary was remorseful as he addressed me. "He's a wolf that got away when I was still part of the Venandi's group. He'd been part of a rabid wolf pack that we'd tracked from Maine to Kansas. When we took out the others, I'd found him half alive from wounds he'd taken during the battle. He'd been the Alpha, but he wasn't rabid. He'd somehow found a way to control the ones who were."

The men all leaned forward, including Jasper. "How is that possible?" he muttered.

Gary heard him. "I don't know. He learned how to siphon their power into him. I watched as he started to heal himself at an abnormally fast speed, even for shifters." More shuffling in the background. "The leader of my group had us take him back to headquarters for study. I'd been in charge of interrogation." His voice went cold. "There are a lot of things I'm not proud of that keep me up during the nights sometimes. This is number one on my list."

I didn't want to hear what Gary had done. He was my hero, I didn't want that to change. Jasper, being the sweet man that he was, somehow knew. He took the phone from my ear to hand to Seth. I couldn't hear anything but the others could. Jasper tilted my face back as he looked down at me.

"I got you." He pressed his lips to mine.

I closed my eyes as I felt his kiss wash over me. I wanted to sink even more into him but he pulled back after only a few seconds. "Not yet, sweetie." He pressed his lips to my nose gently. "Soon."

Sighing, I pulled my hood over my head again as I nestled my cheek over his heart. Listening to it, everything faded away, even the rest of the conversation. He was safe, warm, sexy, and I swore I heard purring deep within his chest.

I wasn't sure how much time had passed as I dozed while the phone conversation continued. I was so content, I jumped a little when Jasper stroked the side of my cheek.

"Gary wants to talk to you again." He handed the cellphone to me.

"I'm here." I fought a yawn.

"Hey, squirt, I know you have a lot of questions. I promise to tell you soon. I'm going to get everyone packed here and be there in a few days to help your friends find this guy. Okay? I need you to promise to follow all of their directions. Keep the house on full lockdown, even during the day."

"I will. You have a lot of things we need to go over, Gary." Like the huge secrets he kept from Mom and me.

"I know, squirt. I know. I promise I'll go over everything with you once I'm there. I'm calling in my friend that I told you who would come help you, too. He'll probably arrive before I do."

We said goodbye and hung up. I looked around the room at the guys. Jasper squeezed my waist as he held me in his lap.

"So, what happens now?"

"Now, we lock down the house. Eat some breakfast. Go over the information we received from Gary, and see if we can find this fucker before the help arrives. If not, we'll find him with your stepfather and his friend."

Breakfast was a quiet affair as we all ate in silence. Jasper had finally let me go as we all sat around the island again. I missed having the windows open, the house had started to feel smaller because of everything being locked up, but I understood the reason why, so I didn't try to convince them to open at least one.

The images from yesterday continued to flash through my mind. The rogue wolf shifters eyes haunted me, even while I was awake. He'd been covered in blood when he'd attacked us. Did that mean another person was dead? If it hadn't happened to me, I probably would have been questioning the guys' sanity. I wondered what happened to the things we'd brought for the picnic. I could replace everything, even my drawing pad, but Grandma's quilt wasn't replaceable.

"Did the quilt survive?" I was next to Seth, helping to dry the dishes.

He handed me the skillet to dry. "Yes. I think it's torn in a few places, but it should be easy to patch. I can help with that. We grabbed everything we saw. Your art supplies are fine," he gave me a small smile, "besides one pencil. That one didn't make it."

I sighed in relief. "Thank you. Again. I don't know what would have happened if you guys hadn't come."

Seth placed his hands on the corner of the sink as he looked over to me. "You were brave. Stupid, but brave. You saved Axel. For that, you have my eternal gratitude, but you risked your life. What if that hadn't worked?" He leaned his face toward mine.

I shrugged looking at the skillet that was dry. "I had to do something. I couldn't just run away. I didn't know about Axel being a shifter. Besides, everything fears fire, right?"

"Becca." His breath was warm against my cheek. I looked up at him from the corner of my eye. "Let us protect you from now on, okay?"

I nodded placing the skillet on the rack to be put away later. I turned to look up at him. He hadn't moved and his face was still close to mine.

"Are you going to explain what you all meant about how good I'll taste?"

Seth's cheeks flushed slightly and guilt flashed across his face briefly. "Um, well. You know we all like you."

A thrill shot through me as hope fluttered within my chest. "Uh-huh."

He rubbed his face with his hands and I laughed when he finally noticed that his hands were still wet and covered in soap suds. He playfully flicked the soap at me as he grabbed the drying towel.

"This really is a conversation we should all have together after the threat is gone. Just know that we all like you, even Axel, and we need to talk about it."

Axel liked me? The thought of all of them liking me like I liked them made me giddy. For once, I didn't think of Felicity.

She'd played with Axel the whole summer. I knew it broke some kind of friend code, but I liked him, all of them, and I was tired of trying to push myself away from him for her.

"You know I like you, too." I touched Seth's chest. "Whatever this is, I feel it."

CHAPTER 15

Becca

The day passed quickly. The guys took turns sleeping throughout the day. I worked on my painting.

Cody was lounging on the couch while I painted. He was the one on 'guard duty' now after switching out with Jasper. He'd been unnaturally quiet for him. I kept sneaking glances over my shoulder at him.

"Do you want to see it?"

My brush went sideways on the canvas at the sudden question. I cursed silently, but turned to look at him.

"See what?"

His arms were behind his head with his right leg over his left knee. His foot moved to a beat that only he knew of.

"See my wolf. Meet him." His eyes danced as they met mine.

Excitement raced through me with a little bit of fear. Would he look like the rogue that had attacked us? I shook my head. Even if he did, this was Cody we were talking about.

"Yes! I do! Are you sure it's alright?" I glanced toward the hallway that led to the bedrooms.

He grinned as he pulled himself into a sitting position without using his hands. Show off. I wished he'd done that with no shirt on so I could have watched his muscles.

"It's fine. I'll move the couch a little, he's big. As long as we aren't too loud, the others will stay asleep. They're all pretty wiped out."

"You're not tired?"

A flash of fear moved across his face but it was gone so quick that I had doubts I'd even actually seen it.

"Nope. I usually only sleep for a few hours at a time anyway. This is normal for me. So, want to meet my wolf? He wants to meet you. More like show off, but same thing."

"Yes!" I put my brush down without cleaning it. This was way more important. I'd buy a new one if I needed to. "I really want to meet your wolf."

Cody bounced up from the couch before pushing it backward several feet. When he turned around, his hands were on his waist.

"I'm going to have to get naked." His smile was impish. "You can watch if you want." He shook his butt a little.

Slapping a hand over my mouth to stifle my giggle, I turned to the side. "No, I'm not going to ogle your man goodies right now."

"Darn." Cody sighed dramatically, but I heard the sounds of his clothes coming off.

It took everything in me not to peek. I wanted to. So badly. I counted to ten slowly in my head. It had been quiet for a few seconds. There was a shift in the air. I looked over. My mouth dropped.

Cody looked nothing like that monster. He hadn't been kidding, if anything, he'd under exaggerated. He was huge. If he hadn't moved the couch, he wouldn't have fit in the space. Cody's wolf was black, like his hair, but it gleamed in the light. He had an adorable white strip of white fur that started at his muzzle and looked like it moved down his back. His grey eyes, slightly darker, stared up at me.

Cody's wolf spread his legs, his tail went up as it started to wag, and his mouth opened in a happy grin. I hadn't realized I'd been holding my breath until he took a step toward me and it whooshed out.

"Oh, Cody. You're... I don't have any words. Can I touch you?"

He dipped his head once as he came to stand in front of me. His head was even with my chest. Dear God, he was huge. My hands reached out, hesitantly, to touch his head and ears. SO SOFT. My fingers ran over his head to his back as I resisted the urge to hug him.

"You're so soft!" I scratched behind his left ear. My laugh was low as I tried not to wake the others up when he closed his eyes, his tongue lolling out the side of his mouth as he leaned more into the scratch.

Cody pressed his face into my stomach as I continued to pet him. I had a hard time trying to come up with a word that could explain what it felt like to see him. Everything seemed inadequate. I wondered if he'd respond the way dogs do when you scratch at the base of their tail. The wicked thought spurred me on. Using my two hands, I started to scratch down his back, biting my lip in amusement when his wolf made a low groan of pleasure.

When I reached where his tail met his back, I scratched harder, more vigorously. His reaction was priceless. He groaned again but his body fell to the floor limp. I found myself kneeling to be able to keep doing it. His eyes were closed as I continued for a few more minutes. When I pulled back, I couldn't hold in my giggles. I laid on my back next to him giggling into my hands.

"You're so flipping cute, Cody," I managed to get out.

The air shifted again and Cody was no longer his wolf. He had my hands pinned next to my head as he straddled me within seconds. I didn't even have a chance to say anything. My eyes were too busy roaming his chest in awe. He had faint black hair along the middle of his chest, moving down that I hadn't been close enough to see. His nipples were a dark dusky color. As my eyes followed the line of his hair, I had to snap them back up to his face, my own flooding with blood, as I remembered he was naked, not just shirtless.

He was breathing heavily above me but his lips were smirking. "You like my wolf." He looked proud of himself as he said it. "You weren't even a little afraid. I knew you wouldn't be."

"Why would I be afraid of you? You're still Cody. Your wolf is amazing."

"I know." Cody bent down, his face was right above mine. "I'm going to kiss you now."

"Oh, um, okay."

Stuttering was unflattering but Cody didn't bat an eye as he pressed his lips to mine again. My eyes closed as I let myself feel his kiss. It was possessive, hard, and felt like everything was right. I was the one who pressed my tongue into his mouth first this time.

He hummed happily at my tiny bold step. His tongue pulled me further into his mouth as breathing became something to worry about when I was dead.

Everything blurred as I found myself sitting up, our lips separating briefly as my shirt flew off onto the floor. My bra followed seconds later.

My hands dug into Cody's scalp as he pulled from our kiss to nibble his way down my neck to my chest. My nipples were so hard that when he finally licked at the left one, my hips bucked as I whimpered. He moved from one to the other, teasing me, while tugging my pants and panties off. As the cool hair hit my now naked body, goosebumps appeared.

Cody sat back slightly. His eyes were filled with hunger as he looked down my body and back up again. When we looked at each other, he licked his lips.

"You're everything I've ever needed and wanted, Becca. I'm going to make you cry for release." He kissed me hard again but only briefly.

I gasped as he pulled my legs apart, he angled them so my knees were bent. He kissed the inside of my left thigh as he gazed at me. If his gaze could actually make someone melt, I'd be a puddle by now.

"Try to be quiet." He bit my thigh teasingly. "We don't want the others to hear, do we?" The mischievous nature of his was going to be my undoing as he kissed down my thigh.

My legs automatically wanted to close but he blocked them using his own body as his breath blew gently over my pussy. My hands fumbled, but with nothing to hold onto, I clenched them together. I felt his hands spread my lips slowly as I closed my eyes. My whole body was a quivering mess at this point.

When his tongue touched my pussy, dragging upward to flick at my already sensitive clit, I came apart. Cody hummed low in his throat as his tongue pressed inside of me, claiming me possessively.

His right hand kept my hips from bucking as he continued to drive me insane with his tongue, it wasn't long before he sucked my clit, using light pressure from his teeth. I saw stars as I climaxed. A whimper tore from my throat as he didn't let up until my knees gave up and my legs just became jelly.

Cody pulled himself away slowly as he kissed up my body. He squeezed my hips as he hovered over me again. His lips parted slightly.

"I could taste you all day and never get tired of it." His voice had turned husky. His hips moved; I felt his cock brush along my stomach.

"Wait." I took a deep breath. He froze. "Cody, what about protection?" I blushed even redder, if that was possible.

His body relaxed as he kissed me, dragging me down again into pleasure. Cody pressed his lower body against mine, making me shudder again at the feel of his cock.

"Don't worry. Unless we're mated, you can't get impregnated by us." He peppered kisses along my cheeks and forehead.

Releasing a sigh, mostly because his touch was everything I had been craving, but knowing it was safe, I wanted to keep going.

Feeling a little bolder, my hands touched his chest, running along his muscles that twitched slightly at my touch. As they traveled lower, I felt them flex, even in the middle of sex, he still got me to laugh. My laughter trailed off as my fingertips brushed along his tip. Cody held himself above me and I heard him suck in his breath as I began to explore his length.

His skin was softer than I thought it'd be but as my hands stroked down his length together, I felt stirrings in my pussy, knowing he'd be inside of me soon. That's when I grinned up at him as I brought my hands up his back as I pulled myself up to kiss his chin.

"I want you, Cody. Please." My voice wavered.

"Anything for you, maiden."

Cody kept our eyes locked as he moved to push up inside of me. At first, it hurt as I adjusted to his cock. It had been a few years since I'd had sex. To say I was out of practice was beyond an understatement.

He pulled out slowly when he'd gotten about halfway before he pushed back in again, this time going further. It was a few times before he was finally all the way inside of me. We were both shaking a little. I knew he was holding back. He could probably crush me in his arms if he wanted, but he was being so gentle.

My hands trailed up his back again as his first thrust sent me reeling. My nails dug into his back as he picked up the pace. I found that my hips moved unconsciously to match him. I needed more. Harder.

I didn't know I'd spoken the last two things out loud but Cody moaned softly before he moved within me faster, our thrusts making our bodies rock together faster and faster. The bare floor felt like the softest cloud while we kissed again.

"Shhh, don't wake them," Cody whispered against my lips as another moan slipped through my lips.

I didn't care. Anyone at this point could hear and I wouldn't stop. Cody's body made mine crave his in a way I'd never felt before. What would it feel like to do this with the others? I dragged my nails up his back around to his chest. Time was lost as our touches and kisses faded into each other.

When Cody reached between us to rub my clit in time with his thrusts, my head flew back as I came. I couldn't stop the shout that came out of me. Cody seemed to stop caring as he sped up his thrusts until I felt him jerk and warmth spread within me.

We were both breathing like we'd run a marathon as we came down from our love making. Cody pressed his forehead to mine. A few moments later, he pulled from me as he rolled onto his back, pulling me into his arms.

"They heard."

Cody

I hadn't been able to stop. When she'd touched me in my wolf form with tenderness instead of backing up in fear, I'd lost all hope of common sense. All thought had fled when she scratched my wolf's tail end. She'd wanted this as much as I did. She felt like Heaven in my arms. I squeezed her to me. There was nothing hard about her. Her softness was everything I wanted. Being inside of her had felt like I was nineteen again having my first time with a girl, but better.

My mate was loud. It was adorable how she kept trying to be quiet when I'd asked her to, so we wouldn't wake the guys. If only she knew I didn't care if they woke up. Which they had right after I'd finished tasting her for the first time. Her breathy moans were Heaven to my ears.

Seth's voice had come through to me. One of them had transformed so they could talk to me. He'd been annoyed, but he'd also been happy. I could feel their need for our mate through our lines, even a little embarrassment from Axel. Our bear was adorable with how modest he was sometimes.

"They heard." I'd dropped that tidbit after we'd both reached our climax. My hands were stroking her sides, her back, and her hair as she lay on top of my chest.

She froze when I said it, but I chuckled at her horrified expression.

"It's alright, my fair maiden. There's nothing to worry about." Keeping my arms around her tightly, so she couldn't escape I said, "they'll just be jealous that one of them wasn't first. I got to be." My grin was large, it felt like my face was going to split apart but I couldn't hide how happy being with her had made me. Even now, holding her, was everything it should be.

She screwed up her nose as she narrowed her eyes at me. "This is going to be a thing, isn't it?"

Blinking at her innocently. "What?"

"You trying to mess with the others using me."

The laughter came through the connection from all three of them.

Jasper's voice was like silk. *Oh, she has your number, doesn't she, pup?*

I just shrugged as I continued to look at her. "Would it really be so bad if I liked to tease them with your beautiful sighs, moans, and gasps of pleasure?"

Her face went that sexy red. This time, she tried to move but I wouldn't budge. I was enjoying this way too much.

"We haven't even talked to the others," she whispered softly. "What if they aren't okay with this? I don't want to hurt anyone. I like all four of you. I want all four of you. How is that fair?" Her eyes swirled with desperation.

Enough of that. Seth wanted to wait but there was no way we were going to when she was thinking this was a bad thing that had happened between us.

Guys, get out here. We need to tell her. About the mating and all of us. Jasper, would you mind grabbing a robe for her?

I felt Jasper's love as the connection broke. He must have been the one to transform. I sat up, pulling Becca with me. I cupped her face in my hands, making her look up at me.

"Becs, the guys are coming out. We're all going to talk to you, clear the air, so that you know exactly where we stand with you. It might not be the best of times to do this, but I'm not going to let you sit here and worry yourself over nothing."

"What? But I need to get dressed!" She pushed at my chest. "Cody, my clothes."

I snorted. "They're a little everywhere at the moment. Besides, your pants might be a little uncomfortable until you clean up, right? Jasper is going to bring a robe."

"Why can't I just go to the bathroom, clean up, and come back?"

I just raised my eyebrow up at her. She avoided my eyes as she puffed out her cheeks.

"...I'd come back."

I stayed silent.

"Oh, fine!" She glared at me as my wolf bounced in place enjoying her attitude.

Doors closing signaled the guys coming into the living room. I stood, pulling her with me again but pushed her around the couch so that she was semi covered. The guys would love to see her naked, but she probably wasn't ready for that quite yet.

Jasper was first. He passed me, running his eyes down my body as he gave a smirk. My cock twitched again but I tried to focus on the issue we had at hand. He held his hand over his eyes while his other hand held out the robe to Becca.

"Here, sweetie. This is Axel's. I stole it when he was putting on his pants. It should be super big, comfy, and warm." Jasper spoke in his velvet voice that always won all of us over when he wanted something.

"Thanks, Jasper," Becca whispered shyly.

I heard her putting on the robe as I glanced up at Seth, who came to stand in front of me, invading my space. He wasn't pleased with me. I averted my eyes and tipped my neck to the side. His bite was quick and painful, but it was gone a second later.

"You're going to need a spanking later, pup," he murmured softly enough that Becca couldn't hear it. My cock responded yet again. He looked down and smirked, before handing me shorts.

Dear Moon Goddess, please, let this work out. The shorts had to be his because I had to tie them as tightly as I could to keep them on. His amused look told me he'd done it on purpose.

Axel was the last one to walk into the room. He held a box of baby wipes from the shared bathroom and the waste basket. He walked past us to stand in front of Becca. He kept his face averted as he offered them to her without saying anything, but the back of his neck, arms, and legs were deep red.

"Thank you, Axel," Becca barely managed to whisper, but she reached out to squeeze his hand in thanks. She looked at the rest of us. "He's the only gentleman right now." She stared at Seth until he looked down, laughing under his breath. Jasper was in the kitchen, but I caught that his shoulders were shaking. She glanced at me. When I didn't look away, she pointed at me, to the wipes, and back to her but lower.

"Oh!" I turned around again. "Sorry."

"Boys. Perverts. All of 'em," her voice grumbled. She knew we heard, but it just made all of us laugh harder silently. "Alright. At least that makes things better. Axel, Jasper, thank you."

I turned around to see her figure dwarfed in Axel's robe. I knew he was pleased because his nostrils flared as she walked around the couch. It trailed on the floor behind her but pretty much every inch of her was covered besides her hands and face. She sat on the couch, curling her legs up on the seat.

Axel went to where she'd been behind the couch to push it back to where it'd been before. Becca let out a surprised squeak but laughed up at him. She reached up to touch his cheek.

"I'm so happy you're better. You scared me, teddy." Her fingers moved along the scruff on his chin.

His eyelids fluttered. That was one of his sensitive spots he liked to be touched. I grinned, knowing he was getting even harder than he'd been before.

Seth cleared his throat. He gently pushed me to sit on the arm of the couch as Axel sat next in the middle of the couch, next to Becca. Jasper came back from the kitchen, handed her a bottle of water, and sat next to Axel, leaning his head against my arm.

Seth sat on the ottoman facing all of us. He stared directly at Becca. Damn, I wished at times like these that we could communicate without one of us being in our animal forms. He ran a hand through his hair before rubbing the back of his neck.

"Alright. We had planned to talk to you about this after the danger had passed, but, obviously, we can't hold it off any longer." He glanced at me before looking back to her.

"Becca, we all like you. We all want to be with you. It's fair to everyone because we're a pack."

She blinked at him, confused. "So, because you're a pack, that forces you to like the same person?"

Seth shook his head. "No, my sweets." Laughter filled his voice. "Let me explain a little better. Most shifters are born, about ninety percent of our population is shifter born. Only ten percent are made. That number is so low because most humans don't have the right genetic make up to be able to survive the change that comes with a bite from our animals." He gestured to all of us. "We're all shifter born." He waited for her nod of understanding before moving forward. "Of the population, only about fifteen to twenty percent of that are women. None of those were made."

"Why such a drastic difference?" Her curiosity got to her.

Jasper leaned forward a little so she could see him. "It's just genetics. Our animals are part of us, but separate. They're their own beings. It takes a lot of strength, mental and physical, to be able to work in tandem with them. We assume that the minds of women, when they're bitten, just can't handle the animal counterpart, and their bodies reject them. As for shifter born, women just aren't born very often. We haven't figured it out, but a theory is that nature does it to keep our population down."

She nodded as she leaned back. "Ok, so little women. Many men."

I snorted at her humor. My wolf's tail moved rapidly.

"Right. So, because of that, most women have more than one mate." Seth crossed his arms across his chest. "We're a little different from most packs. Usually, packs stay to one species.

We're all different, the only one that I know of, but we all have the connection of packmates because our animals have claimed us as male mates to each other." He paused a beat waiting for her to understand that.

If he was worried that she'd be upset, he shouldn't have been. We all smelled her arousal. Jasper rubbed his cheek along my own in pleasure at her smell.

"Oh." She had her hands over her face, peeking through a gap in her fingers at all of us. "Like, you're... um... lovers?"

Seth growled, his chest rumbling as his tiger basked in her smell. "Yes. Lovers. Does that bother you?" We all knew it didn't.

"No! Of course not! Everyone should love who they want, as long as it's consensual." She looked up at Axel. "What about you? You were trying to date Felicity. How did that work?" Her hands fell into her lap as her nose scrunched.

"I stepped away from the family, sexually, while I pursued Felicity. If we'd dated, or gone further, I'd have asked her to mate with us, introduced her to the world of shifters."

She pursed her lips. "And the others were okay with it?"

"Not really," I spoke up. Axel swung his head around sharply to look at me in surprise. "But we wanted Axel happy. So, we said yes. That's what you do in a pack." Axel's eyes were pained, but I reached out to grip his chin. "We love you, bear. Stop being upset about it. It all worked out for the best." He nodded slowly so I let him go.

Becca cleared her throat. "Ok. You're all male mates to each other. How do I come in?"

I snickered, but Jasper nipped my forearm, reminding me to behave.

"In every group of mates, a woman is the one who grounds us, or completes us. Until we have that connection, our animals are restless. Once a group is complete, the powers within them build."

She was quiet, but I didn't like her thinking face.

"That doesn't mean you're a means to an end," Jasper spoke softly at her. "This connection we have with you is special. We've never felt it before with anyone else. We WANT you as our mate, our center, because of you. You're smart, funny, talented, you give back just as much as you take. You complete us, even without being mated. I started falling for you without knowing it that first night in the garden."

Her face flooded again. I was never going to get tired of making her blush. I wanted to see her blush all over her body. I bet her toes were adorable when they were bright red. Jasper nudged my side as my thoughts careened off. He knew me well enough that he didn't have to read my thoughts to know what I'd been thinking.

"This is all a lot to take in. I just thought that I'd date you, not end up mated." She tested the word. "It's a little fast, plus, I need to talk to Felicity."

Axel took her hand in his great, big paw. "We both need to talk to her. As for all of us, we can take it as slow, or fast, as you want. We just wanted to let you know that we want you, in whatever way you'll give us." He brought her hand to his lips, kissing her fingers. "We also didn't want to hide the fact that we are all together in that way, too."

She squirmed again. The blush looked like it wasn't going away anytime soon. Her arousal was starting to get to all of us. A wicked idea formed.

"Would you like to see?"

She narrowed her eyes at me. "The last time you asked me something similar, I ended up naked on the floor."

Axel choked as he tried not to groan. Jasper shifted, clearly uncomfortable, if his bulge was anything to go by, and Seth was literally vibrating in his seat. I stood, deciding that since Axel was right next to her, he'd be the perfect guinea pig for this demonstration.

As I moved to him, there was a flash of blond hair, and Jasper was straddling Axel. He glanced back at me and pointed to the seat he'd vacated.

"You had fun a little earlier. It's my turn to show Becca what she has to look forward to."

My wolf gave a mock growl but settled in to enjoy the show. I didn't need to worry about feeling left out. Seth grabbed me into his lap, his arms steel, keeping me still.

"Behave, naughty wolf. I'll punish you later." His eyes were glued to Becca, watching her reactions to what was going on.

"Promises, promises." My snide remark earned a pinch on my ass that caused a yelp.

Axel's hands rested on Jasper's hips, from this vantage point, I got to watch as he squeezed Jasper's ass tightly as Jasper stroked his hands through his hair.

"See, Becca, one thing that's so sweet about Axel. He loves to be petted. Everywhere." Jasper's purr was loud.

"R-right." Becca clutched her knees to her chest as she watched as if she were dying of thirst. It made me happy to see that she might be cautious about mating, but she would enjoy seeing us together.

"Shut up, Jasper," Axel growled softly. His right hand came up to grip his hair, pulling it tightly before he slammed their mouths together. Both of them groaned.

I could feel Seth's hardened cock beneath me and grinned happily. This night was going to be so much fun.

CHAPTER 16

Becca

Watching Jasper basically devour Axel's mouth was so much better than watching gay porn. The little moans from Axel were the icing on the cake as Jasper held onto his shoulders tightly. Jasper started to gyrate his hips against Axel's when my phone went off with Felicity's ringtone.

All the blood drained from my face as I looked for my pants that had been thrown somewhere when Cody and I had done the dirty deed. Spotting my pants near the table by the front door, I scrambled from the couch.

"Sorry, guys!" I slipped but caught myself as I stumbled to my pants. "Hello?" I took a breath and held it to calm down.

"Hey! What's shaking, bestie?" Felicity's cheerful voice had my shoulders slumping in guilt.

"Hey, Felicity. I thought you were busy this week?"

"Yup, but Wyn is in charge of my training this week, I did really well today, so he let me have an hour off to just relax. He says hello, by the way. How's the art going?"

I glanced over at the guys as they all stared at me. Swallowing, I went down the hall to my room for the illusion of privacy.

"It's going really good. Several new pieces are already done for the portfolio!" I sat on my bed.

"That's awesome, can't wait to see them." Her voice dropped in volume after a second. "Um, have you talked to Axel? Or seen him lately?"

My guilt pressed down on me like a boulder. The start of an attack was right around the corner as I fought to focus. "Y-yeah. I have. A lot, actually."

"A lot?" Her tone was disbelieving. "You've been hanging out with these guys and are okay with it all? How is your anxiety?" I heard a beep. "Hey, switch to video."

Internally, I moaned. I was going to have to do this. I owed it to her. I just hoped that she forgave me. Eventually.

Her face filled the screen. She looked like she was glowing. Her hair was down, she had very little make-up on, yet she could still stop cars if she walked across a crowded street.

"Ok, tell me!" Her grin made her look years younger.

"Um, well some bad things have been happening out here. I didn't want to leave. I had to do some things I could only do here. So, the guys moved into the cabin with me because the security system is better here. Gary thought it was a really good idea."

Her grin slowly faded the longer I talked. "You haven't told Axel that I'm still trying to figure out my feelings, have you?" Her voice was hesitant and I could hear the lie in her tone.

I sighed. "No, I haven't. That's going to be something you have to do, Felicity. What changed? You still haven't told me. You don't even look happy when you say his name anymore. Did you meet someone at the family thing?"

She looked to the side. She was a really bad liar. "Sort of? It's really hard to explain. I still want to see Axel when I come visit at the end of the summer."

I bit my lip, the sharp pain helped me focus on her and not the black that was edging around my sight. "Felicity. I like Axel," I said it softly, but I knew she heard it when she whipped her face back to the phone. If I didn't tell her now, I might not have the courage to tell her again in the future.

"What?" She laughed. "That's a joke, right?"

I shook my head. "I'm not joking. I really like Axel. I've gotten to know him, all of them really, the past month and a half. They're kind."

"How can you like Axel? We were practically dating during school!" She pressed her lips together. "Becca, you can't like him. You just can't."

"I know you liked him, Felicity, but you just said that you found someone new you're seeing. You have been avoiding Axel almost all summer."

"It's not like it was my choice!" She was frustrated as she snapped at me. "I have to be with him. He's mine, Becca. You need to back off."

Uh, what? My spine stiffened.

"No. You treated him like trash this summer. You're as good as 'broken up' when you acted like his feelings didn't matter. I love you, Felicity. You're my best friend. I was hoping that this would go better, but it didn't." I offered her a tight lipped smile. "I'm going to hang up. We can talk when you're ready. Tell Wyn I say hello."

Hanging up on her was probably one of the hardest things I'd ever had to do. I stared at the phone in my hands. I'd made my choice and I wouldn't regret it. These men made me feel safe, but more than that, I felt like I could really be myself around them and they wouldn't care if I was broken.

There was a knock on my door. Jasper opened it slightly before stepping in.

"Hey, hun." He had a soft expression on his face as he looked me up and down. "You know we heard that. I just want to make sure that you're okay." He grinned slightly. "You made Axel blush. I got a picture for you."

I snorted out a laugh. "I'm okay. Or, I will be. Could I have a hug?" A hug sounded really good right about now.

"That," Jasper stepped in front of where I sat on the bed before he knelt on his right knee, "I can do that." He didn't hesitate to wrap me into his arms.

Sighing out the breath I'd been holding, I relaxed into him. He kissed my cheek before slowly pulling away.

"Even though we would all love to keep going where we'd left off, we need to go hunting again. Your stepfather sent a text to Seth while you were in here. He gave us a location he's almost a hundred percent sure that this rogue is hiding out at. It's about ten miles north up the mountain. He's probably still recuperating from the wounds you gave him." He brushed his thumb along my lower lip. "You'll be safe here. We won't be gone long. If we find him there, we'll take care of him. If not, we'll wait for your stepdad. His 'friend' should be here sometime in the evening. He agreed that you staying here would be safer than having you coming along with us into danger."

My heart gripped in fear as I took a deep breath. They had to do this. They were really the only ones who could. Unless the Venandi showed up, but Gary said those guys were bad. They'd try to kill the guys, too.

"Okay. I promise to stay inside." It would do no good to argue. I wouldn't be able to offer any kind of support. What happened with the monster earlier had been a lucky chance.

We both stood up. He held my hand tightly as we moved to the living room. The others were standing, waiting for us. Seth stepped up to us and pulled me into his arms. Jasper went to my back, enveloping me between the two of them. Cody, not to be outdone, jumped onto Seth's back where he reached around to touch my cheek.

I laughed at his antics as Axel came forward to join the group hug. My eyes closed in happiness as we all stayed touching each other for several minutes. Wishing for this to never end, I gave a sad noise as they stepped back together.

"We'll be back before you know it." Seth cupped my cheeks. "We'll have our cell phones with us. You can call us if you need anything, alright?"

"Mmm." His hands were so warm, I really didn't pay attention to what he said.

"Becca," Jasper chuckled from somewhere behind me. "I like this version of her. When she didn't like to be touched sucked. This is much better."

"I like her however she wants to act." Cody was still monkeyed on Seth's back. He stuck his tongue out at Jasper and I giggled as Seth removed his hands from my cheeks.

"Are you sure one of us shouldn't stay here?" Axel crossed his arms.

"I'll be fine," I said before anyone else. "You know what that thing did to you. It's better if you all are together. That way no one gets hurt. I'll be fine inside the house." I touched Axel's arm. "Could we talk for just a minute?"

He gazed down at me as he nodded. "Of course." Uncrossing his arms, he took my hand in his and pulled me further away from the guys. They'd still hear us, but I appreciated the gesture.

"Axel, I know you heard my conversation with Felicity. Are you okay? Was it alright that I told her all of that?" My questions came out rushed as I started thinking that he might be unhappy that he hadn't gotten a chance to talk to her on his own.

"Of course, it's alright." His gravelly voice was soft as he kissed my fingers. "I'm not sure when it changed, exactly, but the longer I've been away from her with no contact, I can't exactly remember why I liked her so much in the first place. That's never happened before. No one has ever taken me away from my pack.

We'd all agreed years ago that we would stick together until we found a mate that would fit with all of us. I was extremely selfish. I have a lot to make up to the guys."

"Damn right you do!" Cody's voice carried across the floor. "You have months and months of hard sex to make up for lost time!"

Axel squeezed my hand as we both laughed together. His shoulders relaxed. It looked like this had been weighing on him.

"We'll talk more about this when we get back." He gave me a soft kiss that made a shiver go up my spine.

I nodded as we walked back to the others.

"Do I get to see everyone's animals?" The idea perked me right up.

Arms wrapped around my waist pulling me into a toned chest. Cody rested his chin on my shoulder.

"It's only fair. You met my wolf. Right, Seth?" he teased him.

Seth had been looking out the windows to the back deck. "I don't see why not. We won't have time to do a proper introduction, but you could put our cell phones around our animals necks. That would actually be helpful." His stunning eyes locked onto mine as he turned his head back to look at us.

"We'll change outside, it'll be quicker. Cody, get our cell phones ready. Jasper, you know where to go?" The ease that he held himself as he gave orders was distracting.

I wondered if he was bossy in the bedroom, too. Most likely, based on our kisses. I slapped my cheeks. It was no time to get lost in a fantasy. Just because I slept with Cody didn't mean I was going to just jump into the other guys arms. Now, if only I could actually make myself believe that.

Several minutes later, I found myself out on the deck with the guys around me. The sun was high in the sky as it beat down on us. I held the cell phone holder necklace things that they wore when they shifted into their animals. I could still barely believe that they weren't human. Even though I'd seen Axel and Cody change.

"Better close your eyes, love, if you don't want a show." Jasper came forward to kiss my forehead one last time. "See you in a few hours."

"Alright, let's shift, lads." Seth removed his shirt, throwing it to the side. He smirked at me as my eyes roamed his chest.

Dear God. They all had their shirts off in seconds. I was close to having a bloody nose. Totally overloaded by muscles galore. As soon as Seth's hands went to his waist, my eyes shut tightly. The sounds of the rest of their clothes joining their shirts had me squirming as I fought to keep my eyes closed. I would not peek!

Who was kidding? I wanted to peek. Slapping my hands over my eyes, I opened my right eye to look through the small gap between my fingers. I didn't see any of them naked, I'd been too slow, but my hands slid from my face as I looked at what was before me.

I'd seen tigers at the zoo, just like most people did. But seeing them at the zoo was nothing like standing three feet from one. Seth's head was big, really big. His body was sleek as his fur practically glimmered in the sunlight. The colors of his fur were fascinating. His black stripes moved in a waving fashion along his body. He had to be at least ten feet in length. His tail moved slowly from where he sat patiently.

When he yawned at me, flashing his sharp, long, and very big teeth, I snorted. "You don't scare me, pussy cat."

There were sounds of chuffing around me. The others seemed to be laughing, or at least trying to. Seth stood from sitting, taking the two steps to be directly in front of me. He rubbed his head against my stomach. I took that as permission to sink my fingers into his fur and sighed. He was a little scruffy on top but as my fingers sunk into his coat, he was fuzzy and soft. Behind his ears were especially soft. He seemed to approve since he pushed his head more, which made me stumble backward.

Instead of falling, my back hit a solid and very furry side. Axel was making sure I didn't fall. I smiled brightly at him. I couldn't resist, I ran my cheek along his side. A yip from my side brought my attention to an unnaturally big fox.

Jasper had to be the size of a large dog, like a lab or slightly bigger. He was all a dark red along his body, except for his feet and face. He looked like a much larger version of the fox I had painted.

"...How?" My whisper was soft as I touched Jasper's ears gently. "My painting... it's you. But, how?"

His head titled as his nose pressed against my arm. "Right. We can talk about that later." I placed the necklaces over their necks, kissing their noses. "Be safe."

The last one to get his cellphone was Cody. He'd sat further away, letting me say hello to the others' animals. His fur didn't reflect the light, it was like it swallowed the sunlight. After I placed his necklace over his neck, I hugged him tightly.

"Come back to me."

Cody licked my cheek as we pulled apart. His grey eyes were bright and he winked at me slowly, making me laugh.

Seth pushed the door open as he pointed with his humongous paw inside.

"Fine. I'm going." After the door shut, I activated the security system. The guys gave me one last look before they were running off the deck and into the forest. "Tigers, foxes, wolves, and bears, oh my," I whispered softly as the shutters blocked my view of the outside.

Becca

Try as I might, I couldn't focus on anything but the worry that rolled in my gut. I'd resorted to pacing in the living room. I'd tried to work on my art, any medium, really, but I stared at the supplies and couldn't sit still.

I'd even started to bite at my thumb nail. This was a bad habit I had kicked years ago. I sighed softly after what had to be my two hundredth sweep of the house. They'd only been gone an hour, it wouldn't do anyone any good if I made myself sick with worry.

Deciding that I would watch TV, I relaxed against the couch. My left foot began to tap as I surfed through the local channels, but I tried to ignore it. When I stopped on the news, I put the remote down and away from me so I wouldn't keep flipping through the channels.

Nothing on the news indicated that the police had been able to find the killer of the body from the other day. They were advising everyone to stop going on hikes, or if they do, to make sure they had protection and went with someone else.

I snorted at that. None of that would stop that monster. He'd just have a second meal if there were two people. A cold chill ran down my spine as goose bumps ran over my arms. I knew it wasn't cold in the house. I looked around but everything was in its place. I ignored it, pulling the throw on the back of the couch over my shoulders.

Several minutes later, the doorbell rang. At first, I thought it had been the TV, but it rang again a minute later. What the hell? Maybe someone was lost? Remembering Gary's words and Seth's, I approached the door and looked through the peephole that was designed so the person outside didn't know it was there.

"Hello? Who is it?"

A man stood on the stoop, his hands were in his front pockets.

He was bulky, he made me think of a body builder, but it wasn't a good look on him. He looked ordinary enough, a square jaw with a little scruff, black hair sprinkled with grey. He wore sunglasses.

"Hi. I'm a little lost. I was trying to get to Winter Park? My GPS keeps running me in circles. I saw the lights were on outside, I thought I'd see if anyone was home to give me better directions." His words were muffled and low.

My stomach twisted. That was plausible. GPS, unless it was satellite, around these parts did tend to freak out. I tapped my fingers against the door as I thought. I wasn't going to invite him in. I wasn't that stupid. Even if this whole fiasco hadn't happened, I wouldn't. I was alone here and he was a lot bigger than I was.

"Hello?" he called out again.

"Yeah. Still here. I can give you directions. Do you have a pen and paper?"

The man shook his head. "No, I don't. I could type it on my phone?" He pulled a phone from his pocket but his lips turned downward. "Damn it. I'm on three percent battery life."

I sighed, this time in annoyance. Who let their cell phone get that low? He didn't have a charger in his car?

"Stay there. I'll write down the directions and give them to you."

"Thanks. I appreciate it."

I was still wary about this guy, but it wasn't like I could just let him keep going around lost. Not with that asshole out there. It took less than a minute to write up directions from here through Tabernash to Winter Park.

Now, the question was how I was going to get this to him. I wasn't going to open the door. I might be able to get the paper to go under the door. I'd have to lift the security door a little to do that, but it would have to do.

"If you'll step back a little, I'm going to slide the paper under the door for you," I called out as I pressed the button to move the security door a few inches.

I'd folded the paper in half so it should have been easy to slip under the teeny crack between the floor and door, but it wouldn't fit. Even when I flattened it out again, it wouldn't budge.

"Sorry, I don't see it." His tone sounded annoyed but more muffled.

Damnit. I was going to have to open the door a centimeter to get this out to him.

"One second." I set the security door to shut after five seconds. That would give me enough time to open the door, shove the paper out and close it before it started to close up again. Easy. The guys were going to kill me.

As soon as the security door was up enough to open it, I unlocked it, cracked it open, and basically flicked the paper out. Just as soon as I tugged the door to close it, the handle was ripped from my hand. In less than the five seconds I had set, the door was ripped off its hinges.

Horror had my throat closing up. The man took off his glasses after he brushed his hands together. He threw the glasses to the ground revealing eyes that were white save a slit of black for his pupils. His smirk transformed his ordinary face into something evil and disgusting. His muscles were moving under his clothes. He rolled his neck.

"That was a nuisance. You've made my revenge more complicated since you came here without the Venandi."

I scrambled backward, my eyes looking at the security panel next to the door. There was no way that I'd be able to activate the noise alarm with him next to it. I was one second from a panic attack that would get me killed.

"Yes. Run, little human. Let me taste your fear." His sneer made my body freeze on instinct. "Did the Venandi tell you what they did to me?" He took a look at the panel. "You know you can run out the door if you want. I'll even give you a head start."

If I ran out of the house, there would be no chance I'd survive. There really wasn't a big chance I'd survive anyway, but at least in the house, I had the emergency lock down room Gary showed me in the bathroom. I just had to figure out how to get there without dying first.

"Not a talkative prey, are you? That's alright. You know, you're the first one in years who's been able to hurt me enough that I had to leave to heal. Clever, using the lighter and aerosol can to make a flame torch."

He pulled back his arm as he slammed his fist into the security panel. When he yanked his arm out of the wall, he dragged out wires, dropping them at his feet.

"There. Now, we don't have to worry about all these silly security precautions that didn't do you much good. Now, where was I?"

Every step he made toward me, I took a large step backward, moving slowly toward the hallway. He seemed like he wanted to talk. Cliché villain move, but it might work in my favor. I knew that I was pale, my knees shook, but I had to fight to stay focused. The panic attack that I felt building in my chest wasn't easy to keep pushed away, but I had to focus on getting to the bathroom. After that I could panic.

"Ah, yes. You know, when you first showed up here, I was so angry that the Venandi wasn't with you. My perfect plan ruined." He went to the television that was bolted to the wall and I took another step into the hallway. "Did he tell you what they did to me!?"

He was repeating himself. He wasn't all there, which made him ever more dangerous, if that was possible. I jumped when the TV flew across the room to shatter against the island in the kitchen. The monster's face had started to elongate when he turned to look at me.

"I wanted to make him watch as I killed his family in front of him. First the son, the girl, you, then the wife. I'd take you and your mother, even as I tore open your stomachs to spill along the floor." His shirt seams began to rip as he continued to shift slowly.

I didn't understand why he wasn't changing as fast as the others, but it gave me more time to continue moving backward.

"You're sick." I was almost there. But the bad news was that he had me caged in. I couldn't get around him if I tried.

"Maybe." I could barely understand him now as his voice was more of an animal growl. "You just had to show up alone. I was going to wait until he showed up, even if it took another year." His fist punched through the master bedroom's door to his left. "But when you brought that pack here? Into my territory? I decided killing you and them would still leave me with some satisfaction. It might even bring the Venandi after me."

He turned to the side, ripping the master bedroom door away. "You've let them into this house!" His muscles all over his body stretched, moving as he grew. He stepped into the room, throwing his head back in a howl as he left my sight.

This was my only chance. I ran as fast as I'd ever run before. My bedroom door banged against the wall as I rushed to the bathroom. I wasn't going to waste time closing it. He'd just break through it anyway. There was another howl before the sounds of a large body breaking through the doorway.

A scream ripped through my throat as I made it into the bathroom. My hand slapped onto the hidden panel just as the monster appeared in front of me.

I wasn't fast enough. Just as I touched the red button that slammed the bars down within milliseconds, the monster had my other hand in its mouth. I screamed again as it bit down, hitting bone. My right hand slapped the orange button as pain radiated up my hand to my whole body.

It was trying to pull me through the bars, but they had to be made of something even stronger than he was because he was trying to pry them apart with his claws as he yanked me into the bars. My head smacked into one, making my head spin. The sound of the security screen, as it tried to close but was stuck because of his claws, sounded like a dying animal.

The monster jerked back, letting my hand go just enough that I was able to pull it back to me. I scrambled backward before falling on my ass. The growling coming from him as he snapped his jaws, had me pulling myself into the bathtub. The monster let his claws go from the bars and the security screen slammed shut.

It took what felt like forever to pull out my phone. Using my good hand as I tried to ignore the pain, or even looking at the wound, I pressed my call button next to my favorite contact list. Only the guys and my family were on it since Jasper had grouped the numbers together for emergencies. I'd have to thank Jasper for his smart thinking if I survived this.

The phone rang twice before a concerned deep voice answered.

"Becca? What's wrong?" Axel's voice helped push my panic attack away.

I opened my mouth but I couldn't get anything to come out. My whole body had begun to shake uncontrollably. My left hand started to feel like it was on fire. I couldn't move it at all.

"H... he... help..." I finally managed to whisper.

There was a loud bang on the other door that led to the twin's room. The monster howled again. I heard it trying to rake through the screen. The noise was like nails on a chalkboard.

"Fuck. Fuck. We're coming, baby."

The phone fell from my hand to the bottom of the tub as the shaking got worse. My mind began to become fuzzy and felt light.

I needed to try to slow down the blood loss. My limbs were heavy as I struggled to pull my shirt off. I couldn't get it over my damaged hand, which was fine since I was going to use it on that hand anyway.

I wasn't sure how much time passed. The monster had continued trying to get into the bathroom, he'd even tried to go through the wall from the hallway. Whatever this room was, it kept the thing out. When the monster became frustrated, I heard it destroying everything it touched within the house. My artwork was probably trashed.

A chuckle escaped my throat. I was dying and all I cared about was my art. My body became cold everywhere. My eyes felt heavy as I struggled to keep them open. If they closed, I wouldn't wake up again. I couldn't even tell if I was shaking anymore.

I caught myself nodding off more and more as the destruction of the cabin continued. I was so tired. All the pain was gone. There was nothing but the cold.

I wanted the guys. I wanted to be held. I wanted all of this to end. I wanted to be able to say goodbye to them. Kiss them before I died. Fate was cruel. I'd finally found my home with them and now, I was going to leave them.

Darkness surrounded me. I couldn't keep my eyes open anymore. I just didn't have the strength.

Good bye. I love you, guys.

I knew I was crying. I knew I couldn't reach them in time.

I focused on a picture in my mind of all of them together. At least I had that as everything just faded to black.

CHAPTER 17

Seth

When we got to the location that Gary had given us, it was apparent that the rogue wasn't here. His scent was everywhere, at least we confirmed this was where he'd been hiding. Jasper had the best nose, so he was put in charge of looking for clues before we left the area to search for him in the surrounding area.

It's strange. His scent just ends in places. It's not natural. He doesn't get into the trees. It's just like he stepped into water to disappear. Jasper was calculating as he thought deeply.

Perhaps he has some kind of technology or magic. Cody chimed in as he circled the area we determined the rouge was sleeping.

This guy is smart. Axel growled through the connection.

He is. Cody, I want you to go north for ten miles. Axel, go east. Jasper, stay here and see if you can find anything. I'll go west. We need to sweep the whole area. This fucker needs to die.

I raced off to start sweeping the area. Where was this guy if he wasn't here? The Rocky Mountains were huge. Without anything besides his scent that kept disappearing, it was like finding a needle in a haystack. Cody was most likely correct that this rogue was using technology of some sort or magic.

Magic was rare for shifters outside of an Alpha's pack magic. We knew some humans possessed it and vampires tended to have a little bit of it. If this rogue had it, we could be in for a long haul. This sweep of the area would most likely lead to nothing, based on our experience so far, but I wanted to make sure that he hadn't killed again near his location. It could lead to more deaths if the authorities came here. They wouldn't stand a chance if he attacked while they tried to do their job.

A sudden panicked thought ran through me. My paws dug into the forest floor as I rode out the feeling.

Report. Who's hurt? There was silence. I couldn't be that far from my pack that they couldn't hear me.

BECCA! Axel's roar of rage that was underlined with fear shattered our connection, giving me a sharp headache that would fade in minutes. That had never happened before.

What's happening? Tell me! Cody's voice sounded like an echo through the broken connection.

I had to shake my head to get the echoes to dissipate as Jasper joined in with Cody as they demanded an answer from Axel.

ENOUGH! My tiger and I sent our alpha power through to all of them. My power slowly pieced back the connection. *Axel, what is going on?*

Becca... hurt... cabin... rogue... Axel's reply faded in and out. He was getting out of range of our connection.

I threw my head back and roared out my fury. Becca was hurt. The rogue was at the cabin? HOW? How did he get around us?

Get to the cabin. I clipped out as I started to sprint as fast as I could to get back to our girl.

I refused to let the fear that I felt control me. My tiger bristled as he gave me more speed. We weren't going to lose her. It wasn't going to happen. I'd be damned if I let it. We hadn't been gone that long, yet it felt like an eternity as I raced to the cabin.

Cody and Jasper met up with me just as we saw the cabin in

the distance. Axel was running around the back to the front. The cabin looked secure. All the screens were down. What the hell was going on? Why hadn't Becca turned on the noise alarm?

Axel's roar echoed through the clearing as we ran around the house.

SHIT! Cody snarled.

The front door was open. Scratch that. The door was halfway across the clearing, near the road. He'd gotten in somehow. That would explain why there was no noise alarm.

Need help, guys. Axel grunted just as I burst through the doorway.

The place was trashed. The sight of all of Becca's artwork littered around the ground in pieces, torn apart, or covered in claw marks fueled my rage. Axel went flying into the far wall as the rogue appeared in the hallway.

He was big. Much bigger than any wolf shifter should be. He looked deformed as one shoulder was larger than the other. His muzzle was crooked and bleeding. He turned his attention when he caught sight of the three of us.

Axel? I couldn't take my eyes off the rogue. He was getting ready to attack.

I'm good.

Good. I snarled, showing all my teeth at this invader. *I want us all to surround him. Cody, his right. Axel, left. Jasper, get behind him.*

I would go at him from the front. There would be no one on one fighting. We were going to take this asshole down and quickly. We needed to find Becca. I let my claws out as I hunched down as the rogue tried to stare me down.

The others slowly moved. The rogue was smart enough not to glance away from me. If he did, I'd be on his neck in no time. He just snarled loudly as they started to surround him. Jasper waited next to Cody, looking for the time where he could get behind him.

We need to rip his head off. Focus on the muscles in his legs, Cody. I want to make him immobile. Jasper, you know what to do. Axel, distract him as you hurt him. Make him hurt!

Just like that, we all moved as one. The rogue howled as he swung out his right arm, but Jasper was too quick to get caught. He bounded around him as Cody lunged for his legs. I lunged at him, managing to sink my teeth into his forearm as he'd pulled back to swing at Axel or Cody.

Red filled my vision. I held on, clamping down through this rogue's arm. My teeth easily went through the bones. My tiger pushed forward, he wanted at this thing that had hurt our girl and bear. I let him.

It seemed like a blur as my tiger shook the rogue's arm, wrenching it out of the shoulder socket. The rogue roared as Jasper appeared on his back, his smaller, but still deadly fangs, sank into the back of his neck. As my tiger went to rip his arm off of his body completely, there was a pulse of power.

I found myself thrown across the room, smacking my head into the kitchen island. My tiger roared but relinquished his control to me so I could find out what the hell had just happened. The others had been thrown around as well. They were coming to their feet, shaking their heads.

What the hell was that? It's the second time that he's done that to me. Axel sounded winded.

Magic. This fucker has magic. Jasper hissed softly.

That changed things. It explained things as well.

As we'd been getting up again, the rogue had changed back to his human form. He smirked at us as he took the arm that was barely being held up with muscle, jerked it up into his shoulder, and a flash of white light occurred. He moved his arm, it was healed.

Alright. This means we need to take him out as one. No making him suffer. We don't know the extent of his powers. It'll be safer for us, and faster, if we just get his head now.

I growled as the man took a step.

"You stupid fucks. This is my territory. You ruined my revenge plan. Well, at least I was able to kill that fucking bitch. I wanted to enjoy it but she locked herself where I can't get her. So, I'll just kill you assholes the way I wanted to kill her." His eyes were filled with madness.

Now.

I dove at him again. The fucker laughed as he shifted. He was even bigger.

Wait! Jasper's shout inside my head made me roll to the left right before I made contact with the rogue. *He's bigger! I think he's losing control of his magic.*

I jumped to the left to avoid the claws of the rogue.

Ok, what does that mean for us? Cody was getting ready to jump into the fight.

Seth, I think if we keep making him use his magic, he'll eventually overload. When he does, he'll be vulnerable. Easier to kill.

Let me make sure I have this right. Claws raked my left side and my snarl rang across the room. *You want us to play cat and mouse? Why?*

The rogue caught Cody in the stomach as he tried to attack him. Power flared again as he threw Cody into the kitchen. He gave a yip of pain as he crashed into the sink, breaking it.

Because of that. Jasper was at Cody's side to check him. *If we can get him to use his powers, keep track right as he uses them, we can avoid taking more damage.*

The rogue had turned to face me again. We were only a foot apart as we began to circle each other. His right shoulder started to bulge as it grew closer in size to the left.

Alright. You guys heard our fox. Try to get him to use his power. Dodge the magic attack. Do not let him escape.

Agreement ran through the connection. The new plan was to fuck with him. I didn't like that we had to waste time. I grudgingly agreed with Jasper, though. If his magic healed every wound we gave him, this was probably the best way.

Axel stood on his hind legs, towering over the rogue. He swiped his claws at the rogue, making a show of it with how slow he swung. The pulse of power went through the room again. Axel dropped to his side, rolling out of the way as the magic made the wall crack.

It went on like this. We'd taunt him, get him to use his magic, we'd dodge or get hit, if we weren't fast enough, and he'd grow again. He was slowing down as he grew.

A few more times should do it.

The rogue threw his head back and howled. I wasn't going to wait. This was it. His neck was exposed as he howled out his fury.

I moved faster than I'd ever moved. My jaw crushed the rogue's throat, my teeth slicing through his muscles like they were butter. I used all of my strength to rip through his throat. His larynx shattered as my jaws snapped shut. There was a weak pulse of power but the only thing that happened was the rogue fell backward. His body began to spasm under my paws as I slammed them onto his chest, my claws digging into his skin. He changed back into his human form. His lips moved as he struggled to speak. That was a little hard to do with a torn out larynx.

Throwing my head back, I roared in victory as his body slowly stopped twitching.

Axel, take the head.

The bear stood in front of me. His paw smacked the rogue's head off his body. It rolled several feet before stopping. The sneer on its face was unsettling. I would address it later. First we had to get to Becca.

I shifted. "Jasper, make sure his body burns. Keep the head.

Axel will help you. Do it now. I need your help, Cody. Grab someone's phone and call Gary."

I strode down the hallway. We'd find clothes later. Becca's doorway was shattered. The rogue had continued his destruction in this room. The smell of blood drew my eyes to the front of the bathroom door that had bars and a security screen. What made my heart ache in fear, was the amount of blood that was spattered and pooled in front of it.

"Cody?" My voice didn't waver. I had to be strong for everyone. I was the Alpha.

"Here." Cody's voice was hollow as he passed me the phone. He, like the rest of us, was covered in wounds and bruises.

"Seth, what the hell is going on?" Gary demanded as soon as I grabbed the phone. "I had the alert that the safe room was activated. Where's my daughter?"

"Can you deactivate the safe room? We need to get to her. We've taken out the rogue. I need to get to her." My tone turned urgent even as I fought to keep control.

"I've done it. Give it thirty seconds. Keep me on the phone, kid. I need to know what's going on. My friend is twelve hours away." Sounds of something hitting a wall happened in the background.

"Right." I put him on speaker.

The bars and security screen started to withdraw. Cody shifted on his feet as he waited until the gap was just large enough to fit through. He scrambled inside.

"Becca!" Her name sounded like it was wrenched from within him.

I was inside the room as soon as I could. What I saw made my blood go cold. Everything faded to black and white.

Cody had Becca in his arms where he knelt inside of the tub. He was covered in blood. Her blood. Her mouth was open slightly, her eyes were shut, and she had her shirt wrapped around her hand but it was soaked through with blood.

He looked up at me, his eyes desolate. "She's freezing." We both could hear no breath or heartbeat.

"Seth!" Gary shouted through the phone.

"She's dead." No. This was all wrong. No. She was our mate. We'd just found each other. She couldn't be dead. It was a lie. I'd finally had hope. Hope for a future with a loving mate with my pack. One who accepted all of us.

Gary was silent except for a sob for several minutes as we stared at our beautiful Becca. Cody was rocking her back and forth.

"Was she bitten?" Gary spoke softly.

"Why does that matter?" Forcing myself to kneel next to the tub, I unwrapped her hand after setting the phone on the edge.

"Just see if she was."

When the shirt fell with a splat inside the tub, my tiger whimpered. I wished I could. Her hand was barely recognizable. It looked more like the meat a butcher's shop hung. Cody refused to look at it as he stroked Becca's hair as he rocked.

"Yeah." I cleared my throat. "Yeah, the teeth marks are clear."

"The body is gone." Jasper walked into the room before stopping in his tracks. "No." He shook his head. "No! Becca!" His legs gave out. I reached out to catch him but Axel was right behind him, holding him up.

Axel's face was blank. His eyes gave away that he was feeling the same loss as we all were. He held Jasper to his chest as he stared at her. Jasper wouldn't stop muttering 'no' over and over again.

"Seth," Gary's voice was strained, "The rogue, he had magic. The tests we ran on him came back as something we'd never seen before. The higher ups wanted to replicate him, make him a perfect hunting machine. We tested him by having him bite some volunteers. The first volunteers all died. As did the second set." Gary let out a shuddering breath. "I had an idea. When our last volunteer was bitten, I injected him with other blood from different shifters. He died, but after an hour, he came back. He was the only one who survived these. We tried it on others. He was the only successful test."

I swung my head to look at the phone in disbelief. "What?" My mind reeled. "You knew that he had magic and you didn't think it was important to tell us?"

"You can get mad at me later," he snapped at me. "You all need to bite her. Your saliva is just as effective as the blood I used. Now. Don't waste any more time. It's the only chance we have. Even if it's a slim chance."

"We can't change her without her consent. She can't give that. She's dead," I snarled. "Women hardly ever survive."

"Seth, I know. But what do we have to lose? I would rather have my daughter angry at me for the rest of her life than have her dead."

"No." My voice was firm.

I could feel the eyes of my pack on me. I knew they didn't agree. I couldn't bring myself to do that to Becca.

"Fuck you, Seth." Cody's strangled voice was soft. "Stop being a fucking martyr. I'm doing it."

My eyes widened in shock. Cody had never spoken to me that way. My tiger growled softly, taking his words as a challenge for Alpha.

"Cody, don't you dare."

His defiant expression was filled with desperation. What happened next shocked me into silence.

Jasper shifted and had his teeth sinking into Becca's right shoulder, hard. He shifted back, climbing into the tub, taking her from Cody. He nodded at him.

"Jasper!" my voice whipped out.

"Stop, Seth. She's our mate. The only one we'll ever have. I'm not letting a chance go to have her with us." He met my eyes calmly. "She would want us to do whatever we could to save her."

My tiger settled. He agreed even as he raged over his mate being dead.

"Fine." My throat was dry.

Cody didn't waste time. He transformed there in the tub. If the situation wasn't so grim, it would be hilarious since he basically was bent in half in the tub as he bit into Becca's other shoulder. His shift was just as quick as Jasper's.

Axel knelt at the base of the tub. I rose to my feet. I backed out of the room to give him room to shift. His bear bit into Becca's left thigh after Jasper pulled her pants off with some struggle. His hands were shaking. Both he and Cody were covered in blood. My chest felt hollow. I had no idea how any of us were going to survive this.

Then it was my turn. Shifting, I stood next to the tub again. It took all of my self control to make myself bite her right thigh. I made sure not to hit her bone. When I shifted back, I wiped my face.

"Is it done?" Gary whispered.

"Yes." Axel picked up the phone.

"Now, we wait. Can you keep me on the line?"

Axel looked to me for permission and I nodded. He was her family too.

None of us left the room while time seemed to stretch on. The only one who did, briefly, was Axel when I asked him to put the front door up, so that anyone driving by wouldn't report it. Thirty minutes finally ticked by.

"We should move her to a bed," Cody whispered. "She's covered in her own blood. We need to clean her."

"Everything is destroyed. The beds in the house are torn to shreds." Axel ran a hand down his face.

"There should be a blow up mattress under the bathroom sink with some sheets." Gary had been silent since we began this torturous wait.

I had something to keep my pack busy. "Cody and Jasper, go clear out the debris from her room. Axel, get it set up after they've cleared it." My hands were as gentle as possible as I took her from Jasper's arms.

Looking down at her heart shaped face, tears filled my eyes finally. I couldn't hold them back any longer as they slipped down my cheeks. I ran my thumb along her cheek. She was so pale. Her lips were so pale, she had no color in her face at all any more.

Pressing my forehead to hers, my tears continued to fall. I started to pray to God, to the Moon Goddess, to anyone who would listen. Just bring her back. Please, just let this work. The sounds of the others moving around in her bedroom slowly faded. The sound of the air mattress being inflated by the air pump filled the room and bathroom.

"Come on, cub." Holding her in my arms, I climbed out of the tub. I took her to the shower, stepping into the water, not waiting for it to warm up.

The water ran red for a long time. Supporting her with one arm, I worked to clean her hair gently. It took about ten minutes for the water to finally run clear.

Axel was there with a towel for both of us. He'd pulled on a pair of sweats. I handed him our mate's body as I took the towels.

"I'll wrap the towel around her and hold her up. Can you remove her wet underwear?" Axel's face turned red briefly.

A small flash of amusement went through me. Our bear was adorable. Even during this grim time, he was protecting Becca's modesty.

We worked together to strip her as quickly as we could. Once Axel threw the ruined garments into the tub, he picked her up in his arms as he took her into her room to lay her on the air mattress. I grabbed the phone where Gary was still on the line, just silent.

Cody sat on the other side of the mattress. He'd found a pair of shorts. He held his knees to his chest as he watched us silently. His eyes were bleak. They hadn't been that way in years, not since the time his family was killed.

Jasper was at the end of the bed. It looked like he'd pulled on a pair of jeans and had the remnants of Becca's drawing pad in his hands. He didn't look up from it as he spoke. "I found your pants outside. Those weren't touched."

"Thank you."

We were closing in on the hour that Gary had said that his friend had come back. If she was going to come back to us, it would be soon. I knew the others were becoming restless, just like me.

"If she doesn't come back in fifteen minutes, she won't at all." Gary cut off his sentence with a sob.

We all stared at her. She was so beautiful. I could almost act like she was sleeping if it weren't for her pale complexion and no heartbeat.

The room was silent as we all waited with bated breath as the clock counted down. The allotted time passed, yet we still waited, saying nothing. After another fifteen minutes, I stood, feeling faint.

"I... we'll be there soon." Gary's anguish rang through the phone line as he hung up.

"She's gone." Those two words made my world shatter around me. "We need to... we need to..."

I'd never felt this before, I couldn't speak. The grief was crushing.

"We need to cover her until her family gets here." Cody stood from where he was curled up to stand in front of me. "Seth." His hands reached to cup my face. "We'll get through this." His words made it feel final. She was gone.

"I'll do it." Jasper stood even as he wobbled.

"I'll find something to eat." Axel stood behind me, hugging me around the waist, letting his forehead press into my back. "I know none of us want to, but our animals need it."

We left the room slowly, seeking the comfort of touch. Jasper stayed behind to cover Becca. I knew Cody wanted to be there but he stayed glued to my side. I scoffed quietly that our wolf was taking care of me. He had such a large, caring heart when it came to everyone but himself.

CHAPTER 18

Jasper

My fox was curled up as tight as he could go. All I felt from him was grief in waves. We'd only known this girl for a small amount, but she'd somehow become so important to us. I ran my fingers down her cheek as I traced her features.

"I'm sorry we weren't here to protect you, my sweet angel." We'd all been crying. I didn't think I'd stop anytime soon. I wondered briefly if I could follow her wherever she'd gone. "You took our hearts with you."

I picked up her limp hand and kissed her fingers. "Your family will be here soon. We'll put you to rest soon."

As I put her hand under the sheet, something in the air shifted. My fox's ears perked up as we looked around the room. It couldn't be the rogue. He was dead. We'd made sure of it. No one could survive what we'd done to his body, especially since his head was separated, too.

I looked back down at Becca and sucked in a sharp breath. There was a little more color in her face. Blinking rapidly, I found myself pressing my ear to her chest, I held my breath as I hoped that there would be a heartbeat.

THUMP. THUMP.

"GUYS!" My scream echoed through the house. There was a crash followed by the thumping of feet racing to the room.

As they appeared in the doorway, I couldn't contain my grin.

"She has a heartbeat."

Cody fell to his knees before Seth grabbed him. Axel turned white. I picked up my phone and redialed Gary's number.

"Yeah?" Gary's voice was hoarse.

"Her heart is beating."

Several sobs came from Gary before he spoke. "Oh, thank God." There was a sniffle. "You guys need to keep her warm. There should be spare comforters or quilts in the hallway closet, if that fucker didn't destroy it. She won't wake for hours, possibly a day. I'm not sure. I've only done this once successfully."

Axel walked into the room with his arms full of blankets. Some were torn but all that mattered was there was enough to cover her. We could always shift and lay against her. Scratch that, I would. I knew the others would.

"Boys," Gary sounded wary. "When she wakes up, she's going to be like a newborn shifter. She's not going to know what's happening, she might get violent."

"We've dealt with new shifters before." Seth was still pissed at Gary for not telling us about the magic.

"Good. My friend will be there soon. He should be arriving within the hour. Do me a favor and don't try to kill him. He's a good friend. He's met Becca. He's also the friend who survived the tests, so he's the best bet we have with making this easier on her. He's a shifter as well. He'll answer all your questions. You'll know it's him when he says 'Six flights to Nantucket'. Yes, it's weird, but it's exactly why we choose it for you."

Before he hung up, I had to ask. "Gary, if he's a shifter now, how is he still alive and part of the Venandi?"

"The whole point of the tests was to get a super soldier. They got one. What they don't know is that he saves most of the shifters he's ordered to kill. He's the perfect undercover mole in the company for our group. At the first sign of the organization wanting to kill him, he'll be gone."

He hung up after that. I glanced between my pack.

"We got her back."

All of us huddled around her. Careful not to get on the mattress, it was very likely our weight would pop it. We didn't want her sleeping on the hard ground. I had her hand clutched in both of mine. Cody was stroking her hair, Axel had his hands under the sheet, stroking her left leg, and Seth was running his fingers along her right shoulder. We were avoiding looking at her torn hand.

We listened as her heartbeat continued to get stronger. Her color slowly seeped back to her normal color. She'd started breathing softly shortly after her heartbeat became regular. It was the most beautiful sound.

I wasn't going to let her go. She wouldn't be more than five feet from one of us. We just couldn't lose her again. Cody had started humming next to her head. It was a song that we used to sing to him when he'd first joined us. It'd been the only thing to help him relax enough at night to sleep.

I'd joined in by starting to softly sing the words, but we were interrupted a few minutes later. A large car pulled along the house. Seth gestured for us to stay as he went out to meet whoever had pulled up. Hopefully, it was this friend we were waiting for.

"Who are you?" Seth's temper was close to the surface. He still hadn't calmed, I couldn't blame him. Not after everything that happened.

"Let's cut the shit. You know who I am, but I'll give you the phrase so Gary can say I followed orders. Six flights to Nantucket."

This guy had balls with his attitude toward Seth's anger. Plus, his voice was deep. I knew Becca would love it. My fox couldn't help but want to meet him.

He got his wish after a minute of silence as Seth led this man to the room.

He was large. He and Axel looked to be pretty equal in muscle mass. He had a strong face, his jaw was prominent, with what looked like a day's scruff. His dirty blond hair was buzzed short, military style. His hazel eyes were narrowed as he looked over us.

"You'll need a lot of meat, based on the looks of everything. We need to make a run to the store."

Seth's face was blank as he stared down the guy. "We know how to take care of a new shifter. Plus, it's polite to introduce yourself."

Cody snickered softly at my side. I gave him a look to behave and he just shrugged at me.

"...Wyn?" The most beautiful voice brought all of our attention to her. Her eyes were barely open as she stared at the guy. "What's going on?" Her tongue wet her lips as she finally looked at all of us. "I feel so weird."

Wyn leaned against the doorway, his eyes had visibly softened as he looked at Becca. "Hey, kid. You've been changed. Welcome to your new life as a hybrid shifter."

CHAPTER 19

Becca

Voices faded in and out as I fought for consciousness. Something was off. It felt like I was floating, but I couldn't put my finger on what it was.

"...introduce yourself."

That voice. It was familiar, I'd heard it before.

"Wyn?" My throat felt like it was dry, it hurt to talk. I blinked a few times. I was in my room, but there was a change in the atmosphere.

Felicity's cousin leaned against the doorway. "Hey, kid. You've been changed. Welcome to your new life as a hybrid shifter."

My brain felt hazy. It took several moments for it to catch up and his statement to make sense.

"What?" Moving my head, I met green eyes with flecks of brown in them that were wide in shock. "Jasper?"

Relief clashed with a painful grimace raced across his face. His large hand reached up to touch my cheek with a tenderness that melted my heart.

"Hey, Becca. It's so good to see your eyes." His thumb ran down my cheek.

My skin tingled at his touch and I felt a loud purr fight to come out of me.

I froze. Jasper furrowed his brow in concern.

"Becca?" He kept his hand on my cheek.

When that purr threatened to come from my chest, it hadn't been me. I sat up hurriedly, the blanket pooling in my lap.

"Turn around," Seth's voice snapped out.

I glanced to the doorway to see Seth standing in front of Wyn, who stared straight into his eyes and a loud grumble released from his mouth.

"Enough," Axel barked from my other side. "Turn around, Wyn, for her modesty."

Modesty? That's when I glanced down and my eyes slammed shut as my arms crossed my chest.

"Why am I naked?!" My outraged squeak would be comical if I wasn't so horrified.

"You don't remember?" Cody was next to Jasper. They were both kneeling on the ground next to where I was. He held up the blanket so I could hold it up to my chest.

I was on an air mattress. I looked around the room in horror. My room was destroyed. Furniture was shattered, torn apart in pieces. Remnants of my clothes were thrown everywhere.

"Remember? Remember what?" A sharp pain rocked inside my head like a ping pong. "Ow." I lifted my hand to touch my temple and stared in horror. Half of my arms skin was shredded. I could see bone and muscle but there wasn't a lot of blood. "Oh God!"

Panic started to set in. My breathing started to quicken, yet that weird feeling from before, which had wanted to purr, pushed at me, calming me. The warmth of something wrapped itself around me, offering comfort.

No one was touching me, though.

"What's happened to me?" It took a few tries before I could ask this. The guys stared at me with looks ranging from sympathy to heartache. Why didn't my mangled hand hurt? That really should hurt, right?

"The rogue, he came after you." Cody was the one to break the awkward silence. His gentle look helped my heart rate slow down. "We got here too late. You were," he glanced away. "Dead. You were dead." His hands ran over his face. "We didn't know what to do. Gary gave us a Hail Mary. We all bit you. You were dead for a little over an hour."

Flash. Visions of a mutated looking wolf-man biting my hand. My screams in the bathroom hadn't reached anyone's ears but mine. Flash.

I gaped up at Wyn. He was just as handsome with his square jaw and buzz cut as I had last seen him. "What did you mean when you called me a hybrid?" I glanced down at my hand as I moved my fingers. There was the pain I'd been expecting, but it wasn't overwhelming. I think I figured it out, but I needed to hear it again.

Wyn's lips twitched in a half smile. He still hadn't moved from where he leaned against the wall near the door. Seth stood between him and the rest of us.

"You're a shifter, now. A hybrid. Like me." He rolled his neck, popping it. "You'll notice that you don't feel that pain? Like there's something moving under your skin?"

Warily, I nodded in confirmation. "Yes."

"That's your other half. Like these boys do, you now have an animal partner. Just a bit more special than theirs." Wyn wouldn't look away from me, even as Seth growled. I didn't mind having his attention on me.

Shifter. I was a shifter? That feeling of whatever was inside of me prodded at me. It wanted to communicate but I had no idea what to do.

"I'm a shifter." I really should be having an anxiety attack.

Why wasn't I freaking out? Or passed out from being overwhelmed?

I did know one thing. I was starving.

At the thought, my stomach grumbled loudly. All the men's eyes went to where my stomach was hidden underneath the sheet. Cody snorted while Jasper smiled softly.

"Why don't we move back to our place and get food for everyone?" Jasper, the voice of reason, reached forward and brushed some hair out of my eyes. "I'd like to get a better look at your hand. It looks like it's mending, but fuel will help it heal all the way."

"Safer, too." Seth moved and I was lifted up into his arms. I squeaked, my good arm instantly wrapping around his neck. "Does your car have room for us?" He glanced at Wyn.

Jasper moved around the bed to stand in front of us and started tucking the blanket that was covering me. My heart melted.

"Thanks." I tried to offer a smile but a yawn broke out.

"Go to sleep, Becs." His almond shaped eyes were gentle. "We'll wake you up when we get there."

I didn't need any prompting. My head rested on Seth's chest as my eyes closed and I sank back into the darkness.

Something delicious was being made. My nose twitched as consciousness returned. As I blinked awake, my arms stretched above my head as I curled my toes.

Looking around me, I was in the boys' house. Specifically, the second floor game room where we'd played video games on the couch under several blankets. My head was in someone's lap.

Axel stared down at me, his eyes tracked my movements before I brushed my good hands fingertips along his brow.

"Hi, big guy." My voice sounded like a frog's croak. "Why so serious?"

That got me a small lip twitch. "We almost lost you, baby." The pain in his voice stabbed through my heart. "We just got you and you died in front of me." His shoulders curled as he leaned forward. He pressed his forehead to mine. "Don't do that again." Tears leaked from his closed eyes onto my cheeks.

Whatever that other presence was inside of me, it whined at me to comfort our mate. My arms went around his neck as I tilted my lips to meet his. It was the most natural move, I didn't hesitate.

He froze against me, but only briefly. His hands moved. One gripped my cheek while the other wrapped around my hip as his tongue pressed into my mouth, touching mine in a brief cordial moment, before a growl rumbled from his chest, and he let loose.

Oh man. His tongue dominated my mouth, leaving me a whimpering mess. The other presence purred loudly. She wanted more. I opened my mouth further to Axel, letting him take over.

A groan came out of me as he pulled back, leaving just a breath between our lips. I looked up into his eyes that looked at me as if I were something precious.

"If you kiss me like that, I might have to." My joke just made him shake his head and fell flat.

"I'll kiss you whenever you want if you promise to not do that again." He kissed my nose and my heart melted. "You taste better than honey."

"Wait, is that really a thing with bears?" I giggled as Axel huffed above me. His fingers brushed some hair from my face.

"Who doesn't like honey?" He pulled back, helping me sit up from his lap. He patted the top of my head. "You feel alright? Dizzy? Do you need any water?"

Taking stock, I ran a hand through my hair, snagging on tangles. My hair must look a mess, but I felt fine. Hungry. Really hungry. Other than that, I actually felt better physically than I had in a long while. Glancing down at my injured left hand, I blinked.

"I'm healed." I brought my hand up to look at it, turning it every which way. There was only a faint pink scar from the middle of my forearm to my pinky finger. "This is really happening." I shut my eyes, took a deep breath, and blew it out. "I can feel something." I pressed my hand to the middle of my chest, between my breasts. "Right here. There's like this other being, or a person?" I looked over at Axel. "Is it what I think it is?"

Axel patted my head gently. "Yes, your animal. We all have the same thing with ours. Mine is a grumpy asshole most of the time."

The being within me purred again. This time, I relaxed and opened up myself to it. It was weird, I hadn't moved from where I sat, but I was suddenly in my center, facing a very large shadow that came into my line of sight.

Beautiful. My animal was huge. Her head came up to my shoulders. She was a tiger, then suddenly, a bear, only slightly smaller than Axel in his bear form. Then a black wolf with a white starburst on her face, and finally, a large fox with the fluffiest tail. She butted her head against my legs.

My fingers buried into her fur and her purr radiated through me. I could understand her without words. I knew what she wanted.

She wanted our mates. To claim them and mark them as ours.

"I want that, too, but you're just going to have to be patient until I work all of this out in my head." Staring into her cobalt eyes that matched mine should have been weird, but it wasn't. "This is new to me, so please."

She changed back into the stunning tiger. She agreed with me, rubbing her face against my shoulder right before my awareness left my center and I was back on the couch.

"Becca?" Axel waved a hand in front of my face. "You alright?"

Fighting a yawn, I nodded. "Yeah, I'm fine. Sorry. I, err, well, I talked to my animal. It was," I tried to think of the words that could describe it. Anything I said wouldn't do it justice. "Amazing."

Axel chuckled. He pulled me into his lap, hugging me tightly. "Our animals are pretty great. I'm glad you're handling this well."

I rested my head on his shoulder. Being in his arms felt safe. "Surprising, isn't it? Normally by now, I'd be a mess of nerves."

The smell of cooking spices and meat distracted me again. My stomach grumbled. "I'm hungry. Like, really hungry." My animal grumbled. She was, too.

"Well, then it is a good thing that you'll finally get to taste my cooking!" Cody appeared at the top of the staircase. He had an apron on that was decorated with cacti. "I made meatloaf, greens, and cornbread."

He had circles under his eyes and he looked exhausted. I was up, across the room, and had my arms wrapped around his middle before I thought about it. I just knew he needed touch.

He pressed into me as we hugged. His nose went to the curve of my neck and he took a deep breath.

"I'm glad you're awake." Cody pressed his lips to the skin peeking through the oversized shirt that I was in.

Now that I thought about it, it wasn't mine.

"Me too. Um. Whose shirt is this?" We stepped back from each other as I raised my arms up. The shirt fell just below my ass. I just about flashed the two of them before I hurriedly moved my arms back down. I was not wearing any underwear.

"That would be Axel's shirt." Cody grabbed my hand. "We didn't want to put anything on under it, in case your animal got annoyed. You transforming for the first time unconscious would probably be a bad thing since she doesn't know any of us, yet."

My animal huffed. She knew them.

Cody led me down the stairs with Axel right behind us. The smell of dinner got stronger and I got even more ravenous. Instead of my stomach making its usual grumble, a loud growl came out of my mouth.

I paused in mid-step. What the heck? I slapped my hand over my mouth. My canines had grown longer.

"Guys?!" My voice came out funny, as if I had a lisp. "What happened to my teeth?"

"You and your animal are hungry. She's probably famished after all the energy she's used to heal your body." Seth met us at the end of the staircase and held out his hand to me. "If you eat something, your teeth should go back to normal on their own." His expression tender, he squeezed my hand. A feeling of calm washed through me.

Jasper and Wyn were already seated at the large table. Seth held out the chair in the middle for me that was next to Jasper. He slid it in after I settled on it. He sat next to me while Axel and Cody sat on the other side of the table, facing us with Wyn.

The food was in front of me. It was all I could concentrate on for the moment as my hands reached out rapidly grabbing various pieces of food.

I didn't even bother with utensils as the food just got shoved into my mouth. A deep rumble was coming from my chest, but it was in satisfaction rather than anger.

I wasn't sure how long I ate like a crazy woman, but when I finally slowed down as I started to feel satisfied, I looked up and froze. All of the guy's eyes were zeroed in on me as I licked the juice from the meatloaf from my fingers.

Cody gave a soft moan. A small thrill raced through me and my tongue flicked out on my lower lip. I watched, fascinated, that all of them, even Wyn, followed my movements. My animal purred in confidence. She liked having all of her mates captivated by us.

My head cleared. What was I doing? All of our mates? She'd included Wyn in that. I didn't even know him!

She flicked her ears at me. She didn't care. He was ours, whether he or I, cared, apparently.

My hands rested on the table as I mentally glared at her.

"Becca? Do you want anymore? I made plenty of everything." Cody's question distracted me from lecturing my animal.

Lecturing my animal. I gave a soft laugh. What was my life now?

"No, I'm full. It was delicious." And it was, I just inhaled most of it without tasting it until the very last few mouthfuls.

Cody ate a bite of his dinner and smiled. "Good. I'll cook for you all the time."

That was really sweet of him.

Wyn cleared his throat, getting everyone's attention. He really was a handsome man, in that scary way.

"Thanks for the food. Can we all talk now?" He pushed his plate away from him a few inches. "Gary should be calling soon. He'll answer any questions you have that I can't answer. But I know you have questions now. I'd rather get done with what I can answer. Then I'd like to get some sleep."

"A shower wouldn't hurt, either." Cody's quip only got me to giggle. The others just rolled their eyes at him while Wyn quirked an eyebrow at him.

Seth shifted in his chair and moved his arm over the back of my chair. I leaned back and his fingers started to play with the tips of my hair.

"Alright. You're a hybrid. Apparently, the only one in existence, until Becca. How has that worked? Shifters need packs to survive." He looked relaxed, but somehow, my animal knew that he'd not relaxed once around Wyn. "Loners are rare."

"I'm not like other shifters. My animal doesn't need a pack like yours do. Even if it did, I've had no choice in the matter. I was made to be the apex prime killer for the Venandi." Wyn's pupils constricted in the light for a few moments. "Unbeknownst to them, I've managed to save most of the shifters they've sent me out to kill. Relocated them to a safe location, for now. I've been working with Gary for several years, even before I was *voluntold* for the hybrid shifter program."

He sighed before he ran a hand along the scruff on his chin. "The Venandi are world wide, but they're fracturing. It's one of the reasons I've been able to do what I've done without them getting suspicious."

Jasper leaned forward, his right hand was tapping on the table. "What do you mean that they're fracturing?"

"It's in part, due to those like Gary, who sabotage their efforts, but it's also the newer generation. They aren't mindless sheep anymore. They're questioning whether what the Venandi believes in is actually just." He met my gaze. "Like my younger cousin, Felicity. She hates their ideals. She's a gentle soul that they're tearing apart."

I didn't know how to feel about that statement. I wasn't shocked to hear that she was part of the Venandi. With the way she had been acting all summer, it explained it. Yet, one thing bothered me.

"If she is part of the Venandi, she should have known that Axel is a shifter, right? Why did she start seeing him?" My animal hissed at the thought of them kissing. Overwhelming possessiveness overtook me.

I stood from my seat, walked around the table, pushed Axel back just enough, and sat in his lap. His arms wrapped around my waist as I laid my head on his chest, listening to his heart beat.

Wyn cleared his throat from beside me. "For new Venandi, they have a graduation requirement where they have to find a shifter, gain their trust, and kill them. There's a spray she would have used that entices shifters. It's only used in these situations because it takes time to work."

Claws sprang out of my fingers as a loud growl erupted from me.

"She what?!" Fur sprouted along my arms in a mess of black, orange, and browns. "He's mine!" The fangs were back.

"Becca? It's okay. I'm alright. She can't hurt me, cub." Axel soothed his hands down my arms as he held me closer to him. "Deep breath."

The fur receded slowly with my fangs, but the claws that had grown were still out. I brought my hands up to look at them. They were sharp, long, and probably lethal.

"What's going on with me?" I was starting to scare myself. First the fangs, I eat like a starving woman, and now this. I had seen red at the thought of Axel being hurt.

"Your animal rages within you. She is unlike those of your mates." Wyn leaned close, briefly glancing up at Axel before he touched my cheek. "You and she must bond. She is multiple animals in one. You must be the alpha, not her. I can help you with learning how to calm her, if you'll let me."

My animal didn't rage on purpose, necessarily. She was more annoyed than anything and protective of whom she viewed as hers. We were a team, she wasn't stupid.

At least that was the message she sent me in reply to his statement.

"Remove your hand from her," a snarl from across the table from Seth had me glancing over. His eyes had transformed into that of his tigers. He was staring at Wyn as his lips pulled back.

Axel's arms tightened around my waist.

"You're not my alpha, cat," Wyn hissed violently.

"Enough. Both of you." Jasper slapped his hands on the table as he stood up. "This is not about you two! This is about Becca! We need Wyn's help, Seth. Wyn, you know that she's our mate, yet you touch her as if you have her permission! You did it to antagonize us." Jasper's hands moved to his side as he curled them into fists. "For the sake of Becca, stop. She seems to like you."

Wyn's shoulders relaxed as he took his hand away from my cheek before holding up his hands. "Alright. I might have done it on purpose. I'll watch myself for now." He sighed. "We'll talk more about this later."

"Felicity obviously hasn't killed Axel. Does that mean she isn't a Venandi?" Changing the subject was the only way I could think of how to defuse the situation.

He turned his attention back to me. "No, she's not been initiated, yet." Wyn seemed fond of Felicity when he spoke. "I'm hoping I can get her out of there before it happens. There's not a lot of safe places, though." He ran a hand down his face. "That's beside the point. Look, I came here because Gary asked me to, and," he met my gaze and a low burning sensation started in my pussy. "You know why."

I did. My animal had been saying it since we'd awoken, I just hadn't had time to think about it. She'd called all of these men my mates, including Wyn. I could sense that Wyn was a good man, somehow. The other guys may not be happy about it, though.

Cody had been quiet this whole time, watching all of us. I looked at him on my other side. He was pushing the remaining part of his food around on the plate with his fork.

"Cody?"

He looked up with a sad expression that he wiped clear. "Yeah? Sorry, I didn't think my input would make any difference."

Cody usually was full of energy, confidence, and humor. It was strange, and worrisome, to see him acting so withdrawn.

I wiggled out of Axel's lap and moved into Cody's. He brushed my hair back from my face. He relaxed almost instantly. I leaned forward and kissed him gently.

Kissing Cody reminded me of right before all of this had happened, when I'd still been human. I wanted him again, and by the feel of his hardening cock, it seemed like we were both on the same page.

His hands gripped my hips as I moved my ass against his cock as our kiss deepened. Another hand gripped the back of my head, tightening around my hair, and pulled me away from Cody, who moved his lips to my neck. I stared up into Axel's heated face.

"Ahem." Wyn cleared his throat. "Maybe you can do that after I've left the room?" A hint of jealousy leaked through his tone.

I shook my head. What was wrong with me? I was as horny as an old goat. "Why can't I stop touching you guys?"

"It's the mating bond." Jasper stood, grabbing his dirty dishes. "I think we all underestimated how strong her animal is. I can barely keep my fox under control."

"Mating bond?" My mind felt a little fuzzy. All I wanted to do was move in Cody's lap for more friction. "She keeps talking about mates. What does this mean exactly? Besides wanting to jump your bones. We talked about all of us being together before this happened to me. Does it have anything to do with it?"

Jasper stood from his seat, collecting his dirty dishes. "It has to be. My fox wanted you before this happened to you, all of our animals did. But now, it's like we can't resist this call that you're sending out." He picked up Seth's dishes as he moved into the kitchen to place them in the sink.

"A call?" My eyes started to shut as Axel rubbed his fingers in my scalp where he'd been holding my hair. "That feels so good."

"Now that you're a shifter," Seth's voice was soft. "Your animal seems to be in heat already. She wants to mate right away."

I pulled away from Axel's touch so that I could look at Seth.

"I'm in heat? So, you guys don't even have a choice in wanting this?"

They all laughed. Including Wyn. That hadn't been what I expected to happen.

"Baby," Seth stood, drawing my eyes to his body. "You're coming with me. Cody, you need to rest. Jasper, Axel, please, show Wyn where he'll be staying while he's here." He moved to stand in front of me, offering his hand. The intensity of his gaze made all thoughts disappear as I slid mine into his. He pulled me from Cody's lap, turned, and walked us across the room up the stairs.

I could hear Wyn's low voice talking to Jasper, but I couldn't make out the words as my whole attention focused on Seth's ass. It was taut and I resisted the urge to sink my teeth into the cheeks.

I stumbled as we got to the second floor. Seth turned to catch me around the waist with a soft chuckle. "Let's talk on the couch for now." He picked me up before depositing me on the soft cushion and sitting next to me.

"Seth?" My body moved on its own and I straddled his waist. His muscles were taut as I settled. My hands ran down his shoulders, my claws had receded at some point and now, I dragged my normal nails down his biceps. "What are we talking about?"

The heat from his skin was intoxicating.

He gripped my wrists in his hands, stopping me from exploring his upper body anymore. His head tipped back on the back of the couch and a strangled groan escaped him.

"Becca, I need to make sure you are sure about this before we move forward." He squeezed my wrists gently enough to distract me from moving my pussy along his crotch. "You know that we all like you, that we all want you more than we can express. You agreed that you wanted us before you were changed, but I have to make sure this is what YOU want, not just your animal." He pressed a kiss to my inner right wrist that made me melt into his chest. "If we mate, the way that she's trying to do, there's no going back. When you were human, you could have walked away from us at any point."

I looked into his devastating blue eyes. "What do you mean?"

"When shifters mate, it's for life." He searched my face, trying to convey how serious he was being. "Our own animals mated with each other long ago. If you become our center with yours, it's forever. No going back. The good news with mating is that you can't become pregnant until you and your animal agree."

"Okay." I shrugged. "Not becoming pregnant is good. The other thing, I kind of figured that was how it was going to be anyway when we talked about this back at the cabin. Unless you guys have doubts?"

"No!" Shouts from downstairs had me giggling as Seth rolled his eyes and his lips twitched as he fought a smile.

"So, I don't see a problem. Except," I paused. I should get this over and done with now instead of waiting to pull off the Band-Aid. "You do know that Wyn is my mate, too, right?"

CHAPTER 20

Seth

 fought to keep my calm as Becca's warmth pressed against my straining cock. Her touch was everything I ever dreamed of. Her scent as a shifter was intoxicating just as much as it was distracting.

A snarl lifted my upper lip at her statement. I'd suspected. Especially with the way Wyn had been watching her since he'd first laid eyes on her. He'd dropped enough obvious hints that it wasn't that hard to understand.

A plate shattered downstairs. Sounded like the others had heard and finally realized. What it meant for our pack was unknown. How we handled this, I had no clue. All I knew was if he made her happy, my tiger would swallow his pride and welcome the man into the pack, but he wouldn't allow him to be Alpha. That was our job.

"Yes, I am aware." My teeth clenched. "You accept him?"

Becca was quiet for several moments, her nose scrunched in thought. I had to resist running my thumb between her brows.

"I'm not sure if I accept him. I do know we can trust him and that he doesn't mean any ill will. I'm not sure how I know that, but I do. I'd like him to stay," she whispered this, but instead of looking away like she would have just days ago, she stared straight at me as she stated it. My chest swirled with pride.

Our mate was strong. She wouldn't back down just because something unexpected suddenly occurred. Her accepting that she was a shifter so quickly was a testament to that.

She shifted on my lap, reminding me of how hard I ached. I let her wrists go so I could clutch her hips, stopping her movement. Delight flared in her gaze as she realized why I'd done that.

"If you want him, we will accept him." It came out strangled as she ground herself roughly onto my cock. I was barely hanging onto my control with a shred. "Becca. You need to stop. I can't hold on for long."

She leaned forward, placing her hands on either side of my head, her breasts coming level with my eyes. Her mouth grazed my ear tip. "Stop holding back. I want you. I want this. *I want pack.*"

I was striding to my room with her over my shoulder within a second. Her excited squeak was cut off as I slapped her ass. My tiger was at the surface. He was ready to mark her as our mate for the world to see.

"You heard our mate." Raising my voice just slightly, I stated, "Wyn is hers. We accept him." My door closed behind me and I tossed Becca onto the bed.

"Take your clothes off." This time, my snarl was laced with my pent up lust and need.

"Make me." Becca lifted her chin. "You're not my alpha, cat." Her hiss was more of her animal than her, but amusement and playfulness radiated from her as she got onto her knees.

I grinned, my canines lengthening in excitement. "Is that how it's going to be?" I started to unbutton my shirt slowly. "You won't win."

She laughed and pulled the shirt off over her head, making me suck in a breath, and beckoned me forward with her finger. "Let's see about that, kitty cat."

I dove at her, tackling her to the bed as she squeaked in delight. My teeth grazed her neck, not drawing blood, but I bit hard enough to elicit a moan from her. My growl caused her to freeze and goosebumps appeared along her skin. I grinned.

"Are you going to behave?" My hands stroked down her sides, grazing her luscious breasts. "Moon Goddess, it's like you were made for us."

Her nipples were pebbled as my hands cupped her breasts. I flicked them with my thumbs, her back arching slightly.

"I don't know what's gotten into me, but I'll behave. For now." Becca licked her lower lip and her palms pushed against my chest. I let her push me onto my back as I growled, pleased as she straddled me. "Seth, is this okay?" She paused at her exploration of my chest.

"Anything you want. My body is yours." I cupped her cheek briefly, pulling her down for a hard kiss. "Everything that I am, is yours."

She closed her eyes briefly. "I want you." She sat up. "Please."

I rolled her to her back as I flipped onto my hands and knees, boxing her within. "Anything you want, Becca." I ran a finger from her lips to the curve of her breasts. "You're so beautiful."

A flush of red appeared on her skin and I grinned as I ran my lips from her nose to her lips, giving her a tender nip, before kissing down to her breasts. Her breathing picked up as my tongue ran around her left nipple before sucking it between my teeth.

Her mewl of pleasure spurred my tiger on. We wanted more. Needed inside of her, to hear her cry out my name.

Becca's scent was tantalizing, her pussy begged to be lapped up. My tongue dipped into her belly button briefly, making her jolt in surprise as I laughed softly. "Ticklish?"

"I didn't know that my belly button could almost make me cum!" She giggled breathlessly as I pushed her legs apart, bending her knees so that she was spread open to me.

Her taste was intoxicating as I took one long lick. Her knees shook as I began to press into her pussy with my tongue, flicking it up when I got to her clit. Her hands clenched the sheets as I continued my assault.

I pushed my middle finger inside of her, softly moaning at how her muscles clenched around it eagerly. Her hips moved as I curled my finger and sucked on her clit.

She really enjoyed that.

Becca

My orgasm came quick and fast. My toes curled as my hips lifted off the bed several inches as I cried out. Seth moved his finger rapidly through my orgasm, making it last longer than I thought possible.

As I panted, his hands moved to my knees and he held himself over me, grinning like a cat who got the cream, as it were. I had the urge to push his head back down to my pussy to wipe that grin off his face.

"Seth." My animal purred, wanting more.

"I know, baby." He reached behind his head, letting down his hair, the curls framing around his shoulders. "Get on your hands and knees."

My animal stretched, offering me an image that I wanted to happen right away. I looked up at Seth as I bit down on my lower lip. His eyes tracked me.

"No. You get on your back. I want to suck your cock." I stretched my arms over my head, making sure my breasts perked up.

His nostrils flared as he thought on it. I didn't wait. My hands pushed him back, we were back to me straddling his waist as I giggled. His hands went behind his head as he gave me a hooded look.

"Suck my cock then, baby." He lifted a brow at me. "Unless you're scared."

Laughter burst out of me as I moved down his legs, pulling off his pants and boxers with his help. His cock stood straight up with a small curve to it. I couldn't wait to have it in my mouth.

I ran fingers along his length, grinning at the hiss of breath he sucked in. I moved forward, kissing the tip, running my tongue along the slit.

The salty taste wasn't completely unpleasant and I took the tip into my mouth, moving my tongue around the edges. I reveled in the way his breathing picked up, my animal purred.

As I swirled my tongue down his shaft, I cupped his balls. They were soft as I gently pulled on them.

Seth hissed, gripped my hair tightly, and jerked my head back. I grinned up at his heavy lidded gaze. His canines reflected the light, making me shiver. I continued to run my hand down his cock, squeezing at the top.

"No more." Seth had me on my hands and knees in the next breath. "You're so beautiful." His rasp was deep behind me.

I squeaked as his palm slapped my ass. The sharp sting of pain faded in a flood of pleasure as he slapped the other cheek. My hands grabbed the pillow in front of me and I buried my face in it to stifle my moans.

His hands ran along my back, making goose bumps pebble where he touched. His thighs pressed against mine and his cock pressed against my pussy. I shuddered.

"Seth. Please." My whimper was pathetic and I didn't care. My animal wanted him to mark us.

"As you wish." Seth's snarl was in my ear, sending a shot of pleasure down my legs.

I cried out as his cock started to push inside of me. He was bigger than Cody and Cody had taken several pushes to get inside of me. I don't know if it was because I was in a different position or my animal did something, but Seth pushed his entire length inside with one stroke.

Oh holy moly.

With every stroke, his palm slapped one of my asscheeks, changing it up after a few thrusts. My ass burned with each smack, heightening the pleasure I could barely take.

My claws flashed out and shredded the pillow as I bit into it. Seth gripped my hips as he pulled out only to thrust back inside of me. Again and again. The sound of our skin slapping together filled my ears as his strokes became faster and rougher.

Seth's weight pressed on top of my back as he leaned forward, pressing kisses along my neck. When he bit down on the right side, I froze as an overwhelming feeling of power washed over me as Seth's teeth pierced my skin. The sharp pain was distant as I rode through the wave of power and pleasure.

When Seth groaned above me, I came as he jerked inside, cumming himself. I collapsed forward, gasping for air. My legs were twitching. Seth pulled me gently over on to my back, his hand coming up to cup my cheek. His touch and gaze was gentle.

"Are you alright?" He tilted my chin up and looked at my neck in pride. "You took my mark easily."

A loud purring sounded in the room. As Seth raised a brow at me, I realized it had come from me. It stopped abruptly as I giggled. I purred!

"I'm going to take that as a yes." Seth kissed me gently. "Your purr is music to my ears." His fingers brushed along where he bit me. It didn't hurt like I thought it would, it was just tender.

My animal brushed her tail out like a fan, reminding me that we now healed incredibly fast. I poked the tender area because why shouldn't I?

"Your turn, baby." Seth grabbed my fingers kissing them. "You can leave your mark on me anywhere you would like."

I blushed looking down his chest to his, still impressive even if it was soft, cock. "Anywhere?" My lips curved at my wicked thought.

He glanced down before jerking his face back up with a look of utter terror. I had to hand it to him, he took a deep breath before he nodded once. "Anywhere." His voice actually went high.

I kissed his chin as I wiggled down his body. "Alright. I'll do it now." His thighs shook. The thought of biting him in his most sensitive area was not a pleasing one to him.

Taking pity on him, I moved my head just as I was about to bite his tip and bit down on his inner thigh, feeling my canines lengthen as they sank into his muscle. His blood spilled across my tongue and it was ecstasy. My instinct was to bite more, harder, but I held back. A splash of warm liquid hit my cheek.

This was Seth. He was one of my mates. A guy that I was falling head over heels for.

I sat up, wiping my mouth and cheek with the back of my hand. Seth looked up at me with an open expression of emotions, and I felt tears prickle in response.

"You're just as bad as Cody, aren't you?" Seth's voice whispered, strained with those emotions. He pulled me to him, resting me on top of him.

Before this summer, I would have freaked out and rolled off right away, afraid that I would have hurt him with my weight. Now, I rested my head over his heart and closed my eyes, listening to the beat. His hands ran gently down my back with soft caresses.

"Whatever comes our way," I looked up at him, "I'm not afraid because I have you guys now."

I'd started to fall asleep again when a knock on Seth's door woke me. The sheets were wrapped around me in a cocoon. Seth went to the door to open it, giving me a very nice back end view because he'd not grabbed a pair of shorts.

"What's up?" He kept his voice low.

"Damn it," Jasper sounded annoyed. "Why didn't you grab something to cover up with? That's not fair." He whined and I slapped my hands over my mouth not to laugh.

Seth leaned against the doorway, raising his arm above his head. "Jasper. What do you need?" His amusement couldn't be disguised, even though he tried to stay serious.

"Wyn went upstairs to the guest room. Cody is passed out in Axel's lap on the couch. They played a game and he was out like a light."

Seth moved to the right, revealing Jasper, who looked exhausted. "Well, my bed is big enough. Get in." He took Jasper's hand and pulled him to the edge of it, looking at me. "Feel up to cuddling with our fox?"

I grabbed Jasper's other hand and yanked him forward, laughing when his face ended up between my breasts. He struggled for a brief second before relaxing and his arms went around my middle. He sighed, his breath warm against my skin.

"I finally get to hold you naked, and I'm so tired." Jasper looked up at me, his emerald jewels shining in the light. "Forgive me."

I ran my fingers through his hair slowly, the strands soft. "Jasper, we have the rest of our lives together." I kissed his forehead gently. "Just sleep and we can worry about everything else later."

Seth got into bed, spooning Jasper and resting his arm across him to hold my hand. "Sleep, my loves. It is safe."

With the combined heat of both of them, my eyes shut on their own as I fell to sleep.

Cody

The inner demons laughed at me. I couldn't provide any kind of substance to the conversation. All I knew was that Becca was alive, a shifter now, and my mate.

Her animal was powerful. The amount of power she was giving off made my wolf roll on his back and expose his neck to her, even if she didn't understand what was happening. The demons were right, I wasn't worthy of her. I always screwed up.

When she'd sensed something was wrong, she'd moved to me. She'd easily distracted me with her touch and kisses. When Axel had pulled her back by her hair, I'd been ready to throw her on the table, fuck whoever watched, and just take her then and there.

Seth took her away to mate with her, which was his right, but it still hurt a little. I wasn't sure why, but I did know it was stupid to be jealous. He was my alpha and as such, needed to mate with her first to establish that connection.

Plus, I'd been her first out of all of us. That helped ease the jealousy.

I went upstairs, sitting on the couch, after I heard Seth's door closed. Jasper led Wyn up to the third floor to one of the guest rooms. Axel came up after he finished cleaning downstairs. It had been his turn to clean after dinner. He found me sprawled across the couch with my legs on the back of it.

He stood in front of me as I looked at him from upside down. The sounds of Becca in the throes of passion filtered through Seth's door and my wolf whined.

"How about a game? We could go old school and play Mario Kart on the Nintendo 64." He grabbed my arm, picking me up like a rag doll to sit up right. "Come on, pup." He turned on the television, plugged in the system, threw the controller at me, and sat down next to me.

I moved so I was pressed against his side. I missed him and I needed touch tonight.

Axel held his controller in his right hand and pulled me into his lap with his left arm. He rested his chin on top of my head as we started to play.

I was in the lead playing as Yoshi when my eyes drifted shut. I was finally able to relax with him being with me, so I fell asleep.

CHAPTER 21

Becca

When the first rays of sun peeked through the curtains, I snuck out of the bed, leaving Jasper curled around Seth. My heart filled just looking at them before my animal reminded me the reason I got out of bed.

Breakfast. I wanted to make breakfast for the guys. I grabbed a pair of shorts and shirt from the dresser that I scrambled into once I closed the door behind me.

As I ran my fingers through my hair, I quietly made my way downstairs. My foot froze in midair as I came face to shirtless chest with Wyn in the kitchen.

"Wyn." I touched his arm. "Hi." The memory of our first meeting flashed through my mind. He'd been kind to me, even though his uncle and aunt hadn't even bothered to care about their daughter, much less a stranger.

He held a cup of coffee. "Good morning." He took a sip. "You're up early."

I stepped around him, ignoring how my animal purred wanting to rub against him.

"I thought I could make breakfast for everyone." The fridge was one of those fancy built in the wall ones. It was over filled with food. I could probably make anything I could think of. "Are you hungry?"

Wyn came to stand next to me, resting his hip on the counter. "I could eat something." The rough drawl hinted at something other than actual food.

My cheeks turned red as I looked at him from the corner of my eye.

"Food, Wyn. Not me." I cleared my throat.

He took another drink of his coffee, as a grin appeared. "That's what I was talking about. You have a naughty mind, Becca." He set down his mug and grabbed two packets of bacon over my shoulder. "Why don't I help you? We can talk." He pulled out a griddle from under the oven.

I watched him move for a few moments before grabbing a carton of eggs. "Okay. Let's cook together."

He was just as big as Axel, and like with Axel, I felt at ease working with him. We didn't speak as the smell of bacon started to fill the kitchen. I cracked the eggs into a bowl to make them scrambled with cheese since that would be the fastest way to cook them.

"When you mentioned training me," I threw the eggshells into the trash can. "What kind of training did you mean?"

Wyn had a large tattoo that ran from the side of his left neck and down his back. It was really distracting, especially since the image of licking every curve of the tattoo kept invading my mind. I wasn't sure if it was me or my animal. Quite possibly both of us.

He turned, catching me staring at him. He flashed another grin filled with teeth. It gave predator vibes. I wanted to run at the same time as jump on him for the ride of my life.

When did this 'heat' thing stop? I scrubbed my face with both of my hands as I tried to focus. I was not some sex-starved teenager. Even if these guys were mine.

"As far as training you, I can help you learn to control your shifts. You will be in charge of what form you shift into, not your animal. It won't be easy, I can feel how strong she is, but you're no push over, are you?" Wyn grabbed a piece of bacon and bit into it.

"Before," I glanced at my hands. "I would have had an anxiety attack even thinking about this. Now, I'm excited." I looked up at him. "Is she going to change everything about me?" It scared me a little thinking about how I may not be the same person anymore.

Wyn put down the fork he'd been using on the bacon. He placed his hands on my shoulders, squeezing gently. "You are still the same person you were before. That doesn't change. What has changed is that you now have the power of your animal behind you. She protects you, gives you her strength." His fingers brushed my cheek. "I was drawn to you when we first met. That was before you'd gained your animal partner. I'm not worried about you changing. If you're worried about your anxiety, she'll stop helping hold it at bay, if you ask her."

Taking a deep breath, I closed my eyes so I could focus on her. She appeared in my mind's eye in the wolf form. She stared at me, calmly, as I stared at her.

"It's true? You've been holding back my anxiety and panic attacks?"

She nodded, a feeling of love washed over me. She pressed her muzzle into my chest as I stroked her ears. She couldn't control being in heat around our mates. That was biological, but she could offer her strength to me until I could handle it on my own.

"Thanks." I pressed a kiss to the top of her nose before opening my eyes again. Wyn still stood in front of me, one hand on my shoulder. "I'm okay."

And I was.

"I think I understand a bit better now." I placed my hands over Wyn's on my shoulder. "She's not just a separate entity. We wouldn't be able to live apart. She is me and I am she. She'll protect me while I protect her."

Wyn offered me a large smile. So large, it almost looked painful. "You just figured out something that took me nearly a year to understand. You are going to be just fine."

I found myself tipping my face up to meet his instinctually. His lips, a little rough, pressed to mine as if we had done this a thousand times. In the same instance, it was also a feeling unlike any other I'd experienced. Our animals harmonized together.

Wyn's animal was different from mine. He was a wolf, lynx, fox, and a hawk. I had so many questions, but they could wait.

His tongue pressed into my mouth, pausing briefly to make sure that I was alright with it. Oh, boy, was I. Clutching his forearms, I pulled him closer. Soon, his lips and tongue were all I could focus on.

He could kiss. It felt like he was fucking my mouth with his tongue. Breathing wasn't a requirement any longer. As his tongue stroked inside of my mouth, heat pooled between my thighs. When he paused to let us both take a breath, I whimpered.

"Don't stop." If I didn't get his mouth back, I'd go insane.

"Oh, Becca, I would continue, but our cooking has awoken the others. I doubt they'll take kindly to seeing me groping you." His hands ran down my arms to grasp my hands in his. "We will have time, have no doubt." He stepped away, moving to the griddle to place more bacon on it. "We'll start training this afternoon. Gary should be here in two days. I spoke with him last night. He's dropping the kids and your mother off at the house in Englewood. We'll have a lot to talk about."

My clit throbbed, wanting his mouth or his cock, but it wasn't going to happen at that point, so I took a deep breath. Thoughts of my stepfather helped cool me down even faster.

"Is there a plan? If the rogue is dead, there's nothing to worry about, right?" I poured the eggs that I'd put in the big bowl into a skillet on the other side of the stove.

"The rogue garnered the attention of the Venandi, didn't he?" Axel's voice came from the stairs.

I still had to get used to that. My hearing was a lot better than it had been when I was human. I don't think it was anywhere as good as the other guys, but it had changed. I added that to the list of things to talk to Wyn about.

Wyn turned to watch Axel come into the kitchen. He came over to me, I felt his heat before I looked up at him. My head thumped against his chest. His dark brown irises had flecks of gold and green in them. I'd never noticed that before now.

"Hi."

He bent to press a kiss to my lips softly. "Good morning, cub." He looked at the skillet, took the spatula from my hand, and started to stir it. "Don't want to burn it."

I relaxed against him as his other hand wrapped around my waist. I let him finish the eggs as I just enjoyed being in his arms. I was trying hard not to just come undone at his touch.

Wyn finished the bacon, placing all of it onto a large serving tray, and started grabbing bread and butter for toast. "Are the others going to head down?" He glanced at Axel.

"Yeah. They're headed down in just a minute."

I was just finishing setting up dishes for breakfast when the other three came down the stairs. I paused to watch.

They were all dressed but their scents wafted toward me and I was back to a horny mess again. I had to clutch the table's edge. Damn it, when was this going to stop happening?

"Sorry, baby." Seth pulled a chair out next to me and helped me into it.

I squirmed. "I said that out loud?"

"Oh yeah." Cody sat across from me, his wicked grin making me groan in embarrassment.

"You're going to be in heat until you've mated with all of us."

Jasper sat on my left, taking my hand in his. "Hopefully after that, it will be less intense." He didn't look like he wanted it to lessen.

"I hope it's not less intense." Axel brought over the eggs and bacon with Wyn. "The smell is intoxicating."

I groaned, my forehead thumped on the table. "Axel!"

"He's right, though." Seth sat on my right. "You'll probably feel out of control until you've mated with the rest of the guys, marking them and receiving their mark." His fingers brushed my hair aside so that he could trace where he'd bitten me.

I almost jolted out of the seat at the pleasure that shot through me.

Seth grinned into the cup he picked up to sip. He'd done it on purpose.

"To continue our conversation," Wyn sat next to Cody, piling his plate with food. "Yes, the Venandi are aware of the situation. They wanted to send a patrol out. Luckily, I was nearby, so I said I would handle the situation." He bit into the toast that he'd over buttered. "I haven't reported back yet, but I should be able to hold them off for a few more weeks."

Seth nodded once as he put some eggs onto my plate. "We figured this would happen since we weren't fast enough to stop the rogue." He placed several pieces of bacon on my plate next and I just shook my head, letting him take care of me. "We can leave this area. They will not find evidence of us in this house, but they'd know there was more than the rogue out here. We wouldn't be able to return here."

This mountain meant too much to me. It was the place where I had the best memories of my father, and the first place where I spent time with my mates. "Never return to Tabernash? No, that can't happen!" I pulled my hand from Jasper's and stood. "Please."

"Cool your jets, sweetheart." Wyn had already finished his first serving. "I doubt we'll have to worry about you guys leaving this area. I have their trust. After a little while, I'll say the rogue has left the area or that I took care of it." He grabbed a piece of bacon off Cody's plate and winked at him as he protested. "I'm not worried. There's always some bigger catch that can distract them. With Gary's help, I doubt we'll have to worry about the Venandi finding any of you, but especially you, Becca."

"Whatever happens," Seth spoke up over Wyn as he finished. "We'll protect you." He glared at Wyn, who narrowed his eyes. "Do not forget who the alpha is here, hybrid. I am the one who leads this family."

Tension snapped in the room as thick as the butter that Wyn had smothered the toast with. I glanced between the two as my animal huffed in annoyance. She pushed me to sit down. It was better to just let them get it out of their system. Wyn might be a hybrid, and very strong, but he was not Seth. We'd both accepted him as the leader of this family when we mated with him first, this was just stupid male testosterone politics.

"Let's take this outside, cat." Wyn stood, turning on his heel to stride to the back door, ignoring Seth, who was right behind him snarling. "Let's just get this over and done with so we can move on."

They both disappeared out the door, leaving it open. I grabbed Jasper's hand again and ran after them. They were already several hundred feet away from the house, facing each other when we got outside. Wyn stood with his arms crossed as Seth removed his shirt.

"What's going to happen?" I glanced up at Axel who came up behind us.

Jasper wrapped his arm around my waist so that Cody, who'd come up on my other side, could hold my hand. I liked that they were constantly touching me. It was comforting after going so long fearing touch from other people because I was afraid I'd freak out with a panic attack. I wanted to rub my face all over these guys and lick every inch of their bodies.

Jasper's nostrils flared as he looked at me, our eyes meeting and his pupils constricted with heat. His arm tightened around me, pulling my body flush against his. He leaned in to kiss me. A terrifying roar sounded in the area, making me jump as I swung my head around to see where it had come from.

Seth had shifted. His tiger, as stunning as ever, stood proud as he faced off against Wyn. I could feel my mouth drop open at the sight of Wyn. He'd transformed into his wolf form. He was nearly as large as Axel was as a bear. He was much larger than Cody's wolf.

Unlike Cody's, Wyn's wolf was white with sections of gray. He reminded me of a very large and deadly looking husky. He was in mid snarl with his sharp teeth on display.

The two began to circle each other. Seth made no noise while Wyn growled, snapping at him. This was really happening. They both could get hurt.

"Why aren't we stopping this?" I wanted to run into the middle of that circle and keep them from fighting, but my animal stopped me.

"If they don't settle this now, it could get dangerous moving forward. This way, they establish who is alpha, and we move on." Axel squeezed my shoulders before resting his chin on my head. "We know Seth will win. When he does, Wyn will have established his order in our pack. I won't fight him for it."

As we watched, Wyn lunged across the circle at Seth while snapping his jaws. Seth didn't move and they went rolling on the ground. Seth's back legs kicked upward, throwing Wyn over his head before rolling to his feet again.

Wyn ended up smacking against a tree across the way. He got back to his feet, shook his head out, and growled. The fur on his back stood up, making him look even larger. Seth's tail just flicked. He honestly looked bored and I fought down a laugh.

They dove at each other at the same time. It was a blur of

different colored fur. The sounds of their bodies hitting each other echoed in the open area. A howl of pain sent a shiver of apprehensive through my body. Wyn had locked his jaws around Seth's neck. Jasper, Cody, and Axel's hands on me tightened as Wyn pinned Seth to the ground.

"Seth!" My cry was covered by Cody's hand, but not fast enough. His ears flicked at my cry and a terrifying roar came from him.

Wyn's teeth were wrenched from Seth's neck and he found himself rolling on the ground as they tore into each other. Fur flew in the air with blood. My animal was fine with this, but the worry started to make my anxiety kick up, even more than my animal was able to hold at bay. As my breathing kicked up, Jasper moved to stand in front of me.

He cupped my face between his hands and blocked my view of the fight. I focused on his emerald eyes, the light made them brighten more. His thumbs stroked my cheeks gently.

"It's okay. This is how dominance is decided between animals. They won't kill each other. I promise." He pressed his lips to mine.

I knew he was trying to distract me, it was partially working, but I could still hear the fight going on beyond him. His left hand moved from my face to hold the back of my head as his tongue pressed into my mouth.

He tasted of fresh limes. I wasn't sure how that was possible, especially considering he just ate breakfast, but he did. My body pressed against his as Cody let go of my hand so that I could touch Jasper's chest.

Except, even though I wanted to continue kissing Jasper because he was delicious, I pushed him away, gently. Even though it was a light touch, he stumbled back a few steps with a startled look.

"Ah!" I grabbed his arms. "I'm sorry about that! I guess I don't know my own strength?"

Jasper laughed as he hugged me. "You're so strong!" His arms tightened around me before he stepped back. "Never apologize for it."

I looked around him at the pair fighting in time to watch Seth smack Wyn in the head with his big paw. Wyn collapsed on his side, several large gashes were bleeding severally.

Seth shifted back on a groan. My eyes couldn't quite keep up. It looked like it hurt, but as he stood there, you wouldn't be able to tell. My animal purred at the marks on his body. He was naked. I took a brief moment to admire it before I ran toward him and Wyn.

"Seth! Are you alright?" I stopped next to Wyn, kneeling as I looked up at Seth, pointedly ignoring his swinging appendage that was rock hard. Apparently, he enjoyed that fight.

"Just fine," he squatted next to me. "That was a great fight." He rolled his shoulder, pressing a hand over his injury on his neck. "He's much stronger than I gave him credit for."

Wyn was passed out, his tongue out. If he wasn't so injured, I'd say he looked cute. I touched the fur by his ear. It was fuzzy and soft. I wondered if he'd let me pet him like Cody had.

"Axel, give me a hand will you?" Seth gestured at Wyn. "Let's get him into a bathtub. When he wakes up and shifts, he can clean up right away."

"Righto, boss man." Axel's big shadow blocked out the sun for a moment. He bent, grabbed Wyn on his uninjured side and carried him over his shoulder like he had done with me before.

I followed behind him, making sure that Wyn didn't wake up and freak out. Seth walked with Jasper and Cody ahead of us.

"Cody, if you try to pinch my ass, I'll have you over my knee and you won't walk for days." Seth didn't even look back when Cody had raised his arm.

"Promises, promises." Cody glanced back at me and grinned. "Would you want to watch, beautiful?"

I giggled, almost tripping as we went inside. "Cody!"

Seth turned to go upstairs with Axel. "I'll be right back after a shower."

That just left Jasper, Cody, and I.

"I'm going to clean up the kitchen." Cody's expression was gleeful. "This means we have a new pack member since Seth didn't kill him!"

"They weren't going to kill each other." I glanced between Jasper and Cody. "Wyn is my mate, too."

"We know." Jasper pushed our shoulders together. "It's just Cody being Cody. It's going to take some time for us to adjust. I think it's going to be just as big of one for Wyn. If not bigger."

"What do you mean?"

Jasper gestured to the couch near the back door. "Wyn's been on his own since he transformed. No pack. He's going to be like you, Becca, experiencing what it means for the first time."

I leaned into his side. "What does that mean, exactly?"

"Shifter packs have hierarchies. I'm sure you've read books about them, yes?" His lip twitched in a smirk at my nod. "Books get some things right sometimes." He started counting off his fingers as he spoke. "Each pack has an alpha that is our leader. He has power, magic if you will, that he gains from being the leader of the pack."

I shifted when his arm went around my shoulders pulling me practically into his lap.

"I'm sure you've already figured it out, but touch is essential in a pack. It brings us closer together and bonds our animals. Most shifters can't function without that fundamental part of a pack. There are some loners who survive without a pack, but it's not ideal for our animals."

"Do all packs mate, like you guys have?" I laid my head on his shoulder, my fingers tracing the wrinkles in his shirt.

His chest moved with his silent laughter. "No. At least, not most. I'm sure there are others out there that do, but it is not the norm." His hands stroked my back now. "Our animals bonded as we did and it progressed into a sexual relationship."

"So, if none of you liked Felicity, except for Axel, why wasn't there more push back from your animals?" I sighed at his hands.

"We wanted him to be happy. He was adamant that what he felt was it for him, we couldn't possibly say no. We figured after she knew about us, we would get to know her." His shoulders shrugged. "It doesn't mean we weren't happy with it, we just decided that we had to give it a try, for him."

Burying my nose in his neck, I kissed his skin. "You all are way too good to be true."

Jasper's chest rumbled. I could hear his purr and I chuckled. My animal stretched confidently. She brushed against me, urging me to claim our fox mate. I reminded her of our earlier conversation and she huffed, but backed off.

"I know that Wyn said he was a loner and doesn't need a pack, but with him being my mate, will he resent me? The rest of you?" I hoped not.

"Becs," he shifted. "If he's experiencing half of the feelings that I have begun having for you, there's no way that he'll be able to stay away from you."

I guess only time would tell. I looked up at the ceiling, my thoughts on the unconscious shifter upstairs.

CHAPTER 22

Wyn

The splash of cold water jerked me into consciousness. I groaned as I stretched out my paws and yawned. I was in a very large bathtub with the shower head raining down on me.

"That was an honorable fight." The bear, Axel, sat on the toilet lid with his hands laced together. "You know what this means now that you've fought for the alpha position of the pack and were left alive?"

I gave a short nod. My animal growled angrily, but he understood as well.

"I'm not a loner anymore." I shifted with a wince, rubbing my jaw. "Are you here to put me in my place?"

The bear gave a shout of short laughter. "I'm not stupid. I know how powerful you are. I'm here just to make sure you heal up so that our shared mate doesn't worry herself into a tizzy about you."

My body relaxed under the spray of water. It may be cold, but my body temperature was high enough that it wasn't a shock to my system after the first splash. I ran a hand through my hair as I looked at Axel.

"I know that this is a lot for everyone. Myself, included. I know you have questions about Felicity. Ask them." It had to be bugging him.

He glanced down at his hands. "The feelings that I experienced when I was with her, those weren't real, were they? They were a product of this 'spray' you talked about?"

I closed my eyes, tilting my head back against the tiled wall. "It's a pheromone spray that has to be used multiple times to become effective. It's why it's only used as the graduation step to Venandi. Her pheromones attracted you to her, like a love spell, the more time you spent with her."

"So, because of the space we've had over the summer, it's worn off on me," he grunted and I could feel the rage rolling off of him.

"She did it on purpose, you know." Squinting at him with one eye, I ran a hand down my chest. "She doesn't want to be a Venandi. She was supposed to have killed you before she left school, but she stalled long enough that my aunt and uncle gave her an extension as long as she trained at the academy this summer."

His shoulders relaxed slightly. "I can't imagine how hurt Becca must be."

These guys confused me. They worried more about our mate, a girl that they hadn't known for very long, instead of focusing on the wrong that had been done to them. My animal grumbled at me. I grudgingly acknowledged that I felt the same pull with her as they did. I just wanted to see her smile.

"She looked ready to kill my cousin. Seems like she's ready to defend your honor." I chuckled, wincing as it pulled on my newly healed wounds. "Damn. That cat can sure use his claws."

Axel's lips twitched in amusement. "He is a bit protective of all of us." He stood. "Welcome to the family, Wyn." He held out his hand to me.

I took it, grunting as he pulled me to my feet. "Just like that?"

He walked to the door, stopping as he opened it. "Just like

that. You have a lot to learn about us, the same we have with you. But Seth's animal has accepted you, and he's the alpha. We listen to our leader. Plus, Becca really didn't give him a choice." He grinned at that as he left the room.

Becca. My own lips curved at the thought of the curvy, spunky kid. She'd gone through Hell, even before the shift. Felicity talked about her a lot. She admired her best friend for fighting her mental demons as hard as she did. I'd wanted to get to know her the first time I'd stepped into their dorm room and saw her speaking with my cousin.

She'd glared at my aunt and uncle without realizing it and I'd been hooked. My animal had gotten a whiff of her scent and wanted to bury our cock deep within her. It had been a very awkward ride back to the compound. Luckily, no one had paid me any mind.

When I'd gotten the call from Gary, I hadn't known that Becca was the same girl. When I'd arrived at the cabin, with it reeking of blood, gore, and pain, I hadn't expected that Gary's stepdaughter survived.

Then I'd seen her. Laying there so pale and barely starting to breathe again. I'd had to fight my animal for control. It wouldn't have done anyone any good if I had raged.

Now, here I was. She was in the same house. She didn't look at me like I was a freak. She acknowledged her animal right away. It had taken me months to get to the control she naturally had in just a few short days.

Plus, she was in heat. With five males that were her mates in the vicinity. The control these boys had was impressive. It took everything within me from yanking her from whichever one she was with and fuck her senseless.

Axel had taken me to the room that they set me up in the first night. I pulled on a pair of jeans as I sat down on the bed with a sigh. This trip to help Gary's stepkid had not gone according to plan. Not that I regretted it, I just had issues with change that I couldn't control.

My phone vibrated on the night stand where I had it plugged into its charger. As I picked it up, I sighed again. It was my aunt, wanting a status update. I went back into the bathroom and shut the door before calling her back.

"Where have you been, Wyn?" she demanded as soon as she answered. "We expected an update over twelve hours ago."

"Sorry about that, Aunt Nina." Not really. "It took some time to get here. I've been tracking the bastard. It just seems like a rogue and, if I'm right, he's already left the area but I've been expanding my search area, just in case I can catch him."

I'd been lying so long to my so-called family for years, it didn't bother me anymore. At first, I'd believed all the lies they spewed about shifters and magic. How only the human race was pure and anything else was an abomination. That changed gradually over time as I got to know Gary. I owed him a lot. He opened my eyes, not to mention saved my life when I'd been thrown into the experiment.

"That's no excuse not to contact us. I was getting ready to send out a patrol to find you." Aunt Nina had a nasally voice that had always been annoying, but now as a shifter, it grated on my nerves to the point of pain. "I want it caught and dealt with, Wyn. It's intelligent for a rogue, I've looked at the autopsy reports of the victims. There was precision in the way it killed them. Bring me its body." She hung up.

I snorted. What body? The guys had taken care of it. They left the head, though. If I had to, I could bring that back with some explanation.

I'd just put the phone in my pocket when it went off again, making me curse. This time, it was Gary. My annoyance lessened.

"She's fine, Gary. As far as I can tell, she's adjusted naturally to the enhanced senses. I doubt she barely notices it. I'm planning on working with her later with shifting into her different animal forms." I grabbed the razor I found in the medicine cupboard with the shaving cream. I started to apply the cream to my face.

"Good. Thank you for being there. I owe you one. I'm dropping the kids and wife off at home later today. I'll head up right after." He sounded exhausted.

I paused as I placed the phone on the counter. With my hearing, I didn't need it on speaker. "Gary, it might be a good idea for you to wait a few more days. I'd like some time to work with her alone, not to mention," I winced as I nicked some skin but it started to heal right away. "She's in heat, Gary." I smirked at the curse he yelled out. "Sorry, but it might make it awkward for you to be here. Let us work this out and then we can all meet up and decide what we're going to do moving forward."

"We?" Gary hissed. "Wyn, what do you mean 'we'?"

Oh, this was just too fun. "I'm one of her mates, apparently." I finished shaving as Gary continued to curse in the background. "So, does this mean I can call you 'dad'?"

He hung up abruptly as I burst out laughing.

I had just finished wiping my face with a washcloth when a knock sounded on the room door. I stepped out of the bathroom. Whoever it was had been quiet enough that I hadn't heard anything. My bet was on the wolf or the fox.

"Enter."

I was wrong. It was Becca.

Becca

The argument I'd had within myself would have been funny if anyone had been able to listen in. Jasper had been concerned when I'd gone quiet after our talk, but I had smiled at him and told him it was nothing.

I argued with myself about coming up to talk to Wyn alone. I knew the guys may not approve of it because they didn't know him, but I did. Kind of. My animal trusted him and he'd not done anything to show that he was untrustworthy.

That's how I'd found myself outside of his door on the third floor. He'd been talking to someone on the phone, but it had been muffled, I couldn't hear clearly. When he'd laughed, jealousy shot through me like lightning. I knocked right after.

"Enter." His voice affected me like Seth's. His voice was a little harder, a soldier taking on the world. He was standing just outside of the bathroom door in just jeans.

My brain short circuited briefly. I took in the muscles of his chest, the clear and defined Adonis belt that dipped below his waistline. But what stood out the most, were the scars that littered his skin. Most looked older, faded. A few were newer and angry looking. I stepped up to him without realizing it and ran my index finger along a pink scar that ran along his collar bone.

"I thought our animals healed us. How come you have so many?" My brows furrowed in concern for him. "These look like they were painful."

He stared down at me quietly, letting me touch him. When I met his eyes, they softened somewhat.

"It might be a hybrid thing. I heal the same as shifters, but bad injuries tend to scar." He still hadn't moved as I continued to explore his scars with my hands. "The same reason why you have the scar on your hand now."

One large scar started at the middle of his stomach and wrapped around his back. I followed it, ducking under the arm he held up so I could keep contact on his skin. The gasp that came from me was soft. His back was worse than his front.

Tears pricked at the corner of my eyes. "How can you stand it?"

He lowered his arm, looking at me over his shoulder. He offered a self deprecating smile. "I don't have much of a choice, kitten." He turned to face me. "Sometimes shifters don't trust a Venandi who is promising to help them."

His expression was tired. He had the weight of the world on his shoulders and he'd been dealing with this all on his own. My arms went around his waist, offering him my strength and comfort. It was really all I could do. When his arms wrapped around my back hesitantly, I relaxed.

I'd been worried that he wouldn't want my touch. Silly, now that I thought of it. He'd been nothing but kind since I'd first met him. Even before this summer, he'd helped me with the smallest thing that had made all the difference to me.

"Becca," that rough voice softened. "I know this is all new to you. I live in a violent world. It's only going to get more violent. I know that our animals have accepted each other, but if this is going to be too much for you, I'll walk away as soon as Gary gets here."

It felt like a knife jerked itself into my heart and twisted. My animal hissed. My arms squeezed his waist as I looked up at him.

"Do you not want this?" I wouldn't force anyone, even if my animal was persistent.

He'd shaven, and his jaw clear of hair made him seem younger. I resisted the urge to touch it.

"Of course I do." He shook his head. "I want you more than I've ever wanted anything in this life, and it scares me. When I met you at your dorm room? I was drawn to you. Not just now. There's just something about you that screams 'home' to me. I don't want you to get hurt because you're with me. I don't think you quite understand how dangerous my life is."

Stepping away from his arms, I started to pace along the floor.

"Look. I get that the Venandi are bad news. I get that you used to be one and now work with Gary to try to stop them. All that means to me is that you're a good person. You've made mistakes. You're trying to save people. I want to be able to help you. Isn't that why you're going to help train me?" I stopped pacing, placing my hands on my hips. "I've changed. I'm not stupid. I can feel how my animal wants to rip her teeth into anyone who could hurt you or the others." I looked down at my hands, spreading my fingers. "Before, I would have been terrified of these thoughts that flash through my mind. Now? I want to help her. I want to help you."

The comprehension that came with that statement froze me for a few brief moments. I could never go back to the way my life had been. Worrying about an art internship when there were lives on the line seemed so miniscule now.

Wyn's hand covered mine and I glanced up. His lips were pressed together in a tight line.

"Becca, I don't think you really understand what that statement means. I'm pretty sure Gary, and your other mates' plan was to talk and come up with a way to hide you from the Venandi. Not to fight them." He squeezed my hand gently.

I narrowed my eyes at him, the annoyance that filled me was also my animals. "I'm not some damsel in distress. I was before, there's no doubt about that. I did die." I stopped him when he opened his mouth. "We can't change that. I wouldn't want to anyway. I can help you and Gary. I know I can. So, I plan to. You'll just have to get used to the idea."

Wyn stared at me silently for several long moments before one chuckle slipped out. "Do the guys know that this is what you have planned? To join the underground movement against the Venandi?"

"Nope. I know they'll help, though." That's just the kind of guys they were. I hoped. "Besides, what did you plan on doing?

The Venandi wouldn't let you just walk away to be with the pack, would they?"

His silence was an answer in itself. I looked at him in triumph.

"That's what I thought."

Wyn shook his head in amusement as a smile graced his face. "Stubborn." He tipped my chin up with the side of his finger. "Beautiful." He bent forward, only a breath away. "Mine." The words barely left him when our lips met.

My animal surged forward in triumph. My hands wrapped around his back as his own moved to my hips, pulling me forward as he pressed us against the wall in two steps. My gasp was covered by his mouth as it felt like his tongue, lips, and teeth took control of my world.

I felt pressure between my thighs as he used one of his legs to spread mine. My hips moved on their own as I ground my pussy against his leg automatically.

A heated growl ripped from him as he pulled away briefly to look down at me.

"Are you sure, Becca? If we do this, I'm here permanently. I'm yours, but you're mine too. I'll kill anyone outside of the pack who dares lay a hand on you." That voice. I was addicted. How it could sound so deadly and sexy all at once was really unfair.

In answer, and with a move that surprised me, I pulled off the large shirt that I'd been wearing like a short dress. I hadn't gotten to the store yet, so I had no bra or underwear either. I 'd begun thinking the guys were putting off a trip for clothes for that reason.

Wyn's pupils widened as his nostrils flared. His hands cupped my breasts, flicking the nipples at the same time. They were already sensitive, so it didn't take much to have me whimpering in need as he leaned forward. His lips latched onto my right nipple as his fingers twisted and pulled my left.

"Oh!" My exclamation was soft but full of need as his teeth tugged. I could feel how wet I was as I moved my hips more against his leg, my clit rubbing against the shorts that still covered my lower half. "Please, Wyn."

His hands moved from my breasts as he released my nipple with a soft pop. His wicked glint had me almost cumming right there. He held my wrists above my head suddenly as he rubbed his jaw along my neck, pressing soft kisses on the tender skin.

"Please what, kitten?" His teeth scraped along my shoulder, on the opposite side where Seth had marked me. "Tell me what you want." His tongue swiped out making my legs shake.

"You. I want you!" I tugged on my wrists but he didn't loosen his hold.

"What do you want from me?" His voice sounded like rocks in a tumbler. "Do you want my cock? Do you want me to fuck you until you can't think straight? Do you want my mouth on your clit with my fingers curled inside of you?"

Oh holy shit. Who knew dirty talk could be so hot? His teeth bit down on my collarbone, making me cry out.

"Tell me, kitten." He bit the spot, harder this time, breaking skin.

The combination of his tongue and pull of his mouth on the spot had me cumming, clenching my thighs tightly around his leg. "I need your cock!"

He released my wrists with a dark chuckle as he picked me up behind my knees. I squeaked clutching his shoulders. His smirk made me want to devour his lips.

"As a reward for answering me, I'll give you what you want." Wyn placed me on the bed, pulling my shorts off in a quick flick of his hand. He looked over me as his eyes bled to black. "God. Your body is perfection." He pushed his jeans down his hips and my mouth went dry. He ran a hand along his length with the right side of his mouth tipped in a grin.

"Last chance, kitten." His face promised the fucking of a lifetime.

"Would you hurry up, already?" In an uncharacteristic move, I spread my legs and ran my middle finger over my clit. "I need your cock."

Wyn was on me in a blink, his large body pressing into mine as our lips met in a clash. I felt his tip press against my walls. I hooked my feet around his hips as he gave a thrust.

A whimper slipped out as he pushed inside of me slowly. It took a moment for my body to adjust around him. He held himself above me on his elbows.

"Doing alright?" His lips pressed against where he'd bitten before.

Nodding, I let out a deep breath. "I'm good."

He gave a final push and his cock was buried inside of me to the hilt. My hands moved to his back dragging down his muscles as he started to pull out of me before abruptly thrusting inside again.

Pleasure built as our bodies moved in sync. Panting breath, heated skin, and moans mixed together.

When he bit down, once again, on my collar bone, giving me his mate mark and drawing out blood, I saw stars as I came, this time, almost passing out. Wyn moaned softly as I felt his own release.

He rolled to lay against my side, his fingers brushing through my hair. My eyes closed at the tender touch.

"You still need to give me your mark." His voice had softened as he continued to run his fingers through my hair.

Opening up my right eye, I didn't want to move. "Now?"

His laugh was barely there. "Yes, kitten. I want to be yours."

Sitting up, mourning the hair petting already, I kissed the middle of his chest. He watched me with hooded eyes.

I wasn't sure where I wanted to mark him until I paused on

his left side of his chest. He raised a brow when I grinned up at him.

"You're mine. You were mine when you first took a step into the cabin." I licked his left nipple teasingly, pleased when he sucked in a sharp breath. Someone was sensitive. I'd have to remember that for the future.

My canines lengthened just as I bit down around his nipple. He gave a shout, his hand coming to hold my head still as I took his blood in my mouth, moaning. I could feel his cock starting to harden against my thigh as I pulled back, licking my lower lip.

The changes my body made with a thought should have still concerned me, but it felt natural now. Easy.

CHAPTER 23
Becca

As I went down the stairs to the second floor a few hours later, I paused as I noticed the rest of the guys on the couch playing a game. I tensed.

Seth was in the middle of it, his arms spread across the back of the couch. He smiled at me, and my shoulders relaxed.

I knew that they were aware Wyn was a mate, but sleeping with him was another thing altogether. Looking at the others, I wanted to make sure we were okay.

Axel was leaning against Seth with Cody in his lap. It made me happy to see them together. Axel must have missed them as much as they missed him. Cody was concentrating on the game as if something important was on the line.

Jasper wasn't there. I glanced around and Seth nodded toward the deck. Jasper stood at the rail, looking out into the woods.

I moved quickly past the TV, with the three of them whistling at me. I rolled my eyes at them as I slipped out the door.

"Jasper?" I didn't want to bother him if he wanted to be alone.

"Hey, Becs." He didn't turn around but held out his arm. I went under the arm to lean against him as he pulled me close. "Just needed some air."

This was quickly becoming one of my favorite things. Cuddling against them.

"Can I talk to you about something?" I looked out at the woods. The sun had started moving across the sky.

"Of course." Jasper moved his attention to me.

"I know we've had the talk, but being with all of you, it's really just fine?" My animal flicked her tail at me in annoyance.

Jasper's arm squeezed my waist as he laughed softly. "My fox wants me to boop you on the nose for that question." He looked back to the woods. "There will be jealousy. I'm jealous that I haven't gotten to have you yet. But we will work it out. You're not human any longer, my love. We're family now. Even Wyn. It'll work itself out. Never doubt our bonds with you and each other. I don't have a problem with Wyn. Like we talked about earlier, I think he's going to be the one who has the hardest time adjusting to all of us." He paused to let me process his words. "I want you. I actually ache with how much I need you to be mine, but it doesn't change the fact that this is your choice and you're in charge of the timeline."

My face flushed at his statement of him being jealous that we hadn't had sex yet. He wasn't pressuring me, and I appreciated him for it.

"You're the reason I can't breathe." Channeling the dark side, I looked at him, trying not to grin. I hoped he got the reference. He didn't disappoint.

"Are you the Death Star? Because you blow me away." He laughed through his own joke as he bent to kiss me.

The taste of lime exploded on my tongue as we stood on the deck and kissed for a long time. My knees were weak by the time we pulled away from each other. Even his cheeks were flushed a little.

"I could kiss you for an eternity and never get tired of it." He pressed a final kiss to my cheek as I fought not to blush again.

Jasper always had a way with words that just weakened me.

"Why don't we do a bonding game night?" An idea popped into my head. I wanted Wyn to get comfortable with the guys. He needed a push to relax. "You guys have karaoke?"

Jasper's emerald eyes glinted against the light. "Do we have karaoke? Is that a serious question?" Laughing, he pulled me back into the game room. "Guys, do we have karaoke?" This, he shouted to them.

Cody jerked off of Axel's lap, groaning as his character was killed on screen. Judging by Seth's snicker, it had been his fault. Cody brushed his hair out of his face as he looked over at us with excitement.

"Really? We can bring it out? Seth said never again after last year's fiasco!" He glanced between Seth and me, with his eyes growing comically large.

I looked at Seth. I pushed out my lower lip, just a little, in a fake pout. He looked at all of us and groaned in defeat.

"Fine. Yes, we have karaoke." He let his head fall back onto the back of the couch with a groan. "Just try not to get the cops called on us again."

"Wait. Cops?" That was a story I had to hear.

"We got drunk and very loud back home. Our neighbors got pissed at one a.m. and called the cops." Axel's amusement was apparent as he watched Seth groan again. "At least our nearest neighbor is with us here."

Cody scrambled up. "I'll grab the machine! Jasper, get Mr. Broody down here! He has to join us." He ran off down the hallway.

Seth sighed as he watched Jasper go upstairs. He patted the seat next to him on the couch. With a streak of mischief, I plopped down between him and Axel, making them move over to give me room.

"You going to sing, cub?" Axel turned off the game with a controller before switching the input on the television.

I shook my head. "Oh no. Not happening. It's like nails on a chalkboard."

Seth ran a hand through his hair. "They are all crazy when it comes to karaoke."

"I wouldn't call it 'crazy'." Axel grinned, a boyish gleam. "We just know how to have fun. Don't think you're not participating, either, Seth." He dodged the controller that Seth threw at him. "Becca will definitely want to listen to you."

Now I was intrigued. I placed my legs across his lap, just in case he tried to get away, and gave him an innocent look. "You sing?"

Those azure eyes narrowed at me, even as he ran his hands along my shins. "Don't think I don't know what you're doing."

I batted my eyelashes at him. "I have no idea what you're talking about. So, singing? Yes?"

He just shook his head as he looked down at my feet and started to rub them, but I saw the tiny smile he tried to hide. I punched the air in success as Axel laughed.

"If I'm singing, so is everyone else." Seth pressed down on the bottom of my feet at once. I felt my soul leave my body as I slumped backward.

"Oh, God. Whatever you want. *Just keep doing that*." My head ended up in Axel's lap as Seth did wonderful things to my feet that should be illegal somewhere. Axel started to run his fingers through my hair which made my eyes close.

I was a goner. A moan echoed through the room as I sank into the pleasure of their touch. It wasn't even sexual and my body was primed and ready.

"I leave the room for five minutes and you guys are trying to get her pants off her again." Jasper's exasperated voice filtered through my haze of pleasure. My eyes slit opened as I looked over to them in concern. I knew we'd just talked, but he said that the jealousy was going to happen for a little while, it still made me worry.

"Don't worry, kit." Seth squeezed my feet one last time before he moved my legs and stood. "Wyn, we're going to be having a karaoke party, why don't you help me grab snacks and drinks from downstairs?" He stopped next to Jasper and whispered something to him.

Axel tugged on my hair, distracting me. His expression was soft. He had no right to look so delectable. "There's still three of us that need to mark you. Once that's been done, we should all settle a little." He'd figured out that I'd started to get worried.

Jasper took Seth's spot, moving my legs so that he could sit before settling them in his lap. He ran his fingers lightly around the skin under my knee. Pleasure shot straight to my pussy and I had to focus on keeping my breathing even.

"Sorry. My fox is being a jealous little asshole. I'm not pressuring you, Becs. Don't think any of us would do that. This is all at your pace, regardless of how much our animals are dickwads." His whisper was laced with guilt.

I couldn't have that. I sat up slowly, giving Axel time to stop petting my hair, as I pulled my legs out of Jasper's lap. I stood from the couch before going to stand in front of Jasper. He looked up at me, his lips parted slightly.

"You guys have never pressured me to do anything." I cupped his face between my hands. "All you've done is show me that it's okay to be myself. I may not be very sexually experienced, but I know my body. *I need all of you.* Just like I need air. Is it strange that it doesn't send me straight to an anxiety attack? We all know I would have freaked out about this before all of this happened. Now that it has? I'm fine with it." I leaned forward, kissing his cheek before moving to his nose. "I want all of you so much that it feels like I'm in a permanent lust filled haze."

That got me a laugh from both of them.

Cody came back into the room from the hallway with his arms full of some type of equipment. It actually looked pretty fancy. He paused as he saw us but grinned when I smiled at him.

"So, does this mean we're having a kinky karaoke party?"

We all burst out laughing as he moved to the TV to start setting up the machine. Jasper pressed his hands over mine on his face before he stood.

"Thanks, Becs." He kissed me gently as he moved to help Cody. They immediately started arguing about what got plugged where.

"You handled that well." Axel was behind me, his big shadow a comfort as I tipped my face to look back at him. He ran a thumb along my jawline. "We'll have fun tonight."

Cody

"I need a hero! I'm holding out for a hero to the end of the night!" The music blared out of the speakers as I belted out the lyrics in a high pitched voice.

Becca was laughing, almost in tears, at my antics. My hips moved with the beat as I rocked out. I jumped on the ottoman as I shook my ass in Wyn's face. The guy started to laugh with Becca.

My wolf was still wary around him. He was a Venandi, after all, but he'd mated with Becca and that's all I needed to know. If Becca was happy, I was happy.

Her laughter and smile kept the demons away. Maybe one day, with her help, they'd be gone completely.

"I need a hero!" My foot slipped on the last note and I ended up flailing backward into Jasper's lap. He grunted at the impact. "Well, hi there, sexy!"

"Bravo!" Becca clapped for me as my score of seventy nine popped up on the screen. "Great job, Cody!" She looked at the others. "Drink up!" She took a shot of tequila like a champ. Her nose crinkled at the taste but she didn't complain.

The guys, including Wyn, all took a drink from what they'd chosen as their drink of choice.

"Okay. Who is the next victim?" I tapped the mic on my mouth as I looked around the room.

Seth avoided my glance as he took another drink of beer. He had moved to sit the furthest away. It was like he was trying to make sure I picked him. I couldn't let him down.

"Seth! My man! It's your turn! Sing us the lovely song of your people!" I threw my hands up in the air as I moved to him. I held out the mic. "I'll even let you pick the song!"

The glare he shot me was supposed to scare me, but with how much fun I was having, I just laughed.

"Please, Seth? I would love to hear your voice." Becca came to my rescue. I didn't even have to look back to see she was using her big, adorable cobalt eyes on him.

His annoyance at me melted away and he took the mic. "I'll get you back for this, Cody. Mark my words."

"Will you spank me?" I made sure to ask the question as he walked around me so that I could rub up against him as I went to sit down next to Jasper.

Seth set up the mic on the stand, staring me down. A thrill ran up my spine and my wolf's tail started to wag. Oh, he was going to definitely spank me later.

He went through the list too quickly for us to see what he

picked as his song, but as it began, I turned to watch Becca's reaction.

As Seth started the first notes in Firecracker by Josh Turner, her mouth dropped open in surprise. The blush that started at her cheeks spread as his voice lowered to match the notes.

Even though he griped about singing, Seth's voice was sinful. He rarely sang because it actually embarrassed him for some reason, but I loved to listen to him. Especially when he would have to growl through some notes.

By the scent Becca was giving off, she was enjoying his voice as much as I was. She didn't seem to notice that we could tell, either. Her attention was solely on Seth, who had started showing off a little by moving to the song.

I adjusted myself since I had begun to sport a boner. Jasper snickered into his hand as he coughed to cover it over.

"You've got one, too." I looked at his crotch, knowing that he was watching me, and I licked my upper lip. My voice was low so we didn't distract Becca from Seth's singing.

"You are such a shit, you know that?" Jasper reached around my shoulders to pull me against him possessively and ran his nose along my neck. "Just wait until tonight."

The end of the song sounded in the room and Becca stood up clapping. We joined her, temporarily ignoring the hard ons that were becoming increasingly uncomfortable.

"Seth, you can sing! That was amazing!" Becca moved to him, wrapping him in a hug as if it was the easiest thing in the world for her. "Look! You got a ninety! The highest so far!"

I still had a hard time believing how easy this was for her. How seamless she seemed to blend with her animal. At the beginning of the summer, just my sudden touch sent her spiraling into an anxiety attack. Now, she touched us as if it was the only thing she wanted to do. We didn't have many shifters that weren't naturally born. Those that got turned were so rare, I had never actually met one until Wyn and Becca, and they were special, even more so.

"Who's next?" Seth kept his arm around her waist as he looked at the rest of us in challenge.

My wolf bowed with his tail in the air. I was just about to offer to sing again when Wyn surprised all of us by standing. He took the mic from Seth with a growing grin that promised a challenge.

"If we're singing country, I'll have to join in. Won't I, kitten?" He cocked a brow up at Becca.

I moaned at how her scent flared around the room at just the nickname. Jasper squeezed my shoulders. He was holding himself back pretty well. Axel had been quiet throughout Seth's song and exchange now, but he shifted in his seat. My wolf yipped in amusement that our bear was just as uncomfortably hard as the rest of us.

Seth handed him the mic with a laugh after they stared at each other for a few moments. I relaxed a little against Jasper. He hadn't been challenging Seth again. He was actually having fun with us.

"Alright, boys." Wyn scrolled through the songs on the screen as Seth went back to the couch with Becca. He sat with her in his lap. She kept her eyes on Wyn. "Let's see how hot we can get our little kitten, mm?"

We all zeroed in on Becca. All the skin she was showing went bright red. She crossed her arms across her chest and she huffed.

"Really? Wyn!" Her reaction was priceless because she tried to sound stern but we could all tell it was a lie.

Wyn started the machine and Nothing On But The Radio started. I started laughing softly, pressing my mouth against Jasper's chest so I didn't interrupt the song. Jasper's chest moved as he held back his own laughter. I looked over at Wyn and had to bite my hand from laughing loudly. He was moving as if he were line dancing as he sang.

It was actually kind of sexy. He had a nice ass.

Axel surprised everyone by standing and moving to stand next to Wyn as he joined him in the line dance. Becca's mouth wasn't the only one that fell open in shock. These two giants moved in sync as Wyn sang out the lyrics.

Jasper couldn't hold it back anymore. His laughter spilled out and mine was right after. Axel winked at us as he turned with Wyn and they both did the next move that ended up showing off their ass to us for a few seconds.

Becca started laughing, her voice added to the song. By the end of it, even Seth was laughing as Axel and Wyn bowed. Wyn got an eighty eight, so he wasn't that bad of a singer either. I didn't think this guy had it in him to have fun.

"That was amazing!" I stood, clapping. "I had no idea you could line dance, Axel."

He snorted. "I'm from a family of bears who isolate from the world and are addicted to country music."

"I didn't know that." Becca squirmed out of Seth's lap. "I don't know a lot about you guys."

"That means that we get to know each other." Axel's hands went to her waist as she came up to him. "We have all the time in the world."

Becca nodded and gave a cute yawn. I had a sudden urge to pick on her, but I held back. The others might really kick my ass if I did that. Although, without knowing her animal, she might like it.

I finished my beer with a loud burp, getting everyone's attention. "Tonight is bonding time and fun! Who's next?" I looked at Jasper. "I vote the fox."

Jasper slapped my ass as the others all agreed. He went over to the machine to look through the songs. Becca moved off toward the deck door. I went with her. She had a look of wonder on her face.

"Becca?" I waved a hand in front of her face but she just grabbed it and laced her fingers with mine.

"Stars." Her soft whisper was full of awe. "I can see."

It was pitch dark outside, but thanks to our animals, we could see just fine. I'd forgotten, stupidly, that Becca hadn't been able to see at all in the dark before. Apparently, I wasn't the only one who'd forgotten.

The others came up behind us and Axel opened the doors so we could step out onto the deck. Becca looked up into the sky. Someone turned off the lights in the game room, letting the light from the stars and moon the only source.

I led Becca by her hand to the rail, letting her lean against it as she gripped my hand in her right as her other gripped the rail. Large tears fell from her. She cried silently as she glanced around.

"It's beautiful." Becca looked over at me and my wolf whined with me. "I never thought I'd ever get to see the stars and moon like this." Her shoulders started to shake and that's all I needed before I pulled her against me. "If becoming a shifter means I can see this every night, it was worth the pain."

Her cheek rested on my chest as we looked up into the sky. The others surrounded us, forming a group hug, which made her laugh through her tears. Even Wyn joined in, standing between Axel and Jasper as we all held her.

We spent the night under the stars. Seth brought out blankets as we took the cushions on the outdoor furniture and laid on the deck. Becca didn't say much, just watched the sky.

CHAPTER 24

Becca

"You know that I can shop for my own clothes, right?" I rubbed my temple as I got into the back of Wyn's rental. "I don't need an entourage. Weren't we supposed to try to work on my shifting today?"

"We will." Wyn turned on the car. "After we finish in town, I'll give you your first lesson."

Jasper and Cody got into the back with me, squishing me between them. Axel got into the front seat. Seth was staying behind because he had a meeting of some kind for his company. I think Jasper was more excited to shop over everyone else.

"Why aren't we taking the Escalade?" Cody grunted as he put on his seat belt.

"Because someone broke the window, and it's in a shop right now getting it replaced, remember?" Axel sent a glare over his shoulder at him. "I got yelled at for that."

"You are the one who technically broke it." Cody stuck his tongue out at Axel, whose eye had begun to twitch slightly.

"Okay, boys." I held my hands up. "Back to my first question. Why can't I shop for my own clothes again?"

"As much as we like seeing you in our clothes," Jasper buckled himself in before turning to me. "You should get your own clothing, including underwear." The tips of his ears turned red. "We need to get you a replacement phone, too."

Oh. I cleared my throat and looked out through the windshield. I knew my face was red. "A new phone would be good. I need to call Mom and Gary." I was not going to talk about my underwear.

"I think purple or green would look good on your skin. Maybe a thong?" Cody decided to talk about it instead.

"Cody! I am not talking about my panties or bra selection." I elbowed him in the stomach. He grunted, rubbing where I'd hit with my elbow. "Besides, it's not like Tabernash has a large clothing selection to choose from."

"I was thinking we would go to Fraser. There's a Murdoch's there." Wyn looked in the rearview mirror. "That way we can get more variety. There's an electronics shop not far from it where we can pick up a phone."

I hadn't been to Murdoch's since my father had been alive. He used to take me so I could go look at all of the farming equipment they had. I forgot that they actually had pretty much everything. They were kind of like Walmart, but more upscale for farmers and ranchers.

The drive wasn't long. Axel and Cody kept us all entertained with their bickering. Wyn tried to hide his amusement but it was easy to see he was enjoying himself. I was still a little tired. I'd stayed up most of the night just staring up at the stars and moon.

"Can we pick up some art supplies while we're there?" I stifled a yawn. "Murdoch's might have a few things I could get."

Jasper squeezed my knee gently. "Anything you want, we'll get."

"I don't even have any money with me." The realization hit me. "Was any of my stuff salvageable?" They hadn't let me go back to the cabin yet.

"No." Axel looked back at me. "We'll cover it. Don't worry about it. It's the least we can do."

"That's not saying that we'll always pay for everything, Becca," Jasper hurriedly spoke as I opened my mouth in annoyance. "Let us do it for now, okay? You can treat us to dinner when we go home."

I snorted. "Good save."

Not long after, we pulled into the parking lot. Wyn pulled up in front of the entryway. "I've got to run a few errands, I'll pick you guys up in about an hour."

Getting out of the car was a fiasco because Cody decided to get 'stuck' in the open doorway.

"Oh no." He leaned back into me, making me fall back with a laugh. "I've fallen for you!" His head ended up in my lap as he cracked up at his own joke.

"You're such a dork." Ruffling his hair, I pushed his shoulders. "Let me out."

He was still laughing when Axel yanked him out by his leg. Cody caught himself before he ended up on the asphalt. Axel offered his hand to me as I got out. He kept my hand in his.

The nostalgic scent of leather hit just as we entered the store. Two years ago, I would have cried from grief just stepping into the building. It'd been over ten years, time healed wounds, but the scars still hurt sometimes. I wondered what he would have thought of all of this. Especially me becoming a shifter.

Actually, he'd have really liked Gary and probably would have loved all of this.

I giggled at the thought of how he'd try to intimidate the guys.

Axel titled his head at me curiously. I just shook mine.

"Just silly thoughts."

He offered a soft smile. "I'm going to go grab some things with Jasper. Will you be alright?"

I raised an eyebrow at him without saying anything. He rubbed the back of his head as he stepped to the left, following Jasper.

"Right. That was probably a stupid question. Have fun?"

Jasper laughed at Axel as they walked toward the other side of the store, leaving me with Cody.

"Fair maiden, shall we procure you some garments fit for a queen?" Cody held out his arm in a gallant fashion. "Whatever you desire, my lady, it shall be yours!"

My animal chuffed in amusement at his antics as I slid my arms through his. My heart warmed as we walked together to the women's section.

"Should we grab a cart?" I hadn't even thought to grab one.

"Becca, I'm the cart. These arms aren't just for cuddles and hot sex on the floor." His outrageous expression had me laughing as we stopped at a few racks of dresses.

I found a few dresses that looked comfortable before I moved to jeans and shirts. Cody stayed near, holding the clothes I decided on.

"I should grab a pair of shoes." I looked down at the oversized flip flops I was wearing.

"Let's grab those after you choose some underwear and try this stuff on." Cody walked off with everything, leaving me no choice but to follow.

He approached the young woman who was manning the dressing rooms. She visibly tittered under his attention.

"Can we get a room? My girlfriend needs to try this stuff on before we buy it." Cody was smooth, I'd give him that. "I'm buying this stuff for her for her birthday!"

I had to stop myself from laughing. The girl didn't have a problem. She glanced between us and I was afraid it was going to be another pizza girl situation, but she surprised me by wiggling her eyebrows at me.

"Seems like you caught quite the catch. Let's get you set up in the back. Do you want her to show off the clothes? There are three mirrors." She led us to the back of the changing rooms. There was a large chair next to the mirrors she told us about that were outside of the multiple rooms. "We're having a pretty slow day, so you shouldn't have to worry about sharing the mirrors."

"Thank you." Cody put the clothes inside the room. "Do you mind if we leave these here while we grab a few more things?"

The girl shrugged. "No problem." She walked off to continue with what she'd been working on before we'd come up to her.

Cody pulled his hair back with a rubber band he had around his wrist. He held up a dark green dress that I had not picked out. It was shorter, I'd need to wear leggings with it, and it was extremely low cut. Placing my hands on my hips, I looked at him.

"Really, Cody?" I had to fight to stop from grinning at his sad expression.

"What? You'd look dynamite in this." He widened his eyes innocently. "Please?"

"You're ridiculous." I took the dress and put it back on the pile of clothes. "You're lucky you're cute." I kissed his cheek. "I'm going to go grab some lady things, you can stay here."

"Aw, but!" he whined but sighed when I just stared at him. "Fine. I'll just wait here. Alone. So alone."

I left the changing room, moving to where the lingerie section of the women's clothing was located. I grabbed my size in multiple colors and styles. Cody was sitting in the chair when I got back. He looked at my arms curiously, but I put the items inside the changing room before he could get a good look.

"I'm going to try on a few things. If I like them, I'll show you." I started to close the door but paused and pointed at him. "Stay there." I shut the door.

I could hear his huff easily. He'd be in here in a second if I let him. The animal inside of me rolled on her back. She wouldn't mind if our wolf came in and I just shook my head at her.

Several of the clothes were too tight and didn't fit comfortably, even though they were labeled my size. The dress that Cody picked out fit like a glove and went to mid-thigh. I could technically wear it without leggings if I was feeling bold enough. That was probably why he picked it.

I put it in the 'keep' pile with most of the shirts and two pairs of the jeans. One pair of jeans I almost chucked out the room because of how they were cut to make bigger women look even bigger than they really are.

When I moved on to the underwear, a wicked idea flitted through my mind. My animal vibrated excitedly. I pulled on the sexiest bra that I'd been able to find, which wasn't that sexy, just a little lace and black. I refused to try on the panties, they would fit.

"Shoot," I called out to Cody. "Could you come help me with the hooks?"

I kept my eyes on the mirror as he opened the door and froze. His eyes ran up my legs slowly, to my stomach, breasts, and finally to my face. Even with cheeks blazing, I offered him a smirk. "Good choice?"

His grey eyes darkened as he stepped into the room, closing the door behind him. His hands went to his pants as he hooked his thumbs under his waistband.

"Damn. I seriously just want to eat you up." His tongue flicked out to lick his lower lip as I watched him through the mirror.

"Are you going to help me or just stare?" My boldness surprised me but it felt good.

Cody stepped up behind me, his hands coming around to rest on my stomach. He pressed his hips against my ass. "You are my salvation." He knelt behind me, using his hands to turn me toward him.

I looked down at him as he looked up at me. I couldn't describe the heat, the emotion, that his gaze held, only that he saw me. He wanted me.

I pushed my shorts down, opening myself up to him as he hooked my right leg over his shoulder as I leaned backward, supporting my back on the cool mirror. My left hand rested on the top of his head, pulling out his hair from the low ponytail he'd placed it in. The band landed somewhere on the floor behind him.

"Keep quiet, Becca. You don't want us to get caught, do you?" His growl was soft, making my knees start to shake. His left hand came around my back and clutched my ass as he brought his mouth to my pussy.

His tongue pushed inside of me, flicking upward at my clit in rapid movements. Cody pushed a finger inside of me, just teasing because as soon as my hips moved, he pulled it out.

"Cody!" My fingers tightened in his hair just as he brought his lips to my clit, sucking on it roughly for several moments making stars flash in my vision. The pressure he applied reminded me of a toy I had at home, except so much better.

He chuckled as his tongue took over. I lost all sense of thought except for how close I was to cumming. With every swipe of his tongue and stroke of his finger, I could feel myself getting to that cliff of pleasure. Just one more and I'd explode.

Cody seemed to sense it, perhaps because I wasn't able to hide the whimper that slipped out, but he pulled his finger out of me with a wicked gleam in his eye.

As I opened my mouth to hiss at him, his canines lengthened and he turned his head just slightly to my right thigh and bit down, marking me as his. My orgasm rocked me to my core. If he hadn't been supporting me, I'd have slid to the ground. It was all I could do to remember to bite my palm to stop my moan.

Cody tenderly moved my leg from his shoulder, licking my

wound that was healing as he did it. He moved his hands to my hips, gripping them tightly so that I didn't stumble as he stood.

"Was that okay? I didn't ask, I just assumed." Fear suddenly flashed in his eyes, showing that hidden pain I'd glimpsed those few times.

I cupped his cheeks bringing his mouth to mine and kissed him with everything I felt for him. My hands moved so that I could wrap my arms around his shoulders as I pulled back slightly.

"I love you, Cody."

That hadn't been what I'd planned to say, but it felt right. I'd realized I was in love with the silly wolf a while back, but I hadn't voiced those feelings because it just hadn't been the time. Now, faced with his pain that I didn't know about, I needed to let him know that I wasn't going anywhere.

Tears filled his eyes, falling gently down his cheeks. "Becca." His voice broke. "I love you, too."

With a little shifting, his pants pushed off his hips and his cock pressed slowly up inside of me. It was easier this time as his cock slid inside of me. I felt like I was filled, that I couldn't move. I didn't need to worry about that. His grip was tight as he pressed me against the mirror moving rapidly.

It was fast, hard, and messy as our tongues fought each other to keep our noise level down. I was worried about breaking the mirror with the strength of his thrusts making my body jerk against it.

My nails dug into his arms as we pulled away from kissing. He tilted his head, offering me the side of his neck and I bit down instinctively. My canines slid in easily, his blood making me growl possessively.

Cody cursed softly as I felt him jerk, cumming so hard, I could feel the excess slowly slide down my legs. My thighs tightened as I shuddered through another release. We both panted as I licked at his new mark on his neck.

The knock on the door would have made me squeak in horror if Cody hadn't covered my mouth. He held me up as we looked at the door. I prayed it wouldn't open.

"Everything alright in there?" It was the worker from earlier.

"Yup." I managed not to giggle. "I just stubbed my toe really hard."

Cody started to shake in silent laughter as he held me. I elbowed him in the stomach, but that just seemed to make him laugh harder.

"Must have been some toe stub." The girl's tone insinuated that she was holding back her own laughter. "I have some customers who will be joining you in the changing room, so if you'd like to finish what you're doing, you'll have a few more minutes."

As we listened to her steps fade away, we both couldn't hold it back any longer. We both burst out laughing. Cody pulled out some tissues from his back pocket and helped me clean up my legs until I could get to a bathroom to properly clean up.

I pulled my borrowed clothes back on as Cody zipped up his pants. His mark from me could be seen clearly on his neck. He tilted his neck to me when he caught me looking.

"I love that you marked me where everyone can see it." Leaning forward, he kissed me gently. "The guys are going to be so jealous."

I rolled my eyes at him. "You're going to rub it in their faces, aren't you?"

"I don't have to do that. They just have to smell you and they'll know." He bent down to grab the rubber band that I'd yanked off of him and put his hair back up. "Or me, for that matter."

"Let's hurry up and get out of here before we commit another crime." I grabbed the clothes I liked while Cody grabbed the pile that we'd leave with the employee so it could be put away. "I'm sure the guys are looking for us by now."

The walk of shame wasn't as bad as I thought it would be. The girl looked up from the clothes she was folding near the entrance to the changing rooms. She grinned at me and I gave one back.

At least that meant we weren't going to be in trouble for having sex in the store luckily. Cody handed her the clothes we didn't pick.

"You two have a *great* rest of your day." I could tell she was resisting laughing. At least we'd given her a story to tell her friends.

I walked quickly away with Cody following.

"I am never going to be able to show my face in this store again." I practically buried my face in the clothes I held in my arms.

"Becca!" Jasper and Axel stood at one of the checkout lines. It looked like they'd grabbed a few things. When we got up to them, I could tell when they realized because their eyes darkened and they sniffed the air.

"Really?" Axel looked at Cody then at me. "Here?"

I couldn't tell if they were annoyed or not. Cody's arm went around my shoulders.

"You guys would have done the same thing." His chest puffed out a little.

Jasper rolled his eyes as Axel just shook his head. "You're very lucky you didn't get caught." Jasper took the clothes from me to place it on the belt to be checked out.

"I like this one." Axel pointed to the dress Cody picked out. Cody glanced at me with a smirk.

"Of course you guys like the one that shows off my boobs."

"We are still guys, darling." Jasper picked up the dress, turning it around to look at it from all sides. "I agree, though. This will look amazing with your skin and eyes."

Axel

"I'm not sure how long I can keep holding off Gary from coming up here." Wyn looked down at his phone, rubbing his jaw. "Not to mention my aunt. I sent her the head of the rogue. The things you can send through the postal service." He amused himself with his own joke. "That should hold them off for a little while longer, at least."

We watched as Jasper, Cody, and Becca looked at phones. She'd changed into new clothes in the restroom at the store after we purchased them. She looked more comfortable, even though I liked seeing her in my shirts.

My bear was in a mood after we scented that she'd mated with Cody. He wanted to mate with her. He was jealous of the wolf and shared images of how he'd like to punish him. I wouldn't mind the spanking. Cody made addicting noises when spanked.

"You doing alright there?" Wyn's question brought my attention back to the conversation. I winced as my hard on rubbed against my jeans.

"I'm just peachy."

He snorted at my answer. "It's strange." He put his phone in his back pocket. "Before I met her, my animal was always just under the surface, ready to strike out. To kill. It didn't matter who. In just the few days with her, he's relaxed for the first time since I changed. He's not yearning for everyone's blood."

I had to grudgingly admire the guy. Having an animal inside of you that could shift into different species had to be overwhelming. He'd been alone, a test subject, and had managed not to go rabid. Dealing with one animal took a lot of control as it was.

"At first, once that hormone started to wear off," I watched as Becca bent over a case to look closer at a phone. "I felt horrible for wanting Becca. I didn't understand how I could be falling for Felicity and, suddenly, want her best friend instead. Becca's never made me feel like our feelings are wrong. She doesn't judge. She's an amazing woman and our beautiful mate." Shrugging, I glanced at him again. "Thank you for coming to help her."

We were quiet during the rest of the time we were in the small electronics shop. Becca ended up choosing the same model phone she'd had before. They were able to transfer her information from the cloud so she didn't lose any data. She immediately went outside to call her mom. Jasper and Cody came up to us.

"I'm starving. Do you think Seth has dinner ready or should we pick something up on the way back?" Cody patted his stomach.

"We can pick up food." Wyn looked like he was trying not to smile. "You must be starving after your romp in the store, yeah?"

"Oh snap." Cody punched Wyn's arm. "You got jokes."

CHAPTER 25

Becca

The conversation went as well as I thought it would with Mom. She was unhappy with me but whatever Gary had come up with seemed to placate her enough that I only got a mild chewing out for not calling her sooner.

"I was worried. Just don't go that long again, young lady." Mom had finished her mini rant as the guys left the shop.

"I know. I'm sorry again, Mom. I've got to go, but I'll talk to you tomorrow." I'd hung up before she'd been able to go off again.

Now I was standing in the backyard across from Wyn after we all had eaten the Mexican food we'd stopped to pick up on the way back. Seth was outside with us, relaxing on one of the chaise lounges as he watched us. The others were inside doing chores.

I changed into some of the workout clothes that we purchased at Murdochs. I wasn't quite sure what to expect with this training Wyn was going to be having me do. He wasn't wearing a shirt, so that was a little distracting.

"Shifting should come easily to you based on how you've reacted to all the other changes." He shook his hands out.

"Why is that?" I copied his movements until I saw him snicker. My hands went to my hips. "Why is this so natural? I feel like I should be overwhelmed. My hearing, sight, reflexes, hell, I'm stronger than I was before! Why am I just jumping in like it's nothing?" I'd had a long internal conversation with myself about this very thing. My animal hadn't been any help, she'd just chuffed at me in amusement.

Wyn rolled his head around his shoulders. "Not sure, kitten. When I changed, I had to fight to stay sane with all the changes. With you, it's like you were a born shifter. Your animal doesn't fight with you like mine did." He glanced at Seth, who just shrugged. "Maybe Gary will have an idea."

I let out a large sigh but shook my head. I was a hybrid shifter. No longer human, yet I still felt human most of the time. Except, you know, the whole having another being sharing my soul thing. Maybe there wouldn't be an answer. It wasn't like this was a normal thing to happen to a lot of people.

"Now, when I first shifted, it hurt. I lost consciousness for the first few minutes and that left my animal in charge. I killed two Venandi before I gained control again when I woke."

Poor Wyn. He'd had to deal with so much shit just because of who his family was. I was glad he'd still ended up being a good guy.

He was a good mate, too. My animal made sure to point that out.

"So, when you shift, try to remember who you are. You'll be confused, especially when you try to stand or walk. You'll have to get used to a new body and how to move." Wyn put his hands on his pants. "You might want to remove your clothes so you don't end up ruining them." He stepped out of his sweats and my brain short circuited for a few seconds.

A rumble in my chest brought my attention back. My animal was enjoying the show right before Wyn shifted. He hadn't shifted into his wolf. This time, he'd changed into his hawk form.

Now, I knew from science classes that hawks weren't small,

but they weren't huge either. I think I remembered a documentary talking about how they could get up to three and half pounds when full grown.

Wyn was much larger than that. He had to be the size of a medium sized child and he was beautiful.

He hopped on his talons.

Well, thank you, Becca. You're fucking gorgeous yourself.

His voice sounded in my head. With a shriek, I fell on my ass in shock.

"What? How!" I looked around in confusion. "I heard you in my head!"

His laughter sounded in my head. *I change into a hawk, and you're concerned about hearing me in your head?*

"Well, excuse me for being a little freaked out. It's not every day that, yet again, another being is in my head!" If my glare could cause physical harm, he'd be crying by that point.

Seth moved from where he'd been relaxing. He came to stand next to me, helping me to get back on my feet.

"That's our fault for not giving you a heads up. When a packmate is in his animal form, we can talk to each other telepathically." He squeezed my hand gently.

"And now I'm pack because we're mated?" I rubbed my temples. "Is that how it works?"

He nodded. "When you mated with me, you became pack. You should be able to talk to Cody too, without any issues. When you've mated with Jasper and Axel, there shouldn't be any issues, although with how close you are with them, you might not have any issues without mating with them. Wyn might have more difficulty since he's not mated to any of us but you."

I blinked. "But he's pack. Wouldn't that mean he can talk to them?"

"He will be able to. But telepathic communication isn't just about being pack. It's about mental bonds. He just needs to work on those and he will." Seth ran his hand over the top of my head in a gentle motion.

I can talk to Seth easily because he's my Alpha. Wyn flapped his wings a few times. *Now, can we continue? Get naked, woman.*

I flipped Wyn off. "I'll get naked when I'm ready!" I looked back up to Seth. "Can I try communicating with the others and you?" The idea of being able to talk to the guys in their heads was entertaining.

You can do anything you'd like, my love. Seth's deep voice rolled through my head and my toes curled. I could hear his animal purring, too.

"Okay, how do I do it?" I rubbed the back of my head. "Do I just think what I want to say?"

Yup. You can also send pictures. Wyn answered me instead of Seth. After his words, a flash of him fucking me from behind made me stumble again. Thankfully, Seth kept me upright as I blushed.

That was unfair! My voice echoed through the connection I felt with Wyn and was satisfied to see him flinch a little. Apparently, yelling was a possibility through telepathy. I thought about the others. *Guys?*

My head was instantly bombarded with their replies all at once.

Becca?

Becs!

You can talk to us! Does this mean you transformed? Hold on, I'm coming out!

Giggling, I hugged Seth. "I did it!"

His warm scent surrounded me as he responded to the hug. "You did. I doubt you'll need to practice since yelling at Wyn seems to have helped you get the hang of it." He laughed under his breath as Wyn flew a few feet into the air and gave a shriek.

Come on, Becca. You can do this. Wyn flew around Seth and I in a circle before landing to hop next to me. *If you can do this easily, I really won't have anything else to do besides teaching you self-defense.*

The sound of a door opening announced the other three guys as they raced across the ground to join us. They were all grinning at me. I was bombarded with hugs from all of them until I could barely breathe.

Okay! Okay! Air is needed, please. I tested it out again, projecting it out in my mind.

Jasper thumped his forehead to mine. *A natural. You are a natural.*

"Alright," Seth stepped back, pulling the others with him. "Let's watch Becca kick ass."

Wyn landed in front of me, gently picking at my leggings with his beak. *Off with the clothes.*

I glanced over at the others guys. Axel got the hint and turned around. Seth followed after with Jasper. Cody just grinned at me, wiggling his eyebrows until my glare had him turn around with a laugh. Next was Wyn, who turned and his tail feathers shook a little. I had to resist the urge to reach out and touch them.

Focus, baby. Wyn's mirth was apparent as he hopped a few feet away. *We can play after.*

I guess I projected that picture to him without meaning to.

I pulled my clothes off quickly and held my arms over my breasts and nether region, as if they hadn't all seen me naked already.

Now, just will yourself to shift. Choose a form, see it in your mind's eye, and feel the change. Wyn flapped his wings from where he stood, still keeping turned for my modesty.

Taking a deep breath, I closed my eyes. My animal pressed against me. She was ready to stretch her legs. I thought about what form I wanted to experience first.

There was a flash of pain that rocked me to my core, but it was gone so quickly, I shook my head rapidly. I wasn't even sure now that there had been pain. It was suddenly warmer than before.

Blinking my eyes open, I jumped in the air. And went pretty high up before thumping back onto the ground, my paws catching me.

Wait.

Paws.

I had paws! And fur. There was a heavy pull on my back. Looking over my shoulder, I yipped in excitement. I had a huge fluffy tail! I was in my fox form. My fur was red and warm. My tail swished in front of my face as I looked back at it.

Wow. Jasper's soft exclamation drew my gaze. He kneeled on the ground and I came up to him, placing my chin on his knee. *How can you be so beautiful?*

Aw. You're such a sweet talker. I fluttered my eyelashes at him. Oh, holy mother of cheese balls. His fingers scratched behind my ears. It was like a million fingers were stroking my hair. It felt so good.

Okay, Jasper. Let's give her a second. Seth's voice made the petting stop. *Becca, can you change back?*

I could, but where was the fun in that? I flicked my tail at him.

Are you able to control your body without fighting your animal for control? Wyn hopped over to where I still sat with Jasper. The hopping was adorable.

I've not had any issues with her yet. Although, she did think you hopping is cute.

Wyn's feathers puffed up. *Let's see if you can change forms simultaneously. Don't push yourself if you become tired. Do just like you did before.*

Stepping away from Jasper, I closed my eyes again to focus. Except this time, nothing happened. No quick pain, no temperature change.

Becca? Wyn prodded at me.

Nothing's happening. I whipped my head around. *Why didn't I change?*

This wasn't good. I couldn't stay an overgrown fox for the rest of my life, even if I was cute and really fluffy. I started to pace.

"Don't panic." Seth squatted down so that he could grab my muzzle. "Change back." His voice deepened and vibrated. There was a slight pressure in my temple. Seth blinked, looking confused. "Why isn't she responding to the Alpha power?"

Wyn shifted and knelt next to Seth. Butt naked. If I wasn't so concerned about not being able to shift back, I'd be enjoying the view.

Alpha power? I pulled my face away from his grip.

"I have certain perks because I'm the alpha. Which includes having the ability to command my pack members to do as I say if I pull on that power." Seth watched me as I started to pace again. "Magic."

I paused. That was kind of cool, but didn't help me at the moment.

Jasper sat on the ground, patting his lap. "Everything has come easy for Becca. We just assumed this would be the same thing." I moved to sit in his lap, tucking my tail under my chin. His fingers ran down my back. "Young shifters sometimes get over stimulated the first few times. It'll be okay, Becs. I have an idea." He looked at the others. "Give us a little bit of time?"

What idea? I looked up at him.

Jasper grinned as his finger scratched under my chin. "Just give it a minute." He glanced back up at the guys. "Please."

I watched the guys through half lidded eyes. Oh man. The scratching under the chin was an aphrodisiac. Seth nodded and they all headed back to the house. I turned my head to make sure I could watch Wyn.

"He certainly has nice assets, doesn't he?" Jasper tapped my nose, catching me in the act.

Yes, yes, he does and he knows how to use them. I giggled.

Jasper picked me up out of his lap, placing me next to him, and started removing his clothes. I whistled telepathically and he threw his head back in laughter before he shifted. I only got a quick look at his body and holy fuck.

Jasper in his fox form was just as stunning as before. His fur was a deeper red than mine. He stretched, his tail shaking at its tip as he shook his fur out. He rubbed our noses together.

Let's have some fun. He bumped against me and took off into the woods. *Catch me if you can!*

I was right behind him. The wind through my fur felt freeing as my legs pumped. I'd never felt this before. Happiness bubbled within me and I started yipping at Jasper. He dodged around trees, under bushes, and even over a small stream of water.

The sounds of birds, little creatures like squirrels, skittered away as we ran around.

I lost him about ten minutes into the chase. I skidded to a stop, ending up rolling over a few times before ending up on my back in a soft patch of grass. I was panting with how hard we'd been running around.

Giving up? Jasper's face appeared above mine. His eyes were lit up in excitement. *Do I win?*

No way. I'm just taking a break. I looked up through the branches into the sky. *This is so different. I'm still me, just more. Does that make sense? I think I'm rambling. I am happy.*

Jasper settled down on his stomach, sniffing my ears, making the fur tingle. *That makes sense. You're not just one soul in your body now, you're two.*

I looked up at the clouds as they slowly moved across the sky.

Jasper, what happens now? When we leave Tabernash and return from summer vacation? Do I go back to school? What about Wyn? He's part of the Venandi. It's not like they're going to just let him leave to be part of our family. And Felicity.

Grief gripped my heart. My best friend turned into an enemy without knowing it. The emotions that I had been holding back, with help from my animal, came rushing to the surface making me whimper.

There was a new world that I was just learning about. That world was in the middle of a war with humans. One of my mates was part of that group, albeit a spy among them, but he risked his life every second he had to be part of that group. He wanted out to be with me. There had to be something we could do to help him and Gary with the Venandi. School just seemed so juvenile now.

Jasper nudged me with his nose, making me look at him. *What happens is that we work together. I have some schooling left, so you go back to school if you want. All that's changed is we watch for signs of the Venandi. As far as Felicity goes, Wyn seemed hopeful that he could help her get out of there. Or something completely different happens. Whatever happens, we'll face it together.*

He was right. Wyn had mentioned that. I licked his nose. *You're a genius, you know that?* I knew what my next steps were going to be, even if they weren't the smartest decision. It would be interesting to see what Gary said.

Jasper nudged his face against mine. A warm feeling filled me as I licked his nose again. *I'm going to try to shift.*

He jumped away just as I thought about shifting. That flash of debilitating pain and I was dizzy for a few seconds. I was standing on just two legs. I wiggled my toes.

"I did it!" Lifting my arms, I looked at my hands. "That's a rush."

"It never gets old either," Jasper's voice had deepened.

I froze, staring at my thumbnail as Jasper moved into my line of sight that I could see out of the corner of my eye.

"Jasper?" I cleared my throat. "I just noticed we're both

naked." I looked up from my thumb and just about started to drool.

Jasper was fit, not nearly as muscled as Seth or Wyn, but he was filled out in all the right places. A tribal tattoo ran from his left part of his chest in swirls of black across to his lower right ribs. It just emphasized his skin tone and his stomach muscles.

"Yes." Mirth danced across his face. "We're both very naked."

Goosebumps appeared along my body. I even shivered as he took another step toward me. I didn't cover myself up as I watched his eyes move over my body. He took in my stretch marks, my droopy breasts, and round stomach and looked at me as if he were starving.

"Say no, Becs. I won't be able to hold back for long." His roughened voice wasn't smooth like normal. He was shaking and it took me a moment to realize it was because he was stopping himself from touching me.

My back straightened as my confidence filled me. Jasper had been the first of these guys to see me for me. My strides took me to stand in front of him with barely a few inches between us.

"Yes." My hand touched his chest. "Don't hold back."

His mouth twisted in a snarl right as he kissed me. The world spun as he gripped my waist with one hand while his other clutched the back of my neck, holding me still as he nipped at my lips.

His body pressed into mine as I lost myself in his unending kisses. His hardened cock pressed into my stomach. I slid my hands between us and took him in them. His chest grumbled out a growl as I explored the veins along his shaft.

"Wait." Jasper pulled away slightly and I froze. "Becca, I need to tell you something first."

He stepped back, my hands fell to my sides, but he kept his one hand on the back of my neck. I stared up at him in confusion as he offered a soft smile.

"I've actually never been with a woman before." A flush of color crossed his cheeks. "It's always just been the guys. That was always enough. I mean, I was attracted to women, but you've seen the guys, I didn't need anything more. Until you."

Everywhere along my skin turned pink. "Jasper." These guys were going to kill me with their sweetness. How could I ever have gotten so lucky? Taking that step toward him that he put between us, I pressed against him. "I'm yours, just as much as the others."

In a second, I was on my back on the soft grass looking up at Jasper, who caged me between his arms. I touched his cheeks, tracing the lines of his face for several moments. His eyes gentled and he kissed the palm of my right hand.

I met him halfway as we kissed. My hands roamed his chest, running them down his pecs. His lips moved slowly along my jaw as I gasped for air.

"Spread your legs," Jasper whispered into my ear, his tongue flicking out along the tender flesh.

I shook as I did as he said. My body cradled his as his cock pressed against my pussy. I was already wet from just being close to him. His hips moved, but he didn't enter me.

No, he decided to torture me instead.

His cock slid along my pussy lips, the tip hitting my clit in a shocking jolt. My own hips bucked off the ground.

"Ah!" My hands instinctively clutched his shoulders as he did it again. And again. "Oh GOD!" His cock rubbing against my clit was a new sensation and I couldn't think. "Jasper!"

"Becs," Jasper's voice was breathless as his thrusts against my clit picked up. "Mark me at the same time." His lips pressed against the right side of my neck, just under my ear. "I'm going to mark your ear. Mark mine as well."

"Oka—! Oh fuck!" My nails dug into his back as his cock finally slid into my pussy smoothly. My legs wrapped around his waist as he leaned further on top of me, picking up speed. It took me a little bit to remember what he wanted me to do. "Jasper."

I pressed my lips to his left ear. He copied my movements on my right side. With each thrust, my legs tightened around his waist.

"Now!" His teeth bit into my earlobe as I did the same on his. My orgasm shook me as his blood splashed across my tongue. He slammed into my pussy roughly twice more as his own release rocked through him. I sucked on his ear after releasing it from my teeth for a second.

"Holy crap," Jasper laughed as he held himself above me on his elbows. He pressed our foreheads together.

"Holy crap is right." I touched my right ear, feeling a small hole. "You literally pierced my ear." I giggled. "We're matching."

He turned his head so I could see my mark on his. He had a slightly smaller hole but he looked so proud. "We are. No one can doubt what you mean to me now."

We kissed again.

Becca

As I stood under the spray from the shower head, my mind wandered. When we got back to the house, everyone had bedded down for the night because we'd ended up romping around the woods for several hours. I'd gone to sleep with Jasper.

The next few days were a blur. Wake up early, go out with Wyn and shift. I was having a hard time shifting back until I relaxed enough. Playing with Wyn, or the others, helped to get me out of my head enough that I could change back.

When I was in an animal form, I was free. My senses expanded and it made me feel like I could take on the world. Then the time came to go back to my human form and I was blocked. None of the guys seemed worried. They had faith I'd get it.

The water started to turn cooler. Rinsing my hair quickly, I hopped out of the shower after turning it off. The guys were all downstairs. I couldn't hear what they were talking about because it was muffled, but I could tell that they were all down there.

My phone went off as I finished pulling on my underwear.

"Hey, Gary." I held the phone to my shoulder with my cheek as I attempted to hop into jeans.

"Hey, kid." Gary sounded tired. "How are you?"

"I'm good." I laid back on the bed, lifted my hips up as I tugged on the jeans. They were easier to get on in the changing room. "Adjusting okay, I guess."

I could hear tapping in the background, like he was hitting keys on a keyboard. "I told Wyn that I would wait until you were ready, but, Becca, I'm worried about you and your mother is about to burst a blood vessel." He cleared his throat. "Wyn told me that you two, er, are, well." The awkward statement he was trying to get at made me laugh as I finally managed to get the new jeans on.

"Mated. We're mated, Gary. The other guys are my mates, too." It was funny how I could say that naturally without even feeling weird about it now. "I have five mates." I said the last part just to mess with him.

"Dang it, Becca." He laughed even though he choked. "As long as you're safe, that's all that matters. We need to talk soon, though. I think it's time I talk to your mother about all of this, too. I plan to do that tonight. Things are getting more dangerous as the days go by. It would be good to get your mates on the same page as well." The tapping stopped. "Something happened last night in Little Rock, Arkansas."

A shiver of fear slid through me and it made my animal flash her teeth. "Something bad?"

Silence for several seconds. "Yeah. Something bad." He sighed. "I can either come up there, or we can talk at home, but it needs to be soon."

"I'll talk with the others. Can I call you in a few hours?" I waited for his agreement before hanging up. I held the phone between my hands as I looked down at it.

I'd known that summer was quickly coming to an end. Now, it would be over within the next day. I smiled as my animal rubbed against me. I let her see that I was happy, not upset, about becoming a shifter.

I took a deep breath. It was time to go back to the 'real' world. Putting my phone in my pocket, I headed downstairs to speak with the guys. It was time to help.

CHAPTER 26

Cody

Her laughter filled the room. I could just stay with my head in her lap all day. Her fingers played through my hair. I knew she was making small braids, but she was enjoying herself, I wasn't going to complain. When she'd come back with Jasper, she'd seemed so relaxed and content. That made me happy, pushing the demons away again.

"Wyn," Becca had told us about her phone call with Gary. "What are you going to do?"

"It'll depend on what we learn from Gary." Wyn had been distant, at least I thought so. We still didn't know enough about each other to really tell. "I wasn't told about anything major that was going to happen from my aunt. It's interesting."

The hybrid shifter was lounging on the other side of the large couch. He was splayed out, his one leg on the arm rest. The man was built like a truck. I wondered briefly how it would feel to have his thighs around my head as I sucked his cock. My wolf grumbled as we got hard.

Becca's fingers tightened in my hair as she tugged on it. "Naughty wolf. What are you thinking that's got you so excited?" Her lips twitched as I looked up at her.

I grinned at her crookedly. "I'm a guy." My eyebrows wiggled and she giggled again. "All I have to do is look at you and it stands straight up."

"Oh dear Lord." Jasper sat next to us with my feet in his lap. He shook his head as he groaned at my reply. "That was terrible, Cody. Terrible."

"If we're going home tomorrow, I'd like to go back to the cabin. I need to clean it up at least." Becca twirled a large section of my hair on her finger.

"We can stop at the cabin before leaving." Seth looked up from the book he'd been reading. "But you don't need to worry about cleaning anything up. We took care of that the first night while you rested."

She looked around at us in surprise. It was like she wasn't used to others helping her. "Why didn't you say something? I could have helped."

"To be fair, your arm was still pretty messed up and you were out of it. We couldn't really ask you to help, now could we?" Seth looked back down at his book. I could see him fighting a smile. "It's taken care of. The door was replaced and we cleaned up the inside. We spoke with Gary about it and he's set up his company to come out soon to fix everything." This time he looked up with a small, apologetic frown. "We weren't able to salvage anything."

Becca sighed as she continued to play with my hair. "I figured that would be the case. He really messed everything up, didn't he?"

"He didn't win. That's all that matters." Axel had been quiet for most of the morning. He was sitting next to Seth but he'd had his eyes closed for most of the time. He'd been disappearing the past few nights and hadn't told anyone where he'd been going or what he'd been doing. Seth didn't seem worried.

"You're right." Her thighs shifted under my head. "Regardless,

I don't want to be separated from any of you." She looked over at Wyn specifically.

He grinned at her and I could smell her arousal. Hell, she could probably smell mine too.

"I'm not going anywhere, kitten." Wyn stretched his arms above his head and his shirt lifted, giving us a very nice view. "You're stuck with me now, remember?"

"Since it's our last night here, why don't we have a barbeque like we did the first day we all met?" She looked at all of us with a hopeful expression. "I really loved that."

"That's a great idea!" Jasper pushed my legs off his lap. "We have all the things here, so we don't even need to worry about grocery shopping. Plus, it'll help lessen the amount of things we have to pack in the cars tomorrow!" He leaned over and kissed Becca loudly. "Brilliant."

"What about me?" Whining, I pushed at his knee with my foot. "I want a kiss, too!"

"You're so needy." Jasper grinned as Becca laughed at my antics. "Sit up so I can kiss you."

Becca's fingers slid through my hair as I did as Jasper said. His hand gripped my chin, tilting my head up. He pressed our lips together softly.

"You're such a brat." His words were soft, meant only for me.

"Yet, you love it." I wrapped my arms around his neck and kissed him but this time, I took control, my tongue pushing into his mouth roughly. He melted under my onslaught as I moved to pull him in my lap but we both froze when Seth cleared his throat.

"As much as we all enjoy watching you two go at it, if you start now, we'll never get the things done for the barbeque." His dry remark just made Wyn snicker.

"I don't know. It smells like our mate was getting into it." Wyn looked at Becca, whose face exploded in red as she flipped him off.

"Actually," Axel stood up. "While you guys get the barbeque all set up, I wanted to show something to Becca. Is that alright?" He took the few steps to stand in front of her and offered his hand. She didn't even hesitate as she slid hers into his hand. "We'll go in our shifted forms, I'll bring a pack that we can put our clothes in."

I glanced up at Jasper curiously, but he just shrugged. Axel usually wasn't very good with hiding surprises, so I really wanted to know what he was planning. Jasper sat in my lap, distracting me as they walked off talking softly.

"Let him have this time." Jasper rubbed our noses together. "We can get this ready without them."

I squeezed his hips.

Becca

"Axel?" He'd been a lot quieter than usual the past few days since our shopping trip into town. "Is everything okay?"

His fingers tightened around mine. "Everything is fine. There's just something I want to show you and going as bears will make it easier to get there." He'd grabbed an empty backpack as we left through the back door. "I'll let you shift first."

We stopped just inside the first line of trees. He handed me the backpack and turned his back to me, giving me privacy.

"Thank you." I touched his back tenderly before undressing and quickly stuffing the clothes into the bag.

With a quick thought, I shifted, barely noticing the pain any longer. My bear was close to my height, only a few inches shorter on all paws. I shook my fur out and pressed my cold nose to his hand.

He tapped my nose playfully before he started to remove his clothes. I turned around to give him privacy even as he chuckled softly at me. The rustle of his clothes being pushed into the pack followed by a groan of his bear let me know I could turn back around.

He was still bigger than me. His bear made a grunting noise at me as he picked up the bag in his mouth and started moving. He paused when I didn't immediately follow.

I jumped on my front paws playfully.

I love how fuzzy you are!

He snorted before starting to move forward again, this time I was right behind.

I'm glad you like my bear. Come on, slowpoke. His happy voice warmed me. *It's just a few miles.*

It was a beautiful day. The sun filtered through the branches as we moved quietly through the woods. Thirty minutes later, I started to hear a small stream of water. We came into a clearing that I knew instantly.

Axel, what are we doing here? I stepped around him and stopped.

The last time I'd been here, everything had been destroyed from the fight between Axel and the rogue shifter. The little playhouse made out of rocks had been knocked around and the furniture just gone.

But as I stood in the sun looking around the small clearing, I shifted back without thought.

Someone had done their best to recreate the scene. New rocks decorated the area with some older I recognized that had splashes of paint on them.

"Axel?" My feet moved on their own as I stepped over the

little border into the playhouse section. "How?" I could feel tears falling on my cheeks.

His heat seared my backside as he came to stand behind me. His hands settled on my shoulders gently.

"I know it's not quite the same, but I wanted to at least try to get it back to as close as possible. It's off my memory, so if we need to move anything around, we can." His lips pressed to the side of my forehead. "I know I probably should have asked, but I wanted to try to do something for you."

Turning around, I wrapped my arms around his middle and buried my face in his chest as I cried. At least with us being naked, I didn't get his shirt wet. His arms pulled me tight against him and he ran his hand down my back in a soothing motion.

"Becca?" He kissed my cheek softly.

"Thank you." Nothing else seemed to even come close to what I could say to him. He knew how much this place meant to me. "It's silly, I know, but thank you. This place, it's not just rocks to me."

"I know." He cleared his throat. "Maybe we should get clothes on, yeah?" His cheeks turned red. "It's a serious situation and I don't want to ruin it."

My brows furrowed for a second as I tried to figure out what he was talking about. That's when I felt him hardening against my stomach. That would explain it.

I started to giggle. I couldn't help it.

"Don't laugh!" Axel shook his head at me as he stepped back. "It's like Cody said. We're guys. You're our mate. I'm surprised I don't have a permanent case of blue balls."

That just made me start laughing even harder. Axel rubbed the back of his head as he joined me after a little while. He bent to the side and picked up the bag with our clothes in it.

"Here." He held it out to me.

Shaking my head, I took the bag, but I put it to the side. I tilted my chin up at him. "Kiss me."

His chestnut eyes darkened as he took in my body slowly. Goosebumps peppered my skin at his look. He took a step closer to me.

"Are you sure? Here?" He was still trying to be a gentleman when I wanted the bear.

"What's a few scrapes and dirt?" I took the last step to bring our bodies together and my hand ran up the middle of his chest. His hair was soft and only a little coarse against my hand.

"Becca." He choked on my name before claiming my lips as his. His tongue took control as one of his hands moved to grip my back and the other held the back of my neck.

Both of my hands moved along his chest as his tongue sucked my soul out of my body. I was shaking after a few minutes, he had to let me up for air.

"I'm going to fuck you now, cub." His hand moved to grip the back of my hair. "I've held back for this long. I kept these feelings hidden thanks to Felicity." He kissed me roughly.

"Talk, talk, talk." I grinned up at him. "That's all you guys do."

He chuckled as his hand tightened in my hair. "Brat."

Then I was in his arms, his hands holding onto my ass as my legs wrapped around his waist. Our faces were level and I took advantage of it, peppering his face in small kisses as he moved, his cock brushing against my pussy with each step, sending a thrill through me.

He bent down, making me bow backward and squeak briefly. He took something out of the bag as he righted himself and kept walking until we were at the base of a large tree.

"Stay still." Before I could ask him what he was doing, his arms left me, leaving me clinging to him with my legs and my arms that hurriedly wrapped around the back of his neck.

"Axel!"

He just laughed as the thing he'd grabbed from the pack came into my view. He'd grabbed a blanket. He laid it on the ground, kicking a few rocks out of the way and my heart melted.

Even though we were both aching for each other, he still took the time to make sure that we'd be as comfortable as possible. He knelt on the blanket and my legs slid from his waist as he lowered me onto the blanket.

"Axel." I touched his cheek.

He kissed my palm, moving his lips from my hand to my inner wrist, biting gently, not breaking the skin. "I want to place my mark here." He met my eyes.

I nodded and that's all he needed. His teeth sunk into my right inner wrist. The pain was fleeting but it made me jerk, even as the pleasure flooded my body. His tongue swiped at the blood that pooled at the mark for a few seconds. He didn't look away from my eyes and I swear I was ready to cum at just that.

Then he moved so that he caged me within his arms. He leaned over me, his hands on either side of my face as he looked down at my body.

"You're mine now." His declaration held a hidden meaning and I smiled.

"I'm yours." I touched the side of his neck. "Now, take me."

He didn't need any more prompting than that. My gasp came out in a rush as his cock pushed inside of me. I winced a little, but all I had to do was spread my legs a little wider to help. When he was inside of me all the way, we looked at each other for a few seconds.

There was no going back. That was never even an option. Felicity would never touch him again. He was mine.

He moved gently at first, but that didn't last long. Every thrust became rougher, the sound of our panting and skin slapping together the only thing in the clearing.

Pleasure built inside of me as I arched my back, needing more. So much more.

When his hands slid under my ass, changing up the position of how his cock hit inside of me, I cried out as my orgasm rocked through me mercilessly.

My canines slid out at the tail end of it and I bit into his right bicep, marking him as my mate forever.

Sensations exploded around us. My body heated as I felt some kind of power rush through it. I screamed, muffling it against his skin as I came again as this feeling rolled through me.

Axel gave a shout as he came, his hips jerked, thrusting into me roughly one last time. He shuddered as he gasped for air.

Our eyes were wild as we rode whatever high this was together.

Seth

"Where do you think they went?" Cody set the pack of sodas from the fridge onto the table we brought outside.

I pressed the pilot light on the grill. "Axel didn't say, but he's been working on something for the past few days. He'd let us know if it was something to be concerned about."

Cody pressed into my side and I wrapped my arm around his shoulders. He'd been having a hard time since Becca changed. He didn't say anything, but I knew how his mind worked. He thought it was somehow his fault. Like he'd thought it was his fault his family was massacred. Mating with Becca seemed to have settled him a little.

"Now that we have Becca, we're going to be okay, right?" He looked up at me with the biggest eyes that always melted my insides. He knew it too.

I moved my hand from his shoulder to the middle of his back. "Everything will be alright, Cody. This family won't be easily defeated."

"Hey, help me bring out the steaks and burgers, slackers." Wyn walked out the back door with his arms loaded down with plates of food to be cooked.

We'd settled our aggression with each other with our fight. There was still trust that needed to be built, my tiger was stubborn about it, but Becca did and that was enough for all of us. He was the oldest, he was close to thirty. I couldn't tell yet if he and his animal would mate with everyone or just Becca. Either way, he was pack now.

"Nah," Cody grinned wickedly. "We like watching you lift heavy things." He ran his eyes down Wyn's body before looking up suggestively, biting his lip in exaggeration.

I had to bite back a laugh. The wolf was not subtle about his attraction.

Wyn shook his head at us as he placed the food onto the table next to the grill. "You're such a flirt. I better keep my eye on you."

When he winked at Cody, I had to hold him up with my arm because Cody got weak kneed. I couldn't stop it. I started laughing.

"And now you've made it nearly impossible to get rid of him." I ruffled Cody's hair as he straightened.

"Who would want to? He's adorable. What a cute pup." Wyn stepped closer, effectively boxing Cody between the two of us. He reached out to tip Cody's face up. "Are you going to behave while we make dinner for everyone?"

Knowing Cody, I held my hands on his hips to make sure he didn't just collapse. He enjoyed being dominated and Wyn oozed dominance. Cody pressed his ass backward against me, stirring my cock.

"Yes, sir," Cody barely managed to reply. His body had gone limp against mine at Wyn's touch.

The man was sneaky. He grinned down at Cody, bopped him on the nose, and stepped back.

"Great! Let's get cooking, guys!" He went back inside to grab more things.

Cody slid into the seat nearest to where we were standing. "Holy crap." He waved his hand in his face. "That wasn't fair! At all!"

"Well, he certainly has your number." I turned back to the grill to check the temperature, but also to stop from laughing at Cody. "This is going to be so much fun."

"Seth!" Now Cody whined. My cheeks started to hurt with how wide my smile was as I grabbed a plate of raw steaks.

"Sorry, Cody," I was laughing as Jasper came outside with Wyn. "No sympathy from me." Especially if that had been a glimpse into what the future held with Wyn.

"What are you guys teasing him about this—!" Jasper began asking a question when an electric shock went through our connections, nearly bringing me to my knees.

Cody jerked in his chair as he clutched the edges of the table. Jasper would have fallen if Wyn hadn't grabbed onto him to stop him. Wyn stumbled as the shock rocked through all of us.

Wave after wave of overwhelming power and pleasure pulsed through me. My mark from Becca on my inner thigh throbbed. I forced myself to stay still as I could feel my magic strength building. It was like I'd inserted one of my claws into an electric socket and the currents were wracking my body.

"What is this?" Wyn's teeth were clenched as his body visibly shook.

A moan fell from me as a surge of pleasure followed the boost in power in my veins. The scent of Becca surrounded us, her lust, her feelings for each of us, and her very essence. A connection formed between all of us, like an invisible string that couldn't be seen, but felt, and snapped into being.

All of us gasped for air. It felt like my blood was on fire. I pushed the curls out of my face.

"Holy shit." I took in the others. They all looked like they'd run a marathon and not done well in it. "This had something to do with Becca." I gave a short laugh as I sat down next to Cody, grabbing a soda and chugging it after opening it. "Fuck. That was a rush."

Cody placed his forehead on the table. He yawned as he turned his face to look up at me. "No kidding." He looked utterly used and spent.

Jasper settled himself into one of the chaise lounges with Wyn next to him. They both were sweating a little.

"I think it probably has to do with her mating with all of us. She must have marked Axel. Now all of our animals are connected. Could her animal have given us such a magical boost?" Jasper was looking at his hands. "I feel like my body is floating. My fox is acting like it's high." He looked upward with his eyes half lidded.

"Let's just take a little bit to get our heads back on." Wyn rubbed his chin. He looked like he was fighting a yawn. "Damn. That wasn't as good as sex, but it came close."

Cody gave a strangled laugh. "Close? I need to change my pants."

CHAPTER 27

Becca

"**B**ecca!" Mom burst out of the house as soon as the SUV was put in park. She ignored Wyn, who was helping me out of the vehicle, pushing him aside to grab me in a tight hug. "You are not allowed to NOT call me for days at a time again!"

I barely felt the crushing hug that she held me in. It was nothing compared to the hugs from the guys that I'd gotten used to. I hugged her back, though, and was careful to make sure I didn't squeeze too hard.

"I'm sorry, Mom. It wasn't something I could control." I had to fight to keep my eyes open.

After getting back to the house last night, Seth had told me what had happened to all of them when I'd marked Axel. On the surface, it didn't seem like anything had changed, but under our skins, something lurked. My animal seemed to enjoy whatever it was.

Seth and Jasper agreed that whatever had happened, it had made all of us stronger. It was like we were all on drugs last night with how good it had felt.

The barbeque had been wonderful. We'd managed to finish

everything that was cooked, lessening the amount that had to be piled into the vehicles this morning.

"If you were still a child, I'd ground your ass for life." My mom continued her small rant as she pulled away from our hug and looked me over. "You look great though. Happy." That's when she noticed all of my guys as they stepped out of the cars. "So, these are your friends?" The way she said friends left little to the imagination. Seemed like Gary had told her about what happened.

Jasper stepped up next to us, smiling. "Hello, I'm Jasper." He took my moms hand. "It's really great to meet you. Becca told us all about you."

My mom looked at him suspiciously, but I could tell she liked him. "I'm Ginny. It's nice to meet you, all of you. Come inside. You can put your things in the garage for now, that way you don't have to worry about it in the car." She turned to lead the rest of us through the garage to inside. "Gary and the twins are playing some kind of video game."

"Go with your mom, baby." Seth pressed a kiss to my head. "We'll take care of the things from the car and catch up. Go say hi to your family."

I gave him a grateful smile as I followed Mom through the door. It had only been a few months since I was here last, but it felt like years. Things were in the same place, but everything was different.

We found Gary in the family room with the twins. They were playing some game, yelling at each other. Milly looked to be winning.

"You cut your hair!" My outburst distracted all of them.

"Becca!" Milly's controller fell to the ground as she jumped up. "You're home!" She rushed to hug me, with Steve right behind her. My hands were full of the twins as Mom turned off the TV.

"Welcome home." Gary walked over to us.

My stepfather was on the wiry side. His glasses always looked like they were lopsided. His smile hardly ever left his face.

"Her friends are coming inside in just a second." Mom wrapped an arm around Gary's waist. "They're all very good looking."

"Please, tell me you didn't flirt with them." Gary looked down at Mom as he teased her.

"They would be so lucky!" Mom gave Gary a mock glare before their attention went back to us.

"Becca, Dad told us what happened! Is it true?" Steve moved around me. "I don't see anything different."

I glanced warily at Mom and Gary. He nodded.

"It's true." I squatted in front of the twins. "I'm a shifter."

Mom gave a small gasp, but otherwise stayed quiet as the twins kept firing off questions.

"Dad said that you have five mates." Milly placed her hands on her hips. "You can't have five mates without our approval." She lifted her chin up as I fought back a laugh. "We don't even know if they're good enough for our sister."

"I want to see you shift," Steve interrupted his sister. He tugged on my hair. "Will you show us?"

"Kids," Mom stepped forward. "Give your sister a chance to breathe. She just got home. Why don't you go get some sodas for everyone? Give us a few minutes?"

It actually wasn't a suggestion and they knew my mom well enough by now, so they went without complaining. I straightened and looked between my parents. There was some strain, even if Mom tried to hide it.

"You can't really be mad at Gary for this, Mom." I held out my hands as she started to say something. "He didn't know that the rogue would be there. If it wasn't for the way he set up the cabin, I'd probably be dead. Plus, it's not like he really hid everything. We did know he believed in this stuff."

The safe room in the bathroom saved me. I owed it to my stepdad to at least try to save him a little of Mom's wrath.

Mom sighed as she stepped away from Gary. She started to pace in the room. "Not the point, Rebecca."

Oh. Full name. She was really pissed. Uh oh.

"The point is that you were hurt and I didn't know of it until just yesterday?" Her voice went up an octave. "That's unacceptable!" I winced a little as she got louder.

"Hunny." Gary stepped in front of her to stop her pacing. "She's okay now. Better. Stronger than she was. Look at her." He turned her to look at me. "What would she normally be doing at this point when you're angry at anyone?"

He was right. Usually by now, I'd have a full blown anxiety attack. I didn't do well with anger, or at least, I didn't used to. I was kind of proud of myself. I was calm and had no hints of anxiety.

Mom narrowed her eyes on me. Whatever she saw gave her pause. She stepped away from Gary to move in front of me. She hugged me again. I could feel a small tremor.

"I was just so scared to hear what happened to you. I didn't believe it at first."

I hugged her back. "I'm okay. I promise, Mom. I've actually never been happier. You're going to love the guys."

Gary came over to us. "I'm going to go introduce myself to your men and catch up with Wyn. Why don't we give you two a little bit more time?" He waited until Mom looked at him with a nod.

When he left the room, Mom pulled away from the hug and moved to sit on the couch, patting the seat next to her.

"Tell me everything. Don't hold back." She straightened her spine as she gestured at me.

The story took a while. I hadn't realized how much had really happened until it spilled from my lips. Mom only interrupted to ask a few questions. When I told her about the girl at the pizza place, her lips thinned and I knew that someone was going to get an angry phone call. She laughed at some of Cody's antics. When I told her about Felicity, she held my hand. We both cried as I got to the part where I realized that I could see the stars. That took a few minutes to get through.

"And now we're all mated. Something happened when I marked Axel. It was just this big rush of euphoria. It was intense, but now, it feels like we're all tied together." I looked down at my free hand. "Even now, I feel them." I placed the hand over my heart. "Are you mad, Mom?"

She shifted, squeezing my hand. "No. I was more frustrated with Gary than anything. I was worried how you'd handle this, but it looks like I don't have anything to worry about." She tilted her head slightly to the right. "Your dad would be proud of you."

Tears pricked at my eyes again. "I thought he'd find this whole thing pretty cool."

She laughed. "Oh, your father would be the first in line to pull your tail, that's for sure."

There was a crash from the kitchen that had us both jumping out of the couch. A shout from Milly about Steve being a clutz made me sigh in relief. Mom touched my arm.

"Let me go meet your boys for real this time." She squeezed my bicep and we went down the hallway to where everyone else had gathered in the kitchen and dining area.

Seth, Wyn, and Axel were leaning against the far wall. Jasper was kneeling next to Steve, helping him wipe up what looked like a spilled glass of milk. Cody was next to Milly. They were whispering something to each other. I'd have to make sure they didn't try any pranks later. Gary was pulling some food out of the fridge.

"So," Mom crossed her arms as she looked at my mates.

"You're my daughters, er, mates?" She stumbled a little over the word. "How do I know you're worthy to be hers?"

"Mom!" My mouth dropped. "You can't ask that!"

Seth and Wyn laughed while Axel offered a smile. Jasper and Cody were quiet, looking at my mother in horror.

Mom placed her hands on her hips, very similar to the way Milly had earlier. "I can. It's my job as your mother. You!" She pointed at Seth, whose smile turned a little predatorial. "Answer the question."

Seth stepped forward, his hands going into his pockets. "We aren't."

What? Now it was my turn to look on in horror. My mom began to tap her left foot as she waited for him to continue.

"Your daughter is a brilliant, talented, and breathtakingly beautiful woman. She has a bright future ahead of her, and we're going to support her the best way we can. There's no one who would be worthy of her." Seth looked at me for a few seconds while he said that. "It won't stop us from protecting her. She's ours now and we won't let her go."

Mom's brow went up. "Well." She looked at Gary, who grinned. "I guess you were right, hunny." She glanced back at Seth. "Alright. Now, let's get those snacks and get comfortable. I have a feeling this is going to be a very long night." She moved to help Gary.

I went over to Seth. "You didn't have to answer her, you know that, right?"

His eyes softened, his hair catching the light. "Yes, I did." He brushed his fingertips along my cheek. "You're everything to us." His lips caressed mine briefly. "We're not going anywhere. Even if your mother is scary." This, he whispered dramatically and loud enough for everyone to hear.

I giggled as the twins laughed as my mom scoffed.

Wyn

As Gary moved with his wife in the kitchen, I motioned to him that I was going to be on the phone and went out into the backyard. My animal was restless. We'd woken that morning to a text from Felicity that made us both wary.

They attacked the Fae's headquarters and lost. Now Dad wants to mobilize everyone for the retaliation that's going to be coming. He said they're going to put me in the first defense squad.

I hadn't responded. I had immediately called Gary before anyone else had woken. The resistance was aware of the attack and making plans.

"Is it finally war?" The sun hadn't even started to rise yet.

"I think it's close. Attacking the Fae was stupid. Suicidal at the current numbers that each group has. The Venandi's numbers have been drastically dropping the past few decades. Even your aunt had mentioned it when I worked for them, attacking the Fae was something they never planned to do until shifters were wiped out. Have you heard from them?" Gary had whispered this, as he had stayed in his room and hadn't wanted to wake Becca's mom up.

That was the troubling thing. Besides the annoying calls before I'd sent the head of the rogue to them, I hadn't heard shit. No demands to come back home. If they'd planned something so violent, they'd have called me.

Unless they suspected something. Shit. Had I fucked up somehow and hadn't realized? I'd woken Seth after the call and shared my concerns. We knew from Becca's conversation, and confirming it with Gary, that something had happened in Little Rock.

"Whatever is happening, our number one priority is our family." Seth hadn't said much after that.

As I looked at my phone, I cursed softly as I hit the call button. My cousin answered on the second ring.

"Wyn?" She sounded exhausted.

"Hey, cus, how's it shakin'?" I focused on the background noise on her end to make sure it was just her and no one else was in the room. There wasn't anyone with her that I could sense.

"You're so weird." I could hear a smile in her voice. "Why didn't you text me back?"

"Sorry, chickie. I don't have that great of service out here. What did your dad say?" I was hoping we had a little bit of time to prepare. Becca didn't even have any self-defense training, I hadn't had the chance to start it yet. "Did he say why they attacked them?"

"You know he wouldn't tell me that. I know there was a meeting, but only the higher ups were in it." There was the sound of rustling clothes. "There was a visitor two weeks ago. He wasn't from the states. When he left, Mom and Dad became really frantic, then this happened."

A visiting hunter from Europe perhaps? They were even more harsh on that side of the world against anything supernatural. It sounded like the only way I was going to find out the reason for attack on the Fae was to talk to my aunt. That would wait until after speaking with Gary and the rest of the group. They needed to learn what was going on.

"Alright. Whatever is happening, it's getting dangerous." I winced, knowing that I was going to be in such trouble when Becca learned what I was about to do. "I'll come get you. Think you can hold on for another forty-eight hours?"

Felicity's voice went even softer. She was only a few years younger than me, but her heart was so young. "I'll have to. Thanks, Wyn."

"Just stay under their radar. I'll be there as soon as I can." I hung up and rubbed the bridge of my nose. This was getting complicated and even more dangerous.

Becca

Getting snacks took longer than I thought it would. Mom went a little overboard with the food while Gary brought out water bottles and soda. The guys helped move everything into the family room and onto the coffee table. The twins were sent upstairs.

I settled on a large bean bag chair near the TV. Seth sat behind me, pulling me against his chest as the rest of the guys arranged themselves around us. Mom eyed us but she didn't say anything, only gestured to the food.

"Eat something." She picked up a bag of chips and tossed them to me. "I won't have anyone in my house hungry."

A rumble of amusement came from Seth's chest as he opened the bag of chips before handing them back to me. He took one and bit into it as Mom nodded satisfied.

"So." Jasper draped his right hand on his knee that he had bent, looking relaxed. "What happened that made you call us away from Tabernash?" His fingers tapped, betraying his nerves.

Gary had brought his laptop from his office. He turned the computer around to show an image of a burning building.

"This is Fair Rock. A local favorite. It also belongs to the Fae. The Venandi, in an unprecedented attack, attempted to destroy it. The building hides a doorway to Fairyland." He set the computer in front of him, pushing some of the snacks together for room. "Before we continue, boys, why don't you tell me what you know of the Fae?"

Wait. My mouth dropped open for a few seconds. Fae? Fairies?

The guys, except Wyn, looked at Seth. Wyn had a fierce glare on his face since he'd come back inside after a phone call he'd thought I hadn't noticed he'd gone outside for. I nudged his thigh with my foot. When he looked at me, his glare disappeared.

"You okay?" I mouthed the words to him. He nodded and squeezed my foot.

"The Fae are our brethren, of sorts." Seth tightened his arms around my waist. "When humans became aware of the Fae, they did what they always have. They tried to extinguish what they saw as different. Since it was different, it didn't deserve to live." He sighed. "The Fae have always had low numbers because half of them can't survive on this plane of existence because of the lack of magic in the air. Only the strong could handle it. For the most part, they tried to stay out of human and other supernaturals business. The Venandi made that impossible after a while."

I looked up at him. He'd looked off into the distance as he continued his story.

"Shifters are actually distant relatives of Fae. Our maker came from Fairyland thousands of years ago. When the Venandi began hunting, and winning, against the Fae, a dark prince gave them something that made hunting shifters much easier. What they gave them, we don't know, but they focused their attention on us, making an uneasy truce with the fairies. That was a few hundred years ago." Hate filed his voice. "Fae are no friends to shifters."

Cody shifted from where he was and leaned against my side. I could feel a little tremor move over him. I wrapped my arm around his middle, squeezing him.

"The Venandi have always kept tabs on the Fae. They want to destroy them just as much as the others. The reasoning that they haven't has been the truce our two species have had, but it was also because of what that dark prince did to ensure the peace. He sacrificed his power into a curse. If the truce was ever broken, the magic would ensure the destruction of the hunters. The details on how that would be done are unknown, but it seems like the higher ups just don't care or found a way around the curse." Gary leaned forward on the couch, his hands resting between his legs. "We need to find out what those details are."

"That's where I come in."

I looked over at Wyn, dreading what he was going to say next. He offered an apologetic smile.

"I've got to go back to headquarters and get the information. I also need to save Felicity. She's been put on the first defense team, she'll die in the first wave of attack." His look of unease made my stomach flip.

Felicity. He had to get Felicity. Did I want her to be saved after knowing that she had planned to kill Axel? That she'd lied to me?

Of course I wanted to save her. I just didn't know if I wanted to be friends, but I couldn't stop Wyn from saving his family. He obviously cared for her.

"You're not going alone." Cody glared at Wyn. "That's asking for trouble."

Wyn looked at Cody with a curious expression. "I can't bring another shifter with me. They'll kill any of you on sight. I'm the only one who can get in and out without suspicion."

"Your mate is right, Wyn." Gary brought everyone's attention back to him. "You can't go alone. It's just too dangerous. There are too many unknowns. I'll be going with you."

That set my mom off. She jerked out of her seat and turned to look at Gary. "Oh, no, you won't! Didn't you just tell me last night that you're not welcome there?!" Fire flared in her eyes and I settled against Seth. This was going to take a while.

Gary and Mom continued to argue for the next several

minutes as the rest of us took bites of food and sips of water or soda. Wyn kept looking down at his phone. I pushed his thigh again with my foot.

"What about me?"

Silence greeted my question as Mom whipped her head to look over at me in growing horror. Gary's brows furrowed but his thinking face popped on.

"No." Wyn didn't even hesitate. "No way."

"Who else can come with you? Do they know instantly if you're a shifter?" I ignored Seth's warning squeeze. "I don't have to go inside, but I can be close, in case you need help."

"If that's the argument," Jasper pulled out his phone. "Any one of us could do that."

I frowned at him. I didn't like that thought at all. Judging by his smirk, I think that was the point, that they felt the same way. I sighed, defeated.

"So, then, what do we do? Wyn isn't going on his own." I pointed at him. "And you knew that would be the response before you even said anything."

Wyn offered me an apologetic wince. "I know, but I can't just abandon Felicity. She's still not a full-fledged Venandi." He reached behind him and rubbed his neck. "I guess it wouldn't hurt to have backup nearby. If something does occur, I can get her out of there with force. I'd just rather not have that happen."

It had to be hard for Wyn. He'd been between the fighting groups for so long. I'd glimpsed his hardened expressions when he didn't think anyone was paying attention. He'd had so much responsibility thrust upon him and he was still so young.

"So, we'll all go with you." I glanced at the guys. "Yeah?"

"Now wait just a second." Mom was still standing with a glare on her face. "You all can't just go to this place! Even I know that's dangerous and stupid." My eyes widened as she turned her glare on me. "I didn't raise you to be stupid."

"Your mother has a point." Gary rubbed his temples. "I think we need to split up. Getting more information on what's happening is important and getting Wyn's cousin, but I need to meet with the leaders of the resistance. I think it's time we come out of the clockwork and present ourselves if the Fae engage. This could turn bloody very quickly and innocent humans and supernaturals will get caught in the middle."

"As much as I don't like it, it makes sense." Seth moved behind me. "We made a promise not to split up this family, but I don't want to leave Becca without protection if we split up."

I looked up at him in surprise. "Protection?"

His lips were pressed together. "If this is leading up to an all scale war with the Fae, it's going to get dangerous. What they lack in numbers, they more than make up for in power. There are some Fae that control the elements. Can you imagine what could happen if they let loose their power?"

"Gary, who is in the resistance?" Jasper stretched his arms above his head, cracking his neck. "You say you work from the shadows, you have to have some powerful allies of your own, right?"

"Yes, I'd like to know this as well." Seth leaned back, making me tip back a little. "We'd always heard rumors of you guys, but never knew there was actually a resistance until you confirmed it."

Gary looked around the room with a frown on his face. He took a minute to himself before he answered.

"I guess it's only fair since you're smack dab in the middle of all of this." He closed his laptop. "Alright. I'll tell you."

Cody moved so that he laid his head in my lap. I stroked his hair almost automatically now.

"Several years before I met Ginny, I had started to dislike all the Venandi stood for. It felt like mindless slaughter at points. My last straw was when a group was sent out to destroy a family of wolf shifters. They weren't part of a larger pack, more like the family you have now, just with kids."

Cody stiffened underneath my hand and Jasper clasped Cody's hand with his. Seth even let out a low growl from behind me.

Gary nodded at them, as if he understood. "When the order was given to kill the kids, I knew that we were in the wrong. It was a massacre thanks to a surprise attack with overwhelming numbers. I went in with the soldiers, even though I was a scientist. The family had been in the middle of dinner. It wasn't until we were clearing out the bodies that I noticed that they'd killed six shifters, but the place settings had seven plates." He looked at Cody, who began to shake. "A young boy was hiding in the front closet that I checked out. I left him there with a warning to not make a sound and I threw the extra plate in the trash without anyone noticing."

Cody's body curled. He wrapped his arms around his knees and buried his face in them. I moved forward to hug him, offering soft reassurances as our other mates surrounded us. Silent sobs with soft hiccups came from him. Seth moved me back after a few minutes and took Cody into his arms, sitting back so he could rock with him. Cody moved his face into the crook of his neck as Seth began to hum a soft tune that the other guys started to join in. Wyn came to my side and held my hand as we watched. Jasper rubbed Cody's back as Axel leaned over them engulfing both Seth and Cody in a large hug. I wasn't sure what I could do.

That had been Cody's family. Gary had been there. Grief shot through me. The horrors that Cody must have gone through.

"Becca?" Cody shifted from Seth's embrace, looking at me with haunted eyes. "Please?"

I was moving without thought as he held out his arms. He pulled me into him and his tears fell onto my chest as I stroked his hair.

"I love you, Cody. That will never change. We all love you.

We're going to protect you." My whispers in his ear were for only him, but I knew the others could hear it.

It took a little bit, but he relaxed and stopped crying with all of us around him.

This explained so much.

"After that night, I started secretly sabotaging little things. They were mostly just inconveniences to them, but if it helped save another life somehow, I was determined to do it." Gary continued after Cody uncurled from Seth's lap but still held onto me. "That's when I met Wyn and discovered we felt the same way."

Wyn nodded. "It wasn't long after that they started the experiments with shifters they captured. A few weeks before the experiment that would have me become a hybrid, we were approached by someone outside of the compound."

Gary ran his hands through his hair as he slumped forward. "He was with the resistance. I still have no idea how they figured out about what I'd been doing, but they knew. He was one of the leaders. The resistance consists of mostly humans, ex-Venandi's who were reported as killed in action, and some other species. This guy was a vampire. First one that I had met." He shook his head. "It's not a big group, but we've grown over the years."

Mom passed him a bottle of water, making him take a sip before he continued. He gave her a gentle smile.

"Anyway, we don't have a name for our group. It helps keep us anonymous. We have several leaders who give out instructions, including the vampire who recruited Wyn and me. When we heard of the attack on the Fae, the leaders called a meeting. They've reached out to the Fae. They're still discussing what we can do. I'm meant to be there, but I wanted to be here and speak with you all before I join them."

"Not to mention he needed to tell his wife about the secret he's been hiding for years," Mom interjected hotly. She was still angry at him. "Smart not to leave until you know that you're forgiven."

Gary looked ready to bolt. "You're absolutely right, dear. I needed to come clean with you before anything else."

I had to slap a hand over my mouth to stop the giggle that formed. It was a serious situation but I couldn't help it. It seemed I wasn't the only one. Cody started to laugh, it wasn't long before we all joined in. Even Gary and Mom.

"Okay," I got my laughter under control. "So what does this mean? We're splitting up? I don't like the idea." It made sense, but I still didn't like it.

"A few of us need to go with Wyn, even if it means we have to hide some distance away. The rest should be with Gary so we can meet with these resistance leaders and find out what they know and plan." Seth sighed. "I hate to say it, but Jasper, go with Gary. If this group is going to go up against the Venandi, you'll have the best chance of negotiating." He ran a hand down my back. "You'll take Cody with you and Becca. Axel and I will go with Wyn."

"What?" Cody shook his head. "We shouldn't separate." There was desperation in his tone.

I reached out to touch his cheek, about to say something when Seth did.

"It's not a good idea to have you anywhere near the Venandi, Cody. You'll go to protect Jasper and Becca. It's not a request, it's an order." His voice hardened and Cody just nodded in defeat.

"Alright, if that's decided, we, at least, have a plan for the next step." Gary stood, offering Mom his hand. "We're going to get some sleep. You're all welcome to stay in the guest room in the basement. We'll figure out more in the morning. I'll make a few calls. We leave bright and early."

Mom took Gary's hand. Before they left the room, she looked at me. "All I care about is that you're safe, hun. So these mates of yours better do their job or answer to me."

We waited until we could hear their bedroom door close. Jasper gave a wince.

"Your mom scares me."

"She scares me, too." I stood, bending backward a little to pop my back. "This is a lot to take in." I looked at my mates. "I was going to tell you guys earlier, but there hasn't been a good time, I guess now is. I want to help Wyn and Gary stop the Venandi. What they've done is atrocious and shouldn't be allowed any longer. I want to join the resistance." I hadn't said this in front of my mom. I knew she would have had a fit, possibly divorced Gary over it.

Well, maybe not that drastic.

Wyn snorted as Seth groaned into his hand. Axel chuckled and held out his hand to Seth.

"Pay up."

I looked at them confused. "What?"

Seth moved, pulling his wallet from his back pocket. He handed Axel a twenty dollar bill. "You won. You were right."

Axel continued to chuckle as he folded the money in half. "I bet Seth that you would want to join the group."

"So, you bet on me?" Feeling a little miffed, but amused, I decided to mess with them a little. "That's not cool."

"To be fair, you did act a little secretive with what you wanted when you could have just told us." Seth stood up, pulling Cody with him. "Why don't we all head down to the basement? Unless you want to stay in your room, Becca?" His lips twitched as he tried not to smile.

"Oh shush." I took Cody's hand. "We're going to have a cuddle pile."

There were still so many questions left.

CHAPTER 28
Becca

Having a cuddle pile was now one of my favorite things. We took a few hours to cuddle, talk about random things, and not focus on the bad things that were happening.

"I knew you guys had mentioned that there were other beings out there besides shifters, but vampires? Fae? What else is out there?" I laid on my stomach using my crossed arms as a pillow. "Are you going to tell me that ghosts are real?"

They just stared at me.

"You are. Ghosts are real?"

Jasper reached out and played with a lock of my hair, twirling it between his fingers. "Every legend has a hint of truth to it. There's a lot out there that humans just dismiss as myth. There's even dragons. Just not on this plane of existence." He laughed at my shocked face.

"Alright. So, a whole lot of shit is real. Got it." I closed my eyes. "I don't like the thought of being seperated from you guys, even if it is necessary. Who knows what's going to happen?"

"It's not going to be for long." Wyn pushed himself up onto his elbows as I opened my eyes. "I'm getting in, getting what information I can, grabbing my cousin, and we're getting out of there." He looked at Axel. "Are you guys going to have an issue with Felicity?"

That was a loaded question. Groaning, I rolled onto my back letting my arms flop out, bouncing off Cody and Seth's stomachs.

"I'm still angry with her." I offered Axel a comforting glance. "Minus the whole hunter thing, she was the best friend I've ever had."

Axel rubbed his jaw. "I don't want to talk to her, but I'm not going to do anything."

"Fair enough." Wyn reached over and ruffled my hair. "She loves you. You were pretty much all she talked about during school. That's why I felt like I knew you before even meeting."

I blushed as I pushed his hand from my hair. "Stop it."

Wyn grinned, making me suck in a breath. "Does hearing about how awesome you are embarrass you?"

"We are not going to have this conversation." I sat up, wiggling off the bed we were all crunched together on. "I want a promise from you guys." I looked over my shoulder at them. "Promise to always come back to me." Worry churned in my stomach, even my animal felt it.

Seth stood and cupped my face with his hands, his thumbs rubbed circles against my cheeks that made me purr. "Close your eyes."

I narrowed my eyes at him before doing as he said. "Why?"

"Take a breath. Do you feel the connection between all of us?"

His hands were warm as I focused on that power that hummed under my skin where each of them had left their mark. With a shock, I noticed something new.

It was like an unseen thread connected me to my mates. Feelings of love, warmth, and kindness flooded the threads.

"No matter where we are, our mate marks connect us." Seth's

soft voice brought my awareness back to the room. "Even if we're separated for a little while, we're tethered together."

His lips caressed mine as he continued to hold my face in his hands. My hands moved to clutch his shirt in my fists. His tongue invaded my mouth, making a soft whine escape from me. Having him touch me with such tenderness made me want to melt into a puddle. The kiss reminded me of the first we shared in front of the pizza place.

"Woman, you take the very air from my lungs." Seth pulled back slightly, his tiger shining through. "We will always come for you."

My knees pushed against each other as my lower body clenched in need. Oh, goddamn it.

"Now, now," Jasper interpreted us. "Do we really want to start an orgy in her parents' house?"

Cody cracked up as Seth groaned and stepped away from me.

"That was like having ice water dumped on me," Seth grunted as he sat back on the bed. "Wyn, when did you want to leave?"

"It's a drive, so first thing in the morning." Wyn held his arm out gesturing for me to climb into his lap. "So can we go back to cuddling?"

Becca

"Are we there yet?"

It was barely seven in the morning. We'd been up since five with the others. They'd left in the guys' Escalade before my group did. I already missed those three.

Gary grumbled under his breath about brats. "No, Becca.

We've still got a little more to go." As soon as we piled into the family car, Gary had turned to us and handed us cloth bags to put over our heads. "Sorry, kiddo. This is to protect the resistance and you."

That had been over an hour ago.

"It's hot under this thing." It's a good thing that I wasn't claustrophobic.

Cody wrapped his arm around my shoulder and squeezed as I leaned into him. Jasper and Cody had put me in the middle seat. Jasper touched my knee gently.

"Do you guys have any idea why Seth had Axel go with them to get Felicity?" On top of annoying my stepdad during the ride, there was really only one thing to do while we traveled and that was talk. "I know he won't do anything to her. I just figured it might have been less awkward without him."

"I'm sure Seth considered that, but I think it was a good idea. The heavy hitters are with Wyn, in case something happens. We'll see them in a few days." Jasper's voice was muffled by the hood. "Gary, what can you tell me about who we'll be talking with?

There was a bump and my body fell into Cody's lap more, the seat belt keeping me from just crawling into it.

"There are three leaders. An ex-Venandi who retired over twenty five years ago. He's a wily old coot, so keep yourself on your toes around him. The vampire, Lario, is originally from France, moved to the states during the Civil War. He built his clan in Louisiana before they were wiped out by a raid. It was dumb luck that he had traveled out of state for some other vampire business. The last is a necromancer. She's one of the oldest people that I've met. She's almost one hundred and forty-two." The car turned left.

"Is the necromancer human?" I had so much to learn. "She raises the dead?"

"Yes." Gary paused. "I mean, technically. Necromancers, along with witches, are humans with a strong magic bloodline."

Cody shifted under me, his hand moved down my back in a soft caress. "Necros raise the dead and command them, but they are also communicators for the dead."

"What does that mean?" The hood was starting to itch. My animal was getting annoyed. "Are we there yet?"

I could hear Cody snickering as Gary cursed.

"I'm not asking to be annoying, Gary. This thing is really itchy and my animal is getting annoyed." She was ready to rip this thing off our head.

"Actually, it's just a few more minutes." Gary sighed. "And to answer your question, necromancers can bring back a person's soul for a minute amount of time. Like a murder victim that can point out their killer."

"A vampire, ex-Venandi, and a necromancer are the leaders of your group." Jasper continued the conversation. "Who will be at this meeting? Have you never tried to recruit any shifters?"

There was a shuffling sound and suddenly, I had to blink as the hood was removed. Jasper's emerald eyes were the first thing that I focused on as he smiled at me softly.

"I figured we were close enough." He pushed back the hair from my face. "Right, Gary?" He looked to the front of the car.

I could see Gary roll his eyes good naturedly. "Shifters." He sighed. "Yes, we're just coming up on the town now."

I looked out the window and blinked. I recognized the road. "Limon? That's where you guys meet?" Mom had worked at the Flying J here for a while until Gary convinced her to work for him. "Why this little town? And why the secrecy? You know that I'm familiar with it."

With a population under two thousand, it was barely a blip on a map. Maybe that was the point.

"So many questions." We started to see buildings as we drove through the main street. "First, yours, Jasper. Lario agreed with Seth, that we need shifters help. Although, he had it a little off. We've tried to approach shifters in the past. I almost lost an arm once. It was mere luck that I figured out that they were a shifter, you lot have learned to hide very well in plain sight. It's just us, the leaders, and a few trusted others. Your safety was guaranteed before we left the house."

Our safety? Did that mean we could have been in trouble for coming with?

Gary turned right, pulling into the parking lot of a Holiday Inn. "Limon is the perfect place to meet every few weeks because it's inconspicuous. Enough traffic flows through here that there are multiple hotels that we can use without arousing suspicion, but it's small enough that most people won't think about looking here."

Gary put the car into park and turned it off. He turned in the seat to look at me. "Becca, these people are dangerous. I work with them, but do not trust them with your secret. Do not tell them what you are. Do you understand me?" He used his *Dad* voice. "They know about Wyn and they haven't used him as they'd like because he's still been part of the Venandi. Otherwise, they'd have forced him to do more dangerous acts than he does now."

Growls came from my two mates. Cody looked ready to kill someone.

"Hold off on that." Gary shook his head and turned, opening the door. "They hold their peoples' lives in their hands. Besides, if we actually do something about the hunters, I doubt we'll need to worry about it anymore." He stepped out of the car.

Jasper grabbed my hand. "Becca, please, do what he asked. Don't tell them what you are. It's doubtful they'll be able to tell, but if they ask, pick only one of your animals, alright?"

I nodded. I could see why Gary waited until the very last second to tell me about keeping my hybrid status under wraps.

Cody and Jasper looked ready to rip someone apart by their limbs.

"I'll keep mum about it, guys. Promise. It'll be okay. Let's get the information that we came for so that Seth and the others don't have to worry about us." I grabbed Cody's hand with my free one and pulled their hands to my chest, kissing the tops of them. "Everything will be alright because we're here together."

They both glanced at each other before laughing softly. Cody kissed me before Jasper did the same. My heart sped up. I was never going to get used to how much they affected me.

A knock on Jasper's window from Gary got us moving. Cody hopped out, going to the trunk and grabbing our overnight bags. We were staying the night in case the meeting went long.

There were only a few other cars in the parking lot as we followed Gary through the entrance of the hotel. My stomach made a soft growl, making me wince. Such bad timing.

Jasper

Thoughts swirled in my mind going a mile a minute. Gary had put his trust in the resistance, but he didn't want them to know about Becca. Could they be just as dangerous as the Venandi?

I needed to see for myself. The Fae weren't just going to sit back against a direct assault. That's why we were here. Our priority was to protect our family, but Seth was looking at the bigger picture. Becca was too.

I hid a smile when Becca's stomach growled as we walked into the hotel. She never failed to make a situation less intense, even if she didn't mean to.

"We'll eat the bagels your mom packed as soon as we get into our room, okay?" It was my turn to hold her around the waist as we stopped behind Gary as he checked us in early.

"We could have eaten in the car if we hadn't had to wear those hoods," Becca grumbled under her breath. "Don't think I'm not telling Mom!"

Gary's shoulders shook slightly as he continued to speak with the hotel employee as he fought back a laugh.

"I don't know." Cody leaned into Becca's other side. "It gave me ideas for later." His hand moved to her ass.

"If you pinch me, you'll sleep on the floor tonight, Cody." She narrowed her eyes at him. "I'm hungry." The warning was clear and the wolf grinned at the challenge.

"Alright. Behave." As much as I'd enjoy the verbal spat that would happen, we were here for a reason.

"Here's your room key." Gary finished at the front desk. "The meeting is in thirty minutes. Eat and relax for a little bit. Go to the meeting room marked on the brochure." He handed me the keys and paper. "I requested a room down the hall instead of next to you."

He looked at Becca with a soft smile. "Eat breakfast and prepare." He ruffled her hair. "I'll see you three in a little bit." He walked off down the hallway to the elevator.

"Alright, you two." Becca clapped her hands together. "Let's go eat."

She grabbed our bags before we could pick them up where we'd placed them.

"Lead on!" She laughed at Cody as he tried to take the bags and she wouldn't let go.

I walked to the elevator, pressed the button, and waited for them to follow. Plans already formed for how we would approach this meeting.

Even though Cody was a goofball, he'd be serious during this meeting because of its importance. He wouldn't allow any harm to befall our mate. Not again. We failed her once, we'd never fail her again.

The image of her still, cold, and dead body would be forever burned into my retinas. It haunted my nightmares.

As we got into the elevator, the two were still arguing about the bags when I took the bag from Becca without a word. Cody groaned as she laughed, threading her arm through my elbow.

"Here's the room key." I gestured to Cody with it. "Why don't you find our room and open it up for us?"

The elevator dinged, opening onto our floor. Cody rushed down the hall, looking at the room numbers until he got to the very end of the hall.

"Here! Only one neighbor. Score!" He went inside as we walked closer to it.

"Hey, you doing alright there?" Becca's soft voice reached my ears. "You're looking pretty serious."

I looked down at her, taking in her large eyes, her lips that were so addicting, and her beautiful hair. How could I have not known she was my mate the first time we met at that party? My fox had. "I'm just making plans on how to approach this meeting. It's frustrating that this happened right after you were turned, making this world even more dangerous to you, but if we can help stop the Venandi? We're game. No one will ever harm you again." Not while there was still breath in my body. My fox huffed in agreement. She was ours.

"Jasper." She stopped us, looking up at me with a soft gaze. "I can protect myself now. I'm not as helpless as I was during the attack. I'm going to help protect you and the others as much as you protect me."

I had to blink for a second. I hadn't given her enough credit. She'd grown so much over the past couple of weeks. I couldn't help the pride that swelled inside of my chest.

"You're right, love." I leaned forward to kiss her roughly. Her sigh of surrender turned me on even more. I'd just started to slip my tongue inside of her mouth when Cody interrupted us.

"As much fun as it is to watch you two make out in the middle of the hallway," he didn't disguise his laughter. "I don't think Becca is big into PDA. Plus, her stomach is probably going to make itself known soon again."

As if on cue, her stomach grumbled and she turned that delicious red color that matched her hair. My cock jerked. If she wasn't hungry, I'd take her right before the meeting to make sure she was covered in my scent.

"Why are you such a butthead?" She walked into the room with me right behind, closing the door.

The room had a single king size bed. I had to hand it to Gary, at least he didn't try to act like we weren't sleeping with his stepdaughter. I placed the bags on the desk near the window. Cody opened up the food container that her mother had given us as we'd left the house.

He handed Becca a foil wrapped bagel sandwich with an apple juice box. She tore into it without a second thought. We both watched, satisfied that she was eating before Cody handed me my own food.

We sat on the bed, quietly finishing the food that had been prepared with love from Ginny. I had to admit, even if it was a few hours, the container and foil kept it fresh and it was good. Not even soggy. I'd have to ask her what she did to make that happen.

"Alright." Cody threw his trash away after he finished. "What do you need us to do during the meeting, Jasper?" He got onto the middle of the bed, sitting cross legged.

"Don't say anything unless absolutely necessary. Gary gave that warning for a reason. We don't promise anything until we speak with Seth." I glanced at my phone. I'd sent a text off to him a few minutes ago. They wouldn't be in Texas for several more hours.

"Works for me." He stretched, smirking at both of us. "You both are pervs. Watching my shirt go up." Cody fanned his face with his hand, pitching his voice high. "You're just embarrassing little old me!"

I threw my head back in a laugh as Becca giggled. Sometimes the things that came out of this guy's mouth were baffling.

"If you promise to behave today, I'll let you do that thing you like." I took a sip from my drink watching as Cody's eyes instantly darkened as Becca looked between us in confusion.

"The thing?" Her nose scrunched as she tried to work out what I was talking about.

Cody tilted his head to the side as he crossed his arms. "I promise to behave and you better not back out of this!"

"What thing?!" Becca snapped at us, now growling that sent a pulse of pleasure through me.

"You'll just have to wait until after the meeting to see, won't you?" I leaned away as she pushed my arm. "Patience is a virtue."

"You did not just say that." Her lips moved in a pout that she didn't know happened when she got annoyed.

"Don't worry about it." Cody leaned forward, balancing on his knees, and kissed her.

He took charge, his hand holding the back of her head. I could see the movements of their tongues and it made me shift as my pants became uncomfortable. A knock on the door had all of us letting out a groan.

"Come on, kids. I've given you enough time to eat breakfast. The meeting is going to be starting here in just a few minutes." Gary's muffled voice reached us. "Let's go."

"Why am I always getting cock blocked with you guys?" Becca gave a loud huff of annoyance as she stood. "Let's get this over with."

I shared a look with Cody. Our mate was adorable.

"Remember your promise." I grabbed my phone and sent a text off to Seth. "I told the others that we'll call after the meeting."

Gary had changed clothes. He was wearing more formal slacks and a button down shirt. He'd even slicked back his hair. Becca stopped behind me.

"Should we have brought more formal clothes?" She kept her hand on the door.

"No. What you're wearing is fine. I'm just a little old school when it comes to these things." He pushed his glasses up his nose. "I was just told that one of the Fae has arrived to speak with us." He rubbed his left shoulder with his right hand. "Becca, please, be careful. Your mother will do unspeakable things, and not the good kind, to me if you get hurt."

Cody draped his arms over me and Becca. "Let's get this over with! We have stuff to do after!"

Gary didn't look impressed but he led us to the elevator. "From what I've been told, our visitor is a Fae who was at the bombing when it occurred." He pressed the ground floor button. "Lario wants to meet you, Jasper, before we go in."

"Is that wise?" I didn't care either way, but I would avoid insulting these people if I could.

"It will be fine. Lario is one that I trust unequivocally." Gary ran his hands down his shirt. "I've never met a Fae before, I'm not sure what to expect."

None of us had, but we knew the stories. Legends had truth.

"The Fae are ancient. Humans are mere babies compared to them. So are shifters. It was a dark Fae that created us. We were created to protect his court with his magic. We're supposedly immune to their powers of persuasion." I counted the points with my fingers. "You can thank them, but they will take it as an admission that they are owed a favor in the future. It's better to not risk it."

"So that means keep our mouth zipped." Becca brought her fingers to her lips. "Got it." She offered a big smile to all of us. "This is going to go fine. We're going to figure out how to work together, make a plan, get the guys back, and kick the Venandi's butts."

"Well, with that logic, it'll be easy sailing." My lips twitched. "Let's do this."

CHAPTER 29
Cody

I knew why Seth sent me with Becca. I thought I'd recognized Gary when we met him, I just couldn't place where. I'd tried to block everything out from that night, but hearing the story, I had relived the memories.

My pack had surrounded me, chasing away the demons. Becca's touch had grounded me. I'd made a promise to myself then that I would be stronger, that I'd protect my mates. The demons inside of me were never going away. The Venandi had assured that, but I would not let them take away my life again.

Seth sent me to guard Becca and Jasper. They were both strong, but I was stronger physically, even with how mentally damaged I was, and that's what made me dangerous. I would become rabid to protect my mates. He also didn't want me anywhere near the hunter's headquarters. My wolf might have snapped if I did. So, sending me to protect these two was the most logical choice.

Becca was hiding it, but she was excited to meet the different species. I had to hide my smile when she looked at me inquisitively. She was pretty much vibrating as we walked.

The meeting room that was reserved was in the middle of the

hotel on the first floor. My wolf's senses stood on end as we got closer. There were several nonhumans in the room. A handsome middle aged man stepped out of the room, closing the door behind him as he noticed us.

"Ah." He offered a nod to Gary. "There you are. I assume this is your daughter?"

Gary stopped us a few feet from the man. I tilted my nose slightly, taking a deep breath. The man didn't have a scent. I focused my hearing, looking for a heartbeat. Nothing. This must be the vampire.

"I am Lario." The man crossed his right arm across his chest and bowed before looking at Becca.

My wolf bared his teeth but kept silent as I stepped closer to Becca.

"Lario, this is Jasper." Gary gestured to Jasper and me. "And this is Cody. Two of my daughter's mates." He actually relaxed for the first time since entering the hotel. Interesting.

Jasper stepped forward and offered his hand to the vampire. "Lario, Gary said you wanted to speak with me."

My wolf lowered his lips, only slightly relaxing as Jasper brought the vampires attention to him and not on Becca.

"Yes." Lario clasped hands with Jasper. "If you'll follow me? Don't worry, we're not going to be out of your sight, wolf." He moved his head to look at me. "I mean your mates no harm." His eyes were black, which was interesting. I hadn't known that was a characteristic of a vampire. "Gary, if you'll head inside?" He waited until Gary squeezed Becca's shoulder and went inside the room, closing the door behind him.

Jasper gestured with his arm. "Lead on. I'll be right back." He offered Becca and I a comforting smile. They moved down the way we'd walked from, stopping about twenty feet away. I could easily hear the conversation, I'm sure the vampire was aware of that. I wondered why he bothered moving down the hallway when we could easily eavesdrop.

"The Fae, Tarragon, has informed us that they've decided on a course of action against the Venandi. He seems particularly interested in speaking with you and your mates that have come." Lario glanced back over at us. "I'm not sure what they have planned, but I get a feeling that they want to use the shifters in their attack. I thought to forewarn you ahead of time."

"That makes sense and doesn't surprise me." Jasper ran his hand through his hair with an annoyed sigh. "Shifters were originally created to guard our creator. They may want to make us be cannon fodder."

Becca's sudden snarl echoed through the hall. I reached out to hold her hand, threading our fingers together. It did what I wanted. It distracted her enough that she quieted herself.

"That was a long time ago. Shifters are not some puppets to be used." I brought her hand to my lips and pressed a soft kiss to her inner wrist. "The vampire is just giving us a heads up before we go back in."

"Just so," Lario spoke from beside me and I fought myself not to jump in the air.

I'd been so distracted with Becca that I'd forgotten to pay attention to where Jasper and Lario were. Jasper hid a snicker behind a cough.

"Let's go in." The vampire held open the door. "You're prepared. Let's get this meeting on the roll." He bowed his head to Becca as we walked by him.

I didn't think that was how that saying went, but I wasn't going to say anything. My shoulders tensed as he closed the door, ending up behind me, but he moved swiftly across the room to where a large table sat with many people sitting around it. He stopped next to an older man and a woman who looked like she'd stepped off a Vogue magazine cover. Gary was sitting next to the older man. A lone man whose aura pushed against my senses, sat at the end of the table alone. He was breathtakingly beautiful. Had to be the Fae. There was an aura of menacing power that he suppressed but I could easily see it.

I'd have to talk to Jasper about this. It might be something shifter related being able to see that kind of power when it didn't seem to bother anyone in the room.

"Please, have a seat." Lario gestured to three chairs that were across from the other people at the table.

I waited until Becca sat in the middle seat. Jasper and I sat on either side of her. My eyes roamed over the people. Most of them were humans. There was a witch next to the necromancer, the Vogue woman. There was the Fae and there was another vampire somewhere amongst the others.

"Everyone, this is Jasper, Cody, and Becca." Lario looked around the table. "They are under my protection while here. Please, be respectful." When he said this, he looked at the Fae.

"I assume you've been caught up?" The man next to Gary spoke to us. He had a large scar from the top of his forehead that slashed across where his right eye used to be and down to his cheek. "I am Abram. I'm ex-Venandi and one of the leaders of this group."

The beautiful woman shifted in her seat. "I'm Volinda. I'm also one of the leaders and a necromancer. I'm sure Gary has told you about us." Her fingers waved in the air. "We're all here to discuss what we should do in regards to the Venandi's attack on the Fae and their violation against their treaty." She looked at the Fae. "This is Tarragon."

The Fae moved his head slightly in a nod. "Shifters. It's been some time since I've seen one of you. You've learned to blend in with the humans very well."

"It is necessary to save our lives from the hunters." Jasper's tone was cool and detached. That was kind of hot, not going to lie.

Becca clutched my knee under the table. It looked like she'd also done the same with Jasper.

"Tarragon has already advised us that the leaders of his people here have determined that the Venandi will be destroyed," Volinda spoke and I noticed it looked like she held her nose up.

"The curse that was placed on the agreement should it be broken has been activated. We've decided to use the magic against all that call themselves Venandi. I will be the chosen vessel to carry the curse and it will strike them within the next week. It will weaken their forces significantly," Tarragon spoke quietly. He hadn't stopped staring at us since we came inside the room. "We are here to propose a temporary alliance. We are looking for the resistance to assist us with taking them out after we've released the curse magic."

"You don't want to risk your own people, even though most of you could probably wave your hand and have Texas under the ocean in minutes. Including yourself." Jasper glanced around the table. "I'm sure I'm not the only one who wants to know why."

The Fae flashed a grin. His teeth were sharp. No one could mistake him for a human with those nasty buggers.

"Smart, one of the first astute observations." He moved his left shoulder in a shrug. "We do not wish to punish the humans in the area for the stupid actions of this group."

Even I knew that was a load of bullshit.

"I'm just going to put this out there." Jasper looked straight at Tarragon. "We will not let you try to use shifters as cannon fodder. You're going to have to work with the resistance on equal footing and come to an agreement before any shifters would begin to consider helping."

That pissed off the male. His aura whipped out in anger, causing the lights behind him to dim.

Becca stiffened next to me and I placed a hand on her back. She could see it as well.

"Come now. You knew this when we spoke before the shifters got here, Tarragon." Lario brought everyone's attention to him by placing his feet on the table, crossing one leg over the other. "Shifters are not slaves anymore. Not to mention, they have long memories. They remember what the Fae did by abandoning them to the Venandi."

The energy around Tarragon dissipated just as suddenly as it appeared. The Fae threw his head back and laughed. It hurt my ears.

"It was worth a shot." He shrugged his one shoulder again. "Alright. We aren't prepared to garner the attention of the human government just now. That means staying in the shadows. What does the resistance ask for?"

Jasper placed his hands in front of him on the table, his fingers on his left hand tapping on the desk. I could tell that he was annoyed.

Gary had been quiet, he was watching the exchanges with a calculating look on his face. Something was going on that I didn't understand.

Abram flipped open a binder that was in front of him. "We're willing to help, but we want to retain the building and all the research materials inside. We also won't allow children to be killed."

"We're not monsters." Tarragon grinned, his teeth showing, which I was starting to realize was a sign of aggression. "All we care about is wiping out their numbers."

Right. Super convincing.

"What will your people be doing while we breach their defenses?" Abram picked up a pen that had been next to the binder.

"I have volunteered to be the one there to release the curse's backlash upon them." Tarragon made an annoyed noise. "We would prefer to leave the actual killing to you."

"That's a load of bullshit!" Becca jolted from her seat next to me and slapped the table with her hands. "Even I can tell you're holding back a shit ton of information!"

I pulled her back down by the back of her seat hurriedly. Shit.

Tarragon turned his full focus on her, his eyes narrowing as he looked her over slowly. Something moved behind his constricted pupils.

Silence filled the room, the only sound was the soft movements in the air from the fan above us.

"Finally. Someone who isn't afraid to be blunt." The menacing aura wrapped around the Fae like dark tentacles. "Of course my species has an agenda. It doesn't have anything to do with the resistance. We're offering to let you take care of a mutual enemy, ending years of death caused by these humans." He looked around the table, pausing on the three leaders before looking back to Becca, who dug her nails into my leg. "If you don't agree, we will slaughter everyone in that compound and burn it to the ground." Finality rang in his voice. Guess he was done talking.

Take it or leave it, huh?

"They took something from you." Lario hadn't moved, much less blinked, while the conversation continued. "That's the true objective."

The only reaction from Tarragon was a slight twitch in his right eye.

"The visitor that met with the Venandi right before they attacked your people, was another Fae." Lario looked at his nails, spreading his fingers as his eyes moved over the tips of his nails. "To be honest, we don't care if this is because of in-house fighting. We will take this opportunity to take out the Venandi headquarters that you've presented to us, but we won't be forcing anyone to assist this if they are not willing." He looked up to meet Tarragon's gaze. "We obviously can't trust each other."

"Trust can be earned." Abram closed his binder. "Give us the day and time and we will be there. We have agents inside right now that we are coordinating with." He stood and several others around the table followed suit. "Lario, I'll leave the details to you." He left the room with five other people following him.

Volinda was the next to stand. She looked at us before turning on her heel and walked out. Half of the people followed.

Lario didn't move from his chair as Gary moved to sit at his side.

"Just like that?" Becca looked at Gary. She was shaking where I touched her, but it wasn't in fear. My mate was holding back from going after Tarragon. She'd grown so much in the past few weeks.

"Shhh, love. Trust me?" Jasper whispered to her so softly, even with my advanced hearing I had a hard time with it.

"This meeting certainly hasn't gone the way I expected it to." Tarragon's aura began to lessen in strength. "I agree to provide the time information. Will a twenty-four hour heads up be sufficient?" He spoke as if he were testing out the phrase.

"Yes. And it will just be you meeting us?" Lario removed his feet from the table, sitting up straight. "Besides releasing the curse, are you going to provide any assistance?" This meeting was like a B rated horror movie on repeat.

"No." Tarragon crossed his arms. "I will not do anything besides being the vessel for the curse's magic. Oh." He offered a fake smile. "The curse will last for twenty minutes. After it wears off, the Venandi will go back to full strength." He stood and snapped his fingers. A folder dropped into Lario's lap. "A peace offering. The blueprints to the whole compound."

There was a sudden drop in pressure as what sounded like

cloth ripping came from the wall behind the Fae. A black portal appeared. Tarragon stepped through it with not another word.

"What the hell was that?!" Becca stood up again, glaring at her stepfather and the vampire. "It sounded like you all had decided what to do even before we got here! Why even bother letting us come here? Why put up this act?"

Jasper pulled Becca into his lap, draping her legs over the chairs left arm as he pulled her close. She huffed but almost instantly relaxed. My wolf grumbled, wanting to be the one holding her.

"I'd like an answer to that as well." Gary looked at Lario. "I'm a little shocked you didn't trust me with this."

"Sorry about that, Gary." Lario opened the folder with one finger. He was trying not to touch it as if he were wary the Fae had done something to it. "That's why I took the fox shifter aside so I could give him a little warning ahead of time."

A warning? I hadn't heard any kind of warning when they'd been speaking before we'd come into the room.

"That's why I didn't say much." Jasper ran his hand along Becca's thigh. "They had their meeting last night is what Lario said. They just wanted to see how we'd react to the news of the Fae. Interesting fellow, though. He obviously was hoping we'd jump at the chance to help take down the Venandi and help out his people."

"That's underhanded!" Becca turned an icy glare at Lario. "Why would you guys do that? We didn't even need to bother to come today if you weren't going to take us seriously."

"Child." A chill filled the room. "You're new to this world, so I am letting your rudeness slide, but keep in mind that I am still a vampire lord." Lario's eyes narrowed as he looked at all of us. "The resistance was created to combat the Venandi and the ultimate goal was to stop them. This is an opportunity that we can't miss. No matter that the Fae have their own issues happening."

He focused his attention onto Gary next. "I didn't tell you so your reactions would be genuine. Tarragon's reaction when we told him that another Fae was responsible for helping the Venandi was telling. They're up to something, but at this time, it's not a concern to us."

Gary rubbed his face, pushing his glasses on to the top of his head. "Alright. I assume we have an actual plan besides the cluster fuck that was this meeting?"

Becca startled all of us by laughing. She slapped her hand over her mouth, trying to stop, but whatever had amused her just made her laugh harder as she tried.

"Mom is going to kick your butt so hard for that." She wiped at the corner of her eyes as tears formed from her laughter. "I'm going to tell her, too."

Jasper shook his head as we watched her and we grinned at each other. It didn't matter that the situation was serious, she made everything brighter.

Once she finished, Lario just continued as if there had been no interruption.

"Yes. Based on intelligence from those inside the compound, the hunters are gathering their forces together. It seems they anticipate retaliation from the Fae. This works in our favor since most of their people will be there when we attack." He pushed the open folder in front of Gary. "The goal is to take out the leaders. If we do that quickly, odds are most of them will give up so we don't have to kill everyone."

Gary held up a blueprint to the light. "These are pretty detailed. Including some areas that we haven't been able to map out yet. You really think this can be done with minimal casualties?"

My index finger started to tap on the table. It was like a broken record.

"At this point, we're taking the risk." Lario met Jasper's gaze.

"I would keep the shifters away. Just a feeling. But we wouldn't say no to your packs assistance, especially the hybrid, Wyn. He'll be imperative in this attack." The vampire pushed himself away from the table. "I think that's enough for now. Talk about it with your family, fox. Let Gary know if you'll be there."

Without another word, he just disappeared, making Becca jump and glance around rapidly looking for him.

"Where'd he go?" She looked shocked. "He went poof! Is that a thing? Can we do that?"

I couldn't hold it back anymore. I started laughing. She was just so cute.

"Cody!" She wiggled to get out of Jasper's lap, but his arms wrapped her up, pulling her into his chest. "Jasper!"

"Sorry, Becca." I took a deep breath. "You just make everything better." She stopped wriggling and a flush appeared across her cheeks.

"That was teleportation," Gary answered her question. "Lario is an old vampire and is extremely strong."

"Teleportation? Seriously?" She took a deep breath, calming down. "That's actually kind of cool." She sighed. "Gary, what was that? I feel like the brunt of a joke."

Her stepfather gave a sigh as well. He pulled off his glasses, rubbing the bridge of his nose. "Essentially, from what I could gather from what was said and what Lario told us at the end, Tarragon wanted to see shifters. It's possible the Fae were hoping to use them again, but you guys were able to put that to rest right away. So, we're attacking the compound of the Venandi in Texas sometime next week. I need to speak with Wyn right away, so why don't we go back to our rooms and meet up later today for dinner? We don't need to leave until tomorrow. This didn't take nearly as long as I thought it would."

We stood, following him out and up to our room. Becca was

quiet until we'd gotten inside the room with the door closed behind us.

"I'm not usually a violent person." She started to pace the room. "But I want to punch every single person in that room in the face." She paused to look out the window. It was almost lunch time. "This whole thing has left me feeling slimy."

Jasper sat on the end of the bed as I leaned against the desk. We watched Becca as she worked through what she was thinking.

"It was a waste of us coming here, that's for sure." I crossed my arms. "There's no way any shifters would help with the way these people have acted."

"I think that was the point, though." Jasper patted the spot next to him as Becca glanced over. "Think about it. Lario spoke in my mind before the meeting to give me the forewarning. The resistance obviously doesn't trust the Fae, but they don't want to waste this chance to achieve their mission, so they played along, but they knew we wouldn't play ball with Tarragon, not after meeting him."

Becca sat next to him on the bed, looking confused. "So was this show for us or for him?"

"Both." Jasper stretched his arms over his head. "I honestly think Lario is someone we can trust. The other two leaders? Probably not, my fox was uneasy with them, but the vamp? Yeah." He yawned in the middle of his sentence. "Sorry. I guess the early morning is catching up. Let's take a nap."

My wolf's tail started moving. Nap time sounded pretty good to me.

CHAPTER 30

Becca

My mind couldn't shut off. Cody and Jasper were snoring away as I stared up at the ceiling. During that ridiculous meeting, my animal had paced. She'd been so ready to attack Tarragon. He rubbed us the wrong way. As for Lario, she hadn't wanted us to rip his fangs out, so I'd take it. She wasn't sure about the other two leaders, especially Volinda. She gave off the vibes of a 'mean girl'.

I sat up, smacking my hands on my cheeks. There was no use worrying myself sick over things that happened. I could only move forward. It sounded like we would be going with the resistance next week because we'd need to support Wyn.

Thinking about Wyn, I pulled my phone out and checked my messages. There was one from Axel letting me know that they were halfway to the compound about an hour ago. I sent him a quick text letting them know I missed them.

I felt for our mate marks, feeling reassured that the ties between all of us were still strong. The two in bed were the strongest since they were right next to me.

Speaking of, I turned a little and took a picture. Jasper was the little spoon while Cody was the big spoon and they were both snoring softly. It was adorable.

My phone buzzed and I smiled as I answered. "Axel, how'd you know I was wanting to talk to you?" I kept my voice low, even though I knew that the guys would wake up to the slightest noise if needed.

"Because I miss you, too." His low rumble made me shift where I sat. "What happened at the meeting? You sound sad."

Was I sad? I didn't think I was. I was disappointed. Gary had talked the resistance up like it was the saving grace for shifters and it turned out that they were a hell of a lot different from that.

"Not sad. Frustrated maybe." I told him what had happened at the meeting. At some point, he'd put me on speaker and I could hear Seth and Wyn grumbling during my explanation more clearly. "I guess the big takeaway is that the Venandi are going to be taken down next week, hopefully. Gary was going to call Wyn about it."

"I didn't answer the phone, kitten," Wyn answered. "I'm driving. I figured if it was important, he'd call back."

"Seth's letting you drive?" I couldn't help teasing them a little.

"Har. Har." Seth didn't miss a beat. "Thanks for letting us know what happened. It certainly gives me a lot to think of."

"We're going to be there when this happens, Seth." I shocked myself as I spoke. "I can't let Gary do this alone. We can't let Wyn be the only one putting himself in danger. Even if it feels like they played a trick on us, I want to stop the hunters. In order to do that, we need to be at this." I took a deep breath moving forward. "We may have to deal with the Fae later on, but shifters deserve to live without the fear of being killed in their homes. I don't want what happened to Cody or me to happen to anyone ever again." I heard a slight crack from my phone. I pulled it from my ear and noticed a dent where my fingers had tightened on the device. Oops. I put it on speaker at the lowest setting.

"Of course we're going to be there, baby." Seth's tone was gentle. "I wouldn't let Wyn handle this on his own, even if he could. You're right. This isn't just about our pack. It's about all shifters' futures. If we can stop these hunters, then my little brother has a chance of finding his own mate in the future without worry. Not to mention future children."

Oh, that's right. I'd forgotten that Seth had a brother. I think he'd only come up in conversation once or twice. My heart warmed how Seth protected his family.

"Kids?" Cody groaned from behind Jasper. "You're talking about our kids already, Seth?"

Wait. What?

Seth's laughter was joined by Axel and a soft chuckle from Wyn.

"Not the time, wolf." He chided at Cody. "We'll let you know once we reach the rental. It'll be a few more hours. You three behave."

Axel took the phone off speaker. "Talk to you soon, Becca. Be careful."

"You too." I hung up, putting the phone on the nightstand. I sighed. I needed to get a protective cover for it since I still didn't really understand my own strength.

"Hey." The bed shifted behind me as Cody draped himself over my back, making me grunt a little. "They're going to be alright. They'll get in and out with Felicity and we'll be back with them in no time." He brushed his nose along my neck, making goosebumps appear along my arms.

I leaned backward into him, soaking up his warmth. My animal purred in contentment.

"I know Seth didn't want you to be close to the headquarters."

I looked at the wall. "I don't like the idea of you being there, either."

Cody's arms tightened around my front. "If I went with them this morning, it probably wouldn't have been good for me. No, not after last night, but we have a few days for me to get my head on straight. I'm not letting any of you near danger without me."

I ran my hands down his arm that had wrapped around my chest. "Just like that?"

His teeth scraped my outer ear, making my breath come out in a gasp. "For you, Becca, I will face my demons head on. They'll fear me, not the other way around, because your love makes me stronger. You just have to trust me. Trust us."

If I could melt into a puddle of goo, I would.

"Now, I have the perfect idea how to cheer you up." Cody pulled back from me. Losing his warmth made me whine a little but when I saw his grin, I knew whatever he planned would more than make up for it.

Cody took his shirt off, throwing it onto the floor. I greedily eyed the curves of his chest as he took his hair out of its braid. He tossed me a mischievous grin before turning his attention on Jasper, who was still sleeping even after the phone conversation. He winked at me right before he flipped Jasper onto his back.

Jasper jerked awake with a start. He started to sit up when Cody pushed him back. His hair was mussed and his eyes were still sleep laden as Jasper looked up at him in confusion.

"Cody, what-?" He cut off with a groan as Cody yanked his jeans and boxers down in one swift move. "Cody!" he protested, yet he didn't move, letting Cody hover over him as Jasper's cock visibly hardened.

"Yes?" Cody's hair brushed Jasper's chest as he bent his face, his lips moving across Jasper's jaw. "Is something wrong?"

My pussy throbbed between my legs as I watched. I knew that

when I'd gotten to watch the guys make out before had been hot, but this was making my brain short circuit.

"We didn't bring any lube," Jasper hissed as Cody bit down on his collarbone. "Ah! Don't draw blood here, asshole!" He thumped Cody on the back of the head but I could tell there wasn't any strength behind it because Cody just chuckled low.

"There's plenty we can do without lube. Don't you want to give Becca a good show? Doesn't she deserve one after not killing anyone in the meeting?" Cody's fangs had sharpened as he glanced over at me briefly. "Right, Becca?"

I nodded eagerly as I moved so I could sit more comfortably. "Yes. I want to watch!"

Jasper let out a laugh that ended on a moan as Cody's hand wrapped around his cock as he sat back so that I could watch Jasper's expressions. Cody's thumb rubbed the top of Jasper's tip slowly in a circle.

"We have to give her what she wants." His tone had deepened into a husky whisper. "Right?" His hand twisted as he stroked upward on Jasper's cock, strangling a whimper from him.

"Right!" Jaspers hands gripped the sheets on either side of him as his hips jerked once as Cody continued to slowly torture him with caresses.

"Good." Cody grinned. "Becca, be a dear and unzip me, would you? Pull out my cock so that I can make our fox whine in pleasure."

I crawled over to him quickly, not even realizing how hot his order was until my shaking fingers were pulling down the zipper on his jeans. He wasn't wearing any underwear as I took him in my hand, pushing down his jeans as far as I could before his ass stopped the fabric.

Cody's cock was throbbing in my palm as I squeezed it slightly. He hissed, grabbing my hand, pulling it off of him before kissing the top of it. "Ah, ah. Can't have you making me burst before I take care of our fox, now, can I?"

"Cody." Jasper's hands moved as he attempted to push Cody back. "Come on!"

Giggling, I sat back again to watch even as my pussy throbbed. I wanted to sketch this scene.

"So eager," Cody growled, trapping Jasper beneath him again, this time thrusting his hips so that their cocks rubbed together. Jasper gave a gasp as Cody reached between them, grasping both their cocks together as he started to rock. "Not enough friction," Cody grunted roughly as his hand moved to the tips of their cocks.

"The lotion from the hotel?" It popped into my head as I scrambled off the bed to grab the tiny little bottle that was on the counter in the bathroom. I slipped leaving the bathroom in my haste to get back to the bed but, thanks to my animal, I was able to prevent myself from flying face first into the doorframe.

Jasper and Cody were locked in a passionate kiss when I got back onto the bed. Jasper had moved his hands to clutch Cody's hair on top of his head as Cody just devoured his mouth. Cody rocked his lower body slowly, their cocks still held tightly in his left hand. I held onto the lotion, just watching until they came up for air. They'd have to eventually, but in the meantime, I just enjoyed the show.

Their kiss started to become sloppy as they moved together slowly. Jasper began to make small noises in the back of his throat which made Cody pull back ever so slightly to let them both breathe in air. He looked over at me.

"Good girl. Becca, open that for me, will you?" He let go of their cocks, sitting back on his heels as he held out his hand to me.

The lotion poured out quickly from the small bottle. Soon, it was emptied onto his palm.

"Thanks, love." Cody's grin made me shiver from the wicked gleam in his eyes. "Now, back to making you squirm."

"Fuck you, Cody!" Jasper hadn't moved. His cheeks were slightly flushed as he watched Cody rub their cocks in lotion. "Would you hurry the hell up?"

Hearing Jasper so flustered made me giggle again. He turned his glare to me, his eyes softening slightly.

"Are you enjoying my torture?" His lower lip went out in a pout that he didn't seem aware he'd done.

"Oh, we both are." Cody leaned forward again now that he'd gotten lotion on both of their shafts. "Now, the real fun begins." He moved his hands on either side of Jasper's head so that he was balanced above Jasper.

Cody started to move his hips, moving like he was inside of Jasper, thrusting quickly. Their cocks slid against each other with each thrust. Jasper clenched the sheets, ripping through them after one tug.

My thighs clenched as Cody began to move faster and faster. Their breathing became ragged and I leaned back slightly on my left hand as I spread my legs, my right hand pushing under my pants to rub at my clit. I moved my fingers to Cody's movements, biting my lower lip as my pleasure built listening to Jasper's cries.

Cody moved in the middle of a thrust, balancing on his left side as he reached down again, holding their cocks together and began stroking them together, his wrist twisting as his hand moved up and down almost as fast as he had been thrusting.

"Oh!" I was close to cumming as Cody groaned. I had to close my eyes as I listened to the two of them reaching their climax. When Jasper cried out Cody's name, I came, unable to stop myself from tumbling over that cliff.

Becca

"If we're done here, why are we staying? Shouldn't we head home?" My words were a little muffled as I chewed on my piece of pizza.

"We can, if you want." Gary took a sip of his tea. "I've spoken with Lario and it seems we're finished. I'm sorry it was such a waste."

"I don't think it was." Jasper had already finished four slices. "Annoying? Most certainly. Yet, we were able to learn some things that will help in the future. So it wasn't a total loss."

"Hey!" I glared at Cody as he attempted to take my second slice of pizza. "There's still some left in the box. Get your own."

"Yours just taste better for some reason." He took a bite out of the one I held in my hand, dodging my smack as he laughed.

"You're a brat." Grabbing my plate, I moved to sit next to Jasper on the bed. "Jasper, he's being mean." I leaned against him, making sure my food was protected.

Cody stuck his tongue out at us before taking another piece from the box. "Spoil sport."

"Alright, children." Gary shook his head with a hint of a smile. "We've paid for the rooms either way. It's up to you."

Swallowing the last of my pizza, I voiced something that had been bothering me slightly. "Can we just go to Texas now? What's the point of Seth and others going in, saving Felicity, and coming back here for all of us to go back within the next day or two? Wouldn't it be easier for all of us if we just met up with them? We could find a place like fifty miles away from the compound to stay out of the radar. I don't know, it's just a thought." It had been awhile since I'd word vomited so much. "I know that all of us there is a danger, but if we're far enough away, it should be okay for a few days?"

Jasper bumped our shoulders together. "I was actually thinking of talking to Seth about that when they reached their destination."

Relief flooded through me. "Good."

"You can take my car. Your mom can come pick me up from here." Gary wiped his hands with a napkin. "I don't see an issue with you going to Texas ahead of time, just be careful. If anything happens to you, your mother will kill me."

Cody didn't voice any objections. The feeling coming from our marks was calm. I knew he said he'd be alright when we went to Texas, I just wanted to make sure. His mouth was full of pizza but he grinned at me, showing a mouthful of chewed up food.

"Ew." I threw a pillow at him as we laughed.

After eating, I helped Gary take the trash out of the room so it wouldn't make the room stink too horribly.

"Hey, kid," Gary paused at the trash can after we threw it away, he looked at a generic art print that the hotel had hung. "Are you really alright? I'm sorry that all of this happened. I never meant..." His voice trailed off as I watched tears start to fall down his cheeks. "When I thought you died." He took his glasses off. "Let's just say that a parent should never have to hear that their child has gone before they have. I know we talked about this briefly before, but I need you to know that you're loved and I take full responsibility for everything. I'm so sorry."

A soft smile formed on my lips and I hugged the man who I called Father now. "I don't want or need any apologies, Gary. Thanks to what happened, I found the guys. I found new strength. I may have died, and don't get me wrong, that was scary, but with your help, the guys brought me back." I squeezed him tightly as he hugged me back. "We're going to help get rid of the bad guys and live a happy life."

"Your mom even mentioned grandkids last night," Gary snickered softly as I stepped away from him in horror.

"Kids? No way! It is way too early for that!" I held my arms up in an X formation. "No way. You can tell Mom that is a negative."

We started back to the room, mock arguing.

CHAPTER 31

Wyn

We took shifts driving, which cut down the twelve hour drive to get to Texas. Plus, Axel drove like a mad man. The compound, ironically called Sanctum, was located just outside of Weatherford on a several hundred acre plot of land. My home away from home.

Right.

The SUV swerved, jolting me out of my thoughts. "Geez. Are you driving as if you were playing a video game?" I flipped Axel off from the backseat even as I grinned in amusement. "Unless you're just being an ass."

"I'm being an ass." The bear didn't even look in the rearview mirror at me as he changed lanes again. "You started mumbling to yourself. It was creepy."

Seth laughed into his hand even as he tried to cover it up. "Okay, you two. We're almost to the hotel." He looked out the window. "Wyn, you're going into the compound alone. You've done it a thousand times, but I want you to be cautious. Get in and get out. Save your cousin. We'll deal with getting more information later. Got it?" He used his alpha magic, making it an order.

I wanted to argue, but the power he held when he used it, made it so I couldn't. Plus, after the information we learned from Becca, it made sense. I had wanted to speak with my aunt and uncle to find out what had made them make such a rash attack, except Felicity came first. I'd get my cousin out and to safety.

"You know, we could leave with Felicity and let the Fae and resistance handle the rest. We don't have to get involved further." Shifting, I sighed as the seat belt tightened. These damn things did not like big people, period.

"I would agree to do that if our mate would." Seth rested his elbow on the window, putting his chin in his palm. "We all know she won't. She wants to help shifters. Taking out the Venandi will do that. She's not going to back down."

"No kidding." Axel snorted. "We just need to focus. We'll get this over and done with."

I eyed the bear. "Are you really alright coming with us?" Felicity had used him after all. Becca hadn't forgiven her yet, either.

"You've asked that a few times already, Wyn. I'm starting to think you care." The cocky bastard finally looked at me in the rearview with a smirk. "I'm fine. I won't want to talk to her, but if it wasn't for her, we might never have met Becca."

"Of course I care." I turned to watch out the window, now refusing to meet his eyes. I wasn't used to the whole expressing feelings thing with others. It came easily with Becca, but with these guys it would take a little bit.

"I think he likes us." Axel laughed as I kicked at the back of his seat.

"Don't tease him too much." Seth didn't move, it looked like he'd closed his eyes. "Everything will work itself out." The GPS on his phone beeped. "Looks like the house we rented for the next few days is close. We'll get food later."

It didn't take long after that we pulled into a small neighborhood. The houses were all the same cookie cutter facades. This would be much easier to deal with the aftermath with Felicity than if we were at a hotel. The house looked small on the outside but I was surprised with the way it was laid out inside. There was plenty of space, especially the amount of rooms would be handy. I wasn't sure if I'd be welcome, or if I wanted to be, in Seth and Axel's bed without Becca. We weren't quite there yet.

"Alright, I'm going to call Jasper. We made good time." Seth rubbed the back of his neck while looking down at his phone. I don't know how he put up with having long hair and it was even curly on top of that.

"I'll call Felicity and set up a time to meet with her later tonight." I walked through the open floor plan to the backyard, if you could call it that, and shut the sliding glass door behind me.

Felicity answered on the first ring.

"Wyn?" She kept her voice low but thanks to my advanced hearing, I didn't have any issues understanding what she said. "Are you almost here?" She sounded terrified.

My animal raged. Felicity was never meant to be a hunter. She was too nice, too kind hearted for this line of work. She just had the misfortune to be born into our family.

"I'm here, kid. I need you to tell me about the shift they have you on today. I'll be coming to get you out in just a few hours." I looked up at the sky. The clouds were darkening in the distance so there might be a storm later, which would actually help with this. "Axel is with me."

She didn't respond for such a long time, I had to pull my cell phone away to make sure she hadn't hung up on me.

"He must hate me." Shame echoed through her response. "I used him and would have killed him."

"Aye, kid, we know. The thing is, though, you didn't. You managed to convince your parents to wait on the last rite. You saved yourself and him by doing that. He's not happy with you, but he isn't going to hurt you." Once we got her out of the compound, I had some connections that I'd use to get her a new identity and send her across the coast, possibly even up to Alaska if I could get the pack leader in Anchorage to agree.

"Do you think Becca will forgive me?" There was the sound of a soft sniffle.

"I'm not sure, cuz." I thought she would, because that's just the way Becca was. She'd even said that she considered Felicity her best friend. They'd have a long road ahead of them, but it didn't mean that they couldn't get over it. "Knowing you, you'll work it out though. But for now, I need you to tell me where you're scheduled to be at the compound in the next few hours."

It turned out that she was on the second outer perimeter tonight. That would make it a bit easier to get in and out unseen since I wasn't going inside the fourth gate to get information from Aunt Nina. She was working with a few guys that I knew. Most of them were jack asses but one of them was actually part of the resistance. He might be able to cover for her long enough to avoid suspicion.

"Meet me at the second inner gate at seven. Don't bring anything with you unless you absolutely cannot live without it. Understand?" I didn't wait for her to acknowledge my command. "I'll see you in a few hours, kid. Stay safe. It'll be over soon."

As I hung up, the sliding door behind me opened and Seth stepped out. He'd put up his hair and looked a little bit more refreshed than he had when we were in the car.

"Hey." He looked around the small yard. "We were going to take a quick nap. You could probably use one, too." This time he met my eyes and my animal shocked me by rolling over on its back.

I had to blink a few times. Ever since we'd fought for the alpha spot, my animal had been a grumpy asshole, even though we accepted that Seth was our leader. Now, all of a sudden, he was completely okay with it? What a bastard.

"A nap sounds good. I told Felicity I'd meet her at seven, so I guess I have a few hours to rest before I need to leave." I put my phone in my front pocket. "We should probably talk before that, though. I want to give you what information I have on the headquarters, just in case."

He nodded, turned to go back inside, and looked over his shoulder as I followed him. "From what you said in the car ride, it's a rather large area."

We stopped at the dining table, sitting across from each other. I could hear Axel in the master bedroom, already snoring softly. It brought a tiny smile to my face before I started to talk.

"The compound has over twenty buildings and I haven't been given access to several. The outer buildings contain the barracks, gyms, and arsenal storage. This includes the first security gate. There's no way to get into the area without going through the security gates and there's a total of four. I'll be going inside the first gate and meeting Felicity. As long as I don't run into any issues, I'll be back within three hours. I've even started reaching out to contacts to see where I can send Felicity so that she's safe." I scratched at the scruff that I hadn't had time to shave the last few days. The rest of the information I explained was how the shifts changed. "I'd still like to get information out of my uncle or aunt." I held up a hand as Seth looked about to say something. "I respect the decision and it's smart to just get in and out."

"Glad to hear it. Your safety is more important than collecting information now that we know what the resistance is planning. Becca would have both our heads if anything happened to you." He grinned. "I'd rather not have that happen."

"Having her mad at me is not something I want to happen. I have a sneaking suspicion that she's even scarier than you are." I crossed my arms. "Honestly, I'm surprised that she's not heading our way after that shit meeting they went to."

Seth's shoulders started shaking in silent laughter as he passed me his phone. My eyebrows rose as I looked down at the message displayed from our mate.

We're coming to Texas. It doesn't make sense to be separated. Plus, you'd be heading back to Texas in a few days again with all of us. We'll just stay far enough from the hunters. No arguments! See you tomorrow!

I laughed, stopping abruptly so I wouldn't wake up Axel.

"She told us, didn't she?" This girl. Even though it would be dangerous, we were enough away it should be fine. "Do you need me to contact the app to extend our stay?"

"No, I will." He looked at me, his face sobering. "You'll come back right after grabbing your cousin. No heroics, got it?"

"Aye, aye, el capitan!" Using two fingers, I saluted him. "Whatever you say!"

Seth shook his head as he stood. "Come on, brat." He walked away into the master bedroom. "Come on."

My animal paced in agitation. It had never been good with waiting. I walked into the room, toeing my shoes off in the doorway. Axel was in the middle of the bed and Seth had just climbed onto the left side. I took a second to look at them. It was a strange feeling, this sense of family that came with being part of their pack. I wasn't sure I'd want any of them sexually. Although, if anyone piqued my interest, it was Cody. The wolf was a brat and I'd enjoy the fight he'd give.

"Turn off the light and get in." Seth yawned even as he wrapped his arms around Axel and laid his head on the bears back. "We won't bite."

Flipping the switch so that the room darkened, I pulled back the covers just as Seth mumbled, "Yet."

I cracked up, waking Axel.

Wyn

Night had already settled across the horizon as I approached the headquarters. I'd done this thousands of times before, but this time, a pit had opened up in my stomach. I fought the nauseous feeling.

Luck was on my side as I pulled to a stop in front of the gatehouse. I knew the men guarding it. There was more security than normal, but that was to be expected since they were waiting for the Fae to retaliate against them.

"Yo, Wyn." Lenny, who was only a few years older than Felicity, leaned out of the window. "It's been a bit, glad to see you back. You heard about what happened?" He was trying to grow a mustache and the result made him look like a hick.

"I heard. Sounds like y'all have been busy while I was away." Handing him my ID, I glanced at the clock. "Aunt Nina is going to have my head for being late."

The kid shook his head, although he really wasn't all that much younger than me. I just had a habit of thinking of anyone younger than me as a kid.

"Yeah, I don't envy you having to report directly to Nina. She scares the piss out of me and the guys here." He handed me my ID back without so much as looking at it. He didn't even move to fill in the log. "You're in luck. Felicity is guarding the second gate tonight."

Normally, I'd bitch about procedure but this would help in the long run if he didn't fill it out.

"Oh, yeah? How's my cousin doing with her training?" My animal started to get annoyed with my small talk.

"Oh, man." Lenny shook his head as he waved at me. "It's just lucky she's the boss' kid." He flipped the switch that lifted the guard rail.

I gave a vague wave through the window as I pulled through the open gate. The drive to the second gate was quiet. The outer buildings were spaced apart. It was the beginning of the night shift so there weren't any patrols out on the road. I had maybe another twenty minutes if I was fast. My animal began to pace within me. Something didn't feel right. He wanted to get us in and out as quickly as possible.

The second gate came into view. The spotlight moved to follow my car as I pulled to the side of the road, in front of the gatehouse. I kept the car on as I stepped out of it, lifting my hand up in greeting. Several men held up automatic rifles until they noticed who I was.

"Ho!" I spotted the man who was in the resistance and a friend. He was older, closer to Gary's age and balding. He actually was a pretty nice guy and I often wondered how he'd ended up with The Venandi.

His eyes widened slightly at my approach, but he schooled his features into a glare. "Wyn. What the hell, dude? It's been forever since you graced us with your presence." We clasped hands and went in for a back slapping hug. "Felicity is ready. She's a terrible actor, so get her out of here quickly." He barely whispered the words, but I heard them crystal clear.

"I just couldn't keep away from your ugly mug, Brad." We pulled apart and I glanced around as if curious to see who else was around. "It looks like you got stuck with the losers for this shift."

There was a round of curses and name calling from the other guards on the shift as they all moved off. Felicity appeared in the gatehouse door. My animal went on guard. She was terrified and I could smell it from where I stood. This girl would never have been able to kill a shifter, much less Axel. She was no hunter.

Brad took the initiative. It seemed he was in charge of this patrol. "Yo. Cadet, come say hi to your cousin. You're due for a break, why don't you go grab us all some drinks?" He passed by her with a nod.

She had no idea that he was in the resistance. She didn't know anything other than I was about to label us both as traitors. I met her halfway, pulling her into a hug.

"Suck it up, kid." I was quick. "You need to hold it together for a few more minutes." I slapped my hands down on her shoulders as I stepped back. "You look great, cus. I don't have to report in for a little bit, why don't we go get some McDonalds?" I made sure to speak loud enough so that everyone could hear. "We'll bring everyone some coffee back." I put my hand on her head and softened my voice. "Go ahead and get in the car. I'll be right there."

I walked over to the gatehouse to speak with Brad again. He leaned against the doorway.

"You have my phone number. Text me your orders and I'll make sure to get you your coffees." I stared at him. "I'll see you later." We shook hands and I turned back to the car.

As I got inside, Felicity was visibly shaking. I reached over and squeezed her hand in mine as I closed the door.

"It's going to be okay. Just a few more minutes." I pulled the car around in a U-turn and headed back toward the first gate. When we were out of sight of the second gate, I spoke, "I need you to get into the back seat and onto the floor. There's a large black blanket on the seat. Cover yourself with it. Be quiet until I say it's safe."

She nodded and crawled into the back without a word. I could hear her shuffling around until there was silence except for her shaky breaths only I could hear. I turned on the radio to an oldies station.

"We're almost done, kid." I pushed down on the accelerator.

This was going a lot smoother than I'd hoped and we were almost out.

It felt like an eternity before the exit came into sight. It looked like Lenny hadn't moved. He looked confused as I slowed, rolling down the passenger side window.

"Wyn?" His brows frowned. "It hasn't even been an hour."

"No, I got orders before even getting through the second gate." The lies just kept falling easily. "Back out to the wilderness."

Lenny nodded, his brows going up. "I don't envy your job, dude." He stepped back as the gate opened. "See you next time."

I pulled through going at a normal speed, but as soon as I rounded a corner, I pushed the car to go over the speed limit.

"Alright, Felicity. We're clear." I looked in the mirrors to make sure that we weren't followed. "Go ahead and come back up here and buckle up."

She appeared and was back in the passenger seat. She clicked herself into her seat belt. Her shaking had gone down a little bit. She'd paled, but I couldn't sense anything wrong, so she'd be alright.

"Here." I handed her my phone. "Order McDonald's coffees for the second gates people. Have it delivered." Brad had been smart. If we distracted the shift with free drinks, they'd not notice she was gone for a longer period of time. "Send a text to Brad and attach him to a group order. That way he can go grab the drinks when they arrive."

She was quiet as she did what I asked. After a few minutes, she set the phone in the middle console, then I looked over to see her crying into her hands.

My heart ached for her. We weren't far enough away for me to risk pulling over but I did reach over and take her left hand in mine and squeezed it.

"It's going to be alright." I hoped I wasn't lying to her.

CHAPTER 32

Axel

"Axel, you're going to make it so we don't get our deposit back if you keep pacing back and forth," Seth chuckled from the couch as he watched me moving. "He'll be fine."

"It's been two and half hours." I rubbed my arms. "I don't know how you're so calm!" My bear was moving within me, just as worried as I was. "That stupid jerk should have texted us by now."

"I'll make sure to tell him how worried you were." Seth grinned at me, knowing that I'd get annoyed.

I stopped in front of him and glared. "You're an ass."

He crossed his right leg over his left and smirked at me. I ignored the excited shiver that went up my spine. He'd done that on purpose.

The sound of the garage opening had us both rushing to the door. The Escalade turned off and Wyn stepped out.

I could breathe again.

That's when I noticed Felicity getting out from the passenger side.

The rage I'd expected never came as she paused and looked at me with wide eyes. She was a beautiful woman, but the feelings that used to flutter in my heart didn't even stir. She was just another woman.

"Hi." She clutched the door handle.

"Hi." I couldn't find any other words at the moment. Telling her off would probably be like beating a dead horse. Plus, I didn't have the urge to do it anymore after laying eyes on her. We were both victims of this situation.

"Everything went smoothly." Wyn handed the keys to Seth before he went to stand next to Felicity. "They've upped security. According to Felicity, the closer to the inner compound you get, the more patrols there are now. My animal was not happy, so it's probably a good thing that I didn't go further inside."

Seth nodded and we moved back inside. "I'm Seth, Felicity. I'm Axel and Wyn's alpha. Are you hungry?"

The petite woman paused in the doorway, obviously uncomfortable and unsure.

"I think food would be great." Wyn wrapped an arm around her shoulder. "You're safe, Felicity. Let's eat and talk."

I moved into the house and went into the kitchen. While Wyn had been gone, I'd ordered some groceries to be delivered. The fee had been a bit steep, but it had been just easier to do than go into a new store without a car.

Pulling out ingredients, I turned on the oven. I watched the others out of the corner of my eye as they sat at the dining room table. Wyn seemed worried, but did a good job of hiding it from Felicity.

"So, Felicity." Seth narrowed his eyes at her but kept a pleasant expression on. "Is there anything you can tell us about what your parents are planning?"

Wyn stiffened. He didn't like seeing Felicity under our alpha's scrutiny but he kept it to himself.

"There was a visitor last week, before they attacked the Fae where they were told there was an entrance to Fairyland. The guy that came in wasn't human. He made a few of the guards piss themselves." Felicity looked down at the table as she talked. "I think he was Fae. He was freaky with how beautiful he was and Mom made sure no one thanked him for any reason. I wasn't allowed in the meeting but when it ended, he just disappeared. From what I could get out of one of the guys who'd been in the meeting, the guy had offered the location and said that if we succeeded in destroying the entrance, the Fae would basically leave the continent because it's the only way back for them here. The only other places are in Asia and Scotland. Dad and Mom felt that it was worth the risk. They didn't even seem concerned about breaking the agreement with them until after the place was attacked."

Wyn scoffed, annoyed. "They're such idiots. It obviously failed spectacularly. Even gained national news attention, I'm assuming that's why they are just preparing for an attack instead of trying to go on the offensive again." He clenched his fists together on top of the table.

"Whatever happened, Mom told me not to talk to you, Wyn. She wouldn't say why, but I don't think they trust you anymore, or anyone." Felicity crossed her arms on the table and rested her head on them. Her voice was muffled. "I think they've gone off the deep end. Dad even shot one of the patrol leaders for voicing an objection against attacking the Fae."

Now that was interesting. I placed the baking tray with the chicken I'd just prepared into the oven. Washing my hands, I turned my full attention on the conversation again.

"Interesting." Seth leaned back in his seat, rubbing his chin. "I wonder if it's possible this Fae did something. Wyn, can you reach out to the resistance and ask someone you trust? If the Fae are the ones who actually started this whole thing, they're up to a whole hell of a lot more than just getting back at the Venandi."

Wyn pulled his phone out and typed on the screen for several moments before setting it back down.

"I've asked Gary to talk to Lario. Felicity, he may want to ask you some questions. You don't need to be afraid though, kid. You're safe now." He reached over and ruffled her hair. She looked a hell of a lot younger than she really was.

"I'm not sure I can help with anything, but I'll do what I can. It's the very least I can do." She glanced back over her shoulder and met my gaze. "Shifters don't deserve what we've done to them."

My bear grumbled and I gave her a nod of acknowledgment.

"Let's focus on one thing at a time." Seth stood. "Axel, I'll help finish dinner. Wyn, why don't you get your cousin set up in one of the other bedrooms until the food is ready?"

Wyn took Felicity's hand and they moved off across the house to where the smaller bedrooms were. She hadn't brought anything with her it seemed. Which was probably smart, but she'd have to start over again.

"What do you think?" Seth pulled out peppers and onions from the bottom drawer in the fridge.

"I think it sounds fishy." I passed a knife to him. "A Fae just shows up, they let him in, and suddenly, they're attacking even though they had a treaty with them. They're attacking extremely erratically."

"Yes, and that's what concerns me. If the Fae are up to something, why now? Why the Venandi? Is it just to get rid of them because of what they've done to shifters and others, or is it because the Venandi are really the only protection humans have against them?" Seth slowly started to cut up the vegetables. "It just opens up a whole new can of worms."

We continued to get dinner put together. We could hear Wyn talking to Felicity softly. She had started to cry at one point. By the time food was ready, she'd quieted down.

None of us talked while we ate. Wyn was on his phone, talking to Gary while he ate in between texts. Seth was in his own little world as he thought on the situation. Felicity finished her dinner quickly, took her dishes to the sink, and went back to the room that Wyn put her in to sleep.

When I started to load the dishwasher, my phone went off with a text. It was from Cody.

So, we're on our way. You know how our mate is. We'll be there in about eight hours, according to the GPS.

I couldn't help the snort that came out. She had told us she'd see us tomorrow. Just not what time.

You guys drive safe. We'll see you when you get here. Felicity is safe and sleeping. Is Becca alright?

I knew it had only been less than a day, but being apart from her now felt like a piece of my soul was missing. I knew the other two felt the same way.

She's fine. She's feisty, I like it. She was ready to jump across that table and pummel that Fae. Oh, I fucked Jasper in front of her. She REALLY liked that.

I had started to take a drink of water when I read that and had to thump my chest as the water got stuck. Jesus. This wolf.

Did you get pictures? Or video?

Cody sent several laughing faces. *Nope. You'll just have to experience it yourself.*

Ass. Be safe.

I put my phone away as I finished my water. I looked up at the sound of a door closing. Wyn came over to the table and sat. He had a frown on his face.

"Wyn?" I sat across from him and handed him a bottle of water.

"Gary agrees with Seth. He sent the information off to Lario. We'll see what they do with it. I have a feeling we're still going to attack the compound as planned next week. There's no way they would allow this opportunity to pass them by. The question now, though, is what happens after?" He took the bottle, removing the cap and sipped the water. "Thanks."

"You know we don't have to be here for the attack." I was curious to see what he thought. "I don't like having Becca here. I know she'll insist, but if all of us agreed, we could probably convince her to let the resistance take care of it."

Wyn shook his head. "No. I couldn't do that. Becca wants to help, but I also owe it to those who helped me in the resistance to help them in this. The Venandi need to be stopped. This may be the only chance we have. Come what may after with the Fae." He held the bottle between his hands, looking down at it. "A friend of mine in Alaska has agreed to give Felicity sanctuary, so she'll be heading out tomorrow afternoon on a flight."

"Really? That's good." Felicity not being here would be less stress for Becca. Although, knowing her, she'd probably still want to talk to Felicity before that. "I heard from Cody. He, Jasper, and Becca are on their way here. They'll probably be here sometime in the very early morning." I noticed his eyes looked slightly glazed. He hadn't slept much during the nap and I knew for a fact he hadn't slept the night before. "It's been a long night. Let's go to bed."

Wyn even let me take his hand and lead him to bed. Seth was sitting against the headboard, working on his laptop. He closed it when we came in. He nodded at me as I gave Wyn a gentle push to the middle of the bed.

"No hanky-panky, promise, but your animal probably could use touch." Not to mention the man, but I wouldn't say that out loud yet.

It was a testament to how tired he was that he didn't give a fight. He just pulled his jeans off, his shirt fell to the floor as he climbed onto the bed to flop on his stomach. He was asleep in mere seconds. I hadn't even managed to get undressed.

"Man has a toned ass," Seth chuckled from where he sat and pulled the comforter around Wyn.

Becca

"Now I know why you never drove when the others were available." I glared at Cody. "You're horrid! Stop playing chicken with the truck drivers! Jasper, say something!"

Jasper just laughed from the front seat, playing a game on his phone. "Let him have his fun. He's not as bad as Axel."

It had just turned six in the morning. We were all hyped up on coffee. When I had said I wanted to go to Texas, the guys had mobilized and we left around eight last night.

We would have left sooner, but I'd ended up watching them give each other blow jobs. Cody was such a brat. I knew I was going to be addicted to watching my mates make love to each other too.

"We're almost there, right?" I closed my eyes so I wouldn't have to see my life flash before my eyes.

"Almost." Cody was laughing at me. "How are you feeling about seeing Felicity?"

Talk about a mood killer. The back of my head thumped against the seat.

"I want to hate her. She lied to me and Axel. She targeted him to kill him, even if she didn't want to." I rubbed my temples. "She's also the best friend I've ever had. She believed in me and pushed me past my comfort zone at school." That felt like years instead of just a few months ago.

"So, I don't know. I'm probably going to slap her before I hug her."

"I find that answer vague and unconvincing," Jasper quoted Rogue One.

"Not helpful!" My eyes opened and I leaned forward to flick him in the ear.

He dodged, grabbing my hand and kissed the inner wrist, making me blush. He didn't even look up from his game.

"That was smooth." Cody slapped his leg as he laughed. "You have to admit he wins with that."

"I'm not admitting anything." I stuck my tongue out at both of them just as I noticed we turned into a cute neighborhood. "We're here?"

"Less than a mile." Cody slowed down just to mess with me.

I ignored him and called Seth. He answered after a few rings. His voice was sleep roughened and my toes curled.

"Baby?"

How could just a nickname make me squirm?

"We're almost there!" I tried not to squeak. "Wake up and let us in."

"Yes, ma'am." I could hear him sit up and the rustle of sheets. "Come get your mates, baby."

Oh, fuck. I dropped the phone and slapped my hands on my cheeks.

Jasper and Cody glanced back at me and both laughed as we pulled into a driveway. The garage door opened to reveal Seth in his boxers and hair down.

The car wasn't even put in park as I threw open the door and jumped out. Seth opened his arms as I basically tackled him.

His scent surrounded me as I took a deep breath. Home. Now everything was okay because all of my mates were close together again.

"Mmm. I missed you." Seth ran his nose up my neck as he

tightened his arms around me. "I didn't think you'd get here this early."

"Cody drove the last few hours." I pulled back a little as the other two joined us. "That cut an hour or so down."

Seth stiffened slightly. "Cody drove?"

Cody grinned and held his hands up. "We're all still alive!"

"He actually was pretty well behaved. Mostly because there weren't a ton of cars out during the night." Jasper clapped a hand on Cody's shoulder. "Good job."

Seth just shook his head, took my hand in his, and had us follow him as he closed the garage door behind us.

"Everyone is still sleeping. It was a late night." Seth didn't turn on the lights inside, not that any of us needed them.

I still loved that I could see in the dark after so many years of being basically blind. I let my eyes take in the décor when a particular scent hit my nose.

Felicity. I'd recognize that perfume anywhere.

Seth noticed when I stopped. He waited until I spoke.

"She's okay?"

He nodded. "Wyn has arranged for her to leave this afternoon for Alaska. She's extremely skittish."

That didn't sound like the Felicity I knew. My best friend was always ready to take on the world. Whatever she'd gone through must have been bad. I took my hand from Seth's.

"Why don't you guys go back to bed? I'm going to go talk to her. Tell Wyn there will be no maiming involved, promise." I crossed my heart with my index finger.

Seth gestured toward where she was staying. "Let us know if you need anything." He bent his head to capture my lips briefly. He used just enough pressure to make my knees shake, and, judging by his smug look, he was fully aware of it. "Come on, trouble maker." He grabbed Cody by his upper arm and dragged him off to the other room where he must have been sleeping. Jasper offered me a hug before going with them.

"Oh, he's asleep!" Cody's tone suggested he was thinking of doing something bad. "CANNON BALL!"

There was a grunt, followed by Wyn cursing up a storm. Cody jumped on top of Wyn. I wish I'd seen it.

I was grinning when I knocked on Felicity's door softly. She was a light sleeper, so I suspected she woke up when we were talking. It only took a few seconds for the door to open and I was face to face with her.

"You look like shit." I could have face palmed. That was the first thing I said to her? Even if it was true, I could've started with something different. Her once bouncy, full of life hair was dull in color, as if it had drained away and the spark in her eyes was gone. She had dark circles underneath her eyes.

Her lips twitched. "You don't look that great, either." Felicity stepped back, letting me into the room. She closed the door after I was inside.

My animal sniffed at her. I'd expected her to rage about being near the woman who'd set her sights on one of our mates, but surprisingly, she was calm, just curious. She didn't have the same attachment to Felicity as I did.

As I faced my best friend, she looked me up and down. She frowned in confusion.

"Somethings different." She rubbed her arms. "Becca? What happened to you?"

"Ah. Um, about that." I forgot that she didn't know. "I, uh, I'm like Wyn. Surprise, shorty?" I shrugged with my palms out.

It took her a few seconds. When the realization hit, her eyes widened and her mouth gaped open comically. "What?"

I sat on the edge of her bed. "I was attacked at the cabin by an ex-experiment of the Venandi. He was out for revenge against

Gary, who turns out is an ex-hunter. The rogue got me instead. I died."

She gasped, her hands covering her mouth in horror as she stared at me. Tears pricked at the corners of her eyes. "Becca!" She threw herself at me, hugging me tightly.

I tried to stay impartial with her, but who was I kidding? She was still my best friend. I hugged her back, making sure not to squeeze too tightly. We cried into each others' shoulders.

After some time I pulled apart from her. I brushed my hair out of my face. "Felicity, we have a lot to talk about and not a lot of time."

She nodded and moved to sit next to me. "I know. I kept so many things from you."

"It's not just that." I took a deep breath. "You targeted Axel. You may not have wanted to, but you still did it." My fingernails grew as my animal growled at the reminder. "Remember how I said I liked him on the phone? It's more than that. I..." Glancing down, I pulled on the bottom of my shirt. "He's one of my mates and I love him." I really hoped he couldn't hear this. I wanted to tell him that I loved him to his face.

Felicity was silent for a little while, until she sniffed. I looked up to see her wiping her eyes free of tears.

"Becca, I am so happy for you." She slowly took my left hand in hers, making sure to avoid the sharpened nails. "I knew you were strong, I just didn't realize how strong. Will we be okay? I've lost my family, except for Wyn, I really don't want to lose my best friend." The last part she practically whispered with defeat. "Please."

My animal suddenly surged forward, taking over my body, shocking me. She didn't transform us, but she gripped Felicity's face in my hands and made her look us in the eyes. Felicity went even paler. I could only imagine what I looked like with my animal in the forefront.

"Family." The words fell from my lips, but it wasn't my voice. My animal let her face go and retreated. I took a gasp of air. "You okay?" My animal flicked her tail at me before curling up to sleep. Apparently, she'd gotten out what she wanted. We were going to have a long discussion about boundaries.

Felicity gulped loudly. "That was freaky."

I nodded. "Tell me about it." My claws retracted. "We'll be okay, Fel. I should tell you, though. Wyn's also a mate of mine."

Her mouth dropped open again. "No shit?"

We giggled and for the next few hours, we talked about everything but shifters and hunters. It was nice knowing that I could forgive her and we could continue our relationship.

CHAPTER 33

Becca

"You're sure this guy in Alaska will keep her safe?" Turning in my seat so I could see both of them, I eyed Wyn, who was driving us to the airport to drop off Felicity.

"Yes, kitten." Wyn didn't look from the road. "I've sent several shifters to him in the past. He's Alpha of the Anchorage pack. He'll make sure she's safe."

"He does know that I was in training?" Felicity's coloring had improved after we'd talked and a shower. "I don't have anything to offer. What am I supposed to do there?"

"He's well aware of who you are, kid. Sero will be the one picking you up. You'll know it's him, he stands out. It might be a bit rough there, I'm not going to lie, but you're a hell of a lot stronger than you give yourself credit for. You can continue school or find a job. Your life isn't the Venandi's any longer." Wyn looked in the mirror at her. "I believe in you."

I had to swallow the squeak that threatened to come out. That had been really sweet. Felicity obviously agreed because she sniffed, fighting back the tears.

"I hate being this emotional. I haven't cried this much

before." She clutched her hands into fists and stared down at them in her lap. "I'm going to make you proud."

Wyn smiled, making my heart skip. He really was a handsome man. I wanted to crawl into his lap right there.

When we got to the airport, I was glad I wasn't the one driving. It was a maze of different lanes. Wyn navigated through everything like a pro. When he pulled up to the curb for drop off, I got out with them.

"Text me as soon as you land." I hugged Felicity again. "Don't let any assholes push you around." I stepped away, wiping my eyes. I wouldn't cry. "I love you."

"I love you, too." She gave me a big smile. "I'll be fine, just like my cousin said. I've got your back!"

Wyn put his hands on her shoulders. "I'm sending some money to the account I told you about earlier. You use that to get anything you need, got it? Don't try to do this alone. I've got your new number and gave it to Sero, too." He handed her a ballcap. "Put your hair up in this and don't remove it until you're on the plane."

I got back into the car to give them a little privacy. Felicity had left the compound without anything except the clothes she wore right now and her phone. I was glad Wyn was looking out for her. It hurt a little because I probably wouldn't see her again for a very long time, if ever.

Wyn got back into the car after about five minutes. I looked over to wave goodbye to Felicity before she walked through the doors. My animal shifted, nudging me.

I looked at Wyn, my heart leapt into my throat. He looked about ready to cry as he pulled his seat belt on. I grabbed his right hand. He offered me a soft smile as he shook his head.

He didn't say anything and that was alright. I didn't let go of his hand as we drove back to the rental house. The drive back was quiet as I watched the scenery go by. There was some traffic so it added an extra half hour to our drive back.

"She's going to be fine." Wyn finally spoke as we pulled into the two car garage. He turned the car off. "She's strong, just not a killer."

Throwing caution out, I scrambled over the console and straddled his lap, my ass pressed tight against the steering wheel. I wrapped my arms behind his neck and held him.

"I'm proud of you. You're an amazing and caring man." I pressed my lips to the side of his neck as his hands gripped my sides. I wanted to say those three words, but they wouldn't come out. Not yet.

"Thanks, kitten." His voice was muffled as he hugged me.

Several minutes went by. As I held him, his body started to relax. I was just about to suggest we head in when there was a wolf howl. I glanced over my shoulder to see Cody standing in the open doorway with his head thrown back.

Wyns body moved under mine as he fought back laughter. "I swear I'm going to spank him."

Cody heard that and just howled louder.

"He'd enjoy that." I laughed with Wyn as we got out of the car. It took a little bit more scrambling on my part and my ass ended up honking the horn, which cracked all three of us up. "Oh hush!"

Inside, music was playing around the house. I found Seth working on his laptop, sitting on the couch. He hadn't bothered putting on clothes besides his boxers.

"We're back." I bent forward and kissed him. His lips were firm under mine and he shifted, suddenly pulling me into his lap. He must have moved the laptop.

He devoured my mouth with his. My hands gripped his shoulders as I soon began to need air even as his tongue pressed harder against mine.

"Not even waiting a few minutes before starting?" Cody's taunt made Seth pull back slightly, letting me up for air. I shuddered as I clung to his chest.

"Nope." Seth held me tighter. "I missed you, Becca." He pressed a kiss to my temple.

"You're going to get that spanking, little wolf. Your smart ass is finally going to earn you a punishment," Wyn growled and the sound made my pussy clench with anticipation. I couldn't wait to watch that.

I wriggled on Seth's lap and he chuckled against me. His lips brushed my ear. "Does that make you hot, baby?"

A whimper escaped my lips as I shifted my hips and ground myself against his rapidly hardening cock. His large hand wrapped around my asscheek and he squeezed, making me groan in delight. "Answer me."

"Yes. I want to watch Wyn spank Cody."

Wyn chuckled and Cody whimpered in anticipation. As much as he loved to dish out the sarcasm, he loved nothing more than a good punishment and to be dominated. Or so I was learning from the guys.

"Good girl," Seth rasped in my ear and held my hips tightly as his pelvis flexed and he ground his cock into my center. Fuck, I wasn't going to survive this. I was going to burst into flames before we even got to any penetration.

Wyn narrowed his eyes and stalked toward Cody, who backed up until Wyn had him pinned against the wall. His hands planted on either side of Cody's head as his tongue darted out to moisten his dry lips. "Does the idea of my palm on your ass excite you, little wolf? You've teased me enough, I think it's time that you pay up."

Cody visibly shuddered underneath Wyn's words and I arched up to see their interaction more clearly. Seth, sensing what I was doing, lifted me and quickly spun me around so my back was pressed against his front. "Now you can watch." He ran his nose along the column of my neck and I shivered against him.

"Cody loves to be spanked. Wyn has been itching to get his palms all over that delectable ass for weeks. I'm surprised he's held out this long."

I glanced around the room to see Axel shifting to adjust himself and Jasper leaning forward slightly to take in the sight. Jasper was another natural submissive, like Cody, but Cody had some dominant tendencies as well. It must be a shifter thing.

Wyn wrapped a hand around Cody's throat as their lips clashed together in a punishing kiss. Seth's fingers deftly worked to unbutton my pants and I arched so he could slide them off, along with my underwear. I worked quickly to pull my shirt over my head and Seth unclasped my bra so I sat completely naked on his lap.

"I'm going to fuck you hard while we watch Wyn spank Cody."

"Yes," I mewled and writhed against him as he trailed light touches along my inner thighs.

Wyn's long fingered hands tipped Cody's head back and he bent low to whisper in his ear. "After I'm done spanking you, you're going to get on your knees and wrap those luscious lips around my cock. I'm going to fuck your face until I spill down your throat." He drew the lobe of his ear into his mouth and Cody quaked beneath him. "And you are going to thank me for fucking your face."

Holy. Fucking. Shit. That was probably the hottest thing I'd ever heard in my life.

He dragged Cody, with his hand still wrapped around his throat, to make his way to sit on the couch. "Strip and then face down over my lap."

The tang of blood invaded my mouth as I realized that I was chewing on my lip so hard, I had broken the skin. Jasper and Axel shifted closer to us and Seth caught the fox's gaze. Something unspoken passed between them and Jasper was on his knees before me in a flash.

Seth held my legs open with his large hands on each of my thighs as Jasper's tongue dragged across my soaking wet pussy. He teased me, drawing out each swipe with a playful glint in his eyes.

My head fell back against Seth's shoulder and Axel tangled his fingers in my hair to wrench my lips to his. "We'll all have you tonight," he growled against my lips and my claws dug into the cushions of the couch, shredding them.

"Yes," I responded and drew his bottom lip in between my teeth. Seth pulled me away and took my place dominating Axel's mouth. All the while, Jasper continued to tease me with his tongue and soft circles around my clit.

"Jasper," I snarled and gathered his hair in my hands. "More."

"Demanding little thing," Cody commented with his usual snark and Wyn growled in response.

"Less talking, more stripping. Unless, of course, you would like me to rip the clothes from your body?"

Cody's eyes brightened and Wyn rose to his feet. Fabric shredded and was tossed across the room. "That will earn you five more strikes, little wolf."

"Can't wait."

When would Cody learn to keep his mouth shut? Probably never.

Wyn

The wolf and his mouth were going to be the death of me.

Primal and dark urges swirled within me, begging to be released, and Cody was more than willing to be on the receiving end of my rough treatment. He was practically begging for it.

And I would more than deliver.

I undid the button of my pants and slid the zipper down, relieving some of the pressure on my aching shaft. Cody's eyes slid down my body and locked onto my cock and a sly smile tilted my lips. "Soon enough. But first, your punishment."

In a smooth move, I sank to the couch and pulled Cody across my lap. He wriggled and fought me for a moment, before settling as I clasped his wrists behind his back. One palm caressed his smooth ass in appreciation as a deep rumble reverberated in my chest. "Ready for this?"

Cody squirmed, trying to free his hands, but I held them tight.

"Stay still or I'll add five more. Trust me, by the end of this, you won't want any more."

"Says you," Cody mumbled and I couldn't help the laugh that bubbled out from me.

"Cody, you are such a little shit," Seth muttered with amusement lacing his words.

Becca giggled, then gasped as Jasper nipped at her inner thigh while two fingers slid inside her pussy. "Jasper," she cried out as his mouth moved back to her clit and started his torture all over again.

My gaze zeroed in on the scene across from me as Seth and Axel each lavished attention on one breast. Our mate was utterly gorgeous as she sprawled out between the three of them. Her eyes blazed with heat as they met mine and I licked my lips. Her animal was close to the surface, enjoying the attention her mates were lavishing on her just as much as her human.

My own beast rumbled his approval along with her. Without warning, my hand lifted and came down on Cody's ass and he cried out in a combination of pleasure and pain. The line between the two was blurred so heavily, and I felt his cock jerk where it pressed into my thigh.

"That was a nice one," Axel murmured as his tongue traced around one of Becca's erect nipples.

"More where that came from." I smirked and my hand landed blow after blow, alternating cheeks as I rained down onto his flesh. Cody made inhuman sounds as I punished his ass, counting out loud as I struck.

"Twenty-five," I breathed out in satisfaction as my hand clenched into a fist and savored the sting of delivering a good and needed punishment. Cody craved to receive this, just as much as I craved to be the one to carry it out.

"Fuck, Wyn, that was..." Cody trailed off on a groan and flexed his hip, pushing his rock hard shaft into my lap.

"Yes, it was, little wolf. Now, it's time to get on your knees. Show our mate how good you can be at sucking my cock."

Becca practically panted at my dirty talk and my own cock begged for release.

Cody scrambled from my lap the second I let his wrists go and dropped to his knees. He glanced over his shoulder and winked at Becca. "Did you enjoy watching that?" he purred. Who knew a wolf could perfect a seductive purr like that?

Becca writhed against Jasper's ministrations and tunneled her fingers through his hair, dragging him more firmly against her. "Cody, suck Wyn's cock. I want to watch."

"Whatever milady desires." He winked and turned his head back toward me. He licked his lips as his hands came up to rest on my still clothed thighs.

I arched my hips and Cody helped pull my pants down my legs. My cock sprang free and Cody wrapped his palm around the shaft and pumped me firmly. My head fell back on a groan and he leaned down to take the tip between his lips.

My fingers tangled in his soft strands as he took me deep into his mouth. My eyes lifted and I met Becca's gaze as the rest of our pack lavished attention on her. A cry left her lips as she shook with her orgasm. My hips lifted and I thrust forward into Cody's mouth, delighting in the way his throat closed around my head.

"Fuck, little wolf," I rasped as his palm cupped my balls and started to explore.

I watched in fascination as Seth moved Becca to impale her on his shaft. The pair groaned while Jasper kept his mouth between them to dart his tongue along Seth's balls.

Fuck, that was hot. I gritted my teeth and roughly thrust my hips into Cody's hot mouth. The pup was practiced and was giving me what was shaping up to be the best blow job of my life.

Becca's cries pierced my ears as my climax started to build. I jerked Cody's mouth from me with a snarl. My fingers tensed in his hair and he smiled with his lips swollen from sucking me. His eyes were bright with desire and deep seated lust.

"Finish him, Cody," Becca cried out as Seth pounded into her from below. "I want to watch him spill down your throat."

Cody hummed his approval and licked his lips before winking at me. I growled with my consent while fisting my cock with my free hand and jerked his mouth down. His lips parted automatically and he took me deep and sucked hard.

Pleasure mounted and turned me into a snarling ball of animal instincts. I fought to keep my eyes open as I watched Seth, Axel, and Jasper pleasure Becca. My gaze couldn't leave hers. We would come together.

"Cum, Becca. Now," I bit out through clenched teeth as my grip on Cody's head tightened and my hips jerked up.

"Yes, Wyn," Becca cried out, my ears ringing with the volume of her pleasure rattling around my head.

Throwing back my head, my mouth opened on a silent cry as my orgasm took control of my body and spilled out of me. Cody jerked against me, but swallowed everything I had to give him. As the last spasm wracked me, I loosened my hold and moved to cup his cheek.

He pulled back, with his tongue darting around my shaft, cleaning every single inch of my still hard shaft. The way I was keyed up, one orgasm wouldn't be enough. Tears trailed down his face, and I wiped them away with the pad of my thumb.

Cody's eyes sparkled with mischief as he kissed my tip before tipping his head up and smiling at me. A small droplet of cum trickled from the corner of his mouth. I swept it up with my fingertip. Cody wrapped a hand around my wrist and drew my finger into his mouth. His warm, wet tongue swirled around and cleaned my flesh.

This wolf was seriously talented with his tongue.

"Good little wolf."

He beamed under my praise and drew back until my finger left his mouth with a pop. My gaze lifted to meet Becca's and then Seth's as he looked over her shoulder. A wicked smile spread over his face and he held Becca's hips still.

"What do you say we try something new?" Seth breathed into Becca's ear.

Becca hummed in question. Axel understood our meaning and rose to his feet and crossed the room into the bedroom. Becca's brows drew together as her eyes swept over the room between me, Cody, and Jasper.

"Do you trust us?"

Becca nodded vigorously at Seth's query and a wide grin tilted his lips. Axel returned with a small bottle of clear liquid. Becca watched the bear as he tossed the bottle between his hands. Dawning washed over her, along with a full body blush. "Oh. Oh!" she exclaimed.

"This is going to be fun." Axel tossed the bottle to Seth, who caught it easily, and rubbed his hands together in delight.

CHAPTER 34

Becca

I watched their movements with careful awareness. Anticipation hummed throughout my body, making goosebumps erupt over my skin. Seth easily lifted me and turned me around to face him. With an arched brow, he took in my features. "You ready for this? For us to fill you and take you so completely, you won't ever want to leave us?"

My brows knit together. "I wouldn't ever want to leave you anyway, but the being filled and taken part sounds rather nice."

Hands caressed along my back down to my ass and squeezed. My hands braced forward onto Seth's chest to keep me anchored. Hot air fanned across my neck and ear as Axel bent down low. "I'm going to be the first to take your ass."

His words sent a sharp spike of need straight to my core. My thighs clenched around Seth and he chuckled as he ran his nose up along my neck. "I think I'll let Jasper have your pussy. He did so well helping to bring you to climax."

Oh hell. Jasper and Axel at the same time. I may split in two.

A soothing hand glided over my back. "We'll go slow, baby. I would never do anything to hurt you." He paused for a moment and smiled against my skin. "Unless you wanted me to, that is."

More heat crept up over my face at the thought of being spanked by Axel like Wyn had spanked Cody. Would I be into it? Probably, but not as hard as Wyn had done.

Axel chuckled. "I think you like the idea of being spanked. I'm sure that we can arrange that later. For now, Jasper, sit on the couch and take Becca from Seth."

Jasper complied, his cock jutting out from his body, hard and ready, as he stood. Before he sat, he bent down and kissed me soundly. "You're so incredibly beautiful."

My fingers tangled in his hair and I tugged his head down to mine for another kiss. Our tongues tangled together as he splayed his large hand over my neck possessively.

Axel landed a soft slap on my ass, making me hiss and pull away from Jasper. I looked over my shoulder at him with a scowl etched on my face. "I was enjoying that kiss."

He smiled and shrugged. "And I wanted to swat your ass. Now, get moving. We need to prepare you."

Shaking his head, Jasper sank down into the couch beside Seth. He wrapped his hands around my waist and pulled me off Seth's lap and onto his own. With his superior strength, he held me up and shifted his hips. In one smooth move, he lowered me down on his shaft, impaling me.

"Jasper," I gasped out his name and my nails curled into the bare skin of his chest.

He rumbled beneath me as his head fell back with his mouth wide open. "Fuck."

Axel placed open mouth kisses along my back as Jasper rocked into me from below. Slow and tender, allowing Axel to start by trailing fingers along my puckered hole. His fingers were slick with lube as he stretched me, preparing me for his large length. One finger. Two fingers. Oh, fuck, I already felt so full.

Seth wrapped a hand around my neck and bent low. "You're doing so good, baby girl."

I cried out as another finger entered me as Jasper moved a little faster. Sweat beaded along my forehead and I reached out to grab a hold of Seth before he could pull away. He took my mouth in a brutal kiss, his tongue plunging in and out of my mouth and matching the rhythm of Jasper's thrusts and the movement of Axel's fingers.

"Mmm," Axel rumbled and withdrew his fingers. "I think you're ready."

"Please," I rasped against Seth's lips. My men chuckled lightly. Cool liquid trailed down along my crack as Axel applied more lube.

"Just breathe. Push out and don't clench up on me." Axel pushed me down further against Jasper's chest before rubbing the tip of his cock along my back entrance.

Groaning, Axel pushed in slowly. "Fuck." His growl vibrated through me, and I pushed back against him before he held me still. "Slow. Can't hurt you."

His bear was close to the surface, adding a deep timber to his voice. A fresh wave of arousal flooded my body and I was like Jell-O in their hands.

Seth's fingers tangled in my hair and angled my head to face him while resting against Jasper's chest. "Breathe with me."

Pressure built within me as Axel penetrated me inch by exquisite inch. I continued to breathe with Seth as he held my gaze captive. His eyes darkened and he licked his lips. "Once Axel and Jasper start fucking you, I'm going to take that mouth of yours."

Axel grunted and moved forward another inch or two. Damn, the man had a lot of inches. Everything felt stretched and filled. The thought of taking Seth into my mouth while Jasper and Axel pounded into me made my pussy clench around Jasper's length.

He hissed out a breath and reached up to cup my breasts before he turned to Seth. "I think she likes that idea."

"I think she does too, boss man." Cody moved into my peripheral vision. He was still naked, and he had his hard shaft fisted in his hand as he stroked it lazily.

Seth chuckled and drew his thumb across my lips, already swollen from kisses from my mates. "She will love it. Because she is our perfect mate in every way."

Axel distracted me from any sappy thoughts by thrusting forward and seating himself fully inside my ass. I sighed in pleasure and wiggled my hips a bit to generate some friction. Jasper and Axel hissed and each wrapped their hands around my waist to keep me still.

"You don't move. We do," Axel breathed huskily into my ear.

"Now, it's time for you to suck my cock, baby girl." A devious grin spread over Seth's face as he climbed to his feet on the couch. His cock bobbed in front of my face, the angle perfect as I took him tentatively into my mouth. He groaned and wound my hair in his fist to gently guide my movements.

"She looks so perfect sitting there with every hole filled." Wyn's voice was rough with desire as he lounged on the opposite end of the sectional. His erection returned with a vengeance as he wrapped a hand around it. "I want her mouth next."

Seth rumbled out his approval as his hips flexed and more of his shaft filled my mouth. Jasper and Axel alternated their thrusts. One in, one out and holy fuck, I could barely think as I was filled with my mates. Pleasure spiked, rolling over my body and making my entire being quake as the orgasm took control of me. I screamed around Seth's cock. His grip in my hair tightened and he shuddered before spilling his seed into my mouth.

I swallowed around him, the salty, tangy flavor lingering on my tongue as he pulled out slowly. My tongue darted out and cleaned him, taking everything I could from him as he ran his fingers through my hair. My orgasm left me boneless. I was a slave to their pleasure as Axel and Jasper filled the room with their grunts and moans.

Wyn smiled as he took Seth's place, leaning down to kiss me soundly before standing before me. "My turn, kitten."

I grinned up at him, my entire body and face flushed with arousal. Cody sidled up next to him and kissed me when he stepped back. "He tastes so good, Becca."

Wyn rumbled his appreciation and wrapped a hand around the back of Cody's neck to bring him in for a kiss of his own. "You had your turn, little wolf. Now it's Becca's."

Cody whined deep in the back of his throat and turned to look at me. "You wouldn't mind me helping out, would you, baby?"

"Ah!" I gasped as Axel landed a slap to my ass and thrust into me hard.

"Answer Cody's question, baby," Axel growled into my ear as he laid another hard slap on the opposite cheek.

"Whatever my mates want," I keened as Jasper flicked his tongue over my nipple before biting down. Pain mixed with pleasure and I was swept up into another orgasm.

Was death by orgasm an actual thing? Because these five were going to make it pretty close. I was already a quivering, shaking mess. Desperate for their touch and their cocks, any way that I could get them.

Seth stepped forward and wrapped a hand around Cody's neck from behind and brought him against his body. "Behave, Cody. You've already played with Wyn tonight. It's Becca's turn. Help, but don't take over."

"Yes, boss man," Cody replied with a hint of snark hidden in his otherwise submissive words.

The wolf really was a brat, but I loved him so much, my heart could barely take it. All of these men had wormed their way into my heart and imprinted upon my very soul. Losing any one of them would destroy me.

Wyn drew his lower lip between his teeth as he rose to stand on the couch. Cody grinned slyly at me and wrapped a hand around the base of Wyn's shaft to hold him ready for me to suck. My jaw ached and the muscles in my cheeks and neck protested my movements, but I shoved the discomfort away and took Wyn deep into my mouth.

Cody moved his hand down to play with Wyn's balls. The hybrid shifter appreciated the touch as his head fell back and he sighed in pleasure. I loved how vocal my men were. I could always tell when they were enjoying something because they never hesitated to give a grunt, groan, or growl in appreciation.

Wyn snapped his head forward, his eyes wide as he glared down at Cody, whose hands had disappeared beneath Wyn's balls. Wyn jerked his head up by his hair. "Did I say you could play with my ass, little wolf?"

Cody's lips tilted up at one corner in his bratty smirk and continued to dance his fingers along Wyn's asshole. "I'm not doing anything…"

I pulled back from Wyn's cock to burst into laughter. "You are so full of it, Cody."

"I would love to be full of his," Cody hummed as he wrapped a hand back around Wyn's shaft. "Fuck, he is so hot and growly. It always makes me hard in an instant."

"Cody," Seth barked in his alpha tone and stepped behind them. "Cut the bratty behavior."

Cody's eyes dropped, but retained their playful sparkle as his hands moved back into visible areas.

"I'm starting to feel a bit neglected down here," Jasper commented with a tender bite along my collarbone.

Axel reached a hand over me and smoothed it down Jasper's damp chest. "Don't be, we're the ones actually inside her."

Seth let out a fierce growl. "Just because I allow it," he responded with a fierce slap to Axel's ass that caused me to cry out as it reverberated through me.

"Alpha," the men all replied in unison and Seth snorted his approval.

I took Wyn back into my mouth and suckled him. Cody resumed his play and the sounds of pleasure soon filled the air around me again.

Seth remained planted behind Wyn, his eyes were bright with control and power. Sensing Wyn getting close to his second release of the night, he stepped behind him and wrapped a hand around his throat. "You are mine too, hybrid. This body belongs to our pack and our mate."

"Fuck, yes." Wyn threw his head back to rest on Seth's shoulder.

Seth bent low to whisper in his ear, "I'm the alpha here and I control when we all cum."

"Yes, Alpha," the men all rumbled.

Seth's upper lip drew back into a snarl as his power washed over us. "Cum. Now."

I fell over the ledge with Jasper circling my clit with the pad of his thumb. Wyn spilled in a rush down my throat. Jasper and Axel in my pussy and ass. A splash of liquid fell against my back and side as Seth and Cody all came too.

Blackness surrounded me as I swallowed and pulled away from Wyn. My entire body was boneless and shaking.

Spent and drained. That was the only way to describe how I was feeling. I whined as Axel withdrew from my ass.

"Shhh, baby," he cooed and ran soothing hands along my flesh. "We'll get you cleaned up and put in bed."

"Love you all," the thought was a brief moment before the darkness took over me.

CHAPTER 35
Becca

"Again!" Seth looked down at me. "Get up, Becca. We're not done."

Coughing, I groaned as I flipped over onto my stomach as I pushed myself to my feet. That hadn't hurt nearly as bad as I thought it would, but the shock to my back made me lose my breath for several seconds.

We were practicing in the backyard. We'd been here for four days already and they'd all been taking turns on helping me learn self-defense.

"Not pulling any punches?" I wiped my pants off as I straightened, moving my leg back so that I could prepare for his next attack.

"No. If we're going to be at the attack on the compound, you need to have some kind of self-defense training. This isn't up for debate." He took a step toward me. "After this, you'll practice with Wyn on fighting in your animal forms."

I was sweating so much that I was tempted to take my shirt off. I was back to borrowing the guys clothes since I'd only packed for one day when we'd gone to meet the resistance. Luckily, the house had laundry, so I only really had to borrow their clothes during workouts.

"When fighting someone, look for weak points. There's no such thing as fighting dirty. There is only survival." Seth moved suddenly, his leg kicking out and catching me behind my knee. I fell to my hands. I'd seen him move, but I hadn't known what to do. "Your only goal is to get away alive."

Time dragged on during this training. I was thankful for the accelerated healing I had, otherwise I'd have been bedridden at the end of it. Even though Seth wasn't holding back, he took steps to not cause serious harm.

"Agh!" I landed on my back again, and this time, it really hurt. "Ow." My spine throbbed.

Seth kneeled next to me, concern evident. "Becca?"

"I'm good." I didn't move, though. "But can we take a break?"

His hand brushed some hair from my face, the gentle touch making me close my eyes. It felt so good.

"Break it is." His hand left my face and there was a shift in the air next to me.

I turned to look at Seth as he laid next to me, he glanced up at the clouds. His brows were slightly furrowed and I couldn't resist running my thumb along his nose.

"Are you worried? About the upcoming attack?" I flicked my finger on the tip of his nose teasingly.

He grabbed my hand, kissing the tips of my fingers. "Of course. I'm worried about what happens after."

The guys had caught me up on what they'd learned from Felicity. I had agreed with them. The more I learned about the Fae, the more I disliked them. My dislike for them was now on par with the Venandi.

Felicity was doing alright, at least according to the texts that I received from her. Apparently, Sero was really hot, but an asshole. She had gone shopping the second day she'd been there and already had a confrontation with some local shifters, but they got their asses handed to them by their alpha before she had to do anything.

Knowing that she'd already had trouble and was protected helped ease my mind with her being so far away now. It helped Wyn, too, even if he didn't say it.

"If the Fae do decide to do something, what would it be?" I looked up to the clouds. "Could it be worse than what the Venandi have done?" A feeling in the pit of my stomach suggested that it would be.

"The Fae are extremely powerful beings. The only reason they're in hiding is because Earth doesn't have the magic that Fairyland does. If they were to find a way to change that, not only shifters will have problems, humanity would be at risk of annihilation." Seth shifted onto his side, leaning his cheek onto his hand. "I doubt that is what's happening, but it's better to be cautious." With his free hand, he used his index finger to trace my cheek to my lips. "After we're done in Texas, I want to introduce you to my brother."

"Yeah? You think he'll like me?" I pushed myself up so I could lean on my hands. "I've never asked you what your brother's name is."

"Oh. That's my fault. His name is—" Seth was interrupted as Wyn opened the sliding door and stuck his head out.

"Hey, love birds. Are you done?" His hair was damp from a shower. "I want to get an hour or two of training with Becca before dinner."

Seth got to his feet and pulled me up with him. He ran his hands down my hair. "She's all yours." He gave me a wink. "We'll talk more later tonight."

"Do you need to rest?" Wyn closed the door behind me as we came back inside.

The furniture in the living room had been pushed against the sides of the wall with the dining room table when we trained inside. The breakables were on the kitchen countertops.

"No." Which was true, my back was fine now. "I need to learn what I can with the time we have."

Wyn cocked his right hip as he grinned. "You're a good kitten." He gestured to the living room. "Let's stick to our smaller forms for now. I'd rather not cause any damage to the house if we can help it."

Shifting back was getting a little easier with how hard we were all working.

"Mr. Biggy is so considerate." Cody strutted into the room. His hair was damp too and I narrowed my eyes.

"Wait. Did you take a shower together and I didn't get to watch?" I pointed at him. "That's rude!"

Ever since that night we'd all been together, Wyn had opened up more to the other men. Especially with Cody. He hadn't taken it all the way with him, yet, but their make out sessions were hot as hell. Plus, Cody really had fun messing with him. I think it was getting spanked that spurred him on.

"Aw." Cody bounced over to kiss me. "Don't worry, fair maiden. You can watch next time."

If I could stop time, this is where I'd do it. I knew that as the days went by, we got closer to the big fight, but I was happy with my pack right now. I'd even spent a few hours yesterday with Axel and Jasper as we reached out to the school. We were pushing classes out and took the semester off. I didn't want to quit school, but this was more important right now.

When Gary called later that evening to let us know that they'd be moving in on the compound tomorrow night with the resistance and Tarragon, I became scared. I tried to hide it.

After all, this had been my idea. I'd insisted that we help them do this, but that still didn't stop me from worrying about Gary and what could happen to all of us if something didn't go right.

I should have known my mates would see through me, though. Axel sat next to me on the couch, turned to me with his arms open for a hug, and didn't say anything. He just waited for me. I practically dove into his arms, as I settled into his lap. His large hands stroked my back as I buried my face in his neck.

"It's going to be fine." His nose brushed behind my ear. "None of us are going inside, except for Wyn, and that's only a possibility."

I didn't answer as I watched the others. Seth was on the phone with Gary and Wyn on speaker. Jasper was listening as Cody sat on the ground in front of Axel, leaning against his legs.

"It should be pretty straight forward," Gary's voice was strained. Seth had put him on speaker. "There's more than enough of us to handle this. Lario is in charge of the frontal assault with his people." My step-father sighed. "The plan is to take hostages. We aren't killing anyone if we can help it."

"There will be casualties, Gary. We both know that my family would never allow anyone to take them alive," Wyn grunted. "If the curse works as intended, though, it will cut those numbers by half."

"We'll meet you at the specified location I emailed to you at eight p.m. Be safe until that time. Becca, your mother sends her love and told me to tell you to remember to brush your teeth." He choked. "And to use protection."

I burst out laughing as he hung up. I could only imagine his face as he said that. The guys all looked uncomfortable, which just cracked me up further. I wondered if Gary knew that I couldn't get pregnant until my animal and I decided to. I wasn't going to tell him, though.

Axel gripped my hips, bringing my attention back to him. His kind, brown eyes melted me from the inside. I could feel his bear reaching out to send his own feelings. I tilted my head just enough so that I could kiss him gently. He'd offered his comfort and calmed me down.

"We'll get this over with and begin our lives together. As a pack." I firmly believed that. Nothing would stop us.

CHAPTER 36
Becca

The hoodie Seth gave me fell to my butt. We were all wearing black, which I thought was a little silly, but considering what was about to happen, it made sense to try to blend as much as we could against the dark. I pulled my hair into the hood.

I'd been worried about Cody on the drive over, but he'd seemed fine. Calm. He was keeping his word.

As we arrived at the meeting spot, it looked like the people from the meeting were already there, including Tarragon. The Fae watched all of us silently as we approached them. I didn't like the look in his eyes.

Gary stood next to Lario, who was wearing a black suit. He was pretty easy on the eyes now that I actually looked and wasn't so pissed off at the resistance. He was the first to move to meet us. He shook the guy's hands in greetings while nodding at me. "Good to see you again, Wyn."

"Lario. Gary." Wyn had been mostly quiet since this morning. His expression now was cut off and detached. "What's the plan?"

"I'm going in with my people. The goal is to incapacitate the guards as quickly as possible. Our people inside report that no suspicions have been raised, which works in our favor." Lario gestured for us to follow him. He led us to the other two leaders of the resistance and Tarragon. He introduced them to my mates.

"One of the last tiger shifters." Tarragon eyed Seth, making the hairs on the back of my neck raise. "Fascinating. Your species was one of the strongest shifters created."

Seth didn't look impressed. In fact, he looked downright bored as he stared down the Fae. "Fascinating." His obvious sarcastic reply wasn't missed by anyone.

"Right." Gary cleared his throat. "Wyn, I'm going in with Lario so that I can deal with whatever they have cooking up in the lab. I'd appreciate it if you were with me." He offered me an apologetic wince. "I need someone familiar with the area and I trust."

"If my alpha agrees, I'll help." Wyn surprised all of us by referring back to Seth.

My heart started to pound. It really was happening. My claws started to grow and I clenched my fists together to hide it. Freaking out wasn't going to help anyone at this point. With one deep breath, my animal helped center me. We had this.

"I'll be going with you." Seth held his hand up when I opened my mouth. "I'm not letting Wyn go in alone. The rest of you will stay out here and offer support as you can, but no engagement unless necessary. Yeah?" His power tugged on the connection between us, offering strength.

It was the right move. If anyone would make sure my stepdad and Wyn were safe, it was Seth. We moved off to the side as the resistance continued to speak amongst themselves.

"You two better come back unharmed." I glanced between Wyn and Seth. "If you get hurt, you're both grounded."

The guys all chuckled at that. They thought I was joking. Seth stepped forward, wrapping his arms around my waist as he pulled me against him. My hands rested on his chest as I looked up at him.

"We'll get in and out quickly. We got this, baby." His azure eyes were bright against the dark. "Trust in us." He kissed me gently, offering comfort and a promise.

Wyn was next after Seth let me up for air. He went to the others as Wyn held me. He was like a rock wall. No emotion showed on his face.

"I'll take care of both of them." He brushed our mouths together gently. "No grounding."

"Alright," a loud voice rang out, garnering everyone's attention. Abram, wearing full body armor, stepped forward. "Groups one through three, we're moving out." He glanced at Tarragon. "On your mark, we'll begin."

Gary walked over to us, gave me a tight hug, before he led Seth and Wyn off to join the second group. My mates gave us reassuring smiles before following him. It felt like my throat was closing. My animal was just as worried as I was, which meant she was having a hard time helping me cope with my anxiety.

Axel came up behind me, resting his hands on my shoulders. "They got this."

I covered his hands with mine as we watched the groups of people moving into the night. Volinda, wearing the most outrageous black dress that was actually a ball gown, was speaking with a few people off to the side of Tarragon.

Who wore a ball gown to a fight?

Jasper and Cody appeared on my sides. They didn't touch me, but their presence helped ease my anxiety slightly.

Twenty minutes passed in silence when Tarragon stepped forward, away from Volinda. "The time is now." He raised his arms over his head.

Just like that, the dark energy that had been around him during the meeting suddenly warped around him. What looked like tentacles whipped around as the wind picked up around him. The Fae's hair lifted as his eyes bled white. His palms turned a sickly green as he began speaking a language that hurt my head. The sound felt slimy as my ears throbbed.

Axel's hands tightened on my shoulders and he pulled me behind him as Tarragon's voice raised. The magic that was building pressed around us like a heavy weight. I started to feel a little woozy. When Tarragon shot his hand forward, facing the compound, the black tentacle-things whipped out, rushing toward the area like a tidal wave. As they rushed past us, the heavy weight lifted and my ears popped, still leaving that sick feeling behind.

So that was a curse. I was glad it hadn't been aimed at us because just being near it was making me feel weak. My animal suddenly stood at attention, bringing my focus toward the compound that was less than a mile away. An explosion rocked the night. If my mates hadn't been there, I know I would have fallen from the force of it.

"What the hell?" I could barely hear Cody as more explosions rang out around us.

I whipped my head around to look at Tarragon. He was laughing. The energy around him started to build again. Volinda, with the remaining resistance members, surrounded him as she demanded an explanation.

"Did you really think that we'd just let these vermin off with a little curse?" Tarragon's voice rang clear as he eyed the resistance members. "Getting rid of your little group in the process is a bonus." He turned his face to look at us. "It's too bad about the tiger. I would have liked to add him to my collection."

Seth

"Something doesn't feel right." Keeping my voice as soft as possible, I looked at Wyn as we waited in the shadows outside of the first wall, near the gate, that surrounded the compound.

"I don't trust the Fae." My hybrid pack member looked up at the ten foot wall.

"As you shouldn't." The vampire leader popped up next to me. If I hadn't been alert, I would have taken his face off with my claws. He smirked, clearly aware of my thoughts. "I fully expect a betrayal. That's why I had Gary give you two those pendants that you put on. They're made of iron. All of the people in the attack groups have them on. It won't offer a hundred percent of protection, but it should help in case our Fae friend decides to try something."

I looked down at the round necklace that Becca's stepfather had handed to me as we'd begun the walk here.

"Did Becca get one of these?" Wyn looked at Gary. "She and the others are the ones still with him."

"No, we couldn't give those in his vicinity one without risking his notice." Gary glanced at this watch. "Don't worry. Volinda has sworn to protect your mates with her life. It's time."

I bit my tongue in annoyance. At least they'd kept the necromancer with the Fae to watch his movements. I still didn't like it.

A gust of wind rocked against us. It was so strong that Gary stumbled. Lario held onto his arm to make sure he didn't fall as magic began to surround the area. My tiger growled, preparing for a fight. Something was coming and it wasn't friendly.

"He's released the curse." The vampire kept his cool as we all looked back to where we'd come from. "And something else." His body jerked as if sensing something I couldn't, and pushed Gary to the ground. "Get down!" He didn't bother keeping his voice down as he screamed for his people to drop.

Wyn tackled me, covering my body with his as a black cloud ascended upon us. I watched in horror as the magic disintegrated the physical wall. A Venandi guard got caught in the cloud and the scream of pain that ripped from his throat would haunt my dreams for years to come. He fell to his knees and it looked like the magic had sucked the life out of him. His skin clung to his bones. He was still alive, barely. He was a skeleton with coverings.

"Don't let it touch you!" Lario's shout was hard to hear, even for me, over the yells and shouts surrounding us.

The black magic pushed forward into the compound. It continued to spread as tendrils expanded from it.

"That is not the curse they said they were going to use," Wyn grunted as he rolled off of me. He looked around as screams in the distance reached us.

"I'm going to kill that Fae." Lario sat up. His voice had turned dangerous as he viewed the magic. "That would have hurt us if it had hit us."

Gary groaned, pulling off his glasses that were cracked. "I think we figured out Tarragon's end goal."

I could have told him that, although with the shared look between him and Lario, they already guessed this would happen. A snarl erupted from me.

"If you thought this would happen, why risk it?" If Becca or the others had been caught in this, the thought terrified me to the point I started to shake.

"Given the chance to put a stop to the Venandi, no matter how brutal," Lario met my gaze unflinching, "my people and I are prepared for the sacrifice."

Watching the cloud move further into the compound, I pulled Wyn to his feet with me. "We're going back to our mates. You can obviously handle this without us."

Gary nodded as we turned and ran back the way we'd come. The air was thick with the leftover magic.

Becca

"Becca!" Jasper shoved me to the side as something flew by where I'd been standing. It looked like a purple lightning bolt.

"Take him down!" The necromancer's voice came from the side. She was struggling to her feet as magic blanketed the area. Obviously, she was regretting her dress choice at this point.

Tarragon had proven to be an enemy. He'd planned to betray the resistance from the start. When he'd stepped toward me and my mates, Volinda had ordered an attack on him. I'd gotten to witness her throw her hands into the ground, channeling her magic. What had popped up out of the ground had been animal bones that formed together in misshapen figures that rushed at the Fae as the other witches threw spells at him. It was actually kind of cool until Tarragon whipped out the lightning bolts. He hit two of the witches who hadn't moved since. I really hoped they were just unconscious.

"You need to get out of here." Jasper grabbed my right elbow as we looked around.

My blood turned to ice. Axel and Cody had shifted and were lunging at Tarragon. They were dodging his attacks, but couldn't get close enough to attack him.

"I'm not leaving them." Wrenching my arm from Jasper, I pulled the hoodie over my head. "We're helping them, Jasper. We aren't defenseless." I could feel my limbs shaking with how scared

I was, but I wasn't letting them face this asshole alone. Not when I could help this time.

The rest of my clothes flew off and I shifted into my fox form, choosing speed over muscle.

Guys, we need a plan. I started to run toward Tarragon. Jasper was at my side within seconds.

A plan would be good. Cody let out a yelp as one of the bolts hit the tip of his tail. *Holy Hell, that hurt!*

My animal spun us, rolling when Tarragon threw out a lightning in our direction. The air practically crackled.

You all need to get out of there! Seth's command jolted me momentarily. *We're on our way back, just get away.*

Can't do that, boss man. Axel managed to get behind the Fae, swiping at his backside with claws out. *He seems intent on either killing us or taking us with him. Particularly you.*

I gave out a mental shout when Tarragon formed a sword in his hand of magic and slashed out at Axel, catching his side. There was pain down our mate mark. Rage bubbled inside of me as my animal roared.

Kitten, calm down. Remember, self-defense! Wyn's concern filtered through the rage as I moved around the Fae to get to Axel.

Cody and Jasper attacked him as one, giving me the time to get to Axel, who held his left paw in the air, I could see bone and muscle. The smell of blood hit my senses as I nudged his side with my nose. He sniffed at my neck, his love pushing through the pain in the mark.

I'll be fine.

He's dead. I shifted, changing into my wolf form. My paws dug into the dirt as I pushed Axel further from the battle. *Stay out of his range, Axel.*

Becca, I'm fin—

No. I turned to glare at him. *You'll be a distraction if you try to help now.*

Ouch. True, but ouch. His bear grumbled angrily at me as I nudged his nose. *I'll see about helping the witches who were knocked down.* He limped away from me.

I pushed my feelings into my mark, making sure he knew how much I loved him without saying anything.

Another flash of pain ripped through me, this time it was Cody. I turned in time to see him get hit directly by a bolt.

CODY! All our voices echoed in my head. I couldn't get to him. Jasper stood protectively over him as Tarragon took a step toward both of them.

That's when Wyn swooped out of the sky, his talons dug into Tarragon's left shoulder. The Fae grabbed at Wyn, but he was too fast for him. As he was distracted, Seth came out of nowhere, tackling Tarragon to the ground. Seth let out a roar in his face, his claws dug into his chest as if he were slicing into butter.

The Fae didn't even blink. I whimpered when he punched Seth in the head several times. My mate didn't move but I felt the damage. Seth bit down on the arm that was punching him, drawing out a grunt from Tarragon.

"Enough!" Tarragon gave his own roar as power pulsed from him, throwing Seth off of him.

Seth landed near Jasper and Cody, who had just shakily gotten to his feet.

Guys? Cody? I tried not to let them feel how scared I was.

Stay back, baby. Seth took a step toward Tarragon, who rolled his neck in annoyance. *It's going to be alright.*

I can help! I moved forward stealthily even as Seth and the others grumbled at me.

"As much fun as this has been," the Fae held his uninjured hand out. "I have a compound to destroy." He started mumbling in the strange language from before. The earth trembled as another explosion rocked the night.

I'd managed to stay out of his sight on his right side as he sent more magic out at the guys. Lightning rushing out at them.

Enough was enough. There was no such thing as fighting dirty, especially with this asshole.

I got down, waiting for an opening as Wyn transformed mid-flight into his wolf form, dropping on top of Tarragon. Wyn went for his neck just as Seth leapt at him, too.

Tarragon protected himself, throwing up his hands. I saw my opportunity. My feet pounded into the ground as I dove at the man. My teeth sunk into his flesh and my growl was triumphant as Tarragon made a squeal-like sound as I bit into his penis, ripping it from his body, even though it was nasty. It'd been pretty easy, actually.

Everything seemed to freeze in that moment. For just a second, there was just his screams, then Tarragon was no longer in any pain because Seth and Wyn tore into his neck, cutting off his screams. I spit out his dick, watching a little bit fascinated, as it rolled a few feet. It was disgusting, even more than the guy's body as it fell to the ground, his head almost completely cut off from his neck.

Severed heads are a theme with this family. Wyn came over to me pushing against my side. *I can't believe you bit his dick off.* He gagged and it was such a funny sight that I laughed.

Seth shifted where he was standing over Tarragon's body. I ran my eyes over him to make sure he was alright as well as admired the view.

"Becca, we're going to have a conversation about you ignoring my orders." He knelt in front of me after stepping over Tarragon. "I can't believe you did that." His skin was a little green as he looked over at the offending appendage.

It worked, didn't it? I glanced over to Jasper and Cody. *Cody! Axel! Are you okay?*

CHAPTER 37

Becca

"What do you mean 'no'?" I glared down at my mate. "The healer said you have to take this medicine until it's gone." I held up the bottle that was half empty. "Drink it!"

"No! It tastes gross and I'm fine!" Cody scrambled away from me onto the other side of the bed. "I can sit up! I don't need it!"

Growling, I pounced on top of him. He grunted from the force of it and tried to wiggle away. I plugged his nose with my left hand using my fingers and waited. He was turning blue by the time he gave up and gasped for air. I shoved the rest of the liquid down his throat. When he tried to cough it back up, I moved my hand from his nose to his mouth.

"Deal with it!" My raised voice bounced off the walls in his bedroom. "Stop being so stubborn!"

Once I was confident he'd swallowed it all, I removed my hand from his mouth. He glared up at me.

"Please, Cody. I love you." I pressed my forehead against his. "When you wouldn't wake up after you passed out, I thought my world had ended. The guys felt the same."

Cody huffed and his arms wrapped around my middle, pulling me so that I was laying on top of him now.

"Sorry, fair maiden." He kissed my temple. "I didn't mean to scare you."

I stayed in his arms for a while longer. We'd started to doze off when a knock on the door woke me up. Jasper entered the room with a tray filled with food. Behind him, followed the rest of my pack.

After Tarragon had been defeated, the chaos of the night had continued. Axel's front paw hadn't started to heal and Cody had collapsed with a huge burn on his chest. Even with the advanced healing of being shifters, they were in a lot of pain.

Thankfully, the stuck-up necromancer, Volinda, ended up being able to help with the witches who were still conscious. They'd been working on Axel and Cody's injuries when Lario and Gary returned from the compound that was set ablaze in the distance.

"Gary! You're okay!" I'd shifted back without any problems for once.

"Hey, kid!" Gary covered his eyes and turned his back. "Clothes! You need clothes!"

"Oh." Glancing around, I'd forgotten about the whole naked thing momentarily. Wyn appeared next to me, pulling the borrowed hoodie I'd thrown off earlier onto me. "Thanks, Wyn."

"Well, looks like we missed a lot." Lario stood over Tarragon's body, pushing his boot into the ribs. "Pity. I wanted a piece of him."

"Gary, what happened at the compound?" I wrapped my arms around my middle as I watched the witches working on Cody.

Wyn pulled me against his side. I tried to ignore that my mates were nude and there were other women around getting to see them. Attacking allies who looked at my naked mates was bad.

"The curse stole the lives of anyone who got caught in it. Luckily, most of our people were able to avoid it." Gary rubbed the back of his head. He was covered in dirt. "It interacted with anything that held an electrical charge, hence the explosions. The Venandi are gone. There are only a few survivors from what I can tell so far."

I looked up to Wyn. He'd not shown any emotion but I could feel his arms around me, shaking ever so slightly.

"What about kids?" That has been the one thing I'd agreed on at the meeting. Kids didn't deserve to suffer for their parents' decisions.

"The men we had on the inside got them out this afternoon." Lario came back over to us, holding something in his hand. "Once your mates are stable, we need to move before the human authorities find us here." He held up Tarragon's limp appendage and grinned. "Whoever did this, I owe you a great deal. This is the greatest thing I've seen in a very long time."

"Is that—?" Gary gagged. "Oh Lord."

"That would be Becca. She ripped it clean off." Seth had been with Axel, speaking with the witches. "That's our mate." The pride in his tone made me stand a little taller.

I don't remember much of what happened after that. The adrenaline that had been pumping through my veins disappeared and I'd fallen asleep in Wyn's embrace.

I'd woken up in a bed between Cody and Axel the next day. They were the most injured of our group, but thanks to the medicine the witches gave us to speed up their healing abilities, four days later, they were almost back to one hundred percent.

Cody was a difficult patient. The rest of the guys left him to me when he tried to bite off Jasper's fingers the night before.

"We're having lunch in bed." Jasper set the tray on the nightstand next to me. "As long as it's safe to approach." He narrowed his eyes at Cody.

"Sorry." Cody widened his eyes pathetically. "Don't be mad."

I giggled as they all sat around us. Jasper got behind Cody, leaning against the headboard.

"I heard from Gary." Seth ran his hand along Axel's arm. "Everything seems to be contained. They haven't heard from any other Fae, but they'll all be on alert. Lario sends his regards."

I leaned my head back against Wyn's chest as he picked me up into his lap. We'd spoken to Felicity yesterday. She'd taken the news of her parents' demise surprisingly well. Sero even introduced himself to me over the phone. They'd been arguing about something when they hung up.

"Does that mean our pack is safe?" I reached out my hand for Seth's free one. We were all touching now.

"We're safer than we were before. News of the Venandi's destruction has already reached other shifters. We may have more coming around more often now." Seth squeezed our hands together. "The Fae are up to something. There's no way Tarragon acted alone, but I'm sure his dick being sent to them from Lario will be a good deterrent."

Looking at each of my mates' faces, I smiled. I flooded our mate marks with all of my feelings for them.

"I love you. There's no way anything can stand between us. I can't wait to spend the rest of our lives together."

The End.

The Panda Overlords think severed dick tastes spicy.

BOOKS BY ASPEN

Loved Shrouded In The Dark? Why not take a look at other books by Aspen Black

Shrouded In The Dark

The Ghost Dud Series
Ghost Revelations
Ghost Deceptions
Ghost Confessions
Ghost Transformations

Excalibur's Decision Series
Aryana's Journey

The Silver Springs Library Series
Book can be read as a standalone
Iris Book 9
Silver Skates
 Book can be read as a standalone
Cider Book 9

Secrets of Talonsville Charity Series (%50 of proceeds are donated to charity)
  Knight's Talons

Please visit Aspen and her co-author's group on Facebook
  Aspen Black and Adammeh's Wanderers

Subscribe to Newsletter

Printed in Great Britain
by Amazon